CRY EDEN

Harold Gershowitz

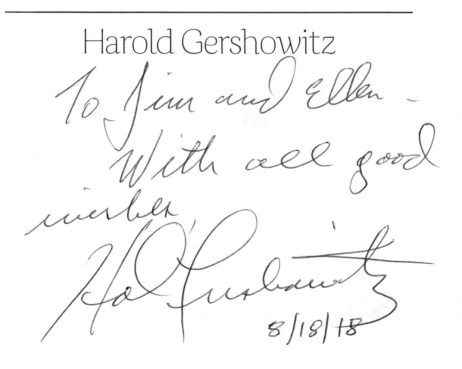

To Jim and Ellen —
With all good
wishes

Hal Gershowitz

8/18/18

ISBN: 978-1724260444

DEDICATION

To my loving wife, Diane, who has during our thirty-three years of marriage played such a vital role in the completion of each of my novels. Diane has been a true partner, reading and rereading each draft of everything I wrote, and candidly sharing with me her reaction to each paragraph, each chapter, and each story. Diane was an invaluable resource in completing my first novel, *Remember This Dream* (Bantam Books), and each of those that followed, *Heirs of Eden*, *The Eden Legacy*, and now *Cry Eden*, all products of Amazon's independent publishing platform—CreateSpace.

And, as always, heartfelt tribute to Bayla, my dear late wife, and to our son Steven, both of whom were lost so very young and whose memories I so treasure. And to our children, Amy, Michael, and Larry, Danny and Jill, and our entire gaggle of wonderful grandchildren, Jennifer, Samantha, Jared, Zach, Ryan, Zoe, Ben, Samuel, and Olivia.

ACKNOWLEDGEMENTS

Sincere thanks to my wife, Diane, and to superb readers Dr. Terri Ketover, Gloria Scoby, Gary Gittelsohn, and Amy Lask, all of whom pored over the pages of my manuscript in search of typos, misspellings, and inconsistencies. Diane's research many years ago into certain aspects of the Middle East conflict influenced my decision to write the trilogy comprising *Heirs of Eden*, *The Eden Legacy*, and, finally, *Cry Eden*.

I would be remiss if I didn't recognize Rema Saadeh Manousakis, who, as a child, fled Jaffa with her family during the fighting in Palestine in 1947. Her journey, which eventually led her to America, closely parallels that of my fictional character Alexandra Salaman. Rema was kind enough to spend many hours reading the manuscript of *Heirs of Eden*, the first book in this trilogy. All three books have benefited from her recollections, observations, and candid sharing of experiences that affected her life and that of Alexandra. I will forever be grateful for the insight Rema provided.

Among those who gave generously of their time to assist me in researching various aspects of the novels that make up the trilogy are Judge Abraham Sofaer, Israeli Brigadier General (retired) Yitzhak Segev, the late biographer Amos Alon, the late Mayor of Jerusalem

Teddy Kollek, and, finally, the late Arab Mayor of Bethlehem Elias
Freij. Mayor Freij and I met in his office during the First Intifada, and
he spoke passionately about the prosperity the entire region would enjoy if only there was peace.

I offer very special thanks to those ordinary, and some extraordinary, Israelis and Palestinians who were willing to candidly share with
me their stories, their frustrations, and their hopes and dreams for this
tortured region they call home. I pay special tribute to those members
of my family, Penina and Grisha Otiker, now deceased, who as young
pioneers managed to escape the Nazi rape of Poland over eighty years
ago and find their way to Kibbutz Yad Mordechai in British Mandate
Palestine. They have produced three generations of Sabras—native-
born Israelis who have defended their country while seeking peace
with their neighbors.

A treasure trove of previously top secret and otherwise classified
documents are now unclassified and available to the public. Numerous
articles, essays, biographies, and memoirs published during the past forty-
five years have greatly illuminated the events surrounding the 1973 Yom
Kippur War. Among the many sources I utilized in researching *Cry Eden*
are the Office of the Historian of the U.S. Department of State, the Combat
Studies Institute of the U.S. Army Command and General Staff College,
the American-Israeli Cooperative Enterprise, the National Archives of
the United States, and the *British Journal of Middle Eastern Studies*.

Our understanding of the role played by the United States during the Yom Kippur War has been greatly enhanced by the declassi-
fication of minutes of high-level meetings between the senior-most
officials of the United States and the belligerents in the war, the de-
classification of transcripts of numerous telephone conversations between U.S. Secretary of State Henry Kissinger and President Richard
Nixon, and conversations between Kissinger and White House Chief
of Staff Alexander Haig, Soviet Ambassador Anatoly Dobrynin,
Israeli Ambassador Simcha Dinitz, and Secretary of Defense James
Schlesinger, to name but a few.

Of particular interest to me were declassified, but previously "top secret," minutes of meetings, such as the meeting on Monday January 14, 1974, attended by Anwar al-Sadat, President of the Arab Republic of Egypt; Ismail Fahmy, Minister of Foreign Affairs; Major General Mohammed Abdel Chani el-Gamasy, Egyptian Army Chief of Staff; Henry Kissinger, U.S. Secretary of State; Ellsworth Bunker, Ambassador at Large and Head of U.S. Delegation to Geneva Peace Conference; Joseph Sisco, Assistant Secretary for Near Eastern and South Asian Affairs; and Peter W. Rodman, National Security Council staff.

I found the writings of Abraham Rabinovitch (*The Yom Kippur War*), Simon Dunstan (*The Yom Kippur War*), Henry Kissinger (*Crisis*), Evan Thomas (*Being Nixon*), Robert Slater (*Golda*), and Abba Eban (*An Autobiography*) to be particularly illuminating.

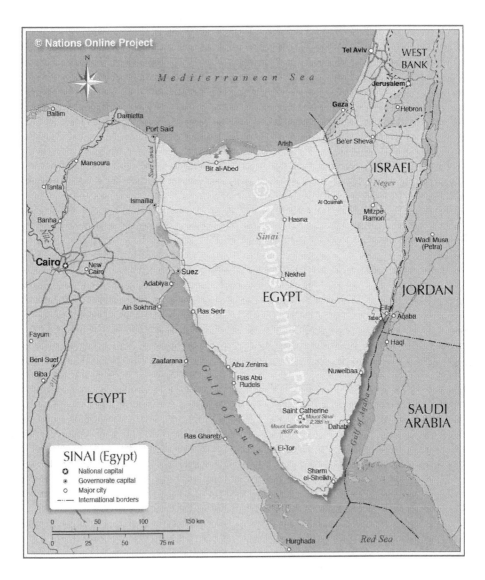

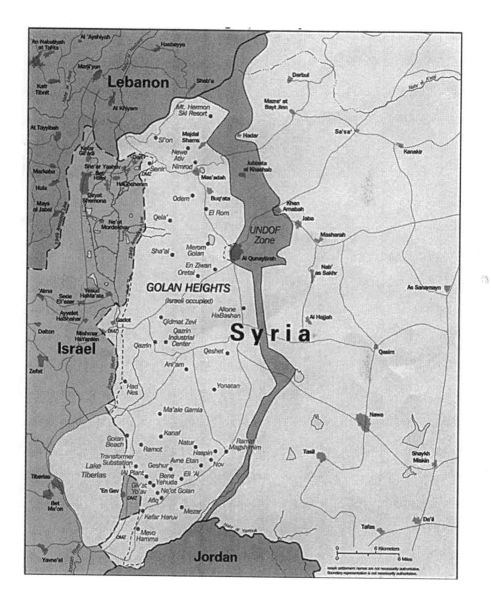

"There is a contest old as Eden, which still goes on—the conflict between right and wrong, between error and truth. In this conflict, every human being has a part."
Rev. Matthew Simpson (June 21, 1811–June 18, 1884)

CHAPTER ONE

SEPTEMBER 25, 1973

It was dusk in Amman, Jordan as the well-polished limousine approached the heliport. The rotor blades of the Royal Jordanian Air Force helicopter idled smartly, rhythmically whipping through the warm air as the automobile pulled to a stop alongside the waiting aircraft. A young army officer opened the passenger door and snapped to attention as three men moved briskly from the automobile, hunched over slightly as they moved under the rotating blades to the helicopter. Moments later the aircraft, emblazoned with the Jordanian coat of arms, slowly lifted off. It arched to the southwest and began the thirty-eight-kilometer flight to the north shore of the Dead Sea, the lowest point on earth at thirteen hundred feet below sea level. The three Jordanians landed about fifteen minutes later. They disembarked and walked a few meters to board the awaiting Israeli Air Force helicopter, the six-pointed Star of David proudly displayed on the fuselage. They flew westward, passing just north of Jerusalem headed toward Tel Aviv, and landed as the sun descended over the Mediterranean. The three men, accompanied by an Israeli Army escort, walked the short distance from the heliport to the modest guesthouse of the Israeli Institute for Intelligence, known the world over simply as Mossad.

Israeli Prime Minister Golda Meir was waiting to greet them. Standing on one side of her was her executive aide, Mordechai Gazit, and on the other side, Zvi Zamir, the head of Mossad.

"Good evening, Your Excellency," the Prime Minister said, extending her hand to King Hussein. "Good evening, Prime Minister Rifai. Welcome, General Talib."

OCTOBER 1, 1973

Amos Ben-Chaiyim smiled as he approached his Mossad supervisor, Benjamin Bar-Levy, in the dining room of Jerusalem's King David Hotel. The two men were a study in contrasts. Amos, an imposing Israeli Sabra, was born on a kibbutz not far from Gaza the same day Adolph Hitler became Chancellor of Germany. He towered just over six feet—well tanned and weathered, his tousled dark hair slightly striated with hints of sun-bleached blond.

Amos hadn't seen Bar-Levy for over two months, not since the Lillehammer disaster, when he was called to assist in the extraction from Norway of colleagues who had badly botched an attempted assassination. Actually, the assassination was successful. It was the victim they got wrong. They had targeted Ali Hassan Salameh, the so-called Red Prince, who they were certain planned the Olympic massacre in Munich. Instead, the hit team shot and killed an innocent waiter from Morocco.

Bar-Levy liked Amos. He considered him one of his most reliable agents. He had nerves of steel, and there was no one smarter.

Amos knew Bar-Levy would be at his favorite corner table hunched behind the *Jerusalem Post*. Bespectacled with his signature wire-rimmed glasses, his older colleague lingered an extra moment to finish the story he had been reading. That's the way his Mossad colleague started every day. First came the news, then everything else. His favorite breakfast—tea, toast, and apricot jam—was still untouched. He looked more like one of the pale, balding clerks at the National Library over in the Gav'at Ram neighborhood than the intelligence operative with the razor-sharp mind Amos knew him to be.

"Must be something interesting, Benjamin, your toast and tea are getting cold."

"Ach, not so interesting—just sad," Bar-Levy replied, tossing the paper down so that Amos could see what he had been reading. Amos had already thumbed through the *Post* that morning and had seen the stark front-page, black-and-white photograph of Israeli President and Mrs. Katair, Defense Minister Moshe Dayan, and other members of the IDF High Command standing solemnly at the Paratroopers Memorial near the Bilu-Gedera Road. BROTHERS IN COURAGE read the boldface header.

"It looks like more will be buried before the year is out," Amos said somberly as he sat down opposite Bar-Levy. Everyone, it seemed, was resigned to the coming bloodshed.

"Maybe before the month is out," Bar-Levy sighed.

"Is that why you wanted to meet this morning? Do you know something?"

"The Hashemite came to meet Golda and told her there will be war."

"King Hussein told her that?" Amos asked incredulously.

"Yes," Bar-Levy answered in a whisper. Then, leaning low across the table to be sure no one could overhear them, he continued, "He came to the guesthouse with Prime Minister Rifai along with their Chief of Intelligence, General Talib. They called for the meeting to warn us Egypt and Syria are planning to attack."

"So, what are *we* going to do?" Amos asked anxiously.

"Golda thinks he's overreacting. She thinks he's an alarmist—afraid he'll lose the rest of his kingdom if war comes. I tend to agree with Golda. Attacking us would be insane."

"I don't think we can dismiss the King's warning. He took an enormous risk to come," Amos replied.

"Look, we all know Sadat is planning some action. They're engaged in the biggest military maneuvers ever, but I can't imagine they're really going to storm the Canal. Their losses would be catastrophic. Our people think it would cost them nearly twenty thousand dead to try."

"We intercepted a report from the Kremlin. The Russians think it would cost Sadat thirty-five thousand men," Amos replied.

"If there is all-out war, we'll lose hundreds, maybe thousands, even though our people are certain we'll have twenty-four to forty-eight hours' warning. We're already at our highest state of alert."

"I don't know why we're not mobilizing all our forces now. If war actually comes, every hour we delay will cost Israeli lives at the front," Amos argued.

"Because Major General Zeira, our know-it-all Chief of Military Intelligence, says an attack isn't imminent. He's so damn sure the Syrians aren't going to do anything without Egypt, and he says Egypt doesn't have the equipment they would need to neutralize our air force. If they're foolish enough to attack, Zeira says, the Arabs will have a disaster on their hands," Bar-Levy said as he spread a healthy splash of apricot jam on his toast.

"Ah, the Concept," Amos answered, a touch of contempt in his voice.

"It makes sense, Amos. The Kontzeptziya, as Zeira calls it, couldn't be more logical."

"It is and it isn't. Our military intelligence people are all so damned positive that Egypt will never attack until they have the planes and ordnance and trained pilots and, most of all, the skill to knock out every one of our airfields. That's the so-called Concept on which we're staking everything. And now we have this warning from King Hussein himself."

"If Golda took Hussein's warning seriously she wouldn't have run off to Strasbourg this week to address the EU Parliament."

"Oh, right. I forgot about that."

"Yes, and before she returns, she's making an unscheduled detour to Vienna to meet with Bruno Kreisky about his decision to close the transit camp housing the Russian émigrés who are in route here."

"This just doesn't make any sense. It's like Nero fiddling while Rome was burning," Amos answered. "It's crazy."

"Right now, nothing is burning. Our military intelligence people all think the Kontzeptziya makes sense. After all, our pilots won the sixty-seven war within the first few hours of fighting. The rest of the week was mostly mopping up behind the fleeing Arabs. They say the soonest the Egyptians and Syrians could even hope to take on our air force would be at least another three years."

"So, this entire Egyptian buildup is all bluster? Is that what you think, Benjamin? You believe the King would come and bring his top people just to bluster?"

"Hussein is an alarmist. We're relying on General Zeira and his military intelligence network. If they think there will be no war until Egypt has the capacity to knock out our airfields, then there will be no war, because Egypt simply doesn't have the capacity to do that—not now, anyway."

"Are you as confident as Zeira that they won't storm the Bar-Lev Line?" Amos asked. "Because I'm not so sure."

"That barrier runs the entire length of the Canal, over ninety miles, except for the Bitter Lake section, which is a barrier itself. How could they possibly scale that wall we've built? It's over sixty feet high and twenty feet wide. Besides, it would take them days to bulldoze their way through all that compacted sand. Dayan says they would need an atomic bomb to break through that wall. How could trucks or tanks breach a barrier like that, especially with our forces throwing everything we have at them? It's crazy."

"Well, the Line may be ninety miles long, but we have only a few hundred men clustered in a couple dozen forts, maybe five hundred, six hundred in all, manning the entire Line. We don't have more than a platoon at any fort—too few to stop an invading army and too many to be expendable. We send reservists to man the whole damned Line, and most of them have never seen combat. If our fortifications at the Line were neutralized by air and artillery for a few hours, the Egyptians could try to punch their way through in enough places to gain a foothold in the Sinai. I don't like it. I don't like it at all."

"Impossible. The Egyptians would be torn to shreds," Bar-Levy answered. "How could they punch their way through that massive wall while our men were firing at them like they were ducks in a shooting gallery? Besides, there are another eighteen thousand men, three hundred tanks, and nearly one hundred pieces of artillery a few kilometers behind the Line. I don't care what the King thinks, an attack doesn't make any sense. Maybe a real army could make a fight of it, but the Egyptians and the Syrians—no, I don't think so. And I'll tell you something else, Amos, and not a word of this to anyone," he continued, barely above a whisper. "We have a source within the Egyptian establishment. I can't tell you who, but trust me, he's worth his weight in gold. He would know if war was imminent, and he hasn't raised a red flag."

Amos knew better than to press Bar-Levy about the identity of the informant.

Bar-Levy nodded slowly, but knowingly. "He is good as gold, Amos."

"Well, maybe it's all a bluff," Amos answered, after a long pause. "Maybe Hussein is part of a plan to get us to the negotiating table."

"What's there to negotiate? Sadat will demand the Sinai, Hussein will demand the West Bank, and Assad will insist we abandon the Golan Heights. We give up everything and what do they give us? Nothing in return—nothing."

"An end to the perpetual state of belligerency—I'm not sure I would call that nothing," Amos replied.

"Do you want to know what will end the state of belligerency, Amos? Our Bar-Lev Line. That's what will end the state of belligerency."

"I don't agree, and Arik doesn't share your confidence in the Line either. He thinks it's just one big stationary target. He'd rather rely on the maneuverability of his armored divisions."

"Ach, Sharon. He's a bulvan, a loud, boorish bull in a china closet. He'd rather just slug it out with the Egyptians."

"Well, at least he's our boorish bull in a china closet," Amos answered.

"Anyway, there's something else I wanted to discuss with you," Bar-Levy continued, abruptly changing the subject. "It's probably nothing, but something's been nagging at me."

"You've piqued my curiosity, Benjamin. So, what's nagging at you?" Amos asked, pouring himself a cup of tea.

"I think the Egyptians are up to something else while all this is going on."

"Such as?"

"I'm not sure. All we know is that they've been quietly buying high-pressure water pumps—a lot of them. They're supposedly for the Cairo Fire Department, but I don't believe it."

"Do you think they've had some major flooding somewhere?" Amos asked.

"No, I don't think that's it. We'd know if there had been any substantial flooding. There's been no unusual rainfall. Amos, our agents tell us they've purchased three hundred high-pressure pumps from some British outfit, and now we've learned that they've gone and purchased another hundred and fifty even more powerful pumps from the Germans. I'm wondering if they have some problem at Aswan."

"That doesn't seem likely. The high dam has been in operation for three years, Benjamin. If there was just a leak in the power plant they wouldn't need hundreds of pumps, and if there was an actual breach in the dam all the pumps in the world wouldn't help."

"Why would they suddenly be buying hundreds of high-pressure water pumps, Amos?"

"Well they sure as hell aren't planning to pump the water out of the Suez Canal," Amos quipped. "After all, Dayan called the Canal the world's greatest anti-tank ditch."

"They're using those pumps somewhere, Amos."

"Or they're planning to. Maybe they just want the pumps available in case of future flooding. The Nile Valley does have a long history of flooding."

"Did, Amos. Flood control is one of the reasons they built the dam at Aswan—remember? No, I don't think it has anything to do with the

Nile overflowing its banks. It has to have something to do with whatever surprise they're planning."

"Maybe it's defensive. Maybe they're anticipating something we might do and want the pumps on hand just in case."

"Maybe … maybe not. It's one hell of a lot of pumping power they've begun accumulating, Amos."

"Think about it, Benjamin. Let's assume they want to make a stab at crossing the Canal. Maybe they're amassing a lot of rolling stock—trucks, tanks, rocket transporters, and the like. Should actual fighting begin they'll want the freedom to move all of that equipment to the front quickly and without interruption. It could be nothing more than a huge abundance of caution. Maybe they just want high-pressure pumps on hand in case we try to impede their movement by using the water in the Canal or even the Mediterranean to make the terrain unpassable."

Benjamin Bar-Levy looked up at Amos, his expression revealing a hint of excitement.

"You know, you might have hit on something, Amos. Their Russian military advisors are all too familiar with the Rasputitsia. Their mud season made the roads impassable and stopped the Germans dead in their tracks on the Eastern Front. I think you may have hit the nail on the head."

"Maybe, maybe not. Let me see what I can find out."

"So, are you still planning to travel to the States this month?" Bar-Levy asked, changing the subject.

"Yes. Just for a few days. I'm going to spend Yom Kippur with Karen's family in Chicago."

Benjamin's lips curled into a half smile as he nodded. "Are you going to see the Palestinian woman too?"

"You mean Alexandra?"

"Yes. I don't mean to meddle. I just thought … being in the States …"

"Yes," Amos interrupted. "I plan to stop in Washington on my way back and spend a day or two with Noah and Alexandra."

"So, they're still together—the Palestinian and the Jew?"

"Benjamin, they've been happily married for five years. Of course, they're still together. They have a son."

"Yes, yes. Of course," Benjamin Bar-Levy replied, smiling politely.

"The boy is named after me, Benjamin. I'm his godfather."

Benjamin's eyes darted to Amos, his expression suddenly serious, a hint of alarm crossing his face.

"His name is Amos?"

"Yes, of course. He's named for me. Does that bother you?"

"The Jewish man, Greenspan, and the Palestinian woman have a child they named Amos?" Bar-Levy asked again.

"Benjamin what is it—why would that concern you?"

Bar-Levy paused, his mind riveted to a seemingly innocuous revelation—the name the Jewish businessman, Noah Greenspan, and his Palestinian wife, the journalist Alexandra Salaman, had given their son. "It's probably nothing," Bar-Levy finally whispered.

"Good, then you should have no problem telling me what upset you about the child's name."

After a moment's hesitation, Bar-Levy looked up at his young colleague.

"Amos, as you know, we've been after Omar Samir ever since you pulled Alexandra Salaman and the Haddad fellow out of Khartoum back in sixty-seven."

"Yes, of course I know. Samir's been elusive as hell," Amos replied. "What does that have to do with Noah and Alexandra's child?"

"Well, a few weeks ago we came close. We raided a house in Yattah, just south of Hebron, where we thought Samir was being sheltered. The place was abandoned. We found nothing very helpful—only some scribbled notes left behind in a desk drawer."

"And?" Amos prodded.

"There was nothing very illuminating in the notes. Except there were two or three references to something they called the Amos Project, or the Amos Operation."

"And you thought it had something to do with me?" Amos asked.

"No, we really didn't think it had anything to do with you. We don't think Samir would have had any way of knowing you were involved in the rescue of the Salaman woman at Khartoum. I don't think you're on their radar at all. Frankly, we concluded that they had some scheme they code-named after the Old Testament prophet."

"Ah, you mean from the Book of Amos. The old prophet prophesied that the King of Israel, Jeroboam, would die by the sword and Israel would be vanquished."

Bar-Levy nodded. "It seemed logical."

"And now you think it could somehow involve Alexandra and Noah's son, Amos?"

"Knowing this Samir character as we do, that could be just as logical—perhaps not very likely, but not illogical either."

"You're thinking they could be plotting to harm the child?"

"As I said, not very likely, but we certainly can't rule that out. Knowing what we know and putting two and two together—I think the Greenspans' son, Amos, could be in danger."

CHAPTER TWO

The Egyptian President, Anwar Sadat, sat in his office contemplating the scores of aerial photographs spread across his desk. The grainy black-and-white images encompassed maybe a quarter of the twenty-three thousand square miles of the Sinai Peninsula—Egyptian land occupied by Israel ever since the disastrous six-day war. His focus, of course, was on the Suez Canal connecting the Mediterranean with the Indian Ocean and separating the Sinai from Egypt and Asia from Africa.

The one-eyed Jewish Defense Minister, Moshe Dayan, had called the Canal the world's greatest anti-tank ditch. And then there was the insulting scar running the entire one-hundred-mile length of the Canal, the scar the Israelis had built of tightly compacted sand six stories high and twenty feet wide—the so-called impenetrable Bar-Lev Line.

All of Egypt will soon be praising my name or cursing it, he thought. *The Jews think we're so incompetent that we would give up the entire Sinai before we'd even try to take it back, and I'm about to risk everything to prove them wrong.*

Sadat slowly relighted his pipe and hunched over the photographs, drawing in a long, slow drag of his favorite Nat Sherman's Highstone.

Quite impressive, the Egyptian thought as he studied the Israeli fortifications. Most of the Israeli forts were built about three miles apart along the entire length of the Canal, just behind the Bar-Lev Line. He could see where the Jews thought the Egyptians would try to cross the

Canal because there the forts were closer together, less than a mile apart. Sadat moved his finger along the X's and other symbols his generals had drawn on the maps depicting, in detail, where the Israelis had placed machine-gun nests, mortar positions, anti-aircraft weapons, minefields, and even designated firing positions for tanks. Lines of hash marks, some of them fifteen rows deep, revealed where barbed-wire had been strung out to protect the men manning the defensive positions. Red arrows drawn over the Canal pointed with precision to places below the waterline where pipelines had been installed. In the event of an attempted Egyptian crossing, the Israelis planned to release enough burning napalm or crude oil through these pipes to sear the air over the Canal and boil the water running through it. An invading army would be incinerated before they could step foot on the Sinai side of the Canal. *Quite impressive, indeed*, Sadat mused, as he relit the smoldering embers in the bowl of his pipe.

***

Omar Samir lay on his back staring up at the ceiling fan as it rotated and groaned ever so slowly above his bed. He had, once again, returned to the New Cataract Hotel, not far from Aswan, to brood. He was in a foul mood. Life had, it seemed, conspired to confound him at every turn. It had been six years since the Palestinian woman, the journalist Alexandra Salaman, had escaped the fate he had so painstaking plotted for her. She had slipped from the absolute hell he had arranged for her in Sudan, and a day hadn't passed since the Arab summit in Khartoum that he hadn't brooded over her escape. He read everything Alexandra wrote and everything anyone wrote about her.

A friend, Ahmed Kahn, a former classmate from Phoenicia University in Beirut, was now a driver at the newly opened Qatari embassy in Washington. Kahn dutifully mailed to Samir every news item from Washington newspapers that mentioned either Alexandra Salaman or her husband, the Jew, Noah Greenspan. Ahmed Kahn had even sent that clipping from the *International Herald Tribune* that had driven Samir to near despondency. There were Greenspan and his Palestinian wife, Alexandra Salaman, holding their child at the ribbon-cutting ceremony on the opening day of a new shopping mall Greenspan's company, Potomac Center Properties of America, had built in the Elmhurst section of Queens, New York. The child, the caption read, was named Amos. *They had the gall*, Samir seethed, *to name their child Amos*. They named the boy, Samir correctly assumed, after the Mossad agent, Amos Ben-Chaiyim, with whom Alexandra had consorted after she fled Beirut—the Israeli who was responsible for the death of Sheik Ali Abdul Shoukri and who had twice snatched Alexandra from Samir's grasp. The *Tribune* photo gnawed at him. And soon, as he contemplated the revenge he was determined as ever to visit upon Alexandra, it was the child's face that crowded his thinking.

CHAPTER THREE

"Markazie!" the *Washington Evening Star*'s senior editor snapped as he grabbed the phone on the first ring.

"Frank, it's Alexandra. I think I have something big."

"Is it going to ruin my day?" he asked sarcastically.

"The only thing that ever ruins your day is when we're scooped by the *Post*. This is not going to ruin your day."

"You think you've really got something?"

"Maybe. It might be nothing, or it might be huge."

"How do you spell huge?"

"W-A-R," she replied.

"Get your ass up here," he answered as he hung up the phone.

Franklin Markazie adored Alexandra Salaman. She was the sharpest reporter he had ever hired. A natural, that's what he'd called her nearly twenty years earlier when she first came on board as a high school summer intern. He was impressed by the first story she had written for the paper. A reproduction of the article was framed and displayed along with other memorabilia on bookshelves behind his desk. She had called the article "Heirs of Eden." The young intern had written, with great sensitivity, about the stress and conflict experienced by a teenage Palestinian girl in love with a Jewish boy named Noah Greenspan. Now she was one of the *Star*'s most widely read columnists. She had also matured into an uncommonly beautiful woman. Her raven-black hair fell to her shoulders, framing a flawless olive complexion, a nod to her father Sharif's Arab lineage. Alexandra's jade green eyes, straight nose, and high cheekbones hinted at the Anglican heritage passed on to her from her mother Samira's side of the family. Samira's father was Egyptian, her mother British. They had met between the great wars when everything from the Jordan River to the Mediterranean was simply British Mandate Palestine, a leftover construct of the failed League of Nations.

"So, what's the big scoop?" he asked as Alexandra walked into his office.

"We don't know if it's a scoop yet. We don't even know if it's a story."

"Whattaya got?" he asked, his curiosity heightened.

"I think Egypt might be about to attack Israel."

"Bullshit," he snapped. "I can tell you for a fact there's not a hint of anything like that in the CIA morning briefs to the President."

"Yeah, those intelligence briefs somebody squirrels over to you every day are pretty amazing."

"And they don't say a damn thing about war erupting in the Middle East."

"That's because they rely on what the Israelis are telling Kissinger."

"You got a better source of information?" he asked.

"What if the Israelis have it wrong?"

"… and you have it right?" he asked, a touch of mockery in his voice.

Alexandra paused a moment to consider her response. "Maybe," she finally answered.

"Okay, you've got my interest. Who told you what?"

"I have a really good source in the State Department office of Deputy Secretary Ken Rush. He says Rush received a memo in May written by someone named Roger Merrick over at the INR predicting that Egypt was going to attack Israel before the end of the year."

"What the hell is the INR?"

"It's the Bureau of Intelligence and Research over at the State Department. It grew out of the old Office of Strategic Services."

"Oh yeah, that's the intelligence bureau George Marshall established shortly after the war."

"Anyway, Merrick seems certain that Sadat is going to attack Israel. Actually, not Israel proper but the Sinai."

"The Egyptians would have to be crazy," Markazie answered.

"Not necessarily. Merrick says all Sadat wants to do is force the United States to get serious about intervening diplomatically. Merrick doesn't think Sadat has designs on Tel Aviv. He doesn't even believe Sadat will try to take the entire Sinai. Merrick says he'll go to war just to get a toehold in the Sinai and force the United States to bring Israel to the negotiating table."

"Why doesn't Sadat just contact the Israelis and tell them he'd like to discuss a peace settlement? Why go to war, for Christ's sake?"

"Merrick says the Israelis aren't interested in trading the Sinai for an agreement with Sadat. They like the buffer the Sinai provides."

"Who the hell is Roger Merrick, anyway?"

Alexandra simply shrugged her shoulders. "I don't know. He wrote the memo."

"Didn't the Israelis build a Maginot Line or something?"

"It's the Bar-Lev Line, and yes, the Israelis think it's impenetrable."

"So, doesn't that sort of end the discussion?"

"Only if it *is* impenetrable."

"Why would the United States even care?"

"Well, think about it. The Russians have been pulling their advisors out of Egypt and Syria."

"Which could suggest that nothing is going to happen."

"Or that the Russians believe something *is* going to happen and they want to get their people and their families out of the way."

"I think you're grasping at straws."

"Also," she continued, ignoring Markazie's retort, "Merrick's memo predicts that American vital interests in the region would be compromised if war breaks out and we help the Israelis."

"You think he's talking about oil when he refers to our vital interests?"

"Frank, we don't have any other interests in the area. Of course he's talking about oil."

"How could the CIA and the whole fucking Israeli defense establishment miss something like a war about to break out?"

"I don't know. They don't miss much."

"Wouldn't the Egyptians be mobilizing their forces. How could they hide a mobilization for war?"

"They are mobilizing. They have major military maneuvers every year. Maybe this year's maneuvers include trying to cross the Canal."

"So, what do you propose?"

"I'd like to do a *gathering storm* column."

Markazie leaned back in his chair to contemplate Alexandra's request. They sat there for several moments, eyes fixed on one another. Finally, he sighed and shook his head.

"No, Alexandra. Sorry. I think the whole thing is far-fetched, and we'll look like we're fear mongering. You've got one guy's opinion over at State, and I'm telling you, there's not a trace of concern coming out of the CIA or out of Kissinger's office. This guy Merrick wrote this memo back in May and nothing has happened. We don't have nearly enough to run with this."

CHAPTER FOUR

General Mohammed Ahmed Sadek was furious. Confined to his home ever since being forced to resign as the Egyptian Minister of War a year earlier, he paced the floors in anger day after day. What the hell did a desk jockey like Anwar Sadat really know about warfare?

You fight to win, Sadek's own words screamed in his mind. He could still hear President Sadat lecturing him about tactics.

I want us to fight within our capabilities, nothing more. Cross the Canal and hold even ten centimeters of the Sinai. That will help me greatly and alter completely the political situation internationally and within Arab ranks.

He knew, of course, that Sadat was exaggerating to make a point, but still he considered the words obscene, and the plan folly. *Cross the Canal and hold even ten centimeters of the Sinai.* The army estimated up to twenty thousand men would be lost trying to cross the Canal—two thousand men a centimeter—inches gained for nothing, Mohammed Sadek thought contemptuously.

***

Sadat was, indeed, obsessed with crossing and holding the Canal. Tel Aviv was not his goal, nor even the Mitla Pass or Abu Ageilla. His immediate strategic obsession was not Israel. It was six thousand miles to the west. He knew that, for Egypt, the road across the Sinai had to detour through Washington.

Sadat carefully gathered up the aerial photographs he had been studying and placed them in a neat stack at the corner of his desk over the map of the Sinai that had been spread out for him to peruse. He took his time lighting his pipe, drew in an unhurried puff or two, and then carefully smoothed out the map with both hands and studied the isthmus that separated the massive plates of Asia and Africa. *Just seventy-five miles across,* he mused. *The Israelis think my armies have to traverse seventy-five miles to reach Israel and that our forces would never be able to do that—and they are right.*

But Sadat knew he had only to move and hold onto a few miles. Sadat was certain that Washington was the key to everything. Nixon had largely lost interest in the Middle East, having his hands full with Watergate, Vietnam, and his preoccupation with pursuing détente with the Soviet Union. Russian hostility to Israel was helpful, but only went so far. Russia could not entice Israel to the negotiating table. Only America could do that. And to get America's attention, Sadat was willing to risk everything to gain no more than a few miles of sand east of the Suez Canal—sand drenched with the blood of Israelis and Egyptians. And now he was ready. Everything had gone according to plan. A mock Egyptian and Syrian mobilization the previous May caused Israel to call up its reserves for, essentially, a false alarm. It disrupted jobs, households, and industry and cost the Jewish state millions. They wouldn't be so quick to mobilize their army again.

Then there was the matter of Palestinian terrorism, which had intensified in the years following the six-day war and commanded the lion's share of Israel's intelligence effort. In rapid succession, an array of Palestinian terror attacks kept all five Israeli intelligence agencies distracted and busy. Mossad, tasked with planning and conducting Israel's worldwide intelligence efforts, was determined to answer every attack. Modin, Israel's military intelligence gathering service, constantly weighed intelligence information from around the world. Shabak was tasked with counter-espionage operations, and Shin Bet, like the American FBI, was responsible for security within Israel proper. Even

Israel's Foreign Ministry Research Department was preoccupied with terrorist threats. The collective focus of Israeli intelligence had become terrorism—and for good reason. In just the past year Israelis had been attacked repeatedly. The PLO recruited Japanese gunmen who unleashed a massacre in the baggage claim area of Israel's Lod Airport, leaving twenty-six dead and eighty others wounded. Then just weeks later, there was the horrible massacre of the Jewish wrestling team at the Olympic games in Munich. And a month after that Dr. Ami Shachori was murdered by a letter bomb that exploded in his office at the Israeli embassy in London. Almost concurrently, Yosef Alon, the naval attaché at the Israeli embassy in Washington, was gunned down outside his home in Chevy Chase, Maryland. And just as Sadat was putting the final touches to his plan to attack across the Canal, Palestinian terrorists hijacked a train in Austria carrying Soviet Jews on their way to resettlement in Israel.

Grizzly stuff, Sadat thought, *but, then again, Palestinian terrorism did serve to distract the Israelis at just the right time.*

Sadat reached across his desk to review one more time the plans his generals had prepared for "Operation Badr."

He picked the battle name himself. It was at Badr that Islam fought its defining battle against the Meccans thirteen hundred years earlier. The Prophet Muhammad himself had been the mastermind of the battle at Badr. Now history would praise or vilify Anwar Sadat for the battle at the Sinai.

The key to success, Sadat knew, was neutralizing Israeli air superiority. Neither his pilots nor his Russian MiG-21s could match Israel's air power. The Jewish state's pilots were simply among the best in the world, and even the ground crews were better trained and battle tested, and the American F-4 Phantoms, while less agile, carried a far greater arsenal of firepower than the MiGs. The entire ground war, Major General Ahmed Ismail Ali assured the Egyptian President, would be fought under the protective umbrella of the new, deadly Russian surface-to-air missiles.

"If we keep to within ten to fifteen kilometers of the Canal, the Jews will have rough going counterattacking our ground troops," General Ismail had said. "The East Bank of the Canal will be a very dangerous place for the Israelis to send their planes."

"And you," Sadat began, his eyes riveted on Baki Zaki Yousef, the young officer who had come up with the audacious plan for storming the Bar-Lev Line. "How confident are you that our plan will work?"

"If General Ali can keep the Israelis off our backs for a few hours we will breach the Line. I am certain. We'll break through at dozens of points from one end of the Canal to the other."

Sadat slowly drew a few puffs from his pipe, holding Yousef in his gaze. "Twelve, maybe fifteen, kilometers of the Sinai east of the Canal. That's all our troops have to hold," Sadat replied.

"The Bar-Lev Line will not be nearly the obstacle the Israelis think it is," Lieutenant Yousef replied. "I am certain."

Sadat smiled and nodded. "You had better be right. We are counting on your plan. With the Canal securely in our hands, Nixon will force Israel to negotiate. For sure, they'll quickly realize that our fight with Jews could easily deteriorate into their fight with Russians. Yes, for sure, for sure, any thought the Americans had of détente would be dead."

CHAPTER FIVE

Noah and Alexandra lay facing one another, still embracing after their lovemaking. It was a rare blithe moment for them. They knew their young son, Amos, would soon come running into their room and leap onto the bed between them, as he did every morning. So Alexandra relished these few moments of contentment with Noah, which would quickly fade as the day moved along and reality intruded—the reality that Markazie had turned his thumbs down on the column she had wanted to write for the Sunday edition, and the reality of war she predicted was about to erupt once again in the Middle East. Roger Merrick over at State had it right, she was convinced. How did everyone else have it so wrong? Did Kissinger even know about the Merrick memo—the memo everyone had chosen to ignore? What if Egypt attacked across the Canal and the Arabs cut off all oil exports to the United States, as Merrick had predicted. It all made sense, Alexandra thought—the massive Egyptian army maneuvers, the remaining Russian advisors suddenly packing up and leaving with their families, the Israelis on high alert. None of this was a secret. Everyone knew, but no one believed the Egyptians would try to take on the Israelis again. The Israelis were among the world's best when it came to espionage. Surely they knew whatever Roger Merrick knew. Then again, why would Amos Ben-Chaiyim be on his way to Chicago to be with Karen for the Jewish holiday if war really was about to break out? Surely Amos would know.

"Penny for your thoughts," Noah teased. "Your mind seems a million miles from here."

"No, just six thousand," she replied, snuggling a little closer. Noah tightened his embrace.

"Well, there isn't anything in the papers that would suggest war is about to break out. In sixty-seven the papers were full of stories, and television provided non-stop coverage of Arab mobs calling for war. There's none of that now."

"Yeah, that's sort of what Markazie says too. None of those CIA memos he somehow gets his hands on mention war either."

"But?"

"But I have a contact over at State who told me about a staff memo that some guy named Roger Merrick wrote back in May that's very convincing. He thinks Egypt is going to attack and that if we help Israel, the Saudis will cut off our oil."

"Are you going to write about that?"

"No. Markazie won't let me. He thinks talk of war is unfounded, and he's not going to let me speculate about it based on a memo by one guy nobody's ever heard of."

"In that case, let's fool around again," Noah whispered, pulling her even closer.

"Forget it, Romeo. Our five-year-old son is going to come running through that door any moment," Alexandra replied, playfully pushing Noah away.

"Just as well," Noah replied, kissing Alexandra hurriedly before pulling back the covers and getting to his feet. "Daoud will be picking me up at nine o'clock for a meeting at the Jewish Council of Greater Washington this morning. They want me to be this year's campaign Chairman."

"Are you going to do it?" Alexandra asked, looking up at him.

"Yeah, I think so. I won't have to do much. They really just want a reasonably high-profile member of the community to be the face and voice of the campaign."

"Interesting that they asked you, don't you think?"

"Well, right now, I'm as high profile as anyone in the Jewish community. Potomac Center Properties of America has opened four major malls and we've optioned land out in Prince George's County in Landover for our next project. We've been in the news quite a bit. Anyway, I'd just be a figurehead. The campaign almost runs itself. There's not much going on. We would just be on the dais for a few fundraising dinners."

"You and your Palestinian wife," she replied coyly.

"Yeah, me and my beautiful Palestinian wife."

"You're going to be the Chairman of the Jewish Council's annual fundraising drive arriving at all these banquets with your Palestinian wife from Jaffa and Daoud, your Muslim driver from Khartoum. Seriously, you don't think that might be a problem?"

"Alexandra, you're one of the most widely read, most popular journalists in Washington. Everyone admires you. Besides this isn't nineteen sixty-seven. There's nothing that would make you controversial."

"You mean nothing that would make me toxic."

"Are you concerned about me accepting this chairmanship? If you are, I won't do it. But don't jump to conclusions about what the Jewish community thinks of you. Everyone I know adores you."

Alexandra shrugged and smiled. "No, of course I don't mind. I just don't want to become a problem for you or for the campaign. But …" she paused.

"But what, Alexandra? What concerns you?"

"What if this *was* nineteen sixty-seven all over again?"

"I don't think it would make a bit of difference."

"I hope you're right," she replied, as she rose and slipped into her bathrobe. "I hope you're right, Mr. Chairman," she repeated, as she turned and walked into the bathroom.

CHAPTER SIX

Omar Samir ripped open the package Ahmed Sayed Kahn had sent from the Qatari embassy in Washington and spread the contents out on the small table in his room at the New Cataract. There wasn't much—just a handful of news clippings from the *Evening Star* that bore Alexandra's byline. There was the column she had written about the pending legislation to establish home rule for Washington D.C., and another about the surprisingly small amount of federal income taxes paid by President and Mrs. Nixon—less than a thousand dollars in 1970 and 1971, while simultaneously receiving a $131,000 tax refund.

Samir peered down at the clippings, his eyes narrowing as he focused on Alexandra's thumbnail-size likeness staring back at him. *God, how I hate that woman*, he murmured under his breath. Then, as he brushed aside the news clippings, he saw the tiny item Ahmed had stapled to an index card under which was scribbled a brief note: "I called the telephone number. It's the *Evening Star*." Samir squinted and held the index card closer to better read what his friend had stapled to it. It was a few lines from the classified ads section of the paper.

Help wanted: Nanny for 5-yr-old
boy-8:00am-4:00pm Monday-Friday
excellent wages. At least five years'
experience+solid references. Call
202 555 2222 ext.101. A.Salaman.

Samir dropped the index card onto the table and leaned back in his chair—his hands trembled.

***

Five hundred miles almost due north, Israeli Lieutenant Benjamin Simon-Tov, a young intelligence officer assigned to the Southern Command Headquarters at Be'er Sheva, handed his report to his commanding officer, Lieutenant Colonel David Gedaliah. It said little more than his prior report warning that Egypt was more than likely going to attack the Canal.

His superior studied the report for several minutes and then turned his gaze to Lieutenant Simon-Tov. Colonel Gedaliah was annoyed and made no effort to mask his displeasure.

"We've been through this before," he said testily. "This says little more than your last report from a few days ago."

"My last report was ignored."

"And there was no attack was there, Lieutenant?"

"I'm telling you, sir, the Egyptians aren't bluffing. They're going to attack," the young Lieutenant replied, his tone almost desperate.

"And what would you have us do, go to war?"

"I'm an intelligence officer, not a tactician. But it is insane that we're not doing anything, with all that's going on immediately west of the Canal. The Egyptians have never amassed so many troops opposite our positions. They are in offensive formation. At night, you can hear half-tracks and other heavy vehicles being moved into position."

"They do this every year, Lieutenant. For five years they've been doing these maneuvers. We'll know when they're serious."

"Not on this scale, they haven't. I'm telling you, they are not just playing war games."

"Last May, we overreacted to their maneuvers and it cost us a fortune. Do you have any idea what it costs to mobilize our reserves—to bring our economy to a standstill?"

"With all due respect, sir, do you realize what it will cost if the Egyptians attack and we've not mobilized?" Lieutenant Ben-Tov replied, a hint of sarcasm in his voice.

"They're not going to attack. They won't risk another disaster like sixty-seven. They know our pilots would tear them to shreds."

"They have Soviet air-defense missiles now. They didn't have any air defense in sixty-seven."

"They won't risk it. They would never attack while our pilots and our American Phantom jets are sitting just minutes away."

"We are seriously undermanned on the Line," Lieutenant Ben-Tov pleaded.

"Lieutenant, we have nearly twenty thousand more men a few miles behind the Line. Do you think the Egyptians are going to try to hack away at the Bar-Lev Line with what we can throw at them with our soldiers and our artillery and our Phantom jets?" Colonel Gedaliah replied, making no effort to hide his growing impatience with the young junior officer.

"Yes, I do," Lieutenant Ben-Tov retorted angrily. "I think that is exactly what the Egyptians are preparing to do. It is crazy that we're acting like nothing is happening over there across the Canal … and we know that Syria has moved over a thousand tanks onto the Golan Heights."

"Yes, and they're all in strictly defensive positions. They're dug in, hulls down."

"Of course they would want us to think they're in defense mode. They can change to offensive positions in minutes."

"It will be years before they would even try to confront us. Our military intelligence doesn't think they could challenge us before nineteen seventy-five or seventy-six."

"The damned Concept isn't going to protect us," the young Lieutenant replied, his voice rising.

"Don't ridicule the Concept. It is simple and it is sensible," Colonel Gedaliah shouted.

"It is insane! It is causing nothing but complacency. The Egyptians are probably dumbfounded that we've done nothing while they've methodically moved over one hundred thousand men opposite us."

"Do you think our most experienced military leaders don't know what's going on?"

"Colonel, with all due respect, we've convinced ourselves that neither Egypt nor Syria will attack before they can neutralize our air force. That's all this Concept is."

"And you doubt that?"

"It's insane to ignore what the Egyptians have put in place on the other side of the Canal, and what the Syrians are doing on the Golan."

"And what would you have me do?"

"I beg you to forward my report to General Zeira and to the Minister of Defense."

"I will do no such thing, Lieutenant. It is totally contrary to the Concept, the very foundation of our tactical thinking. This is the second time you have sounded this alarm. Your report is duly noted."

"You're not going to do anything with my report, are you?"

"Your report will make fools of us both."

"So will an Arab attack," the young lieutenant snapped as he turned on his heels and stormed away without so much as a perfunctory salute.

CHAPTER SEVEN

OCTOBER 4, 1973

Amos marveled at the vitality of America's second city, as he always did on the drive from O'Hare to the lakefront. The six-year-old Hancock Center had now been joined by the Sears Tower, completed just four months earlier during his last trip to Chicago. The two breathtaking giants, both stretching skyward higher than any other buildings on earth, were clearly visible twenty miles away, towering over the city like protective sentries.

It had been a month. He hadn't been with Karen since she took a few extra days to be with him in Israel following the Labor Day holiday in America. They had spent hours, day after day, at his apartment in Tel Aviv satiating one another. Their time together alleviated the stress of being apart and the fear they silently shared of losing one another. The distance between Tel Aviv and Chicago was numbing.

Now he was in America. He was certain this brief interlude with the woman he loved was going to be interrupted by war, but war hadn't come, nor had Israel mobilized its reserves. He could not remember a more stressful time—what with the Munich massacre a year earlier and the unrelenting terrorist attacks ever since. And there was the Lillehammer disaster, and the air skirmishes with Syria the past spring, and now Egypt and Syria on full war footing. *When is it ever going to end?* he asked himself.

Lake Point Tower came into view as soon as his taxi turned onto Lake Shore Drive. He gazed up to the top of the huge contemporary structure, the tallest apartment building in the world, and smiled. *Karen really is on top of the world*, he mused.

She was now a Vice President at Mid America Ventures, a well-deserved promotion following the public offering she engineered for Noah Greenspan's company. She had just been named Chicago's "Rising Star" by a local business journal, and Amos knew the odds were remote that he could convince her to give up all of this to be with him in Israel. Truth be told, he thought she would be crazy to leave her career and the comfort and safety of America, and a robust exciting city like Chicago, to come to the chaos of the Middle East. He questioned whether it was fair for him to even try to get her to come. And, yes, on more than one occasion he had entertained the idea of leaving Israel and moving to America to be with Karen. The only two women he had ever really loved both lived in America. Karen Rothschild and Alexandra Salaman.

He unlocked the door to Karen's apartment with the key she had given him and put down his suitcase in the entry hall. Amos walked into the living room and stood there high atop Lake Point Tower, taking in the view. There, through the glass wall curving around the eastern exposure, he looked out over the brilliant blue expanse of Lake Michigan. He could see Gary, Indiana and Michigan City way off to the south, and to the east and north the lake extended as far as the eye could see. *The damn lake is larger than all of Israel. Shit, so is the Chicago Area*, he thought.

Amos took his time moving from room to room. The apartment was spotless, everything in place. *Well organized—just like Karen*, he whispered under his breath. Then he saw the note she had left for him propped up on the table in the small dining area. He picked up the pale blue, fine-textured linen stationery to read the message, and smiled ever so slightly. She had applied just a hint of her favorite perfume, Yves Saint Laurent's Rive Gauche, to the paper. The faint aroma stirred images of Karen in his mind, and the sensation was pleasantly arousing. He turned his attention to the message she had left for him.

Dearest Amos, I'm counting the seconds until I'm in your arms. I can't wait to see you, to tell you and show you how much I love you. -- Karen

Then he heard Karen insert the key in the door, and he turned to greet her. Sheer joy blossomed across her face as soon as she saw him standing there waiting for her, smiling. Her blue eyes sparkled with excitement and anticipation—her flaxen, shoulder-length hair smartly framing the beautiful and radiant face he so adored. She rushed across the room and threw her arms around him as he pulled her off her feet, embracing her as tightly as he dared.

"Oh God, I've missed you," she said as they kissed frantically.

"And I you, Karen."

They held onto one another for several minutes, neither wanting to let go.

"You must be exhausted," she finally whispered, leaning away from him.

"I was until you ran through the door," he answered, tightening his embrace.

"Do you want to shower and rest for a while?"

"A shower sounds great. Rest is the last thing I want to do."

"Are you hungry?"

"Depends what's being served," he answered playfully.

"Let's order pizza and stay in tonight," she replied. "I don't want to share you with anyone, and I want to hear everything that's happening in Israel."

"Let's not talk about what's happening in Israel," he answered, turning serious for the first time.

"Things are bad?" she replied, more a question than a statement.

"Bad and, I fear, about to get worse."

"Politics?"

"Not at the moment."

"Terrorism?'

"That too, of course. There's always the threat of terrorism in our part of the world."

"But there's something else?" she replied.

"I don't want to talk about it, Karen. Not right now. It will ruin the evening."

"Okay," she answered hesitantly. "Why don't you shower and I'll call Uno's for pizza and get into something more comfortable."

He nodded. "That sounds great."

"There's a large robe hanging next to mine in the bathroom. I bought it over the weekend at Marshall Fields."

"You think of everything."

"I've thought of very little this week except you. You've filled my thoughts, Amos. Just you."

He placed his hands, gently, on the sides of her face and leaned down to kiss her. Karen closed her eyes. He kissed her eyelids softly.

"I love you so much," she whispered.

"I wish this moment could last forever," he answered.

"It can, you know."

He looked into her eyes, a bit sadly she thought, but he didn't reply. He just held her close, and as he did he glanced over her shoulder and focused, once again, on the massive lake that spread, like the Mediterranean, as far as the eye could see. His mind drifted to the Suez Canal, a stretch of a few meters of water that separated the Sinai from the rest of Egypt, and his young countrymen and comrades from the appalling violence he was certain was coming.

The reverie of the moment broken, he smiled and kissed Karen, a bit too hastily, on the forehead. "I'll shower," he said. "Then let's just relax and enjoy the evening."

"What is it?" she asked. "Your mood just changed. I can feel it."

"It's nothing," he lied. "I'm probably a little more tired than I realized. The shower will be good."

"Go," she replied, nudging him toward the bedroom suite. "Just lay your clothes on the bed. I'll put them in the closet."

As he undressed his mind drifted from the splendor and comfort of Karen's world to the hard reality of the world he had left only hours earlier.

***

Amos, deep in thought, leaned forward against the tiled shower wall, his head resting on his forearm as the warm, soothing water cascaded over his head and shoulders. He closed his eyes and just stood there trying to collect his thoughts. He was in the heartland of America, with thousands of miles separating him from whatever was about to erupt in Sinai and on the Golan. Karen eagerly awaited him only a few steps away. Pizza was on the way from Uno's, a casual meal punctuated with their favorite Chianti, and then, later, her bed awaited. He stood there naked, surrounded by luxury and comfort and, yet, a feeling of growing dread. Who was he to question General Zeira and the whole damn high command? Every impulse told him the Middle East was about to erupt, yet he knew his instincts were not widely shared. Zeira and his senior military intelligence officers were so damn positive that all of the Arab maneuvers were a bluff, that there was no chance of war—that the Concept would prove them right. Amos just stood there, motionless, eyes closed, letting the strong stream from the shower flow over him. Then Amos heard the latch of the shower door snap open as Karen stepped in and snuggled closely behind him, wrapping her arms around his torso in a tight embrace.

"Let it go, Amos. You're here, now, with me," she whispered, tightening her embrace even more. Her naked, shower-drenched body pressing against his sent Amos's senses reeling. He turned and took her in his arms, kissing her tenderly, and then urgently.

"Make love to me now, Amos," she cried, turning and reaching back to guide him as she pressed her body against the wet shower wall.

"Yes," she responded excitedly as he entered her, grasping her tightly—one arm firmly around her waist, the other tightly across her torso. "Yes," she cried again and again, almost desperately.

Every nerve in their bodies aroused, every sinew taut, their ecstasy mounted almost unbearably until the intense climax of their lovemaking. Spent and exhausted, they clung to one another, and for several precious moments, the dread that had been dogging Amos for days had been swept away.

***

They were still in bathrobes when their pizza arrived from Uno's. They had spent the balance of the afternoon, after leaving the shower, in Karen's bed—relaxed in tranquil repose as they lay there entwined in one another's embrace. There was surprisingly little conversation between them, neither wanting to summon the troubling thoughts they both knew awaited just beyond the moment. They lay there, content in one another's arms as evening slowly descended over the Chicago lakefront. It was just after six when the Pizza arrived from Uno's.

Amos poured the Chianti as Karen cut through the pizza with a wheeled blade, separating the pie into equal pieces. The television news was droning in the background as they shared the pizza and sipped the Chianti. Walter Cronkite was reporting something about Vice President Spiro Agnew and a Baltimore Grand Jury investigating possible kickbacks. And then there was footage of Nixon urging Austrian Chancellor Bruno Kreisky to keep a transit camp open to Russian Jews who were immigrating to Israel.

"Kreisky bowed to the damn terrorists," Amos said, referring to the recent rail attack by two Palestinian gunmen.

"Let's not speak of terrorism tonight," Karen replied, reaching across the dining table and squeezing his hand.

Amos nodded. "You're right," he answered, returning the gesture.

They ignored the rest of the news chatter emanating from the television set, content to just focus on one another. They were relaxed as they chatted about plans for spending Yom Kippur with the Rothschilds in

Highland Park. Then, just as they finished off the pizza and most of the Chianti, Amos's attention suddenly snapped back to the local television anchor's voice. Amos was certain he had heard the words "high-pressure water pump" amidst the chatter from across the room. He abruptly halted the conversation with Karen mid-sentence, stood, and walked from the dining table, his attention riveted to the television set. The image on the television was of a black plume rising from what looked like a rail freight car. The announcer was explaining that the federal Environmental Protection Agency had been cited by the city of Chicago for violating the city's air pollution ordinances. EPA was demonstrating how retired freight cars could be dismantled by using high-pressure water pumps to cut down the wooden-planked sidewalls, contaminated by the remnants of varied and sometimes live cargo transported over the decades. The high-pressure water pumps literally turned the timber into kindling, which was then used to incinerate the wood planks in the railcars from within. The demonstration was, apparently, successful, even if impractical. The focus of the news report, however, was the power of the water pumps. The news anchor explained that these high-pressure water pumps could not only cut through the thick wooden walls of the freight cars; they could actually cut through steel—"like a knife through butter," the news anchor said, concluding the news segment.

"Oh my God!" Amos exclaimed. "They're going to use the God-damned water pumps."

"Amos, what is it? What are you talking about?" Karen called from across the room.

"The Egyptians. They're going to use high-pressure water pumps to blast through the Bar-Lev Line," he yelled back, his voice tinged with panic. "That's why they've been buying the fucking high-pressure water pumps," he cried.

"That isn't what the TV newsman just said," she replied. "He said something about water pumps that could cut through wood and steel."

"Yeah, yeah, like a knife through butter," he interrupted impatiently. "Karen, we know the Egyptians have been buying hundreds of high-pressure water pumps. We've been trying to figure out why. I thought they might use them to flood the unpaved roads we would have to use to defend against an attack across the Canal … you know, to turn the sand roads into a muddy hell."

"What's the Bar-Lev Line? You spoke of a Bar-Lev Line."

"We've constructed an enormous wall of compacted sand, nearly one hundred miles long. It's six stories high and over twenty feet wide. We thought it would take days for the Egyptians to bulldoze through that wall, while we were firing everything we had at them. We believed that transporting heavy bulldozers across the Canal during a firefight would be next to impossible."

"And?"

"And all they'd have to do is send two- or three-man teams in small rafts with those damn pumps and they'd have an endless supply of water right out of the Canal with which to blast right through the Line. I'm telling you, Karen, that's what they're going to do."

"What are you going to do?" Karen asked, dreading Amos's response.

"Right now, I have to reach Benjamin Bar-Levy. He has to call Dayan right away," Amos answered. "I have to find a secure telephone. I'll call our embassy in Washington. They'll reach Tel Aviv on a secure line."

"Amos, how are you are going to reach anyone at this hour? It's eight o'clock in Washington and three o'clock in the morning in Israel."

Amos nodded. "You're right. I'll try reaching Bar-Levy through the embassy in the morning. I don't know when the Arabs are going to attack the Bar-Lev Line, but now I'm pretty sure I know how. Ramadan began a week ago. I don't know if the Arabs will attack during the month of Ramadan. They're supposed to be fasting."

"What about Yom Kippur?"

"Probably an ideal time to attack," he answered with a shrug.

CHAPTER EIGHT

OCTOBER 5, 1973

Benjamin Bar-Levy listened carefully as Amos explained his theory about how the Egyptians were going to use their recently acquired high-pressure water pumps to destroy the Bar-Lev Line. He assured Amos he would pass the information on to both Zeira and Dayan, but he voiced his doubt. "You know we can turn the Canal into a wall of fire, Amos."

"Have we ever tested the system, Benjamin? Do we even know it would work?" Amos asked impatiently.

"It should work, Amos. We have a huge supply of fuel oil stored along the Canal for just such an eventuality. The Egyptians will never make it across the Canal. If your theory is correct, they will be sending small teams across in light rafts with their water pumps, and as soon as the first rafts burst into flame the rest will turn back. Frankly, I think the idea that they could destroy the Bar-Lev Line with water pumps is rather far-fetched."

"Just pass my theory along to Zeira and Dayan. Will you do that?"

"I said I would and I will, Amos, but Zeira will laugh at you. Our planes would be over the Canal in minutes. An attempted crossing by Sadat would be absolute folly."

Amos sat there after hanging up, just staring at the telephone.

Karen walked over to the small writing desk where Amos was still sitting, leaned down behind him, and wrapped her arms around his shoulders.

"There's nothing more you can do, Amos. Your colleagues in Israel now know of your concern about these water pumps the Egyptians have been buying."

"They're not going to do a damn thing about it, Karen. They're absolutely certain the Egyptians and Syrians are thoroughly intimidated by our air force. We're so damned sure of ourselves, so damned complacent, we're not even calling up our reserves."

"Come on. Let's drive out to Highland Park. My folks can't wait to see you."

Amos reached up and gently took hold of Karen's hands, briefly kissing the backs of each of them. He turned and looked up at her and managed a weak smile. "I'm looking forward to seeing them too," he replied.

Karen drove north on Lake Shore Drive, deciding to take the more scenic, leisurely route to the north shore. Lake Michigan, just off to the east, glistened under the sun as they passed through Evanston. It was four o'clock in the afternoon when Karen turned her Mercury Cougar west onto County Line Road and crossed from Cook County into neighboring Lake County. Amos reached over and squeezed her thigh affectionately. "You calm my nerves, Karen. Just being with you calms my nerves."

***

At that very moment, six thousand miles to the east and under cover of the dark desert sky, teams of Egyptian frogmen quietly slipped into the cool water along the West Bank of the Suez Canal. They swam slowly, seemingly effortlessly, on a straight course just below the water line for about six hundred feet. Their destination—the fuel lines projecting out from the Israeli fortifications on the opposite bank. They carried no supplies other than a single Russian-supplied Spetsnaz combat knife and small waterproof pouches of cement. Upon reaching the pipelines it took only a few moments for the frogmen to carefully and methodically squeeze the cement into the pipes.

***

Dubi Asherov's phone began ringing in London about the time the Egyptian frogmen were climbing out of the water back on the West Bank of the Suez Canal. The seasoned Mossad officer knew that a call that late meant something was terribly wrong.

"Asherov here," he answered tersely.

"I need to meet the boss as soon as possible," the familiar voice answered.

"I'll have the director leave for London immediately after Yom Kippur services."

"He must come tonight," the voice replied.

"But ..."

"Tonight!"

"I'll relay your message as soon as we hang up," Asherov replied haltingly, his voice betraying his sudden anguish.

Two-and-a-half hours later, Mossad Director Zvi Zamir, aboard an EL AL executive jet racing at forty thousand feet, passed just east of Athens, Greece heading northwest—its course set for London.

***

It was nearly ten o'clock when Amos and Karen returned to her Lake Point Towers apartment. They had enjoyed a satisfying dinner with the Rothschilds as a prelude to the traditional twenty-four-hour Yom Kippur fast that wouldn't end until sundown the following day.

Karen pulled a hassock up to the couch. Amos obligingly propped up his feet as Karen snuggled beside him, her legs comfortably curled beneath her. They were relaxed, even sanguine.

"Do you generally fast during Yom Kippur?" she asked, as she squeezed up against him even closer.

He smiled. "Why, are you hungry?" he asked playfully.

"Not for food," she replied.

"Ah, but for observant Jews, eating food isn't the only thing that's prohibited for twenty-four hours. There are five prohibitions."

"No drinking either," she replied.

"And no bathing, wearing fancy shoes, or," he paused teasingly.

"There's more?"

"No sex."

"Really?"

"Really," he answered.

"So, are we going to be observant?" she asked seductively.

He looked down at her, smiling. "Well, four out of five isn't bad."

With that, Karen quickly turned and shifted, straddling Amos's lap. "God, I love you. You'll be gone in a few days, and I don't know when we'll next see each other," she said.

"I'll be back for Thanksgiving, Karen," he replied, embracing her firmly.

Karen pressed even closer, and slowly, deliberately, gyrated her body against Amos as they kissed.

"Oh God," he whispered.

She stood as he became aroused and reached under her skirt to remove her panties. She dropped the silk undergarment to the floor and reached down and unfastened his belt and pulled his slacks and briefs down over his thighs. Without speaking she straddled him again, holding him with one hand as she lowered herself over him, sighing joyfully as he entered her. She moved, slowly at first, and then with growing intensity. Their shared rapture crested several moments later, leaving them both momentarily blissfully exhausted. Amos leaned back against the couch and closed his eyes. Karen, breathless, rested her head on his shoulder.

"I love you," she whispered.

"And I you," he answered.

"One way or another, we have to figure out how to be together, either here or in Israel. I can't stand being away from you, Karen."

"Can't you extend your stay for a while? Can't you take time off?"

"It's a bad time to be away, Karen. I don't know what is going to happen in my country, or when, but I fear we're on the verge of something terrible."

"You mean the war you've been so worried about?"

"Probably."

"When?"

Amos just shrugged his shoulders. "God only knows," he answered.

Karen sighed, gazing over Amos's shoulder to the huge expanse of Lake Michigan. The light of the half-moon shimmered on the waves rolling ashore. In Israel, six thousand miles away, the sky was ominously dark. The morning sun had not yet ascended over the eastern horizon.

***

Prime Minister Golda Meir was awakened by the ringing of the telephone at her bedside table. The call interrupted a relentlessly recurring dream, an awful nightmare in which every phone in her home was ringing simultaneously to deliver news that Israel was in grave danger—that a new holocaust was about to descend upon the tiny Jewish state. But this time the ringing telephone wasn't a dream. It was her most trusted ally, Brigadier General Yisrael Lior, calling.

"It's war—tomorrow afternoon. We think at eighteen hundred hours."

"You're sure?"

"It's from our golden source. He just finished meeting with Zamir in London."

"Zamir is in London? I was with Zamir earlier today. When did Zamir go to London?" she asked, startled.

"He received a call late this evening and immediately flew to London to personally meet with the source."

"Our golden source? Nasser's son-in-law—Sadat's aide?"

"Yes."

"He's certain?"

"Absolutely certain."

"Have Chief of Staff Elazar, Yigal Allon, and Moshe Dayan in my office at seven tomorrow morning. You had better come too, Yisrael. I value your judgment most of all."

CHAPTER NINE

OCTOBER 6, 1973

It was a somber gathering in the Prime Minister's office, as nearly all of Israel, including almost every reservist in the Israeli Defense Forces, was on foot on their way to Yom Kippur services.

"So, Sadat has chosen war," the Prime Minister said, as she sat down at the small conference table in her office early that morning.

"And Assad too. It will be a coordinated Egyptian and Syrian attack," General Lior answered.

"And our source tells us it will be this evening at six o'clock?" she asked.

"Yes," General Elazar replied. "Sadat apparently figures the sun setting in the west will be in our eyes as his troops attack. It makes sense."

"And what is your recommendation, Dado?" she asked, turning to General Elazar.

"Full mobilization and a pre-emptive attack on the West Bank and the Golan as soon as possible," General Elazar answered without hesitation. "That's been my recommendation all week."

"Moshe?" Meir probed, shifting her gaze to the Defense Minister.

Dayan looked from General Elazar to the Prime Minister, shaking his head in disagreement. "The Concept is sound, Golda. This is not the time to abandon the Concept. It has been the backbone of our defense planning for years, and nothing has changed. Neither the Egyptians nor the Syrians can knock out our airfields, and they simply won't attack knowing what our air force can do to them. We shouldn't overreact and force them, in return, to overreact." He paused, turning his attention back to General Elazar before continuing. "What do you think the Egyptians and Syrians will do when they see we've ordered a full mobilization, Dado?" he asked, his voice rising, his tone angry.

"What do *you* think they will do, Moshe?" the Prime Minister asked before General Elazar could respond.

"They may very well turn their maneuvers into the war they are only rehearsing for now," Dayan answered.

"How big are these Syrian and Egyptian maneuvers?" she asked.

"They're enormous," Dayan conceded, following a brief pause.

"How enormous?" she demanded, losing patience with her Minister of Defense.

"The Syrians have thousands of tanks and maybe one thousand pieces of artillery opposite the Golan," Dayan replied.

"And our forces?" she asked.

"We have less than two hundred tanks, and only about fifty pieces of artillery."

"And on the other side of the Suez Canal?"

"The Egyptians have more than a thousand tanks and maybe two thousand pieces of artillery."

"And Egyptian troops?"

"Over one hundred thousand—maybe five divisions," he answered weakly. "But they put on a show of force like this every year," he added.

"Never anything like this, Moshe," General Elazar interrupted.

Prime Minister Meir closed her eyes for a moment to contemplate what she had just been told. "And what is our strength on the Bar-Lev Line?" she finally asked.

"We have about five hundred men on the Line ..."

"Nearly all reservists and cooks, Golda," General Elazar interjected contemptuously, interrupting Dayan.

"... and nearly three hundred tanks a few kilometers behind the Line," the Defense Minister continued, ignoring General Elazar. "We also have eighteen thousand troops in defensive positions backing up our men on the Line."

"And what do the Egyptians have backing up their frontline troops?"

"It looks like they have another four or five divisions west of the Line," Dayan answered.

"Talk to me in numbers, Moshe. How many men are there backing up the one hundred thousand men they have positioned on the Canal?"

"Roughly another one hundred thousand men, Golda."

"And tanks?"

"We estimate another four hundred in reserve."

"God in heaven," she whispered.

"Golda, they won't attack knowing our air force will tear them to shreds in a matter of hours," Dayan responded defensively.

"So, what do you think we should do, Moshe?"

"No pre-emptive strike and no more than twenty thousand men called up from the reserves. We don't want to precipitate a war by mobilizing all our forces."

Prime Minister Meir sat there looking at her generals. "No future Prime Minister should ever find himself or herself in such a predicament," she replied irritably, betraying her dismay and impatience. "No one will be listening to the radio or watching television today. It's Yom Kippur, for God's sake. How will we even communicate an immediate total mobilization to the reserves?"

"We'll broadcast the call-up and begin sending couriers to every synagogue in Israel. Word will spread like wildfire."

Prime Minister Meir closed her eyes and lowered her head into her hand while she contemplated the decision she knew would affect every man, woman, and child in Israel, and largely define her place in history. A moment later, steely eyed and resolute, she looked up and faced her generals.

"No pre-emptive strike." Her voice was firm and deliberate. She paused a moment to consider her next order to her generals. "Order a full mobilization immediately. We have ten hours before they start firing at sundown."

"But Golda, we can totally disrupt their plans if we strike first, as we did in sixty-seven," General Elazar protested.

"Dado, I have a very bad feeling about all of this. I think we are probably going to need a great deal of help from the Americans before this is over, and I know as sure as we're sitting here that neither Secretary of State Kissinger nor Secretary of Defense Schlesinger will lift a finger to help us if we fire the first shot. They won't tolerate another pre-emptive war."

"Golda, a pre-emptive strike will save hundreds, quite possibly thousands, of Israeli lives," General Elazar argued.

"Dado, how many Israeli lives will it cost if we need help before this is over and there is no one willing to help us—not even the Americans?" There was total silence in the room.

"Our best and most experienced military minds do not believe the Arabs intend war," Dayan insisted.

"Yes, Moshe, I hear you," she replied impatiently, ire rising in her voice. "But our best and most experienced military minds, as you say, have left us with a few hundred cooks and reservists facing hundreds of thousands of Egyptian soldiers on the Canal and the same imbalance on the Golan."

Dayan's shoulders sagged. He lowered his gaze to the floor but said nothing in response.

"We have ten hours to mobilize. Our best and most experienced military minds assured me we would have twenty-four to forty-eight hours' warning in the event of war. You have work to do, gentlemen, and very little time in which to do it," Prime Minister Meir said, ending the meeting and dismissing her generals.

***

President Sadat sat at his desk reviewing the plan of attack with his Military Chief of Staff, Saad el-Shazly. The smoke from his pipe filled the office with a pleasant aroma. He puffed slowly, methodically, calmly.

"Our men are ready?" he finally asked, between puffs.

"As ready as we ever will be," Shazly answered.

"The artillery?"

"Two thousand pieces ready to fire at the Israeli fortifications along the Canal."

"Intensity?"

"Ten thousand shells will hit them in the first sixty seconds. The barrage will continue non-stop for the first hour."

Sadat nodded approvingly as he puffed, almost leisurely, on his pipe. "And our friends in Damascus?"

"President Assad is more than ready. He is imploring us to move up the offensive to two o'clock. He believes he can take the Golan and invade the Israeli north by nightfall if we commence operations at two instead of six. The Jews are desperately undermanned on the Golan. Assad wants to attack before Israel can get sufficient reserves to the Heights. If Assad can threaten Israeli population centers in the north by moving down from the Golan Heights, Israel will have no choice but to concentrate its air power on the Golan. That will greatly hamper the Jews' ability to defend against us at the Canal."

President Sadat drew several long, slow puffs on his pipe as he considered his response. Then he simply nodded. "Send word to Assad to be prepared to attack at two o'clock."

CHAPTER TEN

OCTOBER 6, 1973

Amos teasingly, sensually traced his fingertips along Karen's cheekbone to the edge of her ear, and then very slowly down onto the side of her neck as she lay facing him, her eyelids slightly aflutter. She was not quite awake, but no longer in the grip of deep slumber. They had fallen asleep around midnight in the comfort of Karen's bed and the warmth of their bodies as they embraced one another. Traces of eastern sunlight rising above Lake Michigan played at the edges of the drapes, which had been drawn tightly closed the night before. The faint wail of an ambulance racing along Lake Shore Drive seventy stories below wafted up to announce that a new day had begun. It was seven o'clock.

Karen opened her eyes and focused on Amos. He smiled and leaned into her, kissing her forehead.

"I've been watching you sleep," he said softly. "It was like being mesmerized by a beautiful painting."

"You know, you don't have to sweet talk me. You're already in my bed," she responded, her voice peaceful, barely above a whisper.

He reached up and gently brushed back a ringlet of flaxen strands that had fallen across her forehead.

She smiled.

"I would give anything to be able to stop time right now," he said.

She nodded and returned his smile. "I know," she murmured.

He took her gently in his arms and pulled her closer. They lay there for nearly an hour, face to face, embracing one another, contented, blissfully happy.

And then the telephone rang.

Puzzled, she shrugged, wondering who could be calling so early on a Saturday morning, on Yom Kippur no less.

Amos's heart quickened as she leaned over him to reach the telephone.

"Hello," she answered.

"Amos Ben-Chaiyim, please. It's the Israeli embassy calling from Washington."

Karen handed the phone to Amos and lay back on her side next to him, her hand across his chest, her eyes betraying the anxiety she felt.

"Ben-Chaiyim," he answered, taking the phone from Karen.

"We are patching in Benjamin Bar-Levy from Tel Aviv on a secure line. One moment please."

"Amos?"

"Yes, Benjamin. It's me"

"The war … It has begun, Amos. The Egyptians and the Syrians both attacked about an hour ago."

"The Egyptians are crossing the Canal?"

Karen stared up at Amos, wide-eyed with fear. A cold tremble rippled through her body.

"They've unleashed a horrific artillery barrage against us, unlike anything we've ever seen. It's been non-stop for the past hour, and their troops are coming by the thousands in rafts. They've already begun laying bridges across the Canal."

"What about the Line?"

"They're demolishing it."

"With what?'

"They're attacking the Line with powerful water cannons. You were right, Amos. That's what they were buying the high-pressure water pumps for. It's exactly what you predicted."

"Is it working?" Amos asked, panic in his voice.

"The reports are very fragmentary, but, yes, our great impenetrable sand barrier seems to be melting away under the torrent of high-pressure water."

"And our men manning the Line?"

"It looks bad, Amos. They've been pummeled. The Egyptians are coming by the tens of thousands."

"What about our Phantoms?"

"We can't get within fifteen miles of the Canal. The God-damned Russian air-defense missiles are knocking our planes out of the air before we can attack. We've lost a lot of planes and pilots."

"What's happening on the Golan?" Amos asked anxiously.

"We're getting mauled. The Syrians have attacked with over a thousand tanks … a thousand tanks, Amos. I think we're going to lose the Golan Heights before the day is out."

"The reserves … they're mobilized?" Amos asked, his voiced tinged with desperation.

"Yes, this morning, but much later than we should have. It will be hours before we have our reserves at either front. Meanwhile, the Egyptians and the Syrians are hitting us very hard. It looks bad, Amos. Very bad. To make matters worse, the Egyptians have blockaded the straits at Bab-el-Mandeb. They apparently have a couple of destroyers and a couple of submarines there. All of our oil from Iran is shipped to Eilat through the straits. This has been a meticulously planned invasion, Amos."

"I'll get back as soon as I can, Benjamin. Is Lod still open?"

"Yes, but I have no idea how long we'll be able to receive flights from abroad. But that's why I'm calling. We think you should get to Washington and await further instructions."

"Washington? What the hell am I supposed to do in Washington?"

"I don't know yet. But we'll need a team in Washington. Ambassador Dinitz will, of course, be our point person, but you'll be more helpful there than here. I'll keep you apprised of progress at the front."

"Have we spoken to the White House?"

"Yes, but it's confusing. We don't know where Kissinger stands, and we don't trust Schlesinger at all."

"How bad is it, Benjamin?"

"Everything is very fluid right now, but not good. We're taking huge losses, Amos. I saw Dayan this morning. He's distraught ... beside himself."

"So much for the Concept," Amos said under his breath, his voice tinged with contempt.

"Dayan is saying this could mean the destruction of the third temple."

"I assume our wall of fire at the Canal didn't help."

"Totally inoperable. I don't know what went wrong. Some of our people think the Egyptians found a way to plug the pipes."

"What about our men manning the Line?"

"Reports are too fragmentary to be precise, but I think they're being overwhelmed. It's bad, Amos. It's very bad."

Amos paused, realizing the situation at the Canal and on the Golan was too fluid for Bar-Levy to have anything more precise to tell him. "I'll check in at the embassy as soon as I get to Washington so that you'll know how to reach me whenever you need to."

"Get there as soon as you can, Amos. Golda thinks we're going to need Nixon's help. She thinks the battle in Washington may be as important as the battle in the Sinai and on the Golan."

"I'll be in touch as soon as I get to the embassy."

"Dinitz will be expecting you," Bar-Levy replied. Then the line went dead.

Amos hung up and looked over to Karen. She was sitting up in bed next to him, her arms wrapped tightly around her legs, her head resting, sadly, on her knees, tears streaming down her face. "War?" she asked in a whisper.

Amos nodded. "Yes, it's war, and it sounds like we're getting mauled. I have to get to Washington, Karen," Amos replied as he got to his feet.

CHAPTER ELEVEN

Noah and Alexandra were still asleep when the telephone began ringing that Saturday morning. "Hello, who's calling?" Noah answered, only half awake.

"Sorry to call so early, Noah. It's Frank Markazie. Can I speak to Alexandra?"

"It's for you," Noah said, handing the phone to Alexandra. "It's Frank Markazie."

"Good morning, Frank. What's up?" she asked, half awake, as she took the phone.

"Your guy Merrick was right," he replied. "It's war."

"When, where?" she asked, sitting up in bed.

"The Suez Canal and the Golan Heights. We don't know much yet, but the wires are clattering like crazy that the Arabs have attacked on both fronts."

"Skirmishes or real attacks?"

"Who the hell knows, but from the racket on the teletype machines I'd say there's a war going on. We need a major piece for tomorrow's Sunday edition."

"I'll come down as soon as I get dressed," she replied, glancing over to Noah.

"War?" he asked.

Alexandra nodded. "Yep. It sounds like the real thing," she replied, rushing from their bed to the bathroom. "Noah, I had an interview scheduled here later this morning with a nanny candidate. Can you take that? I have to get to the paper."

"I was going to go to Yom Kippur services this morning," he answered. "But yes, I'll meet with the nanny candidate and go to services this afternoon."

"Great. Thanks, Noah. Her name is A'isha Abadi. She'll be here at ten o'clock."

"What did you say her name was?" he asked, somewhat uneasily.

"A'isha Abadi. She's Palestinian ..." Alexandra called from the bathroom.

Noah sat there on the edge of the bed, mouth half open as he considered Alexandra's reply. Momentarily lost for words, he just sat there staring at the bathroom door.

Alexandra stuck her head through the open door. "Just like me, Noah," she said, with a teasing smile.

"Huh?" he replied.

"I said she's Palestinian, just like me."

"I didn't say anything," he said.

"I know, and I know I caught you off guard. I was going to discuss A'isha with you. I've spoken with a number of candidates on the phone, and I really liked this one. I knew you'd be concerned and I planned to discuss her with you when we were both awake this morning."

"Well, we're both awake now," he replied.

"I don't have time now, Noah. I have to get to the paper. Please, just interview her and let me know what you think."

"I think I don't like the idea," he shouted to the open door.

"Noah, please, just interview her. Then tell me what you think," she yelled from the bathroom. "Let's not argue about this before you've even met her."

Noah knew better than to argue with Alexandra while she was rushing to get to the paper.

"Fuck," he murmured under his breath.

"You'll meet her later this morning?" Alexandra asked as she rushed from the bathroom.

"Yeah, yeah, I'll meet her," he replied.

"Love you," she said, kissing him hurriedly on the cheek as she made her way through the bedroom. "I'll call you from the paper as soon as I know more about the fighting in the Middle East."

"Yeah, I'll be anxious to hear," he said.

***

The woman smiled warmly as soon as Noah opened the door.

"I'm A'isha Abadi. You are Mr. Greenspan, yes?" she said, her eyes fixed on his, her voice soft, but steadfast.

Noah stood there, temporarily lost for words. For a moment, he saw only the deep red hijab and matching scarf framing the woman's face.

"Mr. Greenspan?"

"Oh … yes, yes. Please come in," he replied, extending and then retracting his hand hesitantly.

She reached out to shake his hand without wavering. "It's all right for women to shake hands with men in America when it's a business greeting," she said.

"Please come in," he replied, shaking her hand somewhat awkwardly and returning the smile.

She was a slender woman, around Alexandra's height—quite attractive, Noah thought, and smartly dressed in a black blazer over a white blouse, and red slacks and shoes that exactly matched her hijab. He guessed her age to be no more than thirty.

Noah led A'isha Abadi to the living room of the townhouse and gestured for her to take a seat on the couch. He pulled up a spindle-back chair from the game table across the room and sat down opposite her.

"So, I see you currently work at the Qatari embassy. May I ask why you wish to leave … to find other work?"

"You can't imagine how boring my work is, Mr. Greenspan. All I do all day is file papers. The embassy, as you may know, is new. We have boxes and boxes of papers to file. There's no stimulation, no laughter, and no one to talk to. Besides, I love children."

"May I ask if you have interviewed anywhere else?"

"I haven't. I had just begun looking at the help wanted ads in the newspaper when I came across Miss Salaman's, I mean, Mrs. Greenspan's ad. The position just seems ideal, exactly what I'm looking for, and … also, I am truly a great admirer of your wife. I was very excited when she invited me to come for an interview."

"Can you tell me what it is that you admire so much about my wife?"

"Of course. She's a wonderful journalist and a beautiful writer."

Noah nodded his agreement.

"And, of course, she's Palestinian. What an honor it would be to work for such an admired Palestinian woman," she answered.

Noah consider his response carefully, looking into her eyes as he continued. "You know, of course, that I'm not Palestinian?"

"Yes, yes, of course. You're Jewish," she answered without hesitation. "It would be my honor to work for both of you," she replied, without breaking eye contact with him. Her eyes were radiant, her gaze steady.

"I don't know if Mrs. Greenspan mentioned to you that evening work would be required from time to time. I'm Chairman of the Jewish Council of Greater Washington this year. Mrs. Greenspan and I will have a number of evening events to attend and we would, of course, need you to be with our son while we're out," he said, carefully watching the Arab woman for any sign of discomfort.

"I don't mind working late. I assume I would be paid extra for overtime," she replied pleasantly.

Noah nodded. "Yes, yes, of course," he answered, finding her response both disarming and a little disconcerting. Working for a prominent Jew didn't seem to bother her at all.

The next half hour passed quickly as they continued talking about Amos's daily routine and some of the points of interest in the neighborhood, including a nearby park that, Noah explained, was almost always populated by children at play under the watchful eyes of their mothers or their nannies.

"Is your son here, Mr. Greenspan? I would love to meet him."

"No, Miss Abadi. He isn't. He's with my parents today. They're taking him to the children's service for our religious holiday."

"Oh yes," she replied, nodding. "Of course, it's Yom Kippur."

Noah smiled. "Yes, it's Yom Kippur," he said, followed by a brief interlude of awkward silence—the only sound the ticking of an antique Chouteau clock on the mantle over the fireplace on the far side of the room.

"Miss Abadi, I'll discuss our meeting with Mrs. Greenspan later today, and we'll be in touch with you sometime tomorrow. I enjoyed meeting you," he said as he stood and extended his hand to her.

She stood and shook his hand. "Thank you for meeting with me, Mr. Greenspan. I look forward to talking with you after you've spoken with Mrs. Greenspan."

Noah walked her to the foyer and opened the front door for her.

"Good day, Miss Abadi," he said.

"Have a pleasant fast, Mr. Greenspan," she replied, smiling pleasantly as she left the Georgetown townhouse.

Noah stood at the door and watched as A'isha Abadi walked confidently east on Prospect Street toward Wisconsin Avenue. Then, just before reaching the busy thoroughfare, she turned and hurriedly crossed the cobblestone street to where the driver of an awaiting Lincoln Continental opened the rear door of the car for her.

Who in the hell are you, A'isha Abadi? Noah thought as the black limousine pulled away from the curb and turned left, heading north on Wisconsin Avenue.

***

By the time Noah reached Washington Hebrew Congregation that afternoon, Middle East war news dominated every conversation. Noah arrived several minutes before afternoon services were to begin. A sea of men and women, teenagers, and some younger children crowded the sidewalk in front of the temple and the grand lobby leading into the sanctuary. A relentless overwrought din filled the air. Rumors flowed unrestrained and spread rapidly in animated voices. The Syrians and Egyptians, some said, had captured all the territory Israel had occupied following the six-day war. This person heard that Israel had already counterattacked; that person, that Syria was about to invade northern Israel. Was it true that the Israeli Air Force had been decimated? Had Israel really lost thousands of its soldiers? Was Egypt firing rockets at Tel Aviv? Had Russia joined the attack? Would America come to the aid of Israel? Wasn't Nixon an anti-Semite? Would Kissinger be helpful? Wasn't Schlesinger a self-hating Jew? Endless questions with no answers.

Hy and Esther Greenspan spotted their son across the lobby and called to him. He gestured to them just as Amos broke away from his grandmother and raced through the crowd to his father. He was a handsome boy. He had his mother's olive complexion and his uncle Yusuf's dark brown eyes and wavy black hair, but he had his father's smile and dimples. Noah scooped Amos into his arms, hugging him as tightly as he dared.

The Greenspans hurriedly made their way over to Noah and embraced him affectionately. "The news is just terrible, Noah," his mother said.

Noah nodded. "We're hearing more rumor than news right now. I'm not sure we know what's really happening," Noah replied.

"Well, it's not good, Noah. I heard a lot of Israeli pilots have been lost," Hy Greenspan said, shaking his head.

"Yes, I know. I've heard the same thing, but I think it will take a day or two before we really know anything reliable."

"We'll take Amos back to the house and wait for you and Alexandra there. Sharif and Samira are joining us for dinner," his mother replied.

"That's great. I'm glad we'll all be together," Noah said, handing Amos to his father. "I'll pick up Alexandra immediately after the Neilah service and head over to your place."

***

Few people, it seemed, were paying much attention to the concluding service that afternoon. Everyone was eager for the day's news from the *Evening Star* or NBC or CBS, not the ancient news from scripture. Noah wasn't paying much attention either. Conflict in the Middle East always hinted at the potential for tension in his own household.

Neilah, *the closing of the gates.* What did it really mean—the closing of the gates? Who would live and who would die? Or who would be healthy and who would be lame? Or who would prosper and who would fail? Or did it foreshadow, this year, the closing of the gates on Israel—the death knell for the young Jewish nation, barely twenty years old?

***

Noah kept spinning the dial on the car radio, trying to find hard news about the fighting as he headed across town to pick up Alexandra at the *Evening Star.* She was waiting for him at the main entrance on Virginia Avenue and hurried to the car as soon as he pulled up.

He leaned over and kissed her on the cheek as soon as she got into the car.

"How were things at services?" she asked, as he pulled out of the *Star*'s driveway and headed uptown.

"Depressing," he answered. "The war is the only thing people are talking about. There are a million rumors, but no one really seems to know what's happening."

"I've been monitoring the wire stories coming over the teletype machines. It looks pretty bad for the Israelis, Noah. It's hard to tell exactly what's happening, but one thing is certain. That so-called impenetrable Bar-Lev Line was smashed in a matter of hours. The Egyptians have definitely crossed the Canal and are on the Sinai, and the Syrians have crossed the Golan Heights."

"Unbelievable," he replied. "What are the reports out of Israel?"

"The Israelis are saying that a counteroffensive is about to be launched, but they didn't begin calling up reserves until early this morning. We'll know more tomorrow. Amos is flying in from Chicago.

He'll be staying at the Fairfax Hotel over on Massachusetts Avenue to be near the Israeli embassy."

"Amos was in Chicago?" Noah asked, surprised.

"Yes, he was visiting with Karen and was ordered to Washington as soon as the fighting began this morning."

"To Washington?" Noah responded. "That's interesting, don't you think?"

"Yes, but it makes sense."

"We'll learn more from Amos than from all the chatter on the news," Noah said.

"Obviously the Israelis want to make sure Nixon is in their corner," Alexandra answered.

"Is he?"

Alexandra shrugged. "Who knows. He certainly has his hands full with Vietnam and Watergate right now."

"Yeah, all he needs is to get involved with a war in the Middle East."

"I doubt Nixon will stand by and watch Soviet arms dictate the balance of power in the Middle East," she replied.

"I hope it settles down quickly."

"So, Noah, what did you think of A'isha Abadi?" Alexandra asked, changing the subject.

"What did I think of her? She's very poised and bright, very pleasant ... attractive. And, oh yeah, she wears one of those head scarves."

"A hijab," Alexandra responded.

"Yeah, a hijab."

"But what did you think of her?"

"I think we should keep looking."

"You didn't care for her?"

"It's not that, Alexandra. In fact, she's very impressive. But there was something that bothers me."

"Oh?" she replied. "Tell me."

"Well, it may be nothing, but I watched her when she left our house. She walked down Prospect toward Wisconsin Avenue. I assumed she was going to hail a taxi or catch a bus."

"And?" Alexandra asked, curious about what Noah had observed. "Did she have her own car?"

"No, that's just it, Alexandra. She had a chauffeur-driven limousine waiting for her. A big Lincoln Continental. The chauffeur was waiting and opened the door for her. And I got a good look as it pulled away. It definitely had diplomatic tags. I couldn't make out the detail, but I could clearly see the pattern, you know, the diagonal letters DPL before the numbers. What kind of a nanny candidate gets driven around like that?"

"Well, maybe one who currently works at an embassy."

"Yeah, well she does work at an embassy—the Qatari embassy. She said she's bored out of her mind there."

"Well then, that could make perfect sense. The Muslims really don't like single women mingling on the streets. They probably made an embassy car available to her."

"To look for another job? Does that make sense?"

"It very well might, Noah. Qatar is a very conservative Arab country."

"Do you think they know she's applying for a job in a Jewish household?"

"Maybe they think she's applying for a job in a Palestinian household, which she also is doing."

"I don't know, Alexandra. I'm not sure she's the right person for Amos."

"Do you think she would be put off if she knew you were Jewish and that Amos is being raised Jewish?"

"No. She knew I was Jewish. She couldn't have cared less. She even wished me a pleasant fast today."

"Really?"

"Yeah, she did."

"So, what concerns you?"

"Look, there's a war going on over there. The Jewish community is going to be obsessed with the war and with Israel. I'm going to be the face and voice of the Jewish community for the next year. By tomorrow, every Jewish organization in the country will be raising money for Israel."

"So?"

"So, what will people think about my son being looked after by an Arab woman wearing one of those head things."

"It's a hijab, Noah. And what of it? Furthermore, Amos is *our* son, not *your* son. And for the record, I may not be Muslim, but I am an Arab, for God's sake. Our son is being raised by an Arab mother."

"I didn't mean it that way, Alexandra."

"Of course you did, Noah."

"I'm not prejudiced against Arabs," he protested.

"Of course you are," she responded. "Especially now. Everybody in this country is. And I understand that. Don't you think I cringe every time there's another Palestinian terrorist attack?" she said, her voice taut with emotion.

Noah glanced over to Alexandra. He saw there were tears in her eyes. He reached up and squeezed her shoulder affectionately. "I love you, and I don't want us arguing over A'isha Abadi. You interview her, and if you like her, we'll hire her."

Alexandra turned to Noah and smiled appreciatively. "Thank you, Noah. We won't hire her unless we're both comfortable with her."

CHAPTER TWELVE

OCTOBER 7, 1973

It was a typically pleasant early October day in Washington—cloudless sky and balmy temperature, with a mild refreshing breeze caressing both sides of the Potomac. Noah and Alexandra were waiting at the gate when Amos arrived at National Airport just before noon. Her face broke into a broad smile when he appeared at the top of the stairs leading from the plane. He hadn't changed much over the years. He was still the same handsome, somewhat weathered man she first met when she was a student in Beirut. This was the man who, at great risk, came to warn her of the danger she was in and who spirited her to safety in Israel—the man with whom she fell in love during the five years she lived and worked there—the man who rescued her years later when she was held captive in Khartoum following the six-day war—the man after whom she and Noah named their son.

The three of them embraced eagerly as soon as he came through the gate.

"You both look well," he said.

"You haven't changed a bit," Alexandra replied. "And yes, we're well."

"How long will you be in Washington?" Noah asked.

"Who knows," he answered. "I'm not exactly sure why I'm even here. I wanted to get back to Israel as soon as the fighting started, but the agency wanted me here to help Ambassador Dinitz work with the American government."

"Is our government involved?" Noah asked.

"Not yet, but who knows what help we'll need."

"The news is very confusing. I don't think we have a very good picture of what is happening," Noah continued.

"Right now, nothing good is happening. We're taking a real shellacking."

"The news reports make it sound as though the Israelis were asleep at the switch," Alexandra said as they made their way to the baggage claim area.

"I'm afraid we were, Alexandra," Amos replied.

They retrieved Amos's suitcase and continued talking as they made their way to the curb, where Daoud was waiting with their car.

Daoud rushed from the car and embraced Amos as soon as they approached. "Mr. Amooz, Mr. Amooz, I am so happy to see you," he cried.

"It's been a long time, Daoud. It's wonderful to see you too," Amos replied as he hugged Noah's driver.

It had, indeed, been a long time. They owed so much to the Nubian from Sudan, who was so instrumental in saving Alexandra's life six years earlier, following her arrest during the Arab League summit in Khartoum. He had driven through the night from Khartoum to Gondar, Ethiopia to telephone Amos at Mossad. He begged Amos to find a way to rescue her from captivity and certain death, or worse. And when she fled Khartoum with Amos and fellow Palestinian journalist Dany Haddad, she begged Daoud to come with them to America. And so he did.

Daoud opened the door for them and quickly placed Amos's bag in the trunk. A moment later they were headed west on the George Washington Parkway on their way back into the city.

As Daoud turned onto the ramp leading to the Fourteenth Street Bridge spanning the Potomac, Amos shook his head in despair. "The

Suez Canal isn't half the width of the Potomac where we're crossing now. We could stand and watch whatever was happening on the other side of the Canal. Literally, it's not half the width of the river where we're crossing, and we still got caught flat-footed. I'm telling you, there will be hell to pay."

"The Egyptians have really crossed the Canal in force?" Noah asked.

"The entire Canal is in their hands, Noah. All of it."

"Well, it is their Canal," Alexandra interjected.

"Which they crossed to make war on Israel six years ago," Amos replied.

"It sounds as though the war is going badly on the Golan too," Noah said.

"They overwhelmed our defensive positions on the Heights," Amos replied. "We were so undermanned they just bypassed our defenses in several places."

"Have they invaded northern Israel?" Alexandra asked.

"They could have, but they stopped short. They came at us with thousands of tanks. We didn't even have two hundred tanks on the Golan."

"What stopped them?" she asked.

"The meager forces we have on the Heights put up a really heroic fight. The Syrians could have come down from the Heights and taken the bridges over the Jordan before our reserves got there, but they stopped for the night near Mitzpe Gadot. They weren't more than five minutes from the Jordan River. All of northern Israel was vulnerable. Now our reserves are reaching the front lines, and I think the tide may be turning. I'll know more when I talk to Bar-Levy from the embassy."

"What's the latest intelligence from the Sinai?" Noah asked.

Amos sighed. "It's very bad. The Egyptians had a hundred thousand troops across the Canal and on the Sinai in a matter of hours. They're also bringing in hundreds of tanks. Our fighter planes can't get near the Canal because of the Russian anti-aircraft batteries. Our air force has taken huge losses, Noah."

"Any good news?" Noah asked.

"Yes," Amos answered, after pausing a moment to consider his response. "General Sharon has been called out of retirement and is on his way to the front. After what has happened, Arik is the only general whose judgment I trust. He never believed in the Bar-Lev Line."

***

"So, you went to be interviewed at the Jew Greenspan's home?" Ahmed Sayed Kahn asked.

"Yes, I went to the interview," A'isha Abadi replied.

"And?"

"And, I don't know. Mr. Greenspan didn't seem entirely comfortable with me."

"You wore your hijab?"

"Of course."

"You shouldn't have."

"Don't be ridiculous, Ahmed. You don't think he or his wife would have known I was an Arab? Do you think these people are stupid?"

"Did he say when he would let you know what they decided?"

"He said I would hear from him in the next day or so."

"Let me know as soon as you hear something."

"Why is it so important that they retain me?"

"It will be better for your family back in Hebron if they retain you, A'isha," he answered ominously.

"I did the best I could, Ahmed. You asked me to apply for this job and I did. What do you expect me to do?"

Ahmed Sayed Kahn peered into her eyes. His lips broke into a smile, more threatening than reassuring. "We expect you do to as you are told, A'isha."

"You said you just wanted me to keep you informed about what Mrs. Salaman was planning to write each week. You said you just wanted me to keep my eyes and ears open."

"And so we do, A'isha."

"And that's all?"

Ahmed Sayed Kahn glared at her impatiently. "Get the job and be a wonderful nanny to the boy. Is that too much to ask?"

"And all you're interested in is what I see and hear?"

"Have I asked you to do anything more?"

"I'm not stupid, Ahmed."

"No, you're not, A'isha. That's why you will do as you are told," he replied.

CHAPTER

THIRTEEN

OCTOBER 7, 1973

ISRAEL REELING FROM EGYPTIAN-SYRIAN ATTACK
CIA and Mossad Caught Napping
By Alexandra Salaman

But for an obscure and thoroughly ignored memorandum written by a State Department staffer five months ago, it seems absolutely no one in the United States government had a clue that a major war was about to break out in the Middle East. Interestingly, it appears the Israeli military intelligence community was just as ignorant or, at best, complacent, if not incompetent. While it will take many weeks or months before the extent of the military fiasco that Israel currently faces is known, we do know this much:

It appears the Egyptians and Syrians were able to thoroughly deceive the Israeli intelligence community during months, if not years, of preparation for the attack that was launched yesterday with a ferocity not seen since the Second World War. The Syrians and Egyptians made incredibly effective use of deception, denial, and disinformation to lull the Israelis into a state of uncharacteristic complacency.

It appears that Israeli attitudes, distractions, and internal intelligence problems allowed the Arabs to conduct a surprise attack unequaled since Operation Barbarossa in 1941, when German armies attacked the Soviet Union.

The Israelis, it seems, believed their defensive positions along the Suez Canal were impregnable. The so-called Bar-Lev Line was supposed to restrain any attacker for the period it would take for Israel to mobilize its reserve forces. The Israelis apparently believed their decisive victory in the 1967 war would preclude the Arabs from launching a conventional attack until enormous stockpiles of sophisticated weapons and equipment were on hand. The Israelis seem to have assumed that the Arabs were not capable of planning and executing any type of military endeavor other than guerrilla warfare.

Major General Zeira, Israeli Director of Military Intelligence, demonstrated his cluelessness during an interview last Spring.

"I discount the likelihood of a conventional Arab attack. The biggest problem Israeli intelligence faces is to underestimate what we're up against, but an equally big risk is that we would overestimate (and thus overreact). The Arab leadership have their own logic. Thus, we have to look hard for evidence of their real intentions in the field; otherwise, with the Arabs, all you have is rhetoric. Too many Arab leaders have intentions which far exceed their capabilities."

Really? Well, perhaps not.

Sources tell us that ever since the 1967 six-day war Egyptian maneuvers had gotten larger, with this year's exercises involving division-size units for the first time. Israel had to know that Egypt had called up its reserves and that leaves were canceled. We've learned that Mossad agents had even reported air raid and blackout drills were being conducted by the Egyptians, and that there had been extensive stockpiling of war materials.

One factor that has, undoubtedly, complicated Israeli assessments has been the great increase in Palestinian terrorism against the Jewish state. The majority of Israeli espionage and human intelligence assets have been directed at terrorism. Just last year, Japanese gunmen attacked Lod International Airport. Then came numerous terrorist attacks, which led up to the September 5 Munich Olympic Massacre by Black September. On September 19, an Israeli official, Dr. Ami Shachori, was killed in his London embassy office when he opened a letter bomb sent by the Black September organization. Terrorists struck again here in the Washington area on July 1st, when Col. Yosef Alon, naval attaché of the Israeli embassy, was gunned down outside his home in Chevy Chase by members of the Black September organization. The last incident prior to the war involved the September 28th train hijacking of Soviet Jews on their way to Israel via Austria. Conducted by two members of the Eagles of the Palestinian Revolution, this incident occupied the political and military leadership during the week leading up to the war. And these are only a few of the incidents leading up to the attack by Egyptian and Syrian forces yesterday. Also complicating Israeli thinking was what turned out to have been an unnecessary Israeli mobilization last

May at a cost of millions of dollars. When the Arab attack never came, the Israeli Intelligence Corps' creditability was greatly enhanced, as they had originally said no attack would occur. Inextricably, the same Israeli intelligence community was just as certain no attack was being planned this week. They couldn't have been more wrong.

As far as we can determine, only one intelligence operative in the United States, Roger Merrick, a staffer at the Bureau of Intelligence and Research at the State Department, predicted that war was about to break out. Merrick also predicted last May that the Arabs would weaponize their oil to squeeze the United States if we intervened on the side of the Israelis. Apparently, his prediction never reached Secretary of State Henry Kissinger, who, it seems, was caught as flat-footed as everyone else in Washington.

The balmy Indian summer we are currently enjoying may soon turn into a very cold, harsh winter.

***

Amos tossed the Sunday *Evening Star* down onto the dining room table.

"You're upset with what I wrote, Amos?" Alexandra asked.

"Not with what you wrote, Alexandra. It's all true. I'm upset with our people, my colleagues. Our complacency, our arrogance, has produced a fiasco."

"What is the latest news, Amos?" Noah asked.

"Our losses will be in the thousands, Noah. We're undermanned on both fronts, and the Egyptians and Syrians are taking a huge toll on our planes and our airmen. Our tanks are outnumbered nearly ten to one on both fronts. We're consuming at an unsustainable rate all the ordnance we have. I'm very worried that if the Americans don't come to our aid with equipment and munitions we'll have nothing to fight with." He paused before continuing. "Well, I wouldn't say *nothing* to fight with."

"What is that supposed to mean?" Alexandra probed, understanding that Amos was hinting at something very chilling.

"Don't ask," he responded.

"You can't ask a journalist not to ask."

"Don't ask!" he repeated sharply. "Just don't ask."

"Well, let me change the subject," Noah interrupted.

Amos shifted his gaze from Alexandra to Noah. His expression softening. "Yes, that's a good idea, Noah. Please let's change the subject."

"We're interviewing nannies for Amos. What would you think if we were considering hiring an Arab nanny?"

Amos shrugged. "Why not, if she's qualified and you like her? She's an American Arab?" he asked.

"I'm not sure how long she has been here. According to her application, she was born in Hebron."

"Oh, she's a Palestinian. Muslim?"

"She wears a hijab," Noah answered.

Amos shrugged again. "I would check her references carefully, but you would be surprised how well many Muslims and Jews get along in Israel. She knows you're Jewish, Noah?"

"She does. She didn't bat an eye. She even wished me a pleasant fast yesterday."

"You like her, Alexandra?"

"Actually, I haven't met her yet. Noah met with her yesterday while I was at the paper."

"You liked her, Noah?"

"She was quite lovely. Honestly, the only thing I found off-putting was that she came wearing a hijab."

"That shouldn't upset you, Noah. It's a sign of modesty, that's all. Hijab actually means *curtain*. In Israel, many of the orthodox women also wear head scarves—pretty much for the same reason."

"I hadn't thought of that," Noah replied.

"I'm interviewing her tomorrow morning. The hijab doesn't bother me at all," Alexandra said.

"There is one thing I even hesitate to mention, but you should probably know," Amos said. "I don't think it is significant at all."

"What is it, Amos?" Noah asked.

"You know we're still trying to get our hands on Omar Samir."

Alexandra, startled, leaned into the table, across from Amos. "What is it, Amos?"

"Well, we think we came across a house where he had been staying. It was near Yattah, not far from Hebron. It was deserted, but we did find some notes we think were written in his handwriting, although we're not certain."

"What did the notes say?" Noah asked.

"It referred to an Amos Project or an Amos Operation."

"And you think it might refer …?"

"No, Alexandra, I don't think it refers to your son, Amos. Frankly, I don't think it refers to me either. I suspect it has something to do with an attack he is planning against Israel. I think it has to do with the Book of Amos. You know, the prophet Amos, who foresaw the destruction of ancient Israel. I'm only mentioning it because it was mentioned to me … because I know about it, I thought you should know about it."

"Who mentioned it to you?" she asked.

"Bar-Levy."

"Is Bar-Levy … is Mossad concerned about your safety or our son's safety?"

"Not particularly, but he saw fit to mention it to me when he learned your son is named after me. Bar-Levy doubts that Samir even knows you have a child, and he doubts that Samir knows anything about me. He's just being typically cautious."

Alexandra nodded, her expression evidencing concern.

***

Alexandra was impressed with A'isha Abadi, more impressed than she expected to be, or, perhaps, more impressed than she wanted to be. She was the youngest of the women who had applied for the job, and far more personable than the others. The Arab woman had come to America as a child and had taken some courses at the University of Michigan, and while she still had a large family in Palestine, she said she hadn't visited the Middle East since leaving with her parents two decades earlier, when she was still a child. The Arab woman reminded Alexandra of so many of the women she saw every day when she, too, had lived in Palestine, before she and her brother Yusuf and her parents moved, no, *fled*, from the Middle East. Alexandra could understand why A'isha Abadi wanted to change jobs. She was much too smart to be working all day filing boxes of paper at the Qatari embassy. More importantly, five-year-old Amos took an instant liking to her when Alexandra called him in to meet the prospective nanny. At first, Amos seemed more curious about the red hijab than about the woman wearing it. Sensing his curiosity, A'isha Abadi's face broke into a broad and warm smile as she reached up and removed her hijab.

"Would you like to feel my hijab … my scarf, Amos?" she asked. The boy nodded and hesitantly reached out for it.

"It's very soft, isn't it?" she asked, handing it to him. He nodded and returned the smile.

"Wearing it is a custom where I come from. We put it on when we dress each day, just as we put on all of our other clothing."

"It's pretty," he replied.

"If you like it, I'll wear it, and if you don't, then I won't," she said as he handed it back to her.

"I like it," he answered.

Alexandra smiled and nodded approvingly as A'isha Abadi glanced toward her. She admired how the Arab woman had handled Amos's curiosity about the hijab.

"May we call you A'isha, Miss Abadi?" Alexandra asked.

"Of course, of course," she answered, her smile sincere and engaging.

"Let me be very frank with you, A'isha. My husband and I are both very impressed with you, and it's obvious that our son, Amos, has taken a liking to you as well," Alexandra began. "But as you know, Mr. Greenspan is Jewish and we are raising our son Jewish as well."

"Yes, yes, of course. I understand," A'isha replied. "Are you concerned that that matters to me?"

"I would want to know if it does … in any way."

The Arab woman nodded her understanding. "Mrs. Greenspan, I understood who Mr. Greenspan was before we met. I read the newspapers. He is one of the most respected businessmen in this city. His religion doesn't concern me. We are all descendants of Abraham."

"But let's speak honestly, A'isha. Mr. Greenspan, like most Jews, indeed like most Americans, supports the State of Israel. You are Palestinian. If that is a problem for you, I would understand, but we should know that now."

"I don't mean to be impertinent, Mrs. Greenspan, but why do you think that would be more of a problem for me than it is for you?"

Alexandra, momentarily lost for words, simply smiled and nodded ever so slightly.

"Jews have always been connected to Palestine, Mrs. Greenspan—more so than the Ottoman Muslims and the Christians," A'isha continued. "The fighting over there with the Israelis and the Egyptians and the Syrians doesn't concern the Palestinians, and regardless of who wins, the Palestinians will still be a people without a country. Even when Jordan controlled Palestine, there was no Palestine. The fighting is madness, but it doesn't have any influence on how I think about Jews or, frankly, anyone else here in America."

There was a long moment of silence as the two women looked at one another, each taking the measure of the other. The slightest hint of a smile formed on Alexandra's face, which was quickly mirrored by A'isha Abadi.

"When can you begin, A'isha?' Alexandra finally asked.

CHAPTER
FOURTEEN

The clerk at the New Cataract Hotel handed Omar Samir the key to his room. Samir was dog tired. He had enjoyed too much kabob and lamb kofta at El Masry, his favorite restaurant in Aswan. He picked up a copy of *Al Ahram* to catch up on the latest war news and started toward his room when the clerk called after him.

"Mr. Samir, we have a cable for you. It arrived about an hour ago."

"Any other mail for me?" he asked.

"No, sir. Just the cable. It's from America. Washington D.C."

Omar Samir snatched the cable from the clerk and rushed back to his room, flipping on the light switch as soon as he was through the door. The ceiling fan began slowly rotating above the illuminated glass globe hanging from the ceiling. He tore at the envelope nervously, as the fan groaned overhead. His shaking hands crudely pulled the paper from the envelope, tearing it slightly in the process. The cable was from his friend at the Qatari embassy, Ahmed Sayed Kahn. It consisted of only two words, the most exciting two words Omar Samir had heard in years.

She's in!

Omar Samir could not believe it. The Ali Abdul Shoukri cell had actually succeeded in planting an operative in the home of its great enemy. They could now plan to strike the Arab traitor, Alexandra

Salaman, her Jew husband, and, the best target of all, their half-breed son named for the hated Mossad agent Amos Ben-Chaiyim—the Israeli who was responsible for the Salaman woman's treachery and for the death of Ali Abdul Shoukri.

Omar Samir leaned back in his chair to savor what he had accomplished. He could avenge Sheik Shoukri's death, and he could do it at a time and by any means that suited him. Swiftly killing them, he knew, would be an injustice. No, the punishment had to bring joy to the martyred sheik.

***

A'isha Abadi was pleased the Greenspans had selected her to be their son's nanny. She liked all of them. The young boy, Amos, seemed like an easy child to look after, and Alexandra Salaman, well, who wouldn't be excited to work for her? Noah Greenspan seemed friendly enough, a bit wary perhaps about having a Muslim Arab woman looking after his son given all of the tension over the war and the ongoing conflict between the two peoples. She could only imagine the discussions they must have had before selecting her.

That Ahmed Sayed Kahn had directed her to seek the job was troubling, but after all, what harm could there possibly be? What in the world did he think she was going to learn by simply keeping her eyes and ears open? Alexandra Salaman was only a journalist, a prominent one, but only a journalist nonetheless. Did Ahmed Sayed Kahn really think she was going to learn something that important? All of the intrigue was absurd, she thought. It was so unnecessary, so extreme for him to threaten that her family would be better off in Hebron if she secured the job. *What nonsense.* And who was Ahmed Sayed Kahn to imply that he had such power. He was an embassy nobody. She was glad he told her about the job opening but resented his insistence that she apply for the position, and she was put off by his obsession that she be the one the Greenspans hired.

***

A'isha Abadi squeezed five-year-old Amos's hand affectionately as the two of them strolled through Montrose Park along the well-trod path that led to the gardens at Dumbarton Oaks. Her grasp was warm and soft, reassuring rather than restricting. The boy looked up at her and she smiled broadly, her eyes alive and kind, her eyebrows raised welcomingly. Amos couldn't have been happier that he was spending the day with his new nanny.

It was overcast, but pleasantly warm, and a mild and refreshing breeze wafted across the heavily wooded common. The park was, A'isha thought, like an oasis, bordered by an old Georgetown residential neighborhood to the south, and everywhere else nestled in the embrace of the remaining peripheries of Oak Hill Cemetery, Rock Creek Park, and historic Dumbarton Oaks. It was there, in the old estate, where, thirty years earlier, the great powers met and conceived the charter of the United Nations. The quietude and rustic beauty of the park provided an almost surreal escape from the noise of traffic that honked, sped, and screeched along M Street and Wisconsin Avenue, Georgetown's two main thoroughfares.

She had begun working for Alexandra and Noah as Amos's nanny three days earlier, and she thought it was the best three days of her entire year in Washington. She found Noah and Alexandra's Georgetown home on tree-lined Prospect Street so much more pleasant than the Qatari embassy in its leased space in that huge office building on congested and noisy Wisconsin Avenue. A'isha thoroughly enjoyed her time with the child. He looked so much like the young Arab boys she remembered in Hebron. She supposed he also looked like the young Jewish boys who now lived in Hebron as well.

She didn't see much of Alexandra and Noah during the work day, but whenever they were home she found them to be likeable and welcoming. And then, of course, there was their Israeli friend for whom Amos was named. He came by the house each afternoon shortly before the Greenspans returned from work. She knew he was in Washington because of the war in the Middle East, but she had no idea who he was or what he did. She knew only that the child, Amos, was named for him. He was friendly enough, but still he made her uncomfortable. Every conversation with him turned into questions. How long had she been in the United States? How did she learn the Greenspans were looking for a nanny? Where was her family from? Did she still have relatives in Palestine? What had her job been at the Qatari embassy?

Amos was impressed with A'isha Abadi, but also just a bit wary of her. She was both bright and attractive, almost too bright and too attractive to be working as a nanny. He found her to be surprisingly at home in the Greenspan household, given that her employers were a prominent Jewish businessman and a Palestinian Arab woman. He was also surprised at how at ease A'isha, a Palestinian refugee from Hebron, seemed to be around him, an Israeli on assignment in Washington during a war that was raging in the Middle East. If she held any animus toward Israelis, she hid it well, he thought.

There was, however, something odd that gnawed at him. She seemed hesitant, at first, to discuss how she learned of the nanny position she had with the Greenspans. She had told Amos she had seen the position advertised in the help wanted section of the *Evening Star*, but when he asked if there were many nanny positions advertised in the paper she seemed, momentarily, rattled by the question. "I suppose … yes, I think there were," she had answered. It was as though she had been asked a question she hadn't anticipated. It was but a subtlety, but one he had seen before. It was known as *a tell* to experienced interrogators, a hesitation when there was no apparent reason to hesitate. It was, indeed, a tell. A'isha Abadi hadn't been reading the classified ads in the *Evening Star*. Actually, she didn't read the *Star* at all. Ahmed Sayed Kahn had cut out the help wanted nanny ad and brought it to her. "You must apply for this position," he had told her.

CHAPTER FIFTEEN

Amos, Noah, and Alexandra had dinner that night at Billy Martin's Carriage House, a popular, rustic, old-line tavern on Wisconsin Avenue, just a short walk from the Greenspans' home. They asked for a quiet corner table and were seated at a booth in the rear, not far from where Lyndon Johnson dined with friends during the six-day war. The conversation turned almost immediately to the fighting raging on the Sinai and the Golan Heights.

"I think the worst may soon be over," Amos said. "Ambassador Dinitz says Nixon promised Golda that America will replenish our munitions. He said he would replace the tanks and Phantoms we've lost. We're running low on everything, even bullets."

"How quickly can all of that equipment be replaced?" Noah asked.

"America has a huge arsenal. The problem isn't the equipment. The problem is getting it to us. None of your so-called allies will let American planes land to refuel if they're carrying arms to Israel. I understand the only place American resupply planes can land is at an American base in the Azores. Other than that, everything will rely on midair refueling."

"I didn't know the European nations were so against Israel," Alexandra said.

"It's not so much that they're *against* Israel as it is that they're *for* Arabian oil. They're scared to death the Saudis and the Gulf states will cut off their oil if they assist Israel, even indirectly. After all, winter is right around the corner."

"How is the fighting progressing?" Noah asked.

Amos sighed, leaned forward, and paused to gather his thoughts before answering. Noah and Alexandra leaned closer to better hear Amos.

"We've lost at least two thousand men," Amos answered, shaking his head, his voice choked with emotion. "General Sharon attempted a hasty counterattack to relieve our men at the Bar-Lev Line and failed. The Egyptians easily repulsed the forces we had available. I'm telling you, there will be hell to pay. Relative to our size we've lost more men in the past three days than America has lost during the entire Vietnam war. Bar-Levy says we've lost five hundred tanks in the last three days. It's that bad."

"My God," Alexandra whispered. "Where have the Egyptians and Syrians progressed to?"

"The Syrians have been stopped dead in their tracks. I think we'll take the initiative on the Golan in the next day or two. I don't know what Egypt is going to do. Our reserves are finally in position. If the Egyptians go on the offensive beyond the land they now hold on the Sinai, they'll quickly go beyond the anti-aircraft umbrella the Soviets have provided near the Canal. Our air force and armored divisions will decimate them if they leave the safe zone provided by the Soviet missiles."

"Maybe all they want is the Canal back," Alexandra said.

"Maybe … I hope so."

"But you're not so sure?"

"Look, they've bloodied our nose, and they've bloodied it badly. I really think Sadat started this to get the Canal back, but given the magnitude of his success so far, he may go for the entire Sinai. It's hard to stop when you're winning."

"Could he take the entire Sinai?" Noah asked.

"Noah, it would be the biggest tank battle since El Alamein or Kursk during the Second World War, and if it's an open desert shoot-out without Soviet missiles backing up the Egyptians, we'll win."

"Has the airlift started from the United States?" Alexandra asked.

"There's been some bureaucratic stumbling. I don't think Schlesinger is in our corner, but this is turning into Kissinger's show. Kissinger says they'll supply everything we need except laser-guided bombs. We think Kissinger, with Nixon's backing, will do whatever he has to do to keep the Russians from intervening directly, even if it means threatening to send American troops into the region. Nixon is listening to Kissinger, and they're both determined to checkmate any move by the Russians. Ambassador Dinitz told me Nixon ordered the Defense Department to resupply what we've lost."

"That's impressive. I'm surprised Nixon is so supportive of the Jews," Noah interrupted. "Who knew?" he asked whimsically.

"I guess in Nixon's mind there are American Jews and Israeli Jews. He knows he has very little support and a lot of opposition in the Jewish community in America. I don't know that much about who Nixon likes and doesn't like, but I can tell you he likes Israelis. As long as we'll do the fighting, he'll send the equipment. He's assured Ambassador Dinitz that the United States is not going to allow the Russians to determine the outcome of this crisis."

"What would happen if he didn't back Israel?" Noah asked. "Would it be the end for Israel?"

"Israel has other options, Noah. Nothing I even want to think about, but for Israel, losing is not an option. We have options for winning."

"Like what?'

"Don't ask."

"I *am* asking."

Amos peered into Noah's eyes, his expression fearsome.

"DON'T ASK," he repeated, cutting off further discussion.

***

President Sadat looked at the most current battlefield map, took a few puffs on his pipe, and nodded approvingly.

"We've achieved every objective you laid out for us," Military Chief of Staff Saad Mohamed el-Husseini el-Shazly said from across the conference table.

"For sure, for sure," President Sadat agreed.

"Now is the time to get the United States and our friends in the Kremlin to insist on a United Nations resolution to stop the fighting and insist upon an Israeli withdrawal from the Sinai. For the first time, we're in a strong bargaining position," General Shazly said.

"How many men did we lose crossing the Canal?"

"Hardly any. Maybe two hundred."

"Allah was watching over us," Sadat replied. "We thought we might lose up to twenty thousand men. Our Russian friends thought we could lose close to double that trying to cross the Canal."

"It went as planned. The Israelis never dreamed we could do this. They so underestimated what we could do."

President Sadat nodded but did not reply. He just slowly puffed on his pipe as he considered what his troops had accomplished.

"*Just a few centimeters of the Sinai.* That's what you said we needed to get the Americans and the Russians to force the Israelis to negotiate a withdrawal under the auspices of the United Nations. We accomplished that in a matter of hours. Now we hold a fifteen-mile perimeter all along the Canal deep into the Sinai."

Again, President Sadat just nodded. "You did well, General."

The President's praise seemed a bit too perfunctory, General Shazly thought, as a wave of queasiness, quite uncommon to him, radiated through his body.

"Our *troops* did well, Anwar."

"We have to do a little better," President Sadat replied, raising cold, steely eyes to General Shazly. "Our Syrian brothers need help. They have been pushed off the Golan. We have to divert the Israelis from pursuing their counterattack into Syria. Thanks be to Allah, on the Sinai the Israelis are back on their heels. Why not penetrate as far as we can, and secure the Mitla and Gidi Passes, and *then* insist on negotiations at the United Nations? The more land we hold, the stronger our bargaining position."

"With all due respect, Anwar, the Israelis can't really engage us as long as we have the protection of the Russian missiles, but if we move any further into the Sinai we'll be beyond the protective range of the missiles. The Mitla and Gidi Passes are thirty-five miles beyond our missile umbrella. We'll be totally exposed. It will be the totality of the Israeli Defense Forces against our military. The Israeli Air Force will surely attack our men and our tanks. Their tanks will have the added protection of their air force, just as our armored divisions currently have the protection of the Soviet missiles. The handheld, wire-guided anti-tank weapons the Russians gave us will be of no use in a fast-moving, open-field tank battle, and it would be suicidal to move an armored division into range of the Israeli Air Force."

"We have an air force too, General!" President Sadat shouted angrily, slamming his hand down on the conference table. "We have the initiative right now. Whoever heard of stopping when you have the enemy on the run? We can rush one thousand tanks against the Israelis and be at the Mitla and Gidi Passes before they know what hit them. This is no time to stop. We have them on the run, Shazly."

"They're not on the run, Mr. President. They're regrouping in the Sinai, and in the north they're pushing the Syrians off of the Golan. With the Soviet missiles, we have the stronger hand here in the Sinai as long as we fight under the protection of those missiles. The Israelis still have tanks in the Sinai, and they'll be waiting for us. They will protect the passes at all costs."

Sadat looked up at General Shazly, his stare impatient, and his temper short.

"I am your commander, General. I say we push ahead to the passes while we can."

"That is a political decision, Mr. President, not a military decision. Politically, the gamble might pay off. Militarily, it could be a disaster. The battle will consist of our tanks against their tanks, our men against their men, and our planes against their planes. The protection we enjoy from the Soviet missiles will be neutralized if we advance beyond the perimeter we currently hold."

"I have confidence in our men, General."

"As do I, Mr. President. They've achieved every objective we gave them and more. They have fought bravely. But our well-planned offensive was designed around those Soviet missiles. Those missiles were the backbone of our war plan. Neutralize those missiles and you neutralize our entire strategy."

"Send our armored divisions into the Sinai and secure the passes, Shazly," Sadat replied, his voice curt and angry. "That's an order! You will do as I say. Let's really take the battle to the Israelis, while they're still stunned by our successes. Let's show the world who we are."

General Shazly struggled to control his temper. He sat there silently enraged, his heart pounding in his chest, the sound of his own pulse reverberating in his ears. He knew Sadat had made up his mind and that it would be futile to argue any further. He looked into his President's eyes for several moments, incensed by the stupidity of the order he had just been given. After a moment of agonizing silence, he acquiesced with a curt nod. "As you command, Mr. President. Your *political judgment*, of course, must be the last word on the matter. Indeed, the world will see who we are."

***

Golda Meir sat alone in her office and contemplated the nightmare into which she and her country had descended. She was heartsick. Everything now depended on Washington. Ambassador Dinitz and that young man, Amos Ben-Chaiyim, from Mossad had to get Nixon to do something and do it quickly. Words and assurances were not enough. Over two thousand young Israeli soldiers had already died in a battle that had barely begun. There wasn't a family in Israel that hadn't lost someone or had family or friends who hadn't lost someone in the fighting. Henry Kissinger had rebuffed her request for a secret emergency meeting with President Nixon. "It would suggest panic," the Jewish Secretary of State told her.

The reports from the battlefields kept coming in, and they were horrible. Her recurring nightmare had become a recurring reality. It seemed every phone really was ringing with news of devastating losses. So many young Israeli airmen, the pride of her nation, flying the American-supplied Phantoms had been shot down by Russian missiles before reaching their targets. Almost overnight scores of planes had been lost. In just three days more than five hundred Israeli tanks had been destroyed, many by the latest Russian-supplied handheld, wire-guided anti-tank weapons.

Tens of thousands of Egyptian solders had poured through the so-called impregnable Bar-Lev Line in the first hours of battle. The Egyptians hadn't bombed the massive barrier General Bar-Lev's engineers had built, nor had they bulldozed their way through. They had just flushed it away using high-pressure pumps and the water from the very canal Israel's generals had said the Egyptians would never try to cross. *They just squirted it away with their water guns*, she thought.

And now there was an additional crisis. The Israeli Defense Forces couldn't continue to fight in the Sinai and on the Golan without having to use the arms and ammunition Israel was holding in reserve to protect the homeland. Soon they would have to abandon the buffers they had fought so hard to seize during the six-day war for lack of ammunition and equipment. Many of the men in the thick of the fighting were running out of ammunition. Many of Israel's British-made Centurion tanks were down to their last shells, and her air force was being diminished every time it took to the air.

What was delaying the arms the Americans had promised?

***

"It has to be Schlesinger," Amos said as Ambassador Dinitz listened. "Of all people, a former Jew turns out to be the stumbling block. He's more worried about offending the oil-producing Arabs than he is about the survival of Israel."

"The Pentagon will ultimately do what the White House tells it to do. Kissinger is more important to us right now than Secretary Schlesinger. Kissinger isn't going to let the Soviets determine the outcome of this war. He didn't want to believe we were sustaining these devastating losses. At first, his concern was that we'd defeat the

Egyptians and Syrians too fast, but now I think he understands just how desperate our situation is," Ambassador Dinitz replied.

"Simcha, he has to get arms rolling fast or we'll be firing the last of our ordnance in a few days. Nixon and Kissinger may be giving the orders, but, right now, it's up to Schlesinger over at Defense to carry them out. We need massive support, not the trickle Schlesinger is talking about. He can't half-heartedly comply with the White House and, at the same time, worry about upsetting a handful of Arab sheiks."

"I know, I know," the Ambassador lamented. "Dayan is ready to start shipping reserve munitions to the front. He's pleading for assurances that the Americans are not going to leave us with a bare cupboard and nothing with which to defend Tel Aviv, Haifa, and Jerusalem."

"Schlesinger is letting a few Israeli planes land in the United States to pick up supplies, but he's demanding that we paint out Israeli tail markings before they'll load any supplies on our planes. Can you imagine, we're in the fight of our lives and he has us wasting time painting out the Star of David on Israeli Air Force planes," Amos said, making no effort to hide his disgust.

***

Back in Tel Aviv, Benjamin Bar-Levy's hands shook as he read the encrypted Mossad message. It was a copy of an identical dispatch that CIA agents had just sent to William Colby, the newly installed director of the American spy agency. According to the dispatch, six Russian Antonov 22s had landed—three in Damascus and three in Cairo—in the span of a few hours. This was dire news. The Antonov 22s were Russia's largest cargo transport planes. This was the strongest evidence yet that a massive Soviet arms airlift was underway and that, at least now, the United States was aware of it.

Kissinger was furious. As soon as he learned of the arrival of the Antonov 22s in Damascus and Cairo, he telephoned Soviet Ambassador Anatoly F. Dobrynin.

"Anatoly, you must tell General Secretary Brezhnev that he can have détente or he can have war, but he can't have both. Tell him he is fomenting something neither he nor we should want, and the consequences could be devastating." Then he placed a call to Ambassador Dinitz and asked him to come to his office as soon as possible.

CHAPTER SIXTEEN

"Senator Jackson from the State of Washington wants to see me?" Noah asked incredulously as he placed his briefcase on top of his desk. "What's that all about?"

"I dunno," his long-time secretary, Barb, replied. "He was on the other end when I picked up. He just said, 'This is Scoop Jackson from Washington. I'd like to arrange a meeting with Noah Greenspan as soon as possible.' I assume his staff wasn't in yet, so he called himself. It must be urgent, Noah. I told him you could be there at nine o'clock this morning. Daoud is waiting to drive you over to Capitol Hill."

"Why would Senator Jackson want to see me?"

Barb shrugged. "I think you'll have to ask him that, Noah. I'm guessing either it's about the war over in the Middle East or, maybe, he just wants to hit you up for a contribution."

"Probably a contribution," Noah responded. "He'd have no reason to discuss the war with me."

***

Senator Jackson moved quickly from behind his desk and shook Noah's hand enthusiastically as soon as he was ushered into the Senator's office.

"Well, I've heard and read so much about you, Mr. Greenspan. I appreciate your coming on such short notice. I was anxious to talk to you this morning."

"It's a pleasure to meet you, Senator. How can I be of help to you?"

"Actually, I want to be of help to you, Mr. Greenspan, or more specifically, to the Jewish people. I know you head the Jewish Council here in Washington."

"Well, I'm just this year's campaign Chairman. I'm really a temporary figurehead," Noah replied with a laugh.

"Well, they picked quite a year to make you the figurehead, Noah. May I call you Noah?"

"Please, by all means."

"Great, my friends call me Scoop. Please feel free to just call me Scoop. I like that better than Senator when I'm with friends."

"Okay, I appreciate that. So, tell me, Scoop, what's this all about?"

"You may or may not know how perilously this war is going for Israel, but Israel is in desperate straits. She's taken a terrible beating, but it looks like things have stabilized on both fronts. In fact, the tide has turned on the Golan Heights, and so far, Egypt is not pressing beyond the perimeter they've established east of the Canal. Israel's reserves are now in place on both fronts and they're ready to take the initiative."

"That's the reading I have too, Senator. We have a very close Israeli friend who is working with Ambassador Dinitz to expedite arms shipments to Israel." Noah decided not to mention that his friend, Amos, worked for Mossad.

"Well, that's why I wanted to talk to you. I must say, Nixon and Kissinger are, at this point, behind Israel one hundred percent and so is the Congress. But Schlesinger, over at Defense, is moving things at a snail's pace. He's no friend of Israel. He's more worried about the Arabs and their damn oil than he is about the survival of Israel."

"And what do you think I can do about that?" Noah asked.

"Noah, if huge tonnages of shipments don't begin moving and moving fast, I and several other prominent members of the Senate are prepared to unleash a firestorm of protest here on Capitol Hill. We'll need the loud, vocal support of the Jewish leadership all over the country."

"Ah, and that's why you wanted to see me. You want to know I'm prepared to speak out on behalf of the Washington Jewish community."

"Which you head."

"Well, I'm this year's campaign spokesman, but, yes, I'm the current voice of the community. You can count on me to speak out whenever you think it will help."

"Hopefully, Nixon and Kissinger will put a stop to Schlesinger's foot dragging and we won't have to create a national uproar over Schlesinger and his obstruction of arms deliveries. But I can tell you this—Mondale, Bayh, and, believe it or not, Chuck Percy are all ready to begin screaming about the foot dragging over at Defense. They all have their eye on a possible run at the presidency, and they're very ready, even eager, to speak out. The White House doesn't want us pushing them to do what they want to do anyway, and we don't want to create another big controversy with Nixon when we believe he wants to do the right thing. I can almost feel sorry for him, what with that Watergate fiasco, and now this mess with Agnew. But if this drags on much longer, we'll want a national uproar over Schlesinger's stalling at the Defense Department."

"You can count on me to roar," Noah replied.

"So far, Schlesinger has only authorized the delivery to Israel of two Phantoms," Senator Jackson said. "Can you believe that?"

"That's all?"

"So far, that's all. Noah, Israel has lost dozens of planes, not to mention the pilots who flew them. The last thing Nixon needs is us screaming about Schlesinger, but Nixon is going to have to lay the law down to the Secretary of Defense, or Israel is going to be in big trouble."

"I don't know what good it will do, but I'll do whatever I can to help. Just let me know when," Noah replied.

"Noah, I'm told your wife is one of the most widely read columnists at the *Evening Star*. Is that true?"

"It certainly is. She knows the Middle East like the back of her hand, Senator. She's Palestinian, you know."

"Yes, I understand that … Interesting," he replied, his voice trailing off as if to invite further comment by Noah.

"I don't interfere with Alexandra's writing, Senator. She understands this conflict from every point of view. She's lived it."

"Yes, I understand. Yours must be an interesting household."

"Alexandra and I have known one another since we were kids. Our parents are business partners, and her brother is my best friend. In fact, he was the best man at our wedding."

"As I said, Noah, an interesting family."

"And a very close family, Senator."

"I understand she was imprisoned in Sudan following the sixty-seven war."

"Yes, that's true. She was held in Khartoum and terrorized in prison. She's lucky to be alive."

"Rescued by an Israeli, I understand."

"Yes, he's the friend that I referred to earlier—the one who's working with Ambassador Dinitz."

Senator Jackson smiled and just shook his head. "Who knows, maybe there's hope for Arabs and Jews after all," he said as he put his arm around Noah's shoulder and walked him to the door of his office. "I'll be in touch if we need help from the Jewish community," the Senator said. "It's been a pleasure meeting you, Noah."

**

Reluctantly, General Shazly began preparing for an all-out assault on the Israeli forces concentrated just west of the Mitla and Gidi Passes. He knew, of course, that he couldn't maneuver a thousand tanks in the sands of the Sinai without alerting the Israelis. He had no way of knowing how many tanks Israel had salvaged or how many Israel had moved to the Sinai from Israel proper. Nor did he know that General Ariel Sharon, having mounted a failed counterattack and an attempt to have him cashiered for insubordination, was now busy probing the Canal looking for a weak spot at which to attempt a crossing onto the West Bank and into Egypt. Shazly knew the Syrian offensive had run out of steam and that Israeli planes that had been committed to the battle on the Golan Heights would now be free to revisit the Sinai theater. And this time his troops would be unprotected by the Russian anti-aircraft missiles. Once again, General Shazly urged President Sadat to reconsider his order to press the attack against the Israeli forces that had been pushed far to the east of the Canal. Once again, Sadat was adamant, this time threatening to court martial the general if he didn't immediately and faithfully carry out his orders to attack further east into the Sinai.

***

Ambassador Dinitz shook hands with Secretary of State Kissinger and introduced Amos simply as a colleague assigned to assist him during the current emergency. Kissinger assumed, correctly, that Amos was either from Israeli military intelligence or from Mossad. He noted that Amos waited until he and Ambassador Dinitz were seated before taking a seat himself.

Ambassador Dinitz began without wasting time on pleasantries or inconsequential banter. His voice was firm, and he made no effort to hide his frustration in dealing with Secretary Schlesinger.

"Henry, it is obvious to everyone on our side, and I presume at the Pentagon, that the Secretary of Defense is not only unimpressed with your instructions and those of President Nixon, but determined to impede Israel's ability to fight. He is obviously hostile to our cause."

"We've assured you that the United States will help, Simcha."

"You and the President have assured Prime Minister Meir that our losses would be replaced, but your Secretary of Defense has agreed to send only a plane or two a day, and then pause to assess whether the Arabs are getting upset. In effect, he's telling us that if the Arab oil-producing nations get upset, the United States will have to reassess its support of Israel."

"That is simply not our policy," the Secretary responded, his voice low and gravelly, and, Amos thought, tired.

Ambassador Dinitz continued, ignoring Secretary Kissinger's assurance.

"Secretary Schlesinger also told me that America would only send a maximum of sixteen planes. We've already lost over twenty percent of our aircraft, Mr. Secretary. We lose more every day. Schlesinger even refused to let our planes land in the United States to pick up supplies. Then he said he would allow a few to land, but we would have to paint out the Star of David on the tail of the planes. This is a disgrace."

Kissinger looked down at his hands as his complexion grew flushed with anger. While the Secretary of State had no intention of impeding Israel's ability to defend its position in the Sinai or on the Golan, he did not look favorably on a swift and massive Israeli victory, which would only humiliate the Arabs and, as a result, complicate America's position in the Arab world. Schlesinger, however, was unsympathetic to the Israelis, having assumed, incorrectly, that they had started this latest round of fighting.

"Simcha, the Defense Department says we're having trouble chartering aircraft to send supplies," he replied, changing the subject. "The charter companies don't want to offend the Arabs either. They're worried that they'll become the target of terrorists. We're committed to help. You know that. But bureaucracies are cumbersome, and our Defense Department is one of the biggest bureaucracies in the world."

"Mr. Secretary, this isn't a skirmish we're fighting. This is a fight for survival. The roadblocks Secretary Schlesinger is throwing up will mean the assistance you and President Nixon have promised will not arrive in time to be of use *in this particular war*," he replied, hinting ominously at a danger rapidly spinning out of control. "We'll prevail with or without American help," he continued, "but it would be best if your aid arrived in time for us to fight and win *this particular war at this particular time*." His cryptic wording was not lost on Secretary Kissinger. Amos's attention was riveted on the American Secretary of State, Nixon's most trusted national security advisor.

"What is that supposed to mean, Simcha?" Kissinger snapped, raising and focusing his eyes like lasers on Ambassador Dinitz.

"The third temple is not going to fall to Egyptian and Syrian aggression, Henry. That is never going to happen. One way or another, Israel will prevail."

Secretary Kissinger knew, of course, that Ambassador Dinitz was alluding to the Roman destruction of the second temple and the consequent two-thousand-year banishment of the Jews from their ancestral homeland.

"The Russians are standing behind their Egyptian and Syrian allies one hundred percent," Ambassador Dinitz continued, glancing for just an instant to Amos. "Henry, do you think we don't know about the Antonov 22s that are flying non-stop into Egypt and Syria loaded to the hilt with supplies for the Egyptians and Syrians?" The Israeli Ambassador paused to turn once again to Amos.

"How many Antonov 22s landed in Cairo and Damascus yesterday, Amos?" he asked.

"No less than twenty and possibly as many as thirty," Amos replied, without hesitation.

"And how many transports have *we* received from the United States, Amos?"

"None," Amos replied.

Ambassador Dinitz returned his gaze to Secretary Kissinger. "It seems there is no bureaucracy in Russia, Henry—only in America."

"We're doing the best we can, Mr. Ambassador," Secretary Kissinger replied, reverting to the Ambassador's formal title.

"I do not know exactly what is going on here, Mr. Secretary, but if there is a feeling in the American Defense Department or even in your State Department that deliveries to us should be carefully modulated so that we don't defeat the Egyptians and Syrians too swiftly and humiliate them, I can tell you your greater concern should be the devastation this war is inflicting on Israel as we speak. I have secretaries in my office who have lost their brothers and other family members. We are a tiny nation and the losses are affecting every Israeli family. The daily losses we've sustained since this began would be the equivalent of the United

States losing five or six thousand men in one day of battle. It is in everyone's interest that this war be brought to a swift conclusion, and that we're not left without conventional means to defend ourselves."

"We are not 'modulating' as you say. We're contacting every charter company in the country to expedite deliveries."

"Nothing that has been promised has been delivered."

"Supplies are in the pipeline, I assure you."

"We can't shoot from a pipeline."

"I'll talk with Schlesinger again and see what we can do to move things along."

***

"So, you met with Senator Jackson today?" Alexandra asked.

Noah nodded and smiled. "Actually, I call him Scoop now."

"You call Senator Jackson, Scoop?"

"Yes. He said he prefers that his friends call him Scoop."

"And you're his friend?"

"Uh huh. He insists I call him Scoop."

"He must want a really big contribution."

"No, actually, it had nothing to do with contributing to his campaign. He wants me, as head of the Washington Jewish Council, to be ready to scream like hell if the State Department or Defense continues to drag its heals on resupplying the Israelis."

"Are they dragging their heels?"

"Scoop says they are. He says he thinks Nixon really wants to help, but the bureaucracy isn't cooperating."

"So, what did you tell Senator Jackson—I mean, Scoop?"

"I told him I was ready to roar."

"That's just great, Noah," Alexandra replied irritably.

"Well, what could I say—'I'll think about it'?"

"I knew something like this would happen if you became Chairman of the Jewish Council's annual campaign. I just knew it."

"Why are you upset, Alexandra? Of course, I'd be upset if I thought the Nixon Administration was hanging Israel out to dry."

"I understand that, Noah. But you wouldn't be expected to be screaming from the rooftops about it."

"I would be expected to do whatever I could to help, Alexandra."

"Who would expect that of you if you weren't Chairman of the Jewish Council?"

"*I* would expect it of me, damn it."

"Look, Noah, all I'm saying is that I've bent over backwards to maintain credibility with those on both sides of the Middle East conflict. We were displaced Palestinians, but I owe my life to the Israelis. For God's sake, our son, Amos, is named after an Israeli. But still, I've maintained important relationships on both sides. I'm welcome in Arab circles as well as Israeli circles. Both sides trust me, and I've worked hard to keep it that way."

"What does all of that have to do with me expressing my opinion if somebody is holding up arms shipments to Israel after Egypt and Syria attacked her?"

"Senator Jackson isn't asking you to just express your opinion. He's asking you to speak and express outrage on behalf of the entire Jewish community. He wants to count on you to be a provocateur against the Administration."

"Well, what would be wrong with that?"

"What would be wrong is that the news will become *us*. As soon as I write anything that is sensitive to the plight of the Palestinians the news will focus on the Jewish advocate for Israel and his Palestinian journalist wife. I know how these things work, Noah. You and I maintain a balance that works. We've demonstrated that there can be common ground and understanding between Arabs and Jews by the way we live our lives."

"So, you're saying I can't express how I feel about Israel?"

"Of course you can express how you feel. But Jackson isn't simply asking you to express yourself. He's asking you *to make news* about how you feel. He wants you out front advocating for Israel on behalf of the entire Jewish community. You don't see how that could make *us* the news? I'm telling you, the media will begin focusing on *us*, how we get along given the tensions between Arabs and Jews."

"So, we'd be proof that Arabs and Jews can get along just fine—that they can love one another and bring children into the world that know love instead of hate."

"Listen to yourself, Noah. You're making my point. I don't want *us* to become the news, and I certainly don't want our son to become the news. Senator Jackson, *your friend Scoop*, has his eyes on a possible run at the presidency. He's going to be courting the Jewish vote, and he's wrangling you into his corner."

"That's ridiculous," Noah snapped.

"Let me ask you something, Noah. Did Jackson bring me into the conversation during your meeting with him on Capitol Hill?"

Noah hesitated before responding, as Senator Jackson's question about Alexandra played through his mind, *"Noah, I'm told your wife is one of the most widely read columnists at the* Evening Star. *Is that true? Yours must be an interesting household,"* he had said.

"Well, did he?" she pressed.

"Sort of," Noah responded, somewhat reluctantly.

"Interesting, don't you think?"

Noah hesitated again before answering. "Sort of," he repeated.

***

"Mr. President," Secretary Kissinger began upon entering the Oval Office, "we're getting nowhere finding charter aircraft willing to fly supplies to Israel."

"The hell with the charters," Nixon snapped, making no effort to hide his anger.

"Right. That's what I told Jim over at the Pentagon. He's ordered three of our C-5 transports to immediately begin shipping supplies directly to Israel."

"Three! What the hell can we ship in three C-5As?"

"Mr. President, if we send more than three C-5As there's a good chance the Arabs will revolt. Jim is very worried about the Gulf states cutting off oil shipments to us."

"God damn it, Henry, don't you and Schlesinger understand the Arabs will be pissed off at us whether we send three cargo planes or three hundred?" Nixon yelled as he buzzed his secretary and told her to get Secretary Schlesinger on the phone.

"Jim," Nixon bellowed as soon as Schlesinger was on the line. "Look, Jim, I understand that you're worried about an Arab oil embargo. Let *me* worry about that. You get those God-damned shipments in the air right away."

"Mr. President, we're addressing that right now. We're trying to determine what aircraft we can spare that are capable of doing the job."

"God damn it!" the President yelled into the phone while shifting his eyes to his Secretary of State. "This isn't just a battle between Israel and the Arabs. It's a battle between us and the damn Russians. Those bastards in Moscow are sending plane after plane with supplies to Egypt and Syria and we're diddling around trying to determine what aircraft we can spare to supply the Israelis. I'll tell you what we can spare," he thundered. "Send every God-damned plane that can fly if you have to, but get whatever they need moving—now. Not next week, not tomorrow. Now!"

"Yes, Mr. President," Secretary Schlesinger replied.

"And if the Israelis need more tanks send them from our bases in Germany, but do it now!" Nixon boomed.

Within hours, early morning in Tel Aviv, Israelis were awakened by the deafening drone of Lockheed C-5A and C-141 Starlifter heavy cargo transport planes gliding down from the skies, having flown all night from the United States. And the flying cargo giants kept coming throughout the day and night—day after day, night after night. There had been nothing like it since the Berlin airlift. Israelis pulled their cars over to the side of the road to watch, in awe, as the lumbering cargo planes, U.S. AIR FORCE emblazoned on their fuselage, began their

descents. Nearly every Israeli adult, including Prime Minister Golda
Meir, wept at the spectacle.

***

The Egyptian offensive demanded by President Anwar Sadat
quickly made a prophet of General Saad el-Shazly. He had warned
that the attack would be a disaster, and, indeed, it was. The Israelis,
now being resupplied by America, waited and watched in disbelief
as an immense cloud of sand arose over the horizon, kicked up by a
thousand Egyptian tanks and hundreds of armored personnel carri-
ers rumbling eastward toward their positions just west of the strategic
mountain passes. It was to be a rout. The Egyptians quickly lost a quarter of their tanks and a thousand troops. The Israelis, by comparison,
lost only forty tanks, thirty-four of which were quickly repaired and
put back into service. A day-and-a-half later, Israelis under the command of General Ariel Sharon, known to his men as Arik the Lion,
had crossed the Canal and were in Africa. The Egyptian Third Army,
which had so brilliantly crossed the Canal only a week earlier, now
found themselves sandwiched between Israeli forces in front of them
and behind them. No supplies—no arms, no ammunition, no water,
and no food—could reach them. For all intents and purposes, the war
was over. No Egyptian general and no Egyptian army could rescue the
twenty-five thousand Egyptian troops trapped by the Israeli Defense
Forces. The rescue of the Egyptian Third Army could not be directed
from Cairo or, for that matter, from Moscow. The fate of thousands of
Egyptian troops depended, instead, on the American Jewish Secretary
of State in Washington D.C., and his considerable leverage to influence
decisions in Jerusalem.

CHAPTER
SEVENTEEN

Noah and Alexandra didn't speak much during the short drive from their home in Georgetown to the Mayflower Hotel just south of Washington's Dupont Circle. Noah's mind was focused on the remarks he would soon be called upon to deliver to the hundreds of guests at the Israel Emergency Fund Dinner in the hotel's opulent Grand Ballroom. He was anxious for the evening to go well.

Alexandra was unnerved. She knew the audience would be looking from Noah to her, taking measure of any hint of discomfort she evidenced as the only Arab in the room—the Palestinian wife of the titular head of Washington's Jewish community. She knew her family loved Noah, but she also knew they were terribly torn. Their hearts were certainly not with Israel, not with those who had banished them from their homes in Jaffa a quarter century earlier. Her father, Sharif, was Palestinian; her mother, Samira, half Egyptian and half English. Her twin brother, Yusuf, was a staunch advocate for Palestinian rights, and she, a Palestinian American journalist married to the Jew who was now the voice of the Jewish community as it gathered to support Israel in her struggle for survival. If Noah was anxious for the evening to go well, Alexandra was simply anxious for the evening to go quickly.

The Grand Ballroom was packed, and the din was deafening. Alexandra and Noah knew Amos was there, but there was no point in trying to spot him among the mass of guests in the room. Tables set for ten crowded the floor, with barely enough room between them for the wait staff to make their way to the tables they had to serve. Even the balconies lining three sides of the upper level of the ballroom were filled to capacity. Gold leaf accentuated the crowns of the square columns lining both sides of the long ballroom, and huge bright and sparkling crystal chandeliers were suspended along the center line of the ceiling from one end of the room to the other.

Over the dais, just to the left and right of the podium, both the American and Israeli flags were hanging, brightly illuminated by floodlights mounted on the ceiling. The Israeli flag was centered directly over the very place on the dais where Alexandra and Noah were seated. Alexandra knew the press photographers in the room wouldn't resist the temptation to compose their pictures so as to feature the Israeli flag hanging over the Palestinian journalist at the dais—the wife of Noah Greenspan, the Chairman of the Jewish Council of Greater Washington.

The Executive Director of the Jewish Council of Greater Washington stepped up to the podium, welcomed everyone, and introduced the head table guests. Noah and Alexandra were both greeted warmly, as were the other head table luminaries, who included Ambassador Dinitz, Walter Washington, the city's first Mayor, and his wife, and an assortment of high-profile business leaders—the builder, the restaurateur, the hardware retailer, the local movie mogul, the area's leading auto dealer, a prominent judge, and a major philanthropist and his wife, whose social soirées regularly graced the society pages.

The evening's program began with the cantor from the old Ohev Shalom Congregation singing the national anthem of the United States of America and then that of the State of Israel. Alexandra, of course, sang "The Star-Spangled Banner" along with everyone else in the ballroom. She then fell silent as the room filled with the voices of eleven hundred proud Jews singing "Hatikvah." Her eyes drifted down to the card, neatly positioned atop every place setting, on which was printed the transliteration of the Israeli national anthem, along with the English translation.

> *As long as within our hearts*
> *The Jewish soul sings,*
> *As long as forward to the East*
> *To Zion, looks the eye—*
> *Our hope is not yet lost,*
> *It is two thousand years old,*
> *To be a free people in our land*
> *The land of Zion and Jerusalem.*

Tears blurred her vision as she smiled through the agony of it all.

The cantor then tore a piece of challah from a loaf that had been placed on a small table before him, held it up for all to see, and sang the brief Motzi, thanking the Almighty for the bounty of bread He had provided. Few words passed between Noah and Alexandra during the meal, which somehow the hotel staff managed to magically serve to over a thousand guests in a matter of minutes. There was really too much noise in the room for meaningful conversation, and Noah knew that Alexandra was not in the mood for small talk. Neither was he. Noah wanted to deliver his hard-sell appeal for emergency funds to help Israel fight the war on the Golan and the Sinai, and then get home.

After being introduced as a nationally recognized rising star in the world of business, Noah squeezed Alexandra's hand affectionately, stood, and moved to the podium. The room grew silent, but for the sound of several dozen chairs being repositioned to face the podium and a brief chorus of scattered coughs.

Noah looked out over the crowd on the main floor, and up to those staring down from the balconies.

"Thank you all for being here," he began. "I, like all of you, wish I were home in the comfort of my own living room tonight, or perhaps out to dinner with my wife, Alexandra, and a few friends. We all wish we could be somewhere else tonight. But we're here in solidarity with our brothers and sisters who are fighting for survival six thousand miles away. Sadly, we already know that many Israelis did not, or will not, survive this massive attack by the armed forces of Egypt and Syria. We have received word that, already, more than two thousand Israeli soldiers have been killed and many more are casualties. Relative to her size, Israel has, in the last week alone, already lost many times the number of men America has lost so far during the entire war in Vietnam. The latest reports we have from the region are encouraging and, thank God, Israel seems to have turned the tide on the battlefield. However, we cannot fool ourselves. The situation is absolutely desperate. The good news is that the air armada President Nixon launched to resupply Israel is continuing around the clock. The bad news is that it will take years for Israel to recover from this attack, and it will take billions of dollars in aid if Israel is to survive. And that is why we are here. We cannot rely on our government alone to ensure that Israel recovers. We must do our part. All of you know the drill. There are envelopes on every table, and each contains pledge cards for everyone at the table. I have already filled out my card, and I have pledged to match the first million dollars contributed here tonight." Thunderous applause momentarily interrupted his delivery. "So, I've now told you what I'm prepared to do. We would welcome each of you telling us what *you* are prepared to do. The tables are all numbered, so we'll begin with table one. Anyone who wishes to speak should just stand and one of the Council's staff will provide a microphone. No one need feel obligated to speak tonight, but everyone should feel obligated to use the pledge card with his or her name on it to communicate to us how you will help."

And help they did. Some, who could, matched Noah's commitment. A few pledged even more. Almost everyone gave something. By the time the entire room had been canvassed tens of million dollars had been raised to help Israel fund the cost of what everyone simply called *the emergency*.

***

"So, what did you think of the evening, Amos?" Noah asked, glancing into his rearview mirror as they headed over to Massachusetts Avenue to drop Amos off at the Fairfax Hotel.

"Only in America," Amos replied. "Only in America could millions of dollars be raised for Israel over dinner. Quite incredible."

"I was very pleased with the evening," Noah said.

"You should be. You're quite the persuasive speaker," Amos replied.

Noah glanced toward Alexandra, who was leaning back against the headrest, half asleep, her eyes closed.

"You're very quiet, Alexandra," he said, reaching over to take her hand.

"You were great, Noah. Very effective," she whispered, wearily.

"But?"

"No buts. You delivered a great appeal."

"You certainly did, Noah, and your picture at the podium probably will be on the front page of every newspaper in Washington. You raised a fortune for Israel tonight," Amos said.

"But that won't be the picture the editors will select," Alexandra murmured softly, her voice drowsy.

"Who do you think the papers will picture?" Noah asked, surprised by her comment.

"Me," she answered in a whisper, just before momentarily drifting off.

Amos, surprised by her answer, leaned forward in the back seat.

"Why you, Alexandra?" Noah asked.

Alexandra glanced over to Noah, her eyes barely open. "Because I was the Palestinian at the Israel Emergency Fund Dinner sitting on the dais under the Israeli flag."

"You can't be serious," Amos interrupted. "Noah was the news, Alexandra."

"Yeah, I know, but they had more interesting pictures than Noah at the podium."

"But isn't an appeal that raises millions of dollars in a matter of minutes pretty big news? I mean, Noah hit it out of the park, as you Americans say."

"The guy who selects the photos isn't the same guy who writes or edits the story," she replied, yawning as she spoke.

"But I was the main speaker tonight. Won't that pretty much dictate what picture they use?"

"The most *interesting* picture will dictate what picture they use. How many Israel Emergency Fund Dinners do you think are taking place in America?"

"Dozens," Noah replied. "So what?"

"How many with Palestinians at the head table sitting under an Israeli flag?"

Noah glanced in his rearview mirror at Amos, who simply shrugged.

"I hadn't thought of that," Noah said. "I'm sorry if it turns out that way."

Alexandra turned to him and smiled. "I guess we're each, sort of, each other's cross to bear," she answered, smiling.

"Well, I'll be surprised if they run your picture with a story about how much money we raised tonight," Noah said.

"About how much money *you* raised tonight, Noah," Amos chimed in. "Anyway, do you two want to stop in for a quick nightcap?" Amos asked as they pulled into the driveway of the hotel.

"We can't. It's late and A'isha is still at the house with Amos," Alexandra replied. "But thanks for asking."

"How's that working out?" Amos asked, as he opened the rear door of the car.

"She's terrific," Noah answered. "Amos loves her."

"Yes, we're very pleased with A'isha," Alexandra agreed.

Amos nodded. "*Interesting*," he said as he got out of the car.

"What do you make of that?" Noah asked a few moments later as he turned onto Wisconsin Avenue and headed south toward Georgetown.

"You mean Amos's cryptic 'interesting' when we said we liked A'isha?"

"Yeah, I thought he seemed a little surprised that we were pleased with her."

"Well, aren't *you*?"

Noah looked over to Alexandra and nodded. "Yeah. I was certainly skeptical, but she's terrific, and, as you said, our son loves her."

Alexandra smiled. "The Greenspan men and their Palestinian women."

***

Alexandra was busy preparing breakfast when Noah came downstairs to join her and their son in the kitchen the following morning. Amos, still in his pajamas, was scooping up spoonful after spoonful of Klondike Pete's Crunchy Nuggets and watching a rerun of "Woody Woodpecker" on the small TV at the edge of the kitchen counter. The Sunday *Star*, opened to the Metro section, was already on the breakfast table. And there it was, the large color photo under the headline "Area Jews Turn Out to Support Israel." Noah picked up the paper and sheepishly glanced over the top edge to Alexandra.

"Nice picture of you," he said, trying to manage a smile.

"Yes, and I thought they got the color perfect on the Israeli flag too, don't you think?" she replied, a coy smile playing at her lips.

CHAPTER

EIGHTEEN

Alexandra pulled the draft of Sunday's column from her type-writer, arched her back for a moment as she reached for a blue editing pencil, and then began to read.

US and Russia Standoff: Israel on the Offense
By Alexandra Salaman

What a difference a week or two makes. Barely two weeks ago, Israel was overwhelmed by a massive, meticulously planned, and superbly executed offensive by Egyptian forces storming across the Suez Canal and Syrian forces smashing through the Golan Heights. Israel, by far the most formidable military force in the region, inexplicably all but ignored the spectacular buildup of Egyptian and Syrian forces opposite its positions along the Canal and on the Heights. Israel's complacency and overconfidence almost cost the Jewish state, well, everything. Israeli defensive positions along both fronts collapsed within hours of the Arab attack, and Israeli losses have been staggering.

The Soviet Union trained the Egyptians and Syrians and armed them to the teeth. And as soon as the bullets and missiles began flying, the Soviets began resupplying their Arab clients with a massive daily infusion of arms.

Enter the United States.

President Nixon, sensing that this war was as much a contest between the United States and Russia as it was between Israel and the Arabs, ordered the greatest airlift since the Berlin airlift. Israel, resupplied by America and bolstered by its own reserves, swiftly regained its footing, and took the battle to the Arabs. According to reports from Tel Aviv, Egypt has suffered huge losses in what is now described as the greatest tank battle since Kursk during the Second World War.

Meanwhile, Israeli General Ariel Sharon has successfully crossed the Suez Canal and begun attacking Russian surface-to-air missile batteries that had limited the Israeli Air Force's ability to operate within about fifteen miles of the waterway. To add insult to the Egyptians' misery, General Sharon has now succeeded in establishing enough of a force on the West Bank of the Canal to cut off Egypt's Third Army, and this war could well be over. The Israelis, after initially suffering huge losses on the Golan Heights, have pushed the Syrians off the Heights and are now pressing on toward Damascus.

All the Makings of a Russian-American Face-Off.

With Russia and the United States now fully invested in the fate of their allies, analysts agree that we're headed toward the biggest military confrontation since the Cuban Missile Crisis a dozen years ago. Russia cannot allow Israel to threaten Damascus or hold onto the Suez Canal, but that is exactly what the Israelis seem capable of doing at this point. No one thinks Israel is going to be satisfied with simply repelling an attack on its armed forces. The Israelis will continue to fight on the battlefield to secure the strongest possible position for the coming fight at the negotiating table. Meanwhile, with the United States and Russia "all in" on behalf of their respective allies, the world finds itself on the brink once again. Already there are reports that the Russians have sent a massive flotilla of warships and submarines into the Mediterranean to challenge our long-established naval dominance in this strategic waterway. With hundreds of ships and subs armed to the teeth circling one another at sea and non-stop Russian and American air cargo transports flying into the region every day, the danger is that the slightest miscalculation or a nervous finger on a trigger could result in a catastrophic big power dust-up.

The two Arab nations that started this round of fighting are screaming "ceasefire" at the United Nations, but the Israelis seem to be in no hurry to lay down their arms. They are determined to not only re-establish their lines as of October 6, when the war started, but to improve their position on the ground. Meanwhile, 25,000 Egyptian Third Army troops are relying on Moscow and Washington to work out some modus vivendi before they starve to death or die of thirst.

The dangers have been compounded by very serious distractions competing for the time and brain power of our top officials. Nixon's Vice President, Spiro Agnew, has just resigned amid charges of bribery, and the President has to be extremely distracted with the ever-unraveling Watergate fiasco.

The Russians have a disaster on their hands as well. They trained and armed the Egyptians and Syrians who nearly succeeded in crippling the Israeli Defense Forces. But now the United States has checkmated the Russians. The American resupply of Israel, after a hesitant start, has been spectacularly non-stop since the second week of the war and, as of today, neither the Egyptians nor the Syrians have anything to show for their expenditures in arms and blood. Of course, the Israelis have been badly bloodied in the fighting too, and now that they have gained the upper hand in the fighting, they will be in no mood to relinquish their recent hard-fought gains without exacting a price worthy of the battle.

At a minimum, the Israelis can be expected to insist that terms to end the fighting and relieve the trapped Egyptian Third Army be negotiated face to face between Israeli generals and Egyptian generals. That, in itself, would be historic.

Alexandra penciled a few minor edits before forwarding her column to the *Star*'s composing room to be typeset. At about the same time, approximately eight thousand miles away, Soviet General Secretary Leonid Brezhnev completed a draft of a cable to be wired to his Ambassador in Washington that contained a personal message for President Nixon. Dobrynin was instructed to forward the message to Secretary Kissinger for delivery to the President. It urged President Nixon, without delay, to have his Secretary of State fly to Moscow to help compose a joint Russian-American outline of a ceasefire and separation-of-forces agreement.

The tide of battle had clearly turned in the Sinai and on the Golan. Russia's client states were on the verge of complete collapse on the battlefield.

***

Alexandra rushed from work to pick up A'isha and Amos in Georgetown and headed uptown to meet Noah for a quick dinner at the Hot Shoppe at Wisconsin Avenue and Van Ness Street. Noah had just completed a business interview at nearby WMAL Radio, so Marriott's popular restaurant was a convenient place to meet. Besides, the food was always good. Alexandra ordered a child's portion of Pappy Parker's Fried Chicken for Amos and everyone else ordered Mighty Mo's, a Hot Shoppe's triple-decker cheese burger favorite.

"So, what's happening in the world today?" Noah asked as he licked his fingers while chewing a fried onion ring.

"What part of the world do you want to hear about?" Alexandra teased. "North America, Asia, Europe, or the Middle East?"

"Any part but the Middle East," he answered. "We've heard nothing but news from the Middle East for weeks."

"Well, I'm not sure Spiro Agnew would agree with you," she replied.

"Oh yeah. I forgot about him."

"I'm sure the country will too," she answered. "Can you imagine? That crook took bribes in the office of the Vice President."

"Really, I've been running all day. Anything momentous happen?"

"Well, the price of gas is going through the roof."

"Yeah, those bastards are really screwing us, aren't they?"

"And Nixon agreed to turn over those stupid tapes."

"Not exactly a slow news day," Noah replied.

"I don't think I've seen a slow news day in months," she answered. "It looks like this will be a big year for immigration into the United States. I think we'll soon see a flood of refugees coming from Vietnam and Cambodia."

"What a mess we've created," Noah mumbled under his breath.

"Are *you* a refugee, Momma?" Amos interrupted, holding a drumstick suspended in midair.

Startled by her son's question, Alexandra's eyes darted to Noah and then to A'isha. "What? … Why would you ask me that, Amos?"

"Are you, Momma?"

"Momma's an American, just like you and me, Amos," Noah answered, a bit too hastily, a sharp edge to his voice.

"A'isha is a refugee," the boy said to no one in particular.

Alexandra and Noah both looked quizzically to Amos's nanny.

"Are you a refugee, Daddy?" the boy asked.

"No!" Noah answered more sharply than he intended.

"Are Poppa Sharif and Nanna Sammy?"

Noah looked to Alexandra, momentarily lost for words.

"I'm afraid this is my fault," A'isha interrupted. "Amos asked about my accent. He asked why I spoke a little differently. I told him my family came to the United States from another country … that we were refugees."

"But why is he asking if Alexandra and her family are refugees?" Noah asked. Alexandra could see that he was upset.

"I told him my family came to America the same time Mrs. Greenspan's family came here … to get away from the fighting."

"*God damn it*," Noah whispered, barely able to contain his anger.

Amos looked to his father and then to Alexandra, his expression revealing more bewilderment than fright.

"Noah, it's not anything to get upset over," Alexandra said.

Noah held his tongue, but Alexandra knew he was furious.

"Amos, Poppa Sharif and Nanna Sammy brought Uncle Yusuf and me here a long time ago. We were born far away in another country. My great uncle, Anwar, may he rest in peace, brought us to America. We chose to move to America, but we were not refugees."

"Why is A'isha a refugee?"

"It's just another way of coming to America, Amos," Alexandra answered.

"Because everybody was fighting and people had their homes taken away?"

"Yes, there was fighting."

"Was your home taken away?"

Alexandra, lost for words, absently brushed her forehead with the tips of her fingers as she struggled to respond to her son.

"Didn't you like the city you came from?" he asked.

"It was a lovely city, Amos. It's called Jaffa. It's on the sea."

"Then why did Poppa Sharif and Nanna Sammy take you away? Was there fighting where you lived?"

"It's a very long, complicated story, Amos. Someday, when you're older, I'll tell you the whole story."

"Okay," he said, taking a healthy bite of Pappy Parker's drumstick.

***

The ride back was deathly quiet. It wasn't until they passed Mount Alto, where Wisconsin Avenue slopes down toward Georgetown, that Noah broke the silence. He saw that Amos was sound asleep, leaning against A'isha in the back seat.

"A'isha, didn't it occur to you that what you discussed with Amos was a lot for a five-year-old boy to handle? I mean, fighting and people losing their homes. He's only five years old, for God's sake."

"Please, Noah, not now," Alexandra said.

"I'm truly sorry, Mr. Greenspan. Amos asked a simple question and I tried to give him a simple, honest answer."

"That wasn't a simple answer, A'isha. It was an incredibly complicated answer."

"But it was an honest answer, Noah," Alexandra interrupted.

Noah, irritated that Alexandra didn't seem to share his pique over the conversation A'isha had with Amos, decided to let the subject drop. Alexandra knew, of course, that he was angry, and that he had good reason to be. They both knew there would come a time when they would tell Amos about the history of the Greenspan and Salaman families. How, against all odds, they had become so close, how the Greenspans fought to help Sharif and Samira, and how Noah had befriended Yusuf and Alexandra, and how she and Noah had fallen in love, and even why Amos was named after the Israeli who meant so much to both of them. There was so much they planned to tell Amos, but not at a Hot

Shoppe over fast food on a cold rainy night, and not because the whole complicated subject was introduced to Amos by his Palestinian nanny.

**

Noah was lying in bed staring at the ceiling, his hands folded behind his head, when Alexandra slipped under the covers and snuggled up next to him.

"Come on, Noah, some gear didn't shift in the universe when A'isha discussed her status as a refugee with Amos."

"Why do you think she felt a need to tell him that you and your family more or less came here for the same reason and under the same conditions?"

Alexandra shrugged. "It's all true, Noah. I assume she just didn't think much about discussing it with a five-year-old."

"I don't buy it. She's smart as hell. That's a big subject, and you would think she'd understand that it's something you and I would want to discuss with Amos at an appropriate time."

"It wasn't the best judgment, but I don't think it requires all this brooding."

"The story of our two families and of you and me is damn special, Alexandra. It was ours to tell."

"And it still will be, Noah. A'isha was just answering a question about her accent. It may have been more explanation than was necessary, but it didn't create a crisis. Don't make it one."

Noah turned to face her and smiled. "I love you," he said.

"Now *that's* what I call appropriate pillow talk," she answered, squeezing close to him.

"Do you realize how incredible it is that fate picked you up twenty-five years ago, thousands of miles away, and plopped you down in LeDroit Park a block from me?"

"Hmmm," she murmured seductively. "Isn't that all that matters when all is said and done?"

He pulled her tightly against his body. "Yes, *that* is all that matters when all is said and done," he replied, tightening his embrace.

"Hmmm, that's my Noah," she said, reaching down and closing her hand around him.

With that, he rolled over onto her and smiled. "I love you so much."

Alexandra pulled her nightgown up over her hips and parted her legs to receive him.

Their lovemaking was especially passionate that night. They both understood just how special the bond between them was, how unlikely a marriage theirs was, and, most of all, how deeply they cared for and loved one another.

"Alexandra, sometimes I ache just thinking about how much I love you," he whispered. "I really mean that."

"How well I understand that feeling, Noah. There were times, in Sudan, when I couldn't imagine that I would ever see you again. I know what it's like to ache when you love someone so much."

They fell asleep that night in each other's arms, the tensions of the early evening gone, at least for the time being.

***

Shortly after Noah left for work the following morning, Amos simply blurted out what was on his mind. It was an innocent enough question, the kind of question most children ask sooner or later.

"Mamma how did you meet Daddy?"

Alexandra, momentarily surprised, glanced to A'isha and then to Amos.

After a moment's hesitation, Alexandra decided how she was going to answer her son's question. "You know what, Amos? Mommy is going to show you how and where she met Daddy. Would you like that?"

The boy nodded eagerly.

"A'isha, I'm going to call the paper and tell them I'll be a little late. Grab a warm jacket for Amos. We're all going on a little field trip this morning."

***

Alexandra headed her Camaro over to Key Bridge and took the ramp onto the mile-long Whitehurst Freeway, bypassing the congested M Street corridor, and then continued east along K Street for about three miles to Seventh Street. That's where Amos's education began about a Washington he had never known. As soon as Alexandra turned north onto Seventh Street everything changed. Gone were the sleek office buildings, brownstones, and apartment high-rises. Seventh Street still had the appearance of a war zone, with the entire corridor blighted with the hulks of buildings burned out during the riots following the assassination of Martin Luther King five years earlier.

Alexandra glanced into her rearview mirror and saw Amos twisting against his seatbelt, trying to get a better look—trying to comprehend the landscape passing before him. She turned to A'isha, whose attention was also riveted to the urban desolation tucked away in the heart of the nation's capital.

"What happened?" Amos asked.

"There was fighting here and in other parts of the city, and a lot of fires broke out," Alexandra answered.

"When?" Amos asked.

"Just a short time before you were born, Amos."

"Whhhy?" he asked, a slight puzzled tremor in his voice.

Alexandra looked into the rearview mirror again and saw confusion and fright in her son's eyes.

Noah will be furious, she thought.

A'isha turned in her seat to face the boy. "Amos, sometimes, when some people feel they have been unfairly treated for a long time …," she began haltingly, "… even mistreated … they get very angry, and when people remain angry long enough … they sometimes do the wrong thing."

"Like burn everything down?" he responded, looking out the car window as they passed block after block of devastation.

"Yes, sometimes they even burn everything down."

"Do people get hurt?" he asked.

"Sometimes … yes. Sometimes, most times, people can get hurt."

Alexandra hadn't intended to introduce Washington's recent riots into her *field trip* to show her son where she and Noah had met. There simply wasn't any easy way to get to LeDroit Park from Georgetown without passing through one of the corridors in which the riots had taken place five years earlier.

When they reached Florida Avenue, where Seventh Street abruptly changes into Georgia Avenue, Alexandra turned right and headed east three blocks to Fourth Street. There, where Frazier's Funeral Home still dominated the intersection as it did when she first came to this neighborhood, she turned left and drove her son into LeDroit Park.

It hadn't changed much. The once-proud neighborhood looked tired, as it did when she and Noah first met there a quarter century earlier on the steps of N.P. Gage Elementary School. Alexandra drove slowly by the boarded-up, abandoned former For You Market and, a few hundred feet further up Fourth Street, glided to a stop in front of the deserted grocery store that had once been Sharif and Samira's Crescent Market. It was an old, lonely, pathetic structure. It had never been much, but the memories she had of her years there could not be more vivid or more moving. She turned in her seat, tears in her eyes, to look at her son.

"This is where Poppa Sharif and Nanna Sammy brought me and Uncle Yusuf to live twenty-five years ago, Amos. This was our first home in America." Amos just stared, wide-eyed, and nodded his understanding.

"Where did Daddy live?" he asked.

Alexandra waited for a break in the traffic and then made a sweeping, screeching U-turn across Fourth Street and drove the two short blocks to U Street, where the old For You Market once stood across the street. She pulled over to the side of the street, and just sat there for a moment as angry drivers honked and maneuvered around her Camaro.

"Oh God, what memories," she whispered as tears streaked down her cheeks.

"That's where Daddy lived with Daddy Hy and Mommy Esther, Amos," she said, pointing to what had once been one of the hundreds of corner grocery stores, over which lived the mostly white families that labored, often eighty hours a week, scratching out a living in these neighborhoods.

Amos's eyes roamed over the abandoned, graffiti-covered building as he tried to imagine his father growing up at Fourth and U. The steady roar of traffic racing up Fourth Street contrasted with the quiet, tree-lined tranquility of Prospect Street in Georgetown. It had never occurred to Amos that Noah could have grown up in an environment that was any different than his own neighborhood. There were no trees on Fourth Street, no gardens, nothing, it seemed, but a stream of cars and trucks speeding by.

"Now, let's go see where Daddy and I first met."

Amos twisted in his seat to get one last look at Fourth and U as Alexandra headed toward Second and Elm Street, where an old abandoned school stood. Nearly all of the windows had been broken by vandals.

"Come with me, Amos," Alexandra said as she and A'isha opened their doors. She opened the rear door, unbuckled Amos's seatbelt, and lifted him from the car. The three of them walked up the front steps of the deserted school. "Let's sit here on the top step for a few minutes." Alexandra put her arms around Amos's shoulder and squeezed him close.

"These steps, Amos. These steps where you and I are sitting right now; this is the very spot where I met Daddy twenty-five years ago."

"You met Daddy here?" he asked, somewhat incredulously. "How old were you?"

"Just five or six years older than you are now," she answered, smiling warmly.

"You grew up *here*?" A'isha asked, more an expression of surprise than a question.

Alexandra nodded, smiling a bit wistfully.

"And your husband, Mr. Greenspan, too?"

"We met on these steps on my first day as a student in America."

***

Amos fell asleep as soon as they began the drive back to Georgetown. A'isha was, at first, subdued and deep in thought.

"You're quiet, A'isha. Are you all right?" Alexandra asked.

"It's like a fairy tale," A'isha replied softly. "I knew, of course, that you came here under circumstances similar to mine. But I had never given any thought to where Mr. Greenspan came from. I ... I just assumed he came from a rich American Jewish family."

"He *is* from a Jewish American family, A'isha. A very fine Jewish American family. Just not a rich one at the time we met."

"Your families lived in this neighborhood when you were still teenagers?"

"They did. In fact, it was the father of my husband's college girlfriend who gave the Greenspans and my parents the idea of developing modern neighborhood convenience stores. That's how Mr. Greenspan's parents and my parents became business partners."

"You mean the Milk and Honey stores?"

"Yes, they have well over a hundred of them now. My brother, Yusuf, designed them."

"Mr. Greenspan's father must have had a great talent for business."

Alexandra smiled and shook her head. "Not really. He knew how to operate the For You Market well enough. But it was his son, my husband, who pushed his father and my father to undertake something as bold as building a chain of neighborhood convenience stores. The original business plans for Milk and Honey were all written by Noah. He even negotiated the first purchases of old neighborhood grocery stores. He showed his father how to do it. My husband, and my brother, Yusuf—without them, there would never have been a Milk and Honey convenience store chain."

"And *you* went from that neighborhood, LeDroit Park, to Prospect Street in Georgetown. It's a fairy tale."

"No, A'isha, it's America. We had nothing when we came to LeDroit Park, and neither, for that matter, did the Greenspans."

"And whatever happened to that college girlfriend whose father first suggested this idea of going from corner grocers to chain store developers?"

Alexandra's smile turned into a broad grin. "That would be Karen Rothschild. She's engaged to our Israeli friend for whom our son, Amos, is named."

"No!"

"Quite a story, huh?" she answered.

"Quite a story, indeed, Mrs. Salaman," A'isha replied, smiling as she nodded her agreement.

***

"Kissinger is going to Moscow?" Amos asked. "What in the world for?"

"Brezhnev cabled the White House and asked for an immediate meeting with the Secretary of State," Ambassador Dinitz replied.

"In Moscow?" Amos repeated.

Ambassador Dinitz nodded. "The Kremlin knows the war is over, Amos. Their Arab clients gave us their best shot and did a lot of damage … terrible damage. Our losses would be the equivalent of America losing over two hundred thousand men in a week. The war has been a disaster for us."

"So, now that we've turned the tide of battle, Moscow wants to bring the war to a swift end before the Egyptians and Syrians lose any more ground?"

"Exactly. That's what this conference in Moscow is all about. They have nothing to gain from any additional fighting and quite a bit to lose."

"But we *do* have a lot to gain," Amos replied.

"Ironic, but true. A week ago, we were begging for help while the Pentagon moved in slow motion deciding whether they had any cargo planes available."

"Dayan and Elazar will want to move quickly and consolidate every inch of territory we can. If the Russians think we'll agree to an immediate end to the fighting after we've gained the initiative, they're dreaming," Amos said.

Ambassador Dinitz smiled. "A week ago, we would have grabbed at a ceasefire."

"And the Russians wouldn't have been interested, and the Egyptians and Syrians would have rejected it. A week ago, the Russians were demanding that Israel return to the pre-sixty-seven-war lines. What a difference a week makes, eh?"

"Amos, Brezhnev knows Sadat could fall if we progress too far toward Cairo. This adventure is rapidly turning into a disaster for the Russians. We have to gain as much as we can as fast as we can, because a ceasefire is certain to be imposed in a matter of days."

"I presume Kissinger could always stall by calling for a recess for consultations with the President," Amos said.

"Usually that would be the case. We diplomats do that all the time. But Nixon has cabled Brezhnev that his Secretary of State will have full authority to act on the President's behalf. He's compromised Kissinger's ability to stall for time."

"How many of our men are now in Egyptian territory?"

"In the neighborhood of thirteen to fifteen thousand men and scores of tanks."

"I would think Sadat's forces could cross back onto the West Bank and give us quite a fight," Amos answered. "He's got nearly one hundred thousand men on the East Bank now."

"Unquestionably. But it seems Sadat doesn't want a single Egyptian soldier to go back across the Canal. He thinks it would look like a retreat. He's determined not to give up an inch of the Sinai now in his hands."

"Do you think we can trust Kissinger?" Amos asked.

"It's not a matter of trust, Amos. This has become a contest between America and Russia. We've become America's proxy in this deadly game."

"Some game," Amos answered under his breath. "Do you think Kissinger will keep us advised?"

"Well, he's stopping off in Tel Aviv on the way back to the States after the Moscow meeting with Brezhnev. So, yes, I think we'll get a thorough briefing. Then again, so will Egypt and Syria."

"Well, it seems as though the worst is over," Amos said.

"Maybe and maybe not, Amos. Disengagement on the Sinai will not be so easy. The Egyptians have fought better than any of us would have predicted, and their Third Army is still resisting even though they are totally cut off from any further supplies and any military reinforcement. It has been an incredible turn of events, but the Egyptian Army that attacked us has overreached and is now ensnared in a trap of our making."

"But you don't think they'll sue for peace."

"Not a chance; not with Russia backing them. If this truly becomes a contest between Russia and the United States, as your journalist friend predicted in her column Sunday, there's no telling what it could escalate into. The Russians and the Americans have clogged the Mediterranean with warships circling one another, while we're slugging it out on land with the Arabs."

"What do *you* think is going to happen, Simcha?" Amos asked.

"I think Alexandra Salaman had it exactly right in her column Sunday. We could be headed for another Cuban Missile Crisis, and I have no idea who will blink first—the Americans or the Russians."

CHAPTER NINETEEN

Noah really didn't want to take the call from George Markanos, the notorious short-sell analyst from Deutschland Trust. Markanos invariably meant trouble, and Noah had enough on his mind without having to waste time with this Wall Street bottom-feeder.

"Does he know I'm in?" Noah asked when his secretary buzzed his intercom to tell him the analyst was holding.

"Sorry, Noah. I'm afraid he does. I told him you'd just hung up from talking on the phone."

"Shit," he mumbled under his breath. "Barb, just tell callers you'll check to see if I'm available. You don't have to tell them my life's story."

"Duly noted," she replied. "What shall I tell him?"

"I'll take the call. I didn't mean to snap at you, Barb."

"Also duly noted," she answered.

"Hi, George. How's life on the Street?"

"Well, the economy's booming. So I guess life on the Street is pretty good. How's life in the mall?"

"Fully leased, George. That usually means life is good."

"And I see PCPA is now one of the nifty-fifty, Noah. Not bad for such a young public company."

"Well, it keeps us on our toes, George. High price-to-earnings ratios mean high expectations, you know."

"Indeed, I do, Noah. Investors paying over fifty times earnings—that's pretty impressive. Who would have thought shares in Potomac Center Properties of America would become one of America's most prized securities within five years of the company going public?"

"Well, I guess I would have."

"*Touché*, Noah. Good answer. Nothing like going public with strong economic winds at your back."

"Not to mention a well-run company, right, George?"

"*Touché* again, Noah."

"So, what can I do for you?"

"Just checking in, Noah."

"Well, we're expecting our best quarter ever, George. The fourth quarter is certain to cap off a great year."

"Can I quote you?"

"Of course."

"Like I said, just checking in."

"Anytime."

"Say, Noah, just one more thing. Do you have any idea how your tenants' inventories are running?"

"I'm not sure I understand your question."

"You know, are your tenants keeping up with demand; do they have plenty of inventory? Are they scrambling to keep up with demand or are they well stocked?"

"I suppose they're all keeping up with demand. I haven't heard any complaints. I mean, our loading dock is always busy."

"Yeah, I was just wondering. Funny thing, yesterday I went by Johnson and Murphy's downtown store to order a couple pairs of shoes. I've got really big feet, so they always have to order them for me because they only keep two or three pairs in stock and they're constantly running out. But this time they said they had them in stock. I asked, 'How come you have them in stock?' And Maurice, that's the manager I've gotten to know pretty well, he tells me that they've got plenty of everything in stock."

"So, you now have two new pairs of shoes."

"Yeah, one black and one brown pair of wingtip oxfords. Good-looking shoes."

"Glad you're well shod, George."

"Yeah, they're comfortable as hell too. But it got me thinking. Why do they have plenty of everything in inventory?"

"Beats me."

"You know, when inventory builds up, manufacturers slow down production."

"Maybe Johnson and Murphy's need to change their shoe styles to keep up with today's buyers. They've been around a long time, you know. Lots of competition out there today."

"You got any Johnson and Murphy's in your malls?"

"Sure, they're great tenants."

"I wonder how inventory is running with your other tenants?"

"I haven't heard any complaints."

"You might want to ask around, Noah. Might be good to know."

"Not a bad idea, George, but I can tell you no one is falling behind in their rent. Business is pretty brisk."

"Yeah, that's why you're in the nifty-fifty, right, Noah?"

"We're having our best year, George."

"Any new malls on the drawing board?"

"We're always planning ahead."

"Yeah, with your line of credit and your cash flow, you can chase the market anywhere in the country. It's a nice position to be in, huh, Noah?"

"We're fortunate. That's for sure"

"Well, watch that debt-to-equity ratio. Your loan covenants are pretty rigid."

"I'll keep that in mind, George."

"Talk to you again, Noah. Have a great fourth quarter. And be sure to say hello to that gorgeous wife of yours for me."

"Thanks, George. I'll be sure to do that."

Noah sat there staring at the phone for several seconds after hanging up with the short seller. *I hate that prick*, Noah thought, as he reached for the phone and pushed the button for the loading dock.

"Loading Dock, Hank Farley here."

"Hey, Hank, it's Noah."

"Mornin', Mr. Greenspan. What can I do for you?"

"How's activity on the dock?"

"Busy as ever. Lots of trucks in and out every day."

"Anything unusual?"

"Nah, they come and go, just like always."

"They pretty much unload the same quantities as usual?"

"Huh … now that's an interesting question."

"How come? What makes it interesting?"

"Cause they're getting in and out faster. Seems they're delivering less merchandise."

Noah felt his gut tighten. "Thanks, Hank. Just checking."

"Sure thing, Mr. Greenspan. Everything's running smooth as silk down here."

"Always is, Hank. Keep up the good work."

Noah spent the next hour going through the mall and talking with several of his tenants' general managers.

The story was the same at many stores. The backrooms were backing up. Noah hurried back to his office and called Herb Alperson, his accounts receivables manager.

"Hey, Herb, it's Noah. How does business seem to you?"

"Our business is great, Noah. Everyone pays on time. No problems in the receivables department."

"What do our tenants' revenue figures look like?"

"Damn near everyone is up five, six, seven percent."

"Sales increasing that briskly, huh?"

"Well, I don't know about that, Noah."

"What do you mean?"

"I think some … maybe a lot of the revenue increases are coming from price. I'm not so sure all the increases are coming from sales. Stores seem to have pretty good pricing flexibility, and we get a piece of that revenue growth. Hell of a business, huh?"

"Yeah, hell of a business, Herb."

Noah hung up and called Sylvan Garyson at Monument Parking, the company that managed the parking structure at Potomac Center. "Hey, Syl, it's Noah Greenspan, how you doing?"

"Doing great, Noah. How about you?"

"Can't think of much to complain about, but I do have a question. How's the traffic at our garage at the Center?"

"Fair to middlin'. The last quarter's been a little soft."

"Interesting. Revenue at the mall was up pretty nicely," Noah replied. "I wonder why mall revenue is up and parking traffic isn't."

"Well, maybe more people are walking here and having their merchandise delivered. You know, everybody's on an exercise kick."

"Not likely," Noah replied with a chuckle. "Thanks, Syl, let me know if you see any dramatic change, one way or the other."

"Sure thing, Noah. Talk to you later."

"Yeah, talk to you later," Noah replied before hanging up.

Noah pushed back and propped his feet up on his desk the way he did when he just wanted to think. He clasped his hands behind his head and tilted the chair back, staring up at the light fixture hanging in the center of the room. *Shit*, he thought. *I've been so busy looking at prospective sites all over the country, I've ignored what's happening right under my own nose. We have a recession building. Retail revenues are up, but so, apparently, are inventories. We're not enjoying robust sales; we're enjoying robust retail price increases. Manufacturers have to be curtailing production. We're staring a recession in the face and we don't even know it.*

Noah reached for his phone and buzzed Marshall Flynn, his chief financial officer.

"Flynn," the voice answered.

"Marsh, what do our loan covenants say about a drop in the price of our stock?"

"Nothing. Why, do you think someone is about to unload on us?"

"No, I'm a little queasy about our high multiple."

"Noah, every CEO would like to be running a nifty-fifty company. What's worrying you?"

"I'm worried about the economy, especially retail."

"We've had no softening in our leases, Noah. We're fully leased and everyone is current."

"Yeah, I know, but I think inventories are backing up. I'm not sure whether revenue increases are coming from increased sales or increased prices."

"I think you worry too much."

"I wouldn't worry, except for our high multiple. I'm worried that this strong business cycle we're in is about to peak. If I'm right, retail will get hit hard, and here we are sitting with a stock up in the stratosphere."

"Well, Noah, there's not a damn thing we can do about it. If you're right, we'll have to ride out the storm like everyone else."

"But it won't affect our loan covenants if our stock takes a beating. Is that what you're saying? We've got over a hundred million in bank loans on our balance sheet."

Flynn paused a bit too long before answering.

"Marsh …?"

"Well, our loan covenants do have a MAC clause. I suppose if our stock really cratered they could claim a material adverse change and call the loan or insist that we pay down some of it."

"That's bullshit," Noah replied. "The price of our stock has nothing to do with the health of our business."

"True, but these material change clauses are intentionally ambiguous. They have the effect of turning a long-term loan into a demand note. The banks could argue that we couldn't grow as projected because sometimes we use stock to buy commercial property."

"That's bullshit!"

"Yeah, you've already expressed that opinion. But if the banks thought they could improve the loan conditions in their favor by claiming material adverse change, they might try that. You know, maybe asking an extra eighth of a point or some partial pay-down of our outstanding debt."

"So, you think a significant adjustment in our stock price is something to worry about?"

"I don't know that I'd worry too much. I think the odds are less than fifty-fifty that our banks would try to do that. But …"

"But what?"

"You do have some personal exposure."

"What are you talking about?"

"Well, remember five years ago when you developed a great relationship with Bank Parthenon in Athens, Greece after they put up the ransom money overnight to get Alexandra out of that prison in Khartoum?"

"Yes, how well I remember. They were great. They did it as a favor to Petros Koutras, Chairman of Aegean Marine Group, the huge Greek shipping line. Amos Ben-Chaiyim arranged the whole thing through Mossad. How could I ever forget?"

"Well, you might remember you borrowed twelve million dollars from Parthenon that year at very low rates, with the entire balance due in ten years. I think you purchased some personal property in Delaware, over on the Eastern Shore near Rehoboth."

"Yeah, well, that was five years ago."

"But you used PCPA stock as collateral. The stock was in the stratosphere then too."

"Oh shit. That's right."

"Your loan agreement also had a MAC clause."

"You're saying they might call the loan?"

"Nah, not likely, but they sure as hell will want more collateral if our shares crater."

"I forgot all about that."

"You own half the shares, Noah. It shouldn't be too big of a problem."

"Actually, what has me worried most is that son of a bitch George Markanos. He called me earlier today. He smells recession, and you know sure as hell he'll short our stock if the market looks like it's about to go south."

"Fuck him, Noah. If he drives down the share price, he'll just create a great buying opportunity."

"That's true, but every time he shows up, someone winds up suing me."

"Like I said, Noah. I wouldn't worry about it, because there's not a damn thing you can do about it anyway."

"Thanks, Marsh, that's very reassuring."

"Just sayin'."

"It might be a good idea to project how a material decline in our share price would affect our growth plans."

"Yeah, that's probably a good idea. I'll get right on it."

Noah hung up and immediately placed a call to Karen at Mid America Ventures in Chicago.

"Noah, I'm so glad to hear from you," she said as soon as she heard his voice.

"Yes, it's been a while, but Amos keeps us up to date," he replied.

"I'm jealous," she answered. "He keeps me up to date too. You and Alexandra get to spend more time with him than I do."

"He's working really hard dealing with the war. I think he's with the Israeli Ambassador every day."

"Yes. We talk nearly every night. Thank goodness the war seems to have turned around for the Israelis."

"It's been bad. Amos doesn't go into much detail, but he's been very distressed about the losses Israel has sustained. It's been a very bloody war."

"I know you didn't call to talk about the war. What's up, Noah?"

"Has there been any talk of a recession on the Street?"

"Why, is your business falling off?"

"Our revenue is strong, but I get the feeling inventories are backing up a bit here at Potomac Center. I haven't checked with any of our other properties yet. I wanted to pick your brain first."

"As of now, the economy is really very strong. It's been a long bull market."

"Too long, maybe?"

"No bull market lasts forever, Noah. Are you worried about PCPA stock?"

"I have no reason to worry as far as our business is concerned. Revenues are up."

"Price or same-store sales?"

"Funny you should ask that question."

"Why?"

"I think price may be driving revenue at our malls more than sales."

"Not much you can do about that."

"I know. I'm just a little jittery, though, given our high multiple."

"Not much you can do about that, either," she replied. "High multiple, high risk."

"So, no warning signs on the Street?"

"Nope. The ISM and the PMI indexes are still above fifty."

"What are they?"

"They track monthly production and services activity. Above fifty, we're okay. Below fifty, danger ahead."

"Okay. I guess I shouldn't worry."

"Noah, I don't think you have anything to worry about, and if you did, worrying wouldn't help one damn bit. Look, the Arabs are pissed that the Israelis seem to have gained the upper hand in the fighting, and they've already raised the price of oil, from a little over three dollars a barrel to over five dollars a barrel, but so far it doesn't seem to have affected our economy very much, and it hasn't affected Nixon's determination to supply Israel with whatever Israel needs."

"That's a seventy percent increase. How could that not affect our economy? I'm paying seventy cents a gallon at the pump, and last week I was only paying around fifty cents a gallon."

"Well, you can afford it, Mr. Tycoon."

"Yes, but can the people who shop in my malls afford it? Karen, whatever extra money is going into buying gasoline can't be used to buy other consumer goods."

"Your sales are still strong," she replied.

"Yeah, but like I said, many of our tenants seem to have inventory building up in the back of their stores. I think our growth is coming more from price increases our tenants are getting than from increased merchandise sales."

"Our analysts are watching developments pretty closely, and so far, they haven't sounded alarm bells. We expected economic trouble when Nixon took the country off the Gold Standard back in seventy-one, but nothing much happened, other than some inflation. Now *that* really pissed off the Arabs. All of their oil contracts are priced in dollars, and when the dollar fell, their revenues also fell—but our economy just kept rolling along. We have some inflationary problems, but no one is forecasting recession. The Arabs could have placed an embargo on all oil sales to the United States, but they didn't do that. They just reduced oil shipments by five percent. So far that doesn't seem to have hurt our economy very much."

"Not yet, but if raising the price of oil doesn't seem to be hurting our economy, maybe their next step *will* be a total oil embargo."

"Maybe, but that would hurt their economies as much as ours. I doubt they would do that."

"You know, Alexandra says some guy at the State Department predicted this war in May, and he also predicted that the Arabs would weaponize oil if we came to the aid of Israel."

"Well, we'll have to see what they do, Noah. Right now, our economy isn't showing any jitters."

"How are you doing, Karen?" Noah asked, changing the subject.

Karen took a moment before answering. "That's a complicated question, Noah. My life is going well, but I miss Amos terribly, and soon he'll be headed back to Israel, and these constant separations are really hard. At least now it's pretty easy to reach each other on the phone. I don't know what I'm going to do when he returns to the Middle East. And let's face it, I worry all the time. We both know his work can be very dangerous."

"How well I know," Noah answered.

"I have to run, Noah. I'll let you know if we come across any economic news you might find helpful."

"Thanks, Karen. I appreciate that."

CHAPTER TWENTY

Neither Noah nor Alexandra were home yet when Yusuf arrived. He had brought with him a few renderings of exterior elevations for a proposed indoor urban mall Noah was considering on land he had optioned in the nearby Maryland suburbs. They were planning to discuss the proposed project over dinner at Rive Gauche, a short walk from the Greenspans' Prospect Street home. So, Yusuf was surprised when A'isha opened the door for him.

Her face, framed by her scarlet hijab, radiant and quite beautiful, was, for a moment, all he saw. He stood there, awkwardly transfixed, until Amos came running through the foyer excitedly yelling, "Uncle Yusuf, Uncle Yusuf," and leapt into his arms.

"Ah, *you* are the Uncle Yusuf Amos is always talking about," A'isha said, a warm smile blossoming on her face.

"And you must be Amos's new nanny, about whom *he* is always talking," he replied with a grin. "I've heard a lot about you. You're a big hit with my nephew," he said, extending his hand to her.

"Mr. and Mrs. Greenspan should be home any minute," A'isha answered, shaking his hand warmly. "Please come in."

Yusuf, with Amos still clinging to him, followed A'isha into the Greenspans' living room. *My God, she's beautiful,* he thought.

"So, I've heard a lot about you, Mr. Salaman," she said, turning to face him. "You and Mr. Greenspan are quite the team. He builds what you design, right?"

"Well, it would probably be more correct to say I design what he envisions. He's the developer—the visionary. I'm just the architect."

"Mrs. Greenspan took Amos and me to see where you once lived and where you first met Mr. Greenspan."

"Ah, you paid a visit to LeDroit Park," he replied. "That was a long time ago."

"Not so long ago. You and your sister are *still* very young."

"We were eleven years old. You know my sister and I are twins?"

"Yes, she told me. I've heard about your family and Mr. Greenspan's family and how your two families were competitors in those corner grocery stores."

"Yeah," Yusuf replied with a laugh. "They weren't competitors for very long. They decided to become partners instead."

"Yes, it's an amazing story. And you and Mr. Greenspan became best friends."

"Yep."

"And now he's your brother-in-law."

"And still my best friend," he answered. "So, my sister tells me you were from the Hebron area," Yusuf continued.

"Yes, I still have grandparents and aunts and uncles and a lot of cousins in Hebron."

Yusuf nodded but didn't reply.

"There are many more of my people in Hebron than in America," she said.

Yusuf nodded again.

"And your family?"

"All here," he answered.

She smiled. "All American now. Very nice."

"Palestinian American," he replied.

Yusuf's subtle correction wasn't lost on A'isha. "It's almost incomprehensible," she said, following a brief, but awkward pause.

"How so?"

"I think this conversation is in danger of getting too heavy after so short an acquaintance," she replied, smiling.

"A lot of people are fascinated by the Greenspan-Salaman relationship," he said. "The Greenspans are wonderful people, and I guess we Salamans aren't so bad either. Our two families had so much in common when we first met back in LeDroit Park. Noah Greenspan was the first classmate to befriend me, and he and Alexandra found something very special in one another when they were just kids. Noah's parents literally saved my folks when they wound up in America knowing nothing about being neighborhood merchants. Yes, there was always the Middle East thing, but there was so much more that we had in common. I could tell you a million stories about the Greenspan-Salaman relationship."

"I've been very curious about how Amos came to be named after an Israeli," she said.

"Ah, Amos Ben-Chaiyim," he replied. "That's a long story, but I can tell you this: he saved my sister's life—twice. At great personal risk, he saved her life. If it weren't for Amos Ben-Chaiyim there would be no Amos Salaman Greenspan."

A'isha nodded and smiled. "It's an almost incomprehensible story, isn't it?"

"Not when you've lived the story, A'isha. You have to see people for who they really are, not who you've been taught they are."

***

Yusuf and his sister and brother-in-law dined leisurely at Rive Gauche while discussing the land Noah had optioned in nearby Cheverly, a Maryland suburb in Prince George's County, a few miles from the District. Amos was to have joined them but called to say he would probably be late and to start without him.

"The renderings look great, Yusuf," Noah said.

"Do I hear a *but* coming?"

"Yeah, I think so. I'm worried about the competition. You know, the Lerners just opened their mall at Landover, and White Oaks Center is only a few miles west in Silver Spring. The Green Belt area is developing pretty fast already. I think I moved too slow with the land I've optioned. I think there are greener pastures to explore."

"Well, you've got the renderings. Now you just have to find some other land on which to develop them," Yusuf replied.

"And you can bet we will," Noah said. "I love the look. We'll find a place to build."

"Say, would you guys have any problem with me asking Amos's new nanny out?" Yusuf asked, abruptly changing the subject.

Alexandra, surprised by the question, looked to Noah.

"You want to date A'isha?" Noah asked.

"I just thought I might like to ask her out for dinner or a movie, but if it's a problem, I won't."

Alexandra, still looking at Noah, shrugged her shoulders. "I don't see any harm in that. Do you, Noah?"

"I … I guess not," he replied.

"You seem unsure, Noah. If you think it's a problem, I won't ask her," Yusuf said.

"I didn't know you knew her."

"I don't. I mean, I just met her waiting for you guys to get home from work. She seems bright as hell and she's damned attractive. She's great with Amos too. He seems totally at home with her."

"Yeah, he loves her. We're all fond of her," Noah replied.

"But?"

"I guess it's all right. I have a little concern though. You know, that if you really start dating A'isha and it doesn't go well after a while, that it might, you know, affect the rapport she has with us and with Amos. I mean, it's just a thought, not even a concern," Noah said.

"Noah, Yusuf is only talking about asking A'isha to dinner or to a movie. I don't think there would be any harm in that."

Noah thought for a moment and then simply shrugged. "Sure, why not?" he answered.

***

Leonid Brezhnev sat fuming in his Kremlin office. *Kissinger must have double-crossed us when he was in Tel Aviv*, he thought. The Israelis were using every excuse to continue engaging the Egyptians and Syrians on the battlefield after the Russian-American negotiated ceasefire-in-place was to have gone into effect. Barely two weeks after Egypt's successful crossing of the Canal and Syria's brutal assault on the Golan Heights, the Arabs were in retreat everywhere. The Israelis were within artillery range of Damascus, had encircled the Egyptian Third Army on the Sinai, and, if they chose, could probably march on Cairo. Nothing was now going as planned.

"This was never supposed to be a confrontation between us and the United States," he yelled, smashing his fist onto the top of his desk. "That damned miniscule speck of a country, Israel, is not going to make a fool of the Soviet Union." He had to do something to wrest control of events that were now spiraling out of control. *It is all Kissinger's fault. He's given the Israelis the key to America's entire arsenal,* he thought. The General Secretary decided to jolt the duplicitous Secretary of State and his friends in Tel Aviv. *He will have to decide between supporting the Israelis and confronting us*, he thought. And then he began to dictate a fateful cable to Ambassador Dobrynin in Washington. His instructions were for Dobrynin to immediately contact Kissinger and convey his message to him for immediate delivery to President Nixon.

I'll dispense with the usual diplomatic niceties, he thought. And so he began his message to Nixon with *"Mr. President,"* instead of his usual *"My Dear Mr. President."* General Secretary Brezhnev got right to the point, accusing Israel of unacceptable violations of the agreed-upon ceasefire. He then repeated his call for a joint Russian-American military presence to enforce the ceasefire, which he knew was unacceptable to the Americans. Then his cable meandered into a fateful longshot, and a colossal miscalculation, *"... that if you find it impossible to act together with us in the matter, we should be faced with the necessity urgently to consider the question of taking appropriate steps*

unilaterally. Israel cannot be allowed to get away with the violations."
Russia had drawn a line in the sand.

It was late in the evening when Ambassador Dobrynin finally reached the American Secretary of State at home. He carefully read the Brezhnev cable to Secretary Kissinger, dabbing nervously at the beads of perspiration pocking his forehead. Kissinger perfunctorily thanked the Russian diplomat, giving no indication of what he planned to do. He hung up the phone and then slowly dialed White House Chief of Staff General Alexander Haig, while simultaneously processing what was at stake—what he would recommend to the President.

"Haig here."

"Al, I must speak to the President right away, and I think you should remain on the line."

General Haig paused a moment to collect his thoughts. "That won't be possible, Henry," he said. "The President has turned in for the night."

"I understand. Ordinarily, I wouldn't bother him this late, Al, but we have a major emergency situation with the Russians that requires immediate attention."

"Then you'll have to respond, Henry. We can't disturb the President right now."

"For God's sake, is he drun … is he indisposed?"

There was a pause and then, "Yes, Henry, he is very indisposed."

"A historic decision will have to be made tonight, Al. I think the President would convene the National Security Council. It's that important."

"Then my strong advice would be to convene the Council," General Haig replied.

"I think we have to consider a decision that is only the President's to make," Secretary Kissinger replied, his gravelly voice slow, somber, and steady.

"Henry, the President will not be making any decisions tonight, and, as you know, the United States has no Vice President at the moment. Henry, this will have to be your call."

Kissinger took a few seconds to consider his reply. The alternatives facing the country were clear to him. The time for diplomatic sparring had run out. He glanced down at his watch and slowly sucked in a deep breath.

"Al, call an emergency meeting of the Washington Special Actions Group tonight, to be convened as soon as possible. I'll need you and CIA Director Colby, as well as Joint Chiefs Chairman Admiral Moorer, Herb Scowcroft, and make absolutely sure Jim Schlesinger is there too."

"Anyone else from the National Security Council?"

"No, just the Council's Special Actions Group. I don't want the meeting to be any bigger than necessary."

"Are the Russians intervening?" Haig asked.

"They're threatening to. I think they're about to." Secretary Kissinger paused, more for emphasis than for uncertainty. "We have to make sure they absolutely understand, immediately and in no uncertain terms, that we're not going to tolerate that. It will take more than threats or words, Al."

Alexander Haig, a veteran of five campaigns in Korea, including the decisive landing at Inchon, and the Battle of Ap Gu in Vietnam, for which he was commended for extraordinary heroism, nodded his understanding. He looked up at the clock on the wall of his office. It was nine thirty.

"The WSAG team will be assembled here within an hour, Mr. Secretary," Haig replied, using Kissinger's title to acknowledge his authority and power at that moment.

The Jewish refugee from Germany was, once again, about to make history.

***

"Sorry I'm late," Amos said, as he squeezed into the booth next to Yusuf. He barely smiled, and Alexandra thought she saw a slight tremor as he reached over the table to shake hands with Noah.

"Are you all right?" she asked.

He held up his hand as if to say, *Don't even ask.*

"News about the fighting?" Noah asked.

"Not really. I mean, for all intents and purposes, the fighting is really over, at least for now, between us and our Egyptian and Syrian neighbors. We can see Damascus from the turrets of our tanks, and the Egyptian Third Army is completely cut off. We could march to Cairo if we wanted to," Amos replied.

"You don't look like someone whose country is on the verge of victory on the battlefield," Yusuf said. "You look more like someone who has just received horrible news."

"I may have," Amos answered.

"What's happening?" Noah asked.

"Nothing at the moment, but we could be in for a very tense day or two."

"I haven't heard anything," Alexandra said. "I would get a call from the newsroom if anything major happened that pertained to the fighting."

"That's because nothing new *has* happened—yet."

"Oh, I get it," she replied. "You think the Russians are going to intervene and come to the aid of the Egyptians and Syrians."

"That wouldn't have surprised us. They have a huge investment in their Syrian and Egyptian allies."

"What would surprise you?" she asked.

"If we and the Arabs became a sideshow to a Russian-American face-off."

"You mean Russia and America actually duking it out on the battlefield?" Noah asked.

Amos looked down at his hands for a moment, and then raised his eyes to Alexandra. "Off the record, Alexandra?"

"Of course."

"Not a word, Noah … Yusuf."

"Our lips are sealed," Noah replied. Yusuf simply nodded.

"I'll be surprised if what I'm about to tell you isn't in the press tomorrow, but these past two weeks have been nothing but surprises."

Amos leaned forward as though to whisper. He glanced down at his watch and then looked at Alexandra. "The NSC's Special Actions Group is meeting at the White House right now."

"What's the NSC?" Yusuf asked.

"It's the National Security Council, Yusuf," Alexandra replied.

"So, what's the big deal?" Yusuf responded.

"Yeah, why is that so worrisome?" Noah asked.

"Because it's ten o'clock at night," Alexandra interrupted.

"Right," Amos said. "That means it is a previously unscheduled meeting, which means it's being viewed as an emergency. The Special Actions Group is what the name implies. It's an operational group not a policy group."

"Which means?" Noah interrupted

"Which means the Russians have done or are about to do something that the United States probably intends to stop."

"You mean like when the United States and Russia faced off during the Cuban Missile Crisis?" Noah asked.

Amos nodded. "I think it could be every bit as dangerous. Russia's allies have been bloodied on the battlefield. We've neutralized the air-defense missile system the Russians provided their Arab allies. Two weeks ago, the Egyptians, with Russian backing, successfully crossed the Suez Canal and were pushing into the Sinai. Then they blew it. They sent a thousand tanks into the desert to attack us, and our forces mauled them. Now it is *we* who have crossed the Canal and are in Egypt threatening *their* cities. It is their army that is surrounded and desperate for food and water. On the Golan, the Syrians have been pushed back across the Heights and well into Syria. Moscow has to decide whether to call it a day or to come to the rescue of their allies."

"And you think they've decided to come to the aid of Egypt and Syria," Alexandra asked.

"It's Egypt they're worried about. Brezhnev and Kissinger negotiated a ceasefire that isn't holding. The Egyptian Third Army is trapped. Fighting is continuing in spite of the ceasefire, and the Russians are furious. They think they've been double-crossed, and I assume they've let the United States know they aren't going to stand for it."

"Have they been double-crossed?" Yusuf asked.

"The ceasefire isn't holding."

"Whose fault is that?" Yusuf pressed.

"My understanding is that the Third Army has been trying to fight its way out of the encirclement in which they find themselves. That's a provocation."

"And you are using that as an excuse to solidify your position. Is that right?" Alexandra interrupted.

"What are we supposed to do, just let them leave with their tanks and other arms so they can restart the war?"

"So, you think the Russians are planning to intervene?" she asked.

"I can't think of another reason the Washington Special Actions Group is meeting this late at night a couple of miles from here."

"What do you think Israel is going to do, try and take Damascus and Cairo?" Yusuf asked.

"No, of course not, but as long as there is fighting we're going to move as fast as we can, to be in the strongest possible position when the fighting finally stops and we sit down to negotiate a truce. Sharon is now less than one hundred miles from Cairo."

"And who do you think you're going to negotiate with?" Alexandra asked. "The Egyptians and Syrians have never sat down face to face with the Israelis."

"Good question," he answered. "The Syrians have been pushed totally off of the Heights, and they know we're not going to give up any of the Golan. There's not much to negotiate there. Egypt is another story. We have forces on the West Bank of the Canal and they have forces on the East Bank of the Canal. Our General Adan has ensnared their entire Third Army. Their forces are running out of food, water, and medical supplies. They'll negotiate."

"Through an intermediary," Alexandra said.

"I don't think we'll agree to that. I think we'll insist on face-to-face meetings, our people sitting across the table from their people."

"I'll believe it when I see it," Yusuf said.

"Now *that's* a meeting I'd like to cover," Alexandra mused.

"Don't even think about it," Noah laughed. "After Khartoum, your paper can send someone else."

Amos looked from Noah to Alexandra. There were several moments of silence. Noah's laugh had faded into a nervous smile. Alexandra, he thought, looked deadly serious. *She would head back to the Middle East in a heartbeat to cover a story like this,* he thought.

"I doubt very much that there would be any press allowed at all. The Egyptians would never agree to that," he said.

***

Omar Samir sat at dinner in Aswan reading the latest dispatch from Ahmed Kahn. He seethed as he looked at what Ahmed had sent. The dispatch consisted only of Alexandra's last column in the *Star*, and that repulsive newspaper article and photograph of her sitting under the Israeli flag with the Jews at a big banquet in Washington. There was also a brief handwritten note from Ahmed Kahn. He put the note aside and focused on Alexandra's column: *"US and Russia Standoff: Israel on the Offense."* He could barely control his temper. His anger mounted as his eyes focused on the news clipping about the Israel Emergency dinner at which the Jew, Noah Greenspan, spoke and his Palestinian wife, Alexandra Salaman dined.

The Jews, the Jews, the Jews, he thought. *They're going to win again. And the traitor Alexandra Salaman sits in Washington and gloats about it.*

He thought of everything that had gone wrong almost from the moment Alexandra, as a student a dozen years earlier, had walked onto the campus at Phoenicia University in Beirut. They had befriended her, and she betrayed them all before running off with that Israeli agent Amos Ben-Chaiyim. Because of her the attack they had spent so much time planning against Israeli civilians in Ma'alot-Tarshiha had been foiled and their courageous colleagues captured. Because of her his compatriot, Ali Abdul Shoukri, had been gunned down. Alexandra Salaman survived and prospered while his countrymen suffered.

And then there was the perfect trap he had set for her in Khartoum when she was there to report on the Arab League summit following the sixty-seven war. They had her caged in a hell-on-earth prison, and again she escaped. People said some Greek shipping magnate got her out, but Omar Samir knew better. He knew it had to be the same Jew who spirited her out of Beirut. The same Jew for whom she named her only child.

He dropped the newspaper clippings onto the table and picked up Ahmed Kahn's note. *Interesting development. Our A'isha Abadi has been going out with the Salaman woman's brother, Yusuf Salaman.*

Omar Samir sat back in his chair and reread Ahmed's note. *This is good*, he thought. *This is very good.*

***

It was barely dawn when Ambassador Dinitz called Amos at the Fairfax Hotel.

"Come as quickly as you can. I'll be having a number of conversations with Secretary Kissinger throughout the day, and I would like you to be present. I need another pair of sharp eyes and ears with me."

Amos trotted across Massachusetts Avenue and walked briskly the couple of blocks to the Israeli embassy.

"Sit down, Amos," Ambassador Dinitz mouthed, pointing to one of the chairs in front of his desk as he held the telephone to his ear.

"Yes, Henry, I understand," he said into the telephone.

Amos sat down, his eyes fixed on Simcha Dinitz. The Ambassador looked at his young colleague and slowly shook his head. His expression was grim.

"Yes, I will get back to you as soon as I have spoken with Prime Minister Meir," he said.

"What is happening?" Amos asked as soon as Ambassador Dinitz hung up the phone.

"The Americans have gone to DefCon Three in response to Brezhnev's threat to send troops to Egypt."

Amos knew that DefCon Three was one step short of war being imminent. The Americans had moved to a heightened state of nuclear readiness.

"When?"

"During the night. During the Washington Special Action Group meeting at the White House last night. The Americans have started to reposition three naval battle groups in the Mediterranean, and the Strategic Air Command has been put on an increased state of readiness for possible war with Russia. The Russians now have nearly one hundred ships in the Mediterranean, and another dozen are on the way. To make matters worse, we think they are reconfiguring Antonov 22 cargo planes to carry troops. We also learned that East Germany is mobilizing several army units."

"Jesus Christ," Amos murmured under his breath.

"We've made a proposal that Kissinger has pretty much dismissed out of hand. We proposed that we would reposition our troops that are on the West Bank back onto the East Bank of the Canal, and that Egypt would reposition its troops that are on the East Bank onto the West Bank, and that we would agree to a ten-mile non-militarized zone on either side of the Canal."

"What did Kissinger say?"

"He said it would be an insult to Sadat. Both sides of the Canal are Egyptian territory, and he said that Sadat would never agree to abandon the East Bank to us."

"So, what's next?"

"Nixon will pretty much ignore Brezhnev's threat to send his troops into the area. He is going to tell Brezhnev that such a move would be unacceptable and dangerous, and that the United States would, instead, look favorably upon non-military observers being dispatched to the Canal area to oversee a ceasefire. He will tell Brezhnev that the United States would agree to participate with Russia in sending a team of civilian observers to the war zone."

"What do you think is going to happen?" Amos asked.

"I don't know. By now, the Russians know the Americans are on heightened readiness for possible nuclear war."

"It's like nineteen sixty-one all over again."

"It's even more dangerous, Amos. The American and Russian navies are maneuvering menacingly off the coasts of Libya, Egypt, and Israel while the fighting is going on around the Canal. Those naval commanders can fire at their own discretion if they feel threatened. Any wrong move or miscalculation by the Russians or Americans, or by our navy, for that matter, would be catastrophic."

Amos's thoughts drifted to the horrible incident with the *US Liberty* during the sixty-seven war.

"It's not just about us observing the ceasefire, Amos. We really don't know what to do about the Egyptian Third Army. Dayan would like to annihilate them, after what they did to us, but Golda is willing to let them have safe passage back to Egypt if they lay down their arms. How can we let them go with their weapons and tanks and all of their anti-tank weapons? We're not going to give them the means to turn around and attack us again."

"In other words, we want them to surrender."

"Well, we're not using those words."

"You know, the Americans are not going to allow us to further humiliate Sadat."

"Golda is in one hell of a bind, Amos. We've lost thousands of men, hundreds of our men are prisoners of war, our air force has been decimated, nearly five hundred tanks have been lost, and now that we've out-maneuvered the enemy on both fronts, and trapped an entire army, we're expected to just let them go, lock, stock, and barrel, as the Americans say. The Israeli government could fall just like that," Ambassador Dinitz said, with a snap of his fingers.

"Well, we could let the Egyptians be resupplied with food, water, and medical supplies in return for a real ceasefire. As long as they can't fire at us, it would seem we could let them keep their arms."

"This has become more of a political problem than a military problem," Ambassador Dinitz replied. "We haven't figured out how to let them go now that we have them in a vice. Golda is in serious trouble no matter what happens next. We were unprepared and too cocky. Nearly every family has lost someone or has someone in captivity over there. I think Golda is through no matter what happens."

"So, what's next?" Amos replied.

"Assuming Russia backs off and America stands down, Kissinger is going to be all over me to resolve the problem with the trapped Third Army. His patience is wearing very thin, and I don't blame him. America has gone to the mat for us. Nixon has been fantastic. With all the domestic problems he has, and even with the war in Vietnam, he stood by us in our bleakest hour. I can't think of another American President who would have taken such risks for us. Nixon's airlift to us was almost unimaginable, and it isn't as though all of his own people were on board. He showed the Pentagon what a civilian Commander-in-Chief really is. It would have never happened on such a scale with anyone else; not with Johnson, not with Kissinger, and not with Schlesinger. It's quite remarkable."

"So, what do we do next?" Amos asked.

"I don't know. I told Kissinger that no nation in history had ever trapped an invading army and then let it go with all its weapons."

"What did he say?"

"He said the United States, standing by a tiny ally, has gone to the brink of nuclear war and that there was no precedent for that either."

"I take it Kissinger wants to see more cooperation from us."

"He wants the war to be over, and he won't let us destroy Egypt's Third Army. He doesn't want Sadat to be seen as a failure, because that would end any hope of serious negotiations between us and Egypt. He wants both sides to save face, end the fighting, and then, hopefully, begin talking to one another. He wants to start a peace process and has suggested coming to the region himself early in November. He expects all hostilities to be in remission by then."

"So, we just wait to see how Russia reacts to the United States flexing its muscles?"

"As soon as Russia reacts to America's DefCon Three maneuver, assuming it's a constructive reaction, I expect Kissinger will want to see me. He'll turn the screws on us to offer something constructive. I want you on the call, or with me if he wants to see me in person."

"Do you think the Egyptians will agree to face-to-face meetings with us on the battlefield?"

"I don't know. I think they might. Sadat will, at a minimum, want to see something positive come of all of this. He's lost thousands of men too. Somehow, this war has to be a game changer. I can't imagine we'll just go back to staring at one another across the Canal."

"Well, we'll know soon enough," Amos replied.

CHAPTER TWENTY-ONE

Alexandra was in no mood for chitchat when her telephone rang just before the deadline for Sunday's column. She wasn't entirely happy with the draft she had prepared and was anxious to do some serious rewriting.

"Alexandra Salaman," she answered, as she impatiently snapped up the telephone.

"Hi, Miss Salaman, how are you today?" the deep Southern voice asked cheerfully.

Alexandra found her caller's Southern accent jarring, but amusing. *How are you?* came out comically, sounding much more like *How are yeew?*

"I'm fine, thank you," she replied. "I'm a bit busy right now, but how can I help you?"

"Well, I won't keep you. My name is Sarah Jean Bogart and I'm a reporter for the *Blytheville Courier News*. I read your column *every* week, Miss Salaman. I bet the *Courier News* is the only subscriber you have in the Chickasawba district of Mississippi County, Arkansas."

"You're probably right, Miss Bogart. How can I help you?"

"Oh, please just call me Sarah Jean," the voice on the other end responded, oblivious to Alexandra's impatience.

Alexandra glanced up at the clock on the wall of the newsroom and grimaced. She really didn't have time for this conversation.

"Yes, Sarah Jean, how can I help you?" she replied.

"You know, I think you must be the most knowledgeable person in Washington, Miss Salaman. Your columns are *so* good. I read you every single week."

"Thank you. That's always nice to hear."

"So, I was thinkin', who would I call if I needed to know somethin' that was sort of hush-hush in Washington?"

"Well, probably not me," Alexandra laughed.

"Oh, I think you're the smartest columnist at that paper, Miss Salaman. There's not much that happens in Washington that you don't know about."

"Oh, if you only knew how much I don't know about," Alexandra quipped. "But really, I'm quite pressed for time right now."

"Of course, I understand. I can be such a chatterbox sometimes."

"So, how can I help you?"

"You know, in a small town like Blytheville, reporters like me cover everything from births to funerals and everything in between. I even check the police blotters every day."

Alexandra looked up at the clock again and rolled her eyes in agony. *Where in the hell is this conversation going?* she thought. "Look, I hate to be rude, but I'm terribly behind deadline right now. I'm sure you understand, being a journalist yourself."

"Oh, nobody here thinks of me as a real journalist, Miss Salaman. I'm just a little reporter for a little paper in a little town."

"Well, I certainly …"

"Miss Salaman," Sarah Jean Bogart interrupted, "is the United States about to go to war?"

"What? What did you ask?"

"I think we might be getting ready to go to war, Miss Salaman."

"Why in the world would you say that?" Alexandra asked, her attention now riveted to the chirpy voice with the deep Southern accent.

"Well, I'll tell you what I know, if you'll tell me what you know?"

"What …?"

"You've been writing all about that fighting between the A-rabs and the Jews over in the Middle East every week, and you really seem to know what's going on."

Alexandra's agony of only moments earlier suddenly turned into anticipation. But what could some reporter from a tiny newspaper in a tiny town somewhere in Arkansas possibly know that she didn't know?

"Sarah Jean, you've got my attention. So, what caused you to call me?"

"Well, we don't get big stories down here very often, Miss Salaman … like never."

"Yes, I understand."

"So, do you think if I helped you get a *really* big story you could get me a job up in Washington at the *Evening Star*?"

"Sarah Jean, I have nothing whatsoever to do with who the *Star* hires. Really, that's totally out of my league."

"Could you get me an interview with whoever *is* in that league?"

"Is that what this is about, Sarah Jean? You want to trade information for an interview here at the *Star*?"

"What I want, Miss Salaman, is to get out of this shithole of a town. I mean, it's a nice enough place and there's plenty of nice people around Blytheville, but there's no future for me here."

"Sarah Jean, how old are you?"

"I'm twenty-two and faster than an Arkansas white-tailed deer, Miss Salaman."

"I beg your pardon?"

"I may be young, but I can smell out a story faster than a bluetick coonhound can sniff out a pregnant cougar. And, besides, you were pretty young yourself when you began working for the *Star*."

Alexandra sat back in her chair and tried to picture the young reporter. Sarah Jean Bogart was sassy, energetic, and smart, and, Alexandra thought, she sure knew how to command attention.

"So, let's talk about this information you have, Sarah Jean," Alexandra replied, as she reached for a pad of paper and pulled a ballpoint pen from a coffee mug emblazoned with the paper's logo.

"Will you get me an interview?"

"Let's hear what you have to tell me," Alexandra answered.

"I think we're getting ready to go to war, Miss Salaman."

"You learned that in the Chickasawba district of Mississippi County, Arkansas?" Alexandra asked, her voice a bit incredulous. "How did you put it? In the shithole town of Blytheberg?"

"It's Blythe*ville*, Miss Salaman," the caller replied, "and yeah, I think I did learn that here." Sarah Jean paused, like a seasoned reporter, to await Alexandra's response.

"Where, at the American Legion Hall?" Alexandra answered, a bit too sarcastically.

"Nope … I learned it at the Blytheville police station."

"You learned a war might be about to break out, and you learned it at the Blytheville police station? Some cop tell you that?"

"Nope. Just somebody who works in Blytheville."

"What was *Mr. Somebody* doing at the police station?"

"Well, he wasn't actually at the police station. He was stopped for speeding, and the cop made a note on the blotter about why the man was in such a hurry."

"Are you going to tell me the man was rushing to go to war in the Middle East?"

"Not exactly."

Alexandra knew she was being toyed with, but she also was curious whether or not Sarah Jean Bogart was onto something. "Sarah Jean, why was the man speeding? Where was he going?"

"To the base."

Alexandra leaned into the phone as a quiver ran down her spine. "What kind of base, Sarah Jean?"

"Do I get that interview?"

"I'll absolutely talk to our managing editor, Sarah Jean. I promise. Now, tell me to what base was the man speeding?"

"Blytheville."

"Blytheville? Blytheville what? Is there an army base in Blytheville?"

"No, Miss Salaman. It's not an army base. It's the Blytheville Air Force Base."

"You think we're going to war because some guy was speeding to work at the Blytheville Air Force Base?"

"Uh huh."

"Maybe he was just late for work."

"Nope, he told the cop who stopped him in the middle of the night that he was called at home and told to get to the base right away."

"You said it was an air force base?"

"Uh huh."

"So, some airman got a speeding ticket going to work at his base and you think it means the United States might be getting ready to go to war?"

"Uh huh."

"Because?"

"Because Blytheville Air Force Base is a SAC base, you know, a Strategic Air Command base, and they got *nothing* there but those giant B-52s. They're the ones that carry them mother-fuckin' atomic bombs, Miss Salaman."

Alexandra, momentarily lost for words, contemplated what Sarah Jean had just revealed to her.

"Have *you* gone by the base, Sarah Jean?"

"You bet your ass I have, Miss Salaman."

"Did you notice anything … like unusual activity?"

"Oh yeah. The place is hoppin'. Elmer says it was busy all-night last night, and that's really unusual. Usually, at night it's quiet as a church."

"Who's Elmer?"

"Oh, sorry. Elmer Scoggins is the night driver for Blytheville Taxi."

"Did he take anyone there during the night?"

"No, but he drove by a couple of times."

"And?"

"And he said the place was as busy last night as it is during the day … lights on everywhere, and some planes landed during the night, which never happens."

"You say B-52s are based there?"

"Oh yeah. Lots of them. Ever see one of those B-52s, Miss Salaman?"

"No, I can't say that I have, Sarah Jean."

"They are big mothers, Miss Salaman. I figure if there's suddenly a lot of activity at the Blytheville Base, somethin's going on … somethin' big."

"I'm glad you called, Sarah Jean. I really am."

"Will you fill me in on what you find out? You know, with all your connections and all, you'll know who to call to find out what's going on."

"I doubt I'll find out much."

"But will you tell me what you do learn?"

"You know I can't do that, Sarah Jean."

"You gonna get me that interview?"

"Sarah Jean, I'll get you that interview whether I learn anything or not. I'm really glad you contacted me. You've done some first-class investigative thinking. I'll call you after I've spoken to our managing editor."

"Promise?"

"I promise. There's probably nothing to all of this, but you may have sniffed out a major story. It may be something or it may be nothing, but your instincts were perfect. You'll get that interview."

"Okay then, Miss Salaman. My number is 870-555-4461."

"Got it. I'll call, Sarah Jean. I promise I'll get you that interview. I can't promise that you'll get a job, but I sure as hell will get you that interview."

"Okay then. Bye, Miss Salaman."

"Goodbye, Sarah Jean, and thanks. You did some fine work with this."

"Did I do the right thing, Miss Salaman?"

"Call me Alexandra, Sarah Jean, and yes you did exactly the right thing."

"Bye now, Alexandra."

"Goodbye, Sarah Jean."

Alexandra sat there for a moment collecting her thoughts. Then she picked up the phone and called the Fairfax Hotel and asked for Amos's room.

"Hello!"

"Amos, it's Alexandra. I have to talk to you."

"Are you all right?"

"I'm fine, but I want to come over to the hotel right away. Can you meet me in the Jockey Club?" she asked, referring to one of Washington's favorite *in* places for cocktails and power meetings, lunches and dinners. It was right off of the hotel's lobby.

"Sure. I'll go down and get a table now."

Alexandra hurriedly slipped on her coat as she trapped the telephone between her cheek and shoulder and buzzed Frank Markazie's office.

"Markazie!"

"Frank, hold the editorial page until I get back. I think I may have something huge."

"Shit, Alexandra, they're waiting for your copy now. They're goin' nuts down there."

"Just hold the damn page, I've got to run."

"Where the hell you going?"

"To the Jockey Club to meet someone."

"Who?"

"Hold the page, Frank. I'll try to be back within an hour."

"You're going to be the death of me, girl."

"Trust me, you don't want to check out now. I have to run, Frank."

***

Amos was already seated at a small corner table when Alexandra arrived. He stood as soon as she entered the ornate, but dimly lighted dining room. It was quiet except for the soft piano music wafting in from the bar area. She made her way over to the table and gave him a quick hug as she slipped out of her coat and tossed it onto the red velvet banquette. She sat down opposite him.

"So, what's up?" he asked.

Alexandra leaned across the table to be sure no one could overhear her. "Amos, is the United States preparing to go to war?" she asked, her eyes riveted on his.

"What?"

"I'm sure you heard me."

"Why would you ask me a question like that? How would I know?"

"You knew about that emergency meeting at the White House in the middle of the night."

"President Nixon doesn't confide in me, Alexandra."

"I bet Ambassador Dinitz does. You're with him all day."

"Who in the hell told you the United States was preparing to go to war?"

"Sarah Jean Bogart."

"Who the hell is Sarah Jean Bogart? I've never heard of her."

Alexandra smiled. "I've got my sources."

"I don't know, and I couldn't discuss it with you if I did."

She nodded. "I thought you might say that."

"What are you going to do?"

"Write that some people close to the action have reason to think the United States is preparing to go to war."

"You can't do that, Alexandra."

"Why can't I?"

"It would be irresponsible."

"I don't think that's true at all, Amos."

"You can't speculate about something that dangerous without hard evidence, Alexandra."

"Amos, why is the US Strategic Air Command so busy right now, while we're sitting here?"

"Jesus Christ, Alexandra. Who the hell have you been talking to? Who is Sarah … what's-her-name?" Alexandra smiled, more knowingly than coyly.

"Who is Sarah, Alexandra?"

"Abraham's wife. Isaac's mother."

"This isn't funny, Alexandra. You have no idea what you're fooling around with here."

"Actually, I think I do."

"No, you don't."

"Then tell me."

"Alexandra, stay away from this. You write anything that suggests the United States has increased its DefCon alert and you could be responsible for starting a nuclear exchange in the Middle East, or possibly starting World War Three."

"So, it's true."

"I'm not saying anything is true or not true. I'm just telling you that *if* the United States has alerted its armed forces to step up its war footing, the Russians know it and are deciding what to do in response. The worst thing that could happen under those circumstances would be any public leak of the confrontation, because that would deprive the Russians of the ability to de-escalate without losing face. As long as such a standoff is strictly between the Kremlin and the White House either side can change course without being second-guessed by their own people. The last thing people on either side would want is to have to make decisions with the entire world looking over their shoulders."

"Is it true, Amos?"

"Is what true?"

"Has the United States stepped up its defense condition readiness … its DefCon level?"

"I'm not answering that question."

"I think you just did."

"You know, if you even suggest that there is a nuclear standoff between the United States and Russia, I'll lose my job and probably be unemployable for the rest of my life."

"That's absurd. You haven't told me a thing, and I wouldn't write anything that even came close to implying that you or anyone in the Israeli government, or our government, had."

"And who would believe you, Alexandra? My boss, Benjamin Bar-Levy, certainly wouldn't. Mossad would almost certainly suggest to your government the possibility that I was the source, Alexandra. I'm here in America assigned to Ambassador Dinitz. I've sat in on meetings between our two governments. And remember, you and I have a well-documented history, you know."

"Would you know if the United States had gone to DefCon Three?"

"I'm not touching that question with a ten-foot pole, Alexandra."

"Amos, let's just say I came across this story from a totally unrelated source, which is true. How could I just sit on it?"

"Millions of people could die, Alexandra, if such hypothetical maneuvering between Russia and America became public. If what you are speculating about became public, neither side would easily be able to back down. Do you want to be responsible for that?"

"I'm not sure I would want to be responsible for not alerting the public that tomorrow might be Armageddon."

"This is way over your head, Alexandra. I don't know who your source is, but she or he could be in big trouble for leaking whatever it is you think you know."

"You mean Sarah Jean?" Alexandra replied, barely able to restrain her laughter.

"Your source divulging a military alert to you is no laughing matter, Alexandra."

"Actually, it is," she replied. "If you only knew."

"Alexandra, I beg you. Don't speculate in print about a nuclear standoff between the United States and Russia over the fighting in the Middle East."

"What if I'm not the only one who has this story?"

"Are you telling me another newspaper might be onto this story?"

"I think that's possible," she replied with a smile.

"Alexandra, this isn't funny."

"Do you or those geniuses at the Pentagon think you can start preparing an armada of B-52s for war with no one noticing?"

"Is it the *Washington Post*?"

She shook her head.

"The *New York Times*?"

"Amos, you've convinced me to kill the story at the *Star*. I can't promise anything more than that. I'll see if I can get my source to sit on it too."

"You won't tell me who put you onto this?"

"No, I can't do that."

"Do you want to have dinner?" Amos asked, changing the subject.

"I can't. I have to get back to the paper."

"It's almost six o'clock. What's the hurry?"

"I'm on deadline, and I think I had better call … my source."

"You think she might give the story to another paper?"

Alexandra paused to consider his question. "All I can tell you is that another paper definitely has the story."

"Oh shit."

"Let me deal with it, Amos."

"*Wall Street Journal*?"

"I have to go?"

"Your source … anybody I might know?"

"Highly doubtful," she answered as she rose from her chair. "I'll keep in touch, Amos," she said, leaning over and kissing him quickly on the cheek.

***

"Sarah Jean Bogart," the Southern accent answered.

"Sarah Jean, it's Alexandra Salaman."

"Oh, hi, Miss Salaman. I mean, Alexandra. You did say I could call you Alexandra, right?"

"Of course. As long as I can call you Sarah Jean, it's only fair that you call me Alexandra."

"So, we going to war?"

"I don't know."

"Didn't you ask your contacts in Washington. I mean, how could *you* not know?"

"I can ask, but that doesn't mean anyone has to tell me anything."

"Who did you ask?"

"I can't say, Sarah Jean."

"You can't or you won't?"

"Let's just say, I don't think I found enough to go with this story."

"Well, I think I have."

"No, I don't think you have, Sarah Jean."

"You seemed to think so two hours ago."

"Well, I've done some checking, and I've decided that I don't have enough to run with a story like this."

"You don't think you have enough to run with this? You checked and someone in the know denied that there was a story here?"

"That's not exactly what I said, but, yes, I've decided not to pursue this as a story at this time."

"At this time! When would be the right time, when they're sweeping up what's left of Moscow?"

"Look, Sarah Jean, you did a great job here. You did everything right. Your instincts are as sharp as those of anyone I know. I'm just telling you I don't have enough to run with this."

"Well, you know what, Alexandra? I think I do. I think I could write a story that would get picked up all over Chickasawba, maybe all over Mississippi County. I think this story would make the Little Rock papers."

"Sarah Jean, you can't run with this story."

"Holy Christ and Mother Mary. It's true, isn't it? We're about to bomb the Russians."

"That's ridiculous, Sarah Jean. I didn't say that at all."

"Tell me why you're not running with this story."

"I'm just not."

"Well, Alexandra, I just *am*. What do you think of that?"

"Sarah Jean, you can't."

"You give me one good reason why I shouldn't."

Alexandra knew she couldn't say anything that would only sharpen Sarah Jean's determination.

"Because ..."

"Because *why*, Alexandra?"

"Because I couldn't offer you the job of becoming my assistant here at the *Washington Evening Star* if you did that."

There was silence.

"Alexandra, I mean, Miss Salaman ..."

"It's still Alexandra, Sarah Jean."

"Look, I know I'm just a good Christian girl from Mississippi County, Arkansas, who goes to church on Sundays and the movies on Saturdays, and prays to Jesus every night, and I ain't travelled hardly anywhere, but, Alexandra ... you're not fucking with me, are you?"

Alexandra drew in a deep breath and pictured Markazie's reaction when she told him what she had just done. "No, Sarah Jean, I'm not fucking with you. Your instincts are first rate. I'm in the market for an assistant, and the job is yours if you're serious about wanting to come to Washington."

"But I can't run my story about the United States going to war?"

"No, Sarah Jean, you can't. And for the record, I doubt very seriously that the United States is planning to go to war."

"When can I start?"

"How about next month?"

"How about next week?"

Alexandra smiled. "I really look forward to meeting you, Sarah Jean. Just let me know when you plan to arrive. You can stay with my husband and me until you find a place to rent." Alexandra cringed at the sound of her own voice committing to Sarah Jean something to which she had no authority to commit.

"Thank you, Miss Salaman, I mean, Alexandra. You'll never regret this, not ever."

"No, I don't think I will, Sarah Jean."

***

Alexandra contemplated what to do after hanging up with her newly hired assistant. She decided to talk to her boss first, and then Noah. Franklin Markazie was sitting in his office with his feet propped up on the desk when Alexandra walked in.

"What's up, kid? Where did you have to run off to in such a hurry?"

"Have you been reading those CIA briefs you somehow get your hands on every morning?"

"That's how I start my day, Alexandra. You know that."

It was a gamble, but Alexandra decided to take a shot. "So, you sat on the biggest story since the Cuban Missile Crisis."

Markazie looked at her steely eyed. "What are you talking about, kid?"

Alexandra didn't reply. She just cocked her head and gave him a *you know damn well what I'm talking about* look.

"Don't just stand there. What are you talking about?"

"The United States increases its DefCon level and we don't write about it? That's what I'm talking about, Frank."

Markazie sat there staring at her for several seconds before speaking. "How the hell do you know about that, Alexandra?"

"A reporter from another paper called me about it."

"What!"

"Yeah, that's how I heard about it. She wanted me to share what she assumed I knew."

"God damn it," he roared. "There are some things more important than a scoop. First, I would never run anything my source gives me in confidence, especially from something as sensitive as the daily intelligence briefs. But more important, thousands, maybe millions of people's lives hang in the balance. Damn right I sat on it. National security trumps a big story, even if we have something nobody else has. Is that the huge scoop you were running down when you flew out of here a couple hours ago?"

"Yes. I wanted to confirm from an outside source what I had been told."

"So, you must have run to your friend Amos."

"I did, and he convinced me not to touch this story at this time."

"But now you say there's another paper that has the story."

"There is."

"The God-damned *New York Times*?"

Alexandra shook her head. "No, not the *Times*."

"The *Post*?"

"I convinced the reporter who had the story not to run with it."

"Really? Why did you do that?"

"I knew you were sitting on it, so I didn't want anyone else breaking the story."

Markazie sat there for a moment before reacting. "You didn't want us to get scooped, so you talked our competitor out of running this story. Is that what you're telling me?"

"Well, they're not running with it. I can promise you that."

"Did you say it was the *Washington Post*?"

"I didn't say."

"I'm assuming it was the *Post*."

"The story's dead, Frank. I can promise you that."

"How did you kill a competitor's story like that, Alexandra?"

Alexandra could feel her heart pounding in her chest. "I hired the source."

"What the hell do you mean you hired the source. To do what?"

"To be my assistant."

"Alexandra, what in the hell are you talking about?"

"I hired an assistant. I need an assistant, and this reporter is sharp as a tack—great instincts, Frank. She ferreted this story out of clues that would have gone unnoticed by almost anyone else. She's terrific."

"What the fuck are you telling me?"

"I killed a competitor's scoop, Frank ... for national security reasons."

"By hiring the reporter?"

Alexandra just nodded.

"What the fuck is this going to cost?"

"No more than scale, Frank. She's young. She just happens to be really good."

"Did you say she was with the *Post*?"

Alexandra shook her head. "No, she's not with the *Washington Post*."

"Who the hell is she with, Alexandra? Who are we pirating a reporter away from?"

"The *Courier*," Alexandra answered.

"I'll be damned. Of course, the 911th Tactical Airlift Group is stationed in Pittsburgh. I know the commanding officer. He'd shit a brick if he knew some cub reporter at the *Pittsburgh Courier* was onto the DefCon alert. That unit is based at the Pittsburgh International Airport and that reporter must have observed increased activity and made some inquiries and figured out what was going on. I'll bet anything that's what happened."

"Sounds pretty logical to me," she replied.

"When does this new assistant of yours start, Alexandra?"

"Next week."

"That took real *kutspah*, hiring an assistant without clearing it with me first."

"The word is *chutzpah*, Frank, not *kutspah*," she answered, smiling.

"What's her name?"

"Sarah Jean Bogart."

"She go to the University of Pittsburgh? They have a great Communications program there."

"No, I don't think so."

"How long has she been with the *Pittsburgh Courier*?"

"She's been with the *Courier* maybe a couple of years ... I think."

Franklin Markazie nodded. "Good work, Alexandra. You need an assistant. You should have cleared it with me, but you did the right thing, and you kept a story that shouldn't be published out of a damn good competitor paper."

"So, we're good, Frank?"

"Yeah, we're good, Alexandra. That was a gutsy thing you did, but you're right, you've needed an assistant for a long time. You got your assistant and kept this story out of the *Pittsburgh Courier*. It's a story no one should be running with right now. I'd say you did a damn fine day's work."

Alexandra took a few steps over to Frank and kissed him hurriedly on the cheek. "Thanks, Frank, you won't regret this," she said as she turned to leave her boss's office. "And by the way, Sarah Jean doesn't work for the *Pittsburgh Courier*."

"Huh?"

"She works for the *Blytheville Courier*."

"What the fuck is the *Blytheville Courier*?"

"It's the biggest daily in the Chickasawba district of Mississippi County, Arkansas, Frank. I thought you knew that."

"The *Blytheville Courier* has the story. Is that what you're telling me?"

She nodded, smiled, and left the office.

CHAPTER TWENTY-TWO

"You've been very quiet, Alexandra," Noah said as they sat at the breakfast table the following morning. Alexandra nodded and forced a smile. Noah saw there were tears in her eyes.

"This war has gotten to me, Noah. I'm really out of sorts."

"Because?"

She paused before answering.

Noah reached over and took her hand. "Is it because Israel and the Arabs are at each other's throats again?"

"No, it's not that. I know that war seems to be the one constant in the world. I'm watching some war unfolding somewhere every day when I go to work. I accept that there will be endless fighting over there. I can deal with that."

"Have I done anything to upset you?"

"No, honey. You haven't done anything."

"Alexandra, what is it?" he asked, squeezing her hand gently.

"Noah, I'm really very proud of your stature in the community. I don't just mean the business community. I mean the Jewish community too. You are so admired, and you deserve that admiration."

He looked at her quizzically. "Do you feel I've been ignoring you, Alexandra? Because if you do, I'll …"

"No, of course not, Noah," she interrupted. "As I said, I couldn't be prouder of you."

"But?"

She drew in a long breath before responding. "But, I can't continue to go to these Jewish community events with you, not while the war is going on."

Noah nodded, but didn't respond as her words sank in.

"Noah, while the Palestinians aren't involved in any of this fighting, their sympathy is, overwhelmingly, with Egypt and Syria. I know that neither Egypt nor Syria really gives a damn about the Palestinians, but most Palestinians feel that *they* are the real victims. I know they have to resent me, a Palestinian whose family lost its home in the fighting back in forty-eight, married to a Jewish man who is a major advocate for Israel. Noah, I've grown very uncomfortable going to these banquets and fundraisers for Israel."

Noah nodded. "I understand," he whispered.

"I think many of the Jews at these events must be bewildered by our marriage, by me sitting on the dais at all these events. They couldn't be nicer, and we certainly enjoy the friendship of many Jewish couples, Noah, but that picture of me on the dais sitting under the Israeli flag really got to me. It didn't feel right, Noah."

Again, Noah nodded but didn't say anything.

"I'm sorry, Noah. I know how much you enjoy being a leader in the community, and I know how much you deserve the recognition you've earned."

"It doesn't mean shit to me, Alexandra. Sure, I like the stature I have in the community, and I like being successful in the community, just as I like being successful in business. But I'll drop this activity like that," he said, snapping his fingers. "Nothing matters to me as much as you do, Alexandra. There are plenty of people in the community who can do what I've been doing. Do you think I would want to continue doing this knowing it's making you miserable?"

"Your being active in the Jewish community isn't making me miserable, Noah. I'm very proud of you. I'm just not comfortable being on display while you promote Israel and raise funds for Israel, especially during this awful war. I mean, my mother is half Egyptian, for God's sake. I long ago reconciled myself to the idea that Israel has a place in the Middle East, and God knows the Israelis have always been very accommodating to me. Our son is named after an Israeli who has, on more than one occasion, risked his life for me. We both know that at one time Amos, an Israeli, and I were … very close."

Noah looked into her eyes and drew a deep breath. "Do you have any idea how much I love you, Alexandra?"

She smiled through her tears. "Of course, I do. I feel the same love for you, you know."

"I think I should resign as Chairman of the Jewish Council. I'll tell them I'm too busy with work."

"No. You'll do no such thing. I don't want you to do that, Noah. I really don't. If you resigned that would make *us* the news. This isn't about your activity at all. It's about me, Noah. I don't want you to hide from who you are. I really don't. I just don't want to be an ornament at these Israel fundraising functions. Sometimes, when you're speaking at the podium, I glance at the audience and there are a lot of people looking at *me* while you're talking. I think a lot of people are perplexed … bewildered by our marriage. I know people talk about *us*. How could they not?"

"Let me think about it, Alexandra. I don't know if I want to continue doing this without you by my side. You're not an ornament, Alexandra. Not to me, you're not. You inspire me. You give me confidence, and I think you give others hope. I really think people look at us and think—there's hope."

"Sometimes I wonder if people look at us and think, *Why her?* How did Noah Greenspan wind up with Alexandra Salaman?"

"And wouldn't I love to tell them," he replied.

***

"My sister seems very happy with you, A'isha," Yusuf said as soon as they were seated for dinner. Duke Zeibert's was one of Washington's most popular restaurants and just a block away from the Mayflower

Hotel, where Yusuf had reserved a room for the night so that he wouldn't have to drive back to Baltimore.

"And your brother-in-law?"

"Noah seems just as pleased as Alexandra," he answered. "How about you? Has working for Alexandra and Noah been what you expected?"

"Better than I expected," she answered. "They're quite remarkable. Seeing where she and you grew up was very moving. I felt the same way seeing where Mr. Greenspan lived back then, and being at the very spot where your sister and Mr. Greenspan met when they were just children was very special for me."

"Ah, yes," Yusuf replied. "That would be on the front steps of N.P. Gage Elementary School. I remember that moment like it was yesterday."

"Did you know many Jews, before you met Mr. Greenspan?" she asked.

"I don't think I had ever met any Jews before meeting Noah and the Greenspans," he replied.

Yusuf and A'isha continued their conversation throughout dinner. They were soon chatting like old friends who were catching up with one another might talk. The mood was relaxed; the repartee, easy.

"Your parents and Mr. Greenspan's parents are business partners, right?" she asked as they were finishing a shared desert.

"They are, A'isha. We would have never made it here if it weren't for the Greenspans."

"Did you have any problem with your sister dating and then marrying Mr. Greenspan?"

"You mean because he is a Jew?"

She nodded.

"Interesting question, A'isha. I did have a problem when Noah first asked my sister out on a date."

"And?"

"My sister is pretty headstrong—just like my mother. My father gave in after warning Alexandra not to do anything that would bring shame to our family. Thing is, Alexandra was right. Noah *is* a wonderful guy. My parents absolutely love him, and the Greenspans have always been very close to my sister. Noah has been my best friend the entire time I've lived in this country. I would walk through fire for him, and I'm pretty sure he would do the same for me."

"It seems so normal. Two good people fall in love and get married, and yet a relationship like theirs is probably bewildering to millions and millions of people."

"Bewildering is putting it mildly," he replied, as the waiter poured coffee for them. "Their relationship invokes hatred in millions of people. It damn near cost Alexandra her life."

"You mean that horrible incident in Khartoum?"

"Yeah. You heard about that?"

"I guess I did somewhere along the line."

"From Alexandra?"

"I … I don't recall where I heard about it," she replied, holding his gaze, her voice steady. "Maybe from that Israeli fellow."

"Amos?"

"Yes, maybe he mentioned it. I don't remember exactly."

"Huh," Yusuf murmured, as if to say, *That's strange.* Then after a brief pause, "I don't think Amos would have mentioned it."

A'isha shrugged. "I hear so much conversation in the background, I guess I'm not certain where I heard it."

Yusuf nodded. "It's not important."

A'isha smiled, giving no indication of being the least bit flustered by the turn the conversation had taken.

"So, you must be from a pretty liberal family. When I first met you, I didn't think you would go out with a non-Muslim man. Especially unaccompanied."

"You mean because I wear a hijab?"

"Yeah, I guess so."

"Actually, my family isn't very religious. They're pretty Western. So am I, actually. I don't feel strongly about the hijab. I began wearing it every day when I applied for the job at the Qatari embassy. I just got used to it, and I rather like it. When I applied for the job as your nephew's nanny, I could see Amos was curious about my hijab. I took it off and handed it to him. I told him wearing it was a custom where I came from, but if he preferred that I didn't wear it, I wouldn't."

"What did he say?"

"He said he liked it, so I've continued to wear it."

They continued conversing, leisurely and comfortably. Yusuf liked A'isha. She was, he thought, rather delightful, and quite beautiful. She was about his sister's height and looked more like a model than a nanny. Her scarlet hijab complemented her olive complexion, and her dark eyes had an engaging sparkle.

He started to reach across the table for her hand and then, a bit awkwardly, drew back.

She smiled and softly laid her hand over his. "I'm an American girl, Yusuf. I won't faint if you hold my hand."

"I just didn't want to do anything that made you uncomfortable."

"I'm very comfortable, Yusuf," she said, before withdrawing her hand.

He smiled. "I'm glad you're my nephew's nanny."

"I am too. I was excited about this job as soon as it was brought to my attention. I'm glad your sister and brother-in-law retained me."

Yusuf smiled and nodded. "I'm glad the job was brought to your attention too, A'isha."

She returned the smile.

"By the way, who brought the job to your attention, anyway?" he asked.

"What?"

"You said you were excited about the nanny position as soon as it was brought to your attention. I was curious about who brought it to your attention."

"I meant, I was excited as soon as I saw the position advertised in the paper."

"Of course," he replied, his eyes fixed a bit more intently on hers. "Of course."

She reached over and gently clasped his hand. "I've had a wonderful time tonight, Yusuf. I don't get to do this very often; in fact, not at all. This is the nicest restaurant I've been to since I moved to Washington."

"Yeah, Duke's is my favorite restaurant in Washington. I love the onion rolls."

"Well, the meal was delicious. Thank you," she answered.

"I would have wined and dined you, but I didn't think wine would go with your hijab."

"You assumed I wouldn't drink wine?"

"Well, would you?"

"I have few occasions to drink wine, but I believe Muslims should be able to enjoy a glass of wine as long as they never come to prayer under the influence of alcohol."

"Well, I'll keep that in mind the next time we dine together."

A'isha smiled. "I'm glad there will be a next time."

Yusuf drove A'isha to her apartment at Alban Towers, just across the street from the National Cathedral on Massachusetts Avenue. He noted its proximity to the city's mosque a few blocks away. A Greek Orthodox church stood across the street, and the Washington Hebrew Congregation was but a stone's throw away.

"Quite an ecumenical neighborhood you live in," he said as he parked his Corvette.

"I'm happy here. It's close to everything. I moved here because it was pretty close to the Qatari embassy, but it's only a few minutes from Georgetown as well."

Yusuf walked with A'isha to the entrance of Alban Towers and looked admiringly at the facade of the building.

"Gothic Revival," he said after a long pause, as his gaze followed the lines of the building all the way to the top.

"Ah, yes," she responded, smiling broadly. "I forgot you're an architect."

"It's in my blood," he replied, laughing. "May I see you to your door?"

"Of course," she answered.

They didn't speak as the old mahogany-walled elevator slowly creaked its way to the fourth floor. Her studio apartment was at the end of a long hall, and when they reached her door she turned to him and smiled. "I had a marvelous time tonight, Yusuf."

"I did too, A'isha," he replied, barely above a whisper.

She stood there, silently, for a moment as Yusuf looked into her eyes. He hesitated, not ready to turn away, unsure of how to end the evening.

She reached up and pulled the hijab from her head, letting her hair fall to her shoulders. "More comfortable now?" she asked, a slight tease to her voice. With that, he took her in his arms and kissed her, tenderly and unrushed, for several moments. Then he leaned back slightly and smiled as he brushed back with his fingertips several strands of hair that had fallen over her temple.

"Good night, Yusuf Salaman," she said, handing him her key.

He reached over and unlocked the door to the apartment and pushed it open.

"I'll call you tomorrow," he said, returning the key to her.

"I'll count on it," she replied.

CHAPTER
TWENTY-THREE

Moshe Dayan was seething as he argued with his Prime Minister. "Golda, this is war. We were attacked and came this close to utter defeat," he said, holding his forefinger an inch from his thumb to emphasize his point.

"You don't need to lecture me, Moshe. I know only too well the beating we've taken. Do you think I've slept for so much as an hour a night since this nightmare began? Don't you think I want Sadat and Assad to rue the day they ever attacked us? Every time I close my eyes at night I see corpses, the bodies of our boys."

"We cannot let the Egyptian Third Army just pick up their weapons and drive their tanks back to Egypt so that they can attack us again next week, or next month, or next year. No nation on earth would be expected to do that after being attacked by an enemy army."

"I'm afraid we're not just any nation on earth," she replied.

"In the entire history of warfare, any army that found itself in the position in which we have Egypt's Third Army today would be pleading for its life. It would gladly embrace any terms the victor demanded, if only its soldiers were allowed to survive."

"Yes, I understand, Moshe. But don't give me history lessons about this army or that army. We are the Israeli Army, and had *we* been surrounded, we would be depending on the Americans to save us just as Sadat is depending on them to save the Egyptian Third Army."

"But it is *our* army that sustained such enormous losses, and it is *our* army that has, miraculously, turned the tide."

"And it is *we* who were almost out of ammunition, not to mention fighter planes. What did our air force tell us just a day ago—that they could only have fought another three days before they would have had to cease combat operations. Who came to our rescue, Moshe? Where were our friends in Europe?"

"So, the Americans now dictate what we *can* and *cannot* do on the battlefield?" Dayan replied.

Just then, their conversation was drowned out by the roar of an American C-5 flying overhead on its way back to the United States.

The Israeli Prime Minister smiled and raised her eyebrows. "Do you hear that, Moshe? That's the answer to your question. That's the most dependable sound I've heard in a long time. I trust that sound more than all the advice I've heard in the past month. That sound is music to my ears. I dread not hearing that sound throughout the day and throughout the night. If the people who are sending those planes with their precious cargoes say we cannot humiliate Sadat and we cannot destroy his Third Army, then we will end this at the negotiating table and not on the battlefield."

***

Anwar Sadat sat alone in his office, contemplating all that had gone wrong. His pipe sat in an ashtray at the corner of his desk, the ashes smoldering like a remnant of a lost cause. The exhilaration that had coursed through every fiber of his being only days earlier had been extinguished by brutal reality. Now he felt only despair. Barely two weeks earlier his forces had smashed through Israel's so-called impenetrable Bar-Lev Line, and in a couple of days he had tens of thousands men and a thousand tanks firmly established on the Sinai. The Suez Canal, all of it, had been wrested away from the Jews and returned by him to Egypt. His losses during the Canal crossing were in the dozens, not the thousands that everyone had predicted. In one day, he had avenged the years of humiliation the Jews had visited upon his people following Nasser's preening and strutting and threatening and the disastrous sixty-seven war Nasser brought to his people. But now it was the Egyptians who were bloodied and back on their heels. General Shazly had warned him not to press his luck, not to push too far beyond the East Bank of the Canal and the surface-to-air missile umbrella the Russians had provided.

But we had to do something to relieve pressure on the Syrians, and, besides, we had the initiative, he thought. He had inflicted catastrophic losses on the Israelis. How could he not push on? Every additional kilometer he held would strengthen his negotiating position when the big powers finally imposed a ceasefire.

And then there was that horrible day a week earlier when everything changed. His attempt to push on to the strategic Mitla and Gidi Passes, and to engage the Israelis in the greatest tank battle since the Battle of Kursk on the Eastern Front during the Second World War, turned into an historic rout. The Israelis, who were patiently waiting, destroyed hundreds of his tanks, killed thousands of his men, while suffering negligible casualties and losing only about a dozen tanks. The course of the war had shifted like the sands of the Sinai. And somehow, that audacious general, the one the Jews called Arik the Lion, had slipped across the Canal and silenced the Russian missile sites, and in less than a week Egypt's vaunted Third Army was trapped, sandwiched between Israelis to the east and to the west.

What to do? The Russians had demanded a joint Russian-American expedition to enforce a ceasefire. When the Americans balked, Brezhnev threatened to send units of the Red Army to the Sinai with or without the Americans. Nixon and Kissinger responded by putting America's Air Force and Navy on a heightened nuclear alert, and then demanded that the UN send so-called non-aligned observers to oversee a ceasefire. And then there was the cable from President Nixon. President Sadat picked it up and read the portion he had underlined.

> *I ask you to consider the consequences for your country*
> *if the two great nuclear countries were thus to confront*
> *each other on your soil. I ask you further to consider the*
> *impossibility for us undertaking the diplomatic initiative*
> *which was to start with Dr. Kissinger's visit to Cairo on*
> *November 7 if the forces of one of the great nuclear pow-*
> *ers were to be involved militarily on Egyptian soil.*

It was a brilliant message, he thought—probably written by Secretary Kissinger.

Sadat had already expelled most of the Russian advisors that Nasser had brought to Egypt. *Bringing Russian troops back to Egypt is the last thing I want to do,* he thought. He had to decide between the two super powers. His goal had never been to vanquish Israel, only to bring the old lady, as he commonly referred to Golda Meir, to the negotiating table. The Israelis knew Sadat had been ready to talk for some time, but they were still too intoxicated by their past battlefield successes, and too afraid of fracturing their ruling coalition, to talk to him. He couldn't force them to the table now, and he knew the Russians couldn't either. His thoughts turned to the Jewish German émigré who had fled from Nazi Germany to America with his family when he was only fifteen years old—Heinz Alfred Kissinger.

CHAPTER

TWENTY-FOUR

It was well after eleven o'clock when Ambassador Dinitz called Amos at the Fairfax Hotel. "I hope I didn't wake you, Amos, but I thought we should talk."

"No, I was just watching the news."

"I just finished talking with Kissinger. He's very upset with us. He's given us an ultimatum."

"What kind of an ultimatum?"

"Either we agree to allow non-military supplies through to the Third Army right away or the United States will support the UN demand that we pull all the way back to the October twenty-second lines, the lines where our troops were when the UN called for a ceasefire which both sides agreed to and which neither side has honored. He also told me the US Defense Department has proposed that the Americans air-drop non-military supplies to the Egyptian Third Army. Kissinger said he has argued that it would be better for the Third Army to be supplied through an agreement that we work out with the Egyptians. He thinks maybe if they agreed to face-to-face talks it could change the entire calculus in the Middle East—you know, Israelis and Egyptians actually meeting civilly, face to face."

"Didn't we already make the offer to meet face to face with the Egyptians?"

"Yes, but so far, we've heard nothing back from Hafez Ismail, Sadat's National Security Advisor. Kissinger assured us that he passed our offer to meet on to Ismail but held out little hope that the Egyptians would even consider our offer."

"What are our people saying?"

"Not much. Dayan thinks meeting with the Egyptians is a crazy idea. He feels, given the beating we've taken, we should annihilate the Third Army now that we have them trapped."

"That's what any other army would do," Amos replied.

"We're not any other army, Amos. Dayan might, reluctantly, let them retreat with their arms as long as they got the hell out of the Sinai. Kissinger told me in no uncertain terms that the Americans would not let that happen. He actually told me that the humiliation, let alone the destruction, of the Third Army is an option that doesn't exist for us."

"That's pretty heavy handed of him."

"Well, not when you think of the war from his point of view. Kissinger feels, with plenty of justification, that that's exactly what the United States kept Egypt from doing to us. Our arsenal was getting pretty thin before the American planes and ships came with their supplies. They, in effect, told both the Egyptians and the Russians that the destruction of our army was not an option for them."

"What are we going to do?"

"We're playing a little Russian roulette here. Golda has offered to meet face to face to work things out with the Egyptians at a place of their choosing, and with army officers with a rank of their choosing," Ambassador Dinitz replied.

"The problem is that we've been given an ultimatum by the United States. The clock is ticking, and in a matter of hours Kissinger is going to support the UN demand that we retreat to the east, well beyond the Canal."

"You had better get some sleep while you can, Amos. I wanted to bring you up to date. It's morning on the Sinai and I don't know what's going to happen once Kissinger's ultimatum has run its course."

***

Anwar Sadat made a fateful decision as he sat brooding. Israel had pummeled his forces in Egypt's ill-advised run to the strategic desert passes, and the Jews had now crossed the Canal, trapping his entire Third Army—and then there was the breathtaking American support of the enemy.

Kissinger's ultimatum to Israel never ran its course. It was three o'clock in the morning when the Secretary of State was awakened. A cable had arrived from Cairo. Hafez Ismail had accepted the Israeli offer. If Israel would agree to a complete ceasefire and allow the passage of a convoy of non-military supplies to the Third Army, the Egyptians would send a senior officer to meet face to face with an Israeli counterpart. Egypt designated a nondescript spot on the road to Cairo about twenty kilometers west of Suez City.

"I don't believe it," Ambassador Dinitz said when Secretary of State Kissinger called around three thirty in the morning to tell him the news.

"You really are from a land of miracles," Kissinger replied. "Make sure your government doesn't screw this up."

***

"Alexandra, I have big news for you," Amos said as soon as Alexandra answered the phone.

"Amos, is everything all right? It's five o'clock in the morning."

Noah, startled by the pre-dawn call, sat up in bed.

"The Egyptians have agreed to meet face to face with us to negotiate the cessation of hostilities," Amos shouted into the phone.

"When? Where?"

"They want to meet on the road from Suez to Cairo."

"On the road?" she answered.

"Yes, yes, on the road. They've designated a kilometer marker about twenty kilometers west of Suez."

"In a town?"

"No. It's just a spot at Kilometer 101. I suppose we'll erect a tent or something."

"So, the war is over?" she asked excitedly, turning to Noah, her expression joyous.

"Yes, yes, we've agreed to a ceasefire. The guns are silent. We're meeting with the Egyptians."

"Will you be going back to Israel now, Amos?"

"I will, but there will be a slight detour," he answered.

"A slight detour? What is that supposed to mean?"

"Ambassador Dinitz wants me to be an observer."

"An observer of what?"

"The talks."

"The talks—the Israeli-Egyptian talks? You are going to be at Kilometer 101 when the Israelis and Egyptians talk?"

"Can you believe it?"

"No. I mean, I don't know what to say. These talks will be historic. It will be the first time the Egyptians and Israelis have ever sat face to face at the same table. When are you leaving?"

"Probably in the next twenty-four hours. The talks are scheduled to begin Saturday. We're trying to arrange for me to travel on one of the US Air Force cargo planes. Around forty American Lockheed C-5s are flying into Israel every day. I can get down to Eilat from Lod and the IDF will fly me by helicopter to Kilometer 101."

"Can I meet you for coffee or breakfast?"

"When?"

"Right now."

"I think I know what you're thinking, and the answer is no, Alexandra. Don't even entertain the thought."

"In the coffee shop at the Fairfax?"

"There is no coffee shop here."

"Then in the lobby or in your room. Room service can send some coffee to your room."

"No. Absolutely not, Alexandra."

"You won't have coffee with me? Are you mad?"

"No, Alexandra, I'm not crazy, but I think you may be."

"You have no idea what I want to discuss with you. Maybe just an interview for the story I'm going to write."

"I know you better than that, Alexandra. We've been down this road before."

Noah reached over and snatched the phone from Alexandra. "Congratulations, Amos. This is wonderful news."

"Hi, Noah. Sorry to call so early in the morning, but I wanted you two to know as soon as I heard."

"It sounded like you don't want to meet with Alexandra this morning."

"No, I don't, Noah."

"Are you worried that she'll plead to go to these talks with you?"

"I know damn well she will, Noah. She knows history will be made at these talks, and I know how her mind works."

"Well things are different now, Amos. Don't forget, she's married now. She has a husband and a child," Noah replied, looking over to his wife.

"Are you telling me you want me to meet with her about this?"

"Well, it will be one of the biggest stories of the decade, if not the century."

"I don't think Ambassador Dinitz would want me to do that, and I can tell you for sure my boss back in Israel would go through the ceiling if he knew we were even having this conversation. Alexandra isn't one of his favorite people."

"Well, I just want you to know I'm fine with her meeting with you about this if you're fine with it."

Alexandra closed her eyes and lowered her head to her hand. *God, I would give anything to be at those talks, even for just one day,* she thought.

"It's much too sensitive right now, Noah, for me to be talking to the press, and Alexandra *is* the press."

"I bet this will be on every wire service by noon, Amos."

"Put Alexandra back on the line. I'll have coffee with her, but everything we discuss will have to be off the record until I know how we and the Egyptians are dealing with the press. If there's an announcement by our mutual press offices, I suppose it would be all right."

***

Prime Minister Meir didn't have to think twice about who she wanted at Kilometer 101 negotiating for Israel. She firmly believed that had Major General Aharon Yariv not retired as head of military intelligence in 1972, Israel would have been ready when the Syrians and Egyptians attacked. In fact, she believed the Arabs probably would not have attacked. They would have known that Israel was alert and ready and that an attack would have been catastrophic. Yariv, who had immigrated from Latvia to Palestine as Aharon Rabinovich when he was fifteen years old, was a veteran of every conflict Israel had faced. He was but a boy when he joined the Haganah, the para-military defense force when Britain still ruled Palestine. He had led the legendary and most decorated fighting force, the Golani Brigade, and, after Munich, was chosen to lead Operation Wrath of God, charged with the task of identifying, hunting down, and killing every single terrorist involved in the massacre. He had a well-earned reputation as a master of intelligence, and the Prime Minister believed that had Aharon Yariv still been in charge of military intelligence instead of General Eli Zeira things would have been very different. Of that she was certain. But, perhaps most important, at this time and for this task, there was no better negotiator in the Israeli Defense Forces.

Similarly, President Anwar Sadat knew immediately who he would send to face the Israelis at the negotiating table. No one in the Egyptian Army was more reliable than General Abdel Ghani el-Gamasy. He had been charged with the task of dislodging the Israelis from the East Bank of the Suez Canal, a task that he had planned and executed brilliantly. El-Gamasy, the commander of all ground forces for Operation Badr, had accomplished every objective Sadat had given him. The planning and execution of the war had been flawless. The general, like Sadat himself, had been among the first commoners to graduate from the Egyptian Military Academy, over three decades earlier, and had risen through the ranks because of his tenacity and intelligence rather than his social status. Most of all, Sadat knew the pedantic el-Gamasy would be a match at the negotiating table for anyone the Israelis selected to sit opposite him. A shrewd and patient stickler for detail, he would make no concession without exacting an equal measure from the Israelis.

***

It was a little after seven o'clock when Alexandra arrived at the Fairfax. Amos was waiting for her in the lobby. He looked tired but smiled enthusiastically when he looked up from the *Washington Post* and saw her enter the hotel. She rushed over to him and they briefly embraced.

"A historic time," she said, smiling.

"Let's hope it results in good history for everyone," he replied. "I only have a few minutes, Alexandra. I have to get to the embassy. Ambassador Dinitz and I are meeting promptly at seven thirty. I've arranged for room service to serve us coffee in the Jockey Club. I'm afraid I don't have time for breakfast."

"Not a problem, Amos. I don't want to keep you."

"Well, the news is out, so I can't even give you a scoop," he said, holding up the morning *Post*.

"Well, maybe you can do something even better," she answered.

"Such as?"

"Our air force is running cargo planes around the clock to Israel and back, right?"

"Yes, I hope to be on one of them tomorrow. Ambassador Dinitz is trying to arrange that today."

"Amos, I would like to accompany you to the opening meeting. When you arrange to hitchhike on a US cargo plane to Israel, could you arrange to have me accompany you as, say, your assistant? I could, literally, return the next day. I would barely be gone twenty-four hours, and I would be in the company of military personnel at all times. I would never be in any danger."

"No!"

"Why? What could the harm be? You could arrange for me to accompany you when you organize your own flight. It would barely be a round trip to Israel and back, with a few hours spent at the tent or whatever is going to be erected at Kilometer 101. I could accompany you on the helicopter from Eilat to the talks and head back to Eilat after the first meeting ends. I could be on a returning American cargo plane the next day. What possible harm could there be?"

"No!"

"Why? Tell me what is wrong with what I've proposed."

"First, Ambassador Dinitz wouldn't approve it. Second, Benjamin Bar-Levy would have my head if he knew I had arranged such folly, and third, Noah would be furious. He'd probably never speak with me again, and maybe not to you either. Have you totally forgotten what happened the last time you wanted to be a spectator of history?"

"There is no comparison between this and Khartoum. I'm not asking to go off on my own and sneak into a hostile country. I would be with you from the time I left the States until I boarded a US Air Force cargo plane returning to America a day later."

"No, Alexandra. I won't even discuss this with Ambassador Dinitz."

"Amos, when the embassy arranges your travel to Israel with the Pentagon, simply indicate there may be two of you hopping a ride. You could say you'll have an assistant traveling with you. Besides, your government would probably like knowing there's friendly press accompanying you. If the talks begin Saturday, I would be on my way back Sunday or Monday. There's absolutely no danger."

"Noah wouldn't hear of it, and you know it."

"That might be true, and if it is, that will be the end of it, so there's no harm trying. If Noah says no, I'll drop the whole thing."

"Of course he'll say no."

"Let me worry about that. If he says no … it will be no."

"I don't have time for this, Alexandra. Have Noah call me and tell me he has no objection and I'll think about it. Until then, I'm busy and I have no time for this foolishness."

"Fair enough. And if he does say no, I won't be seeing you until you return to the States for Thanksgiving. I assume you'll stop off here on the way to Chicago or on your way back."

"Yes, I'm sure I'll spend some time at the embassy when I'm next in the States. I'm really considering getting assigned to our embassy here or to our consulate in Chicago."

"Karen would be thrilled," Alexandra replied.

"Yes, she would. So would I. This long-distance relationship can't continue much longer. She's at her wits' end, and frankly, so am I."

"I'll call you one way or the other, after I've spoken further with Noah."

Amos nodded. "He would be crazy to agree to let you do this."

"Then there's no problem. If he says no, that will be the end of it."

***

"No! Alexandra, how could you even contemplate such an idea?"

"Noah, I understand how you feel, but this represents no danger whatever. First, if Amos can arrange this, and that's a big *if*, I would be in the presence of American or Israeli armed forces at all times. Furthermore, I would be back home within twenty-four to forty-eight hours. I would only go for the opening meeting, and I would be there with Amos as an observer. I would stay in Eilat overnight. There would be nothing dangerous about this at all, and it would be an incredible story for me. This will be one of the most historic meetings of the century—I mean, a real history-changing event—and, possibly, I could be there when it happens."

"This sounds eerily like the last time you wanted to cover a historic meeting, Alexandra."

"Noah, there's no comparison. This is going to be a joint meeting of Israeli and Egyptian generals practically arranged by the United States. You can't even think of a circumstance in which there would be any danger."

"I may have to be in New York in the next few days, Alexandra. I think George Markanos is about to recommend shorting our stock again, and I may need to begin meeting with institutions in the next few days to assure them that our business is solid."

"What is Markanos concerned about?"

"The economy. He thinks we may be about to lapse into recession, and if he's right, retail will probably get clobbered. PCPA is sitting out there with a huge multiple, so we'd be a sitting duck to get shorted, and that's Markanos's stock in trade—picking stocks to short."

"When would you have to go to New York?"

"I would go Sunday, for meetings beginning Monday morning."

"I'm sure A'isha could stay here with Amos if we could pull this off," she said. "Maybe Yusuf would drive over and spend the day with them."

Noah nodded, somewhat reluctantly. "Yeah, I'm sure she would do that, and Yusuf would probably enjoy spending the day with them if he's free."

"So, can I ask Amos to try to arrange for me to fly with him to Israel and return to the States on an Air Force cargo plane after the opening meeting? I would travel with him and return home a day or two later."

Noah shrugged. "Yeah, I guess so. I'll be surprised if he can work it out, but if he can, why not? It *is* going to be a huge news event. Yeah, if you can be there for the opening of the talks, go for it."

"We'll see what happens. It's probably a long shot. Meanwhile, I have a column to write."

***

ISRAELI AND EGYPTIAN GENERALS TO MEET FACE TO FACE FOR FIRST TIME
By Alexandra Salaman

October 26, 1973 – In a historic development, Israeli and Egyptian generals will meet in a tent at an obscure spot on the road connecting Suez City and Cairo. The spot, Kilometer 101, about fifteen miles from the gates to Suez City, may someday be remembered as the place where a seismic shift occurred in the relationship between these long-time antagonists in the Middle East. Up until now, so-called proximity talks had to suffice when the two sides needed to strike some modus vivendi. Israeli and Egyptian military or diplomatic personnel wouldn't even sit in the same room with one another. "Proximity" talks, from the Latin "proximus," simply meant the two sides would talk with an intermediary from nearby, but different, hotel suites. That, for a quarter century, has passed for diplomacy between the two sides.

But now, both the Israelis and the Egyptians, who have been duking it out since October 6, when Egypt stormed across the Suez Canal and demolished Israel's sixty-foot-high Bar-Lev Line, are ready to shake hands and talk peace. The Kilometer 101 talks will aim at more than a mere disengagement from the current carnage that has cost both countries dearly in blood and treasure. The seriousness of the talks and the promise of the talks are abundantly clear, given the rank of the two military men who will sit across from one another and, perhaps, take important steps toward peace.

It does not appear to us that these meetings at Kilometer 101 are designed to merely hammer out a truce between the two sides. Given Israel's current advantage on the battlefield, having trapped Egypt's entire Third Army, and the incredible pounding the Israelis took in the early fighting, seasoned observers believe these talks are envisaged to begin a process that could actually result in either peace or an end to the state of perpetual belligerency between these two old enemies.

This round of fighting, which may well become known to history as the Yom Kippur War, has been a *game changer for both sides. Israel has, relative to its size, lost in three weeks two or three times the number of men the United States has lost in a decade of fighting in Vietnam. Egypt, in raw numbers, has undoubtedly lost thousands more than Israel.*

Meanwhile, Syria seems to be odd man out in these discussions at Kilometer 101. Syria struck Israel on the Golan Heights at precisely the same time Egypt opened fire on the Israelis at the Suez Canal. The Syrians fought well, as did the Egyptians, but the Syrian offensive ran out of steam in the first few days of fighting, and Israel has taken the battle to the outskirts of Damascus. Syria is in no position to negotiate because Israel now holds substantially more ground than it controlled when the fighting began. Syria's best hope is for Israel to agree to fall back to the Golan Heights, which Israel is probably willing to do.

As the talks at Kilometer 101 begin, Egypt and Israel have a substantial military presence on both sides of the Suez Canal. The two belligerents retreating to their positions before the war commenced is not a likely outcome of the talks, and probably not the primary objective of either side. A phased Israeli withdrawal from the Sinai Peninsula in return for an end to the state of belligerency between the two countries has to be the objective in both Cairo and Tel Aviv. For the first time in a quarter century this seems to be a feasible objective.

Israeli Prime Minister Golda Meir was clearly caught flat-footed by the coordinated Egyptian and Syrian attack. It may take years to sort out how Israel's legendary intelligence services failed to understand what was happening all around them. With an estimated two to three thousand Israeli servicemen killed in the early days of the fighting, nearly every Israeli family has lost someone. While Israel ultimately acquitted itself well on the battle-field, the failure of its intelligence services is certain to produce a protracted state of self-doubt about the country's invincibility. Israel's sense of destiny has been shaken to the core. It is hard to imagine Prime Minister Meir at the helm when the investigation into what went wrong has run its course.

While it is too early for anyone to assume too much, it seems to us that Secretary of State Henry Kissinger may have earned his stripes during this confrontation. With President Nixon almost certainly distracted with Vietnam, the Agnew scandal, the publication of Daniel Ellsberg's Pentagon Papers, and the ever-growing Watergate contretemps, this has been Kissinger's game of chess to play. From where we sit, he has, so far, played the board brilliantly.

CHAPTER
TWENTY-FIVE

"Okay, Alexandra, this is the best I can do. I can secure a seat for you on a C-5, but there is no way you'll be allowed into the tent at Kilometer 101," Amos said as soon as Alexandra picked up the phone at her desk at the *Star*. "At best, you would have to remain outside with the UN personnel who will be on site. I presume, for what it's worth, you can take pictures of the participants as they arrive and as they leave the talks, but Ambassador Dinitz will not hear of you entering the tent or talking to members of the respective negotiating teams. He won't even raise the subject with anyone in the IDF or the Prime Minister's office. This is non-negotiable, and, frankly, I don't think it's worth the trouble to travel all that distance to look at a tent."

"Where are you staying?" she asked immediately.

"I'm booking a room at Hotel Eilat. I'll travel to Kilometer 101 by helicopter. I'm leaving tomorrow morning."

"Book two rooms, Amos."

***

Omar Samir was at breakfast fuming over the latest war news in *Al Ahram* when the bellman came into the dining room calling his name. The war news was terrible. Egypt and Syria had both made a mess of their simultaneous invasions of Israel, and the Americans were rushing arms to the Jews as fast as Israel could use them.

"Mr. Samir, you have a cable from America," the bellman said as he approached Samir's table. "It just arrived." Omar Samir snatched the envelope and ripped it open. The cable was from Ahmed Sayed Kahn, at the embassy in Washington.

SALAMAN WOMAN TRAVELING TO KILOMETER 101 TALKS *STOP* **COMMUTING BY HELICOPTER FROM ZIONIST HOTEL EILAT TO TALKS** *STOP* **A'ISHA TO STAY ALONE WITH CHILD AT GREENSPAN HOME** *STOP* **GREENSPAN TO BE TRAVELING ON BUSINESS** *STOP*

Omar Samir reread the cable several times. His hands shook as he folded the cable and put it in his shirt pocket. Alexandra Salaman was going to be within reach, and A'isha Abadi was going to be alone with the boy in the Salaman home. *This is God's will,* he thought. *I have to think. We'll never have another opportunity like this.*

***

An unnerving quiet filled their space as Noah and Alexandra prepared to turn in for the night.

"I'm having terrible second thoughts about your traveling to these Kilometer 101 talks," Noah said as soon as Alexandra joined him in bed. He pulled her close against his body. "I'm a nervous wreck, Alexandra."

"Nothing is going to happen, Noah. Nothing *can* happen. Kilometer 101 will probably be the safest place imaginable with all the security. And besides, I'm traveling there and back with the United States Air Force, for God's sake. I'll could be home before you return from New York."

"I'm not sure I understand why going halfway around the world to be at Kilometer 101 is so important if you can't be in the tent while the Egyptians and Israelis are meeting."

"Because when I write my column the dateline will read, *Kilometer 101, Suez, Egypt, October 29*. No other paper in the world will be able to carry that dateline. Noah, what I write will be published in every major city on the planet. Every journalist worth his or her salt would give their eye teeth to be standing at that tent when General el-Gamasy and General Yariv meet for the first time."

"That's a lot of travel for a dateline, Alexandra."

"Trust me on this one, Noah. This may be the biggest story I'll ever cover."

"I doubt that," he replied, squeezing her even closer.

"Stop talking and make love to me, Noah," she answered.

"God, I love you," he whispered.

***

A'isha arrived promptly at six thirty the following morning and, after greeting Noah and Alexandra, poured herself a cup of coffee before joining Amos at the kitchen counter.

"I put a couple of slices of bread in the toaster for you," Alexandra said. "It's your favorite, Pepperidge Farms raisin bread."

"Ah, you know everything about me, even what bread I like to toast. That *is* my favorite," A'isha replied, as she reached over and depressed the bar, engaging the toaster.

"There are some fresh jars of jam in the pantry too. I think apricot and blueberry. Take your pick."

"Well, Amos and I won't go hungry while you're away, will we, Amos?"

"Daoud should be here any minute to take Mr. Greenspan to the airport, and my car should be here shortly too. There's plenty of everything in the fridge for lunch and dinner for the next few days. We should both be home sometime Tuesday, Wednesday at the latest. My brother said he should get here by noon, so the three of you should have plenty of time to enjoy the day. I saw that a new movie just opened called *The Biscuit Eater*. It's a remake of a popular children's movie, so I'm sure it would be appropriate for Amos."

"Oh, that sounds like fun. I'll check and see where it's playing."

"Also, we'll be having a guest stay with us for a few days, and she may arrive in the next day or two. Her name is Sarah Jean Bogart. She's going to be my new assistant at the *Star*. She's a reporter from a small paper in Blytheville, Arkansas. I don't think she's travelled very much or very far, so do what you can to make her feel at home. We'll have her stay in the guest room next to Amos's room. She'll be with us until she can find a place to rent here in Washington."

"Oh, that will be nice. I know they have some studio apartments in my building. I'll be glad to check to see if any are available."

"She's a chatterbox, but very smart. I think you'll enjoy her company while she's here."

"This is one interesting household we have here," Noah said. "I'm off to New York. Alexandra is off to the Middle East. And Sarah Jean Bogart is flying in from someplace I've never heard of in Arkansas. We should have some interesting conversation when we're all back together."

"It certainly is the most interesting place I've ever worked," A'isha said as she noted the contrast in dress between Noah and Alexandra. He was dressed in a dark three-piece Brooks Brothers suit; she, in jeans, a blouse, and a sweater. He wore wingtip black oxford shoes; she, Nike running shoes.

"Both dressed for work, I see," A'isha said, smiling.

Noah reached over and squeezed his wife's hand. "I hope we're doing the right thing. I mean, both of us being away at the same time."

"I know, Noah, but everything will be fine. We'll both be back in a day or two, and Amos is excited to be spending a couple of days with A'isha."

"Oh, I know. I'm not concerned about Amos," he answered. "He adores A'isha. It's the idea of you and me flying off at the same time to different places so far apart that has me a little off balance. It's not a big deal, really. It's just unsettling for me—but, you're right, we'll both be busy as hell, and before you know it we'll both be flying home."

At just about that moment, the car from the Israeli embassy turned onto Prospect from Wisconsin Avenue and slowed to a stop in front of the Greenspan home.

"Time to run. Have good meetings in New York, Noah," Alexandra said, throwing her arms around him. "Don't let Markanos get under your skin."

"You be careful, Alexandra. Try to get as much sleep as you can on the trip over. I'll be at the Waldorf if you need me."

"I'll try calling whether I need you or not," she replied.

They held onto one another for an extra moment, both laboring to convince each other, or perhaps themselves, that this was going to be just another brief work-related separation.

Alexandra turned to the kitchen counter and stooped down to embrace her son. She straightened up, holding Amos tightly in her arms as she did.

"Oh, I'm going to miss you so much, Amos," she said, swaying ever so slowly as she did. "Mommy will be back in three days, and I'll think of you every moment while I'm gone," she said. Amos tightened his grip on Alexandra, hugging her affectionately. She pulled back just enough to look into Amos's eyes.

"I'm going to picture your gorgeous eyes in my mind every night when I go to bed, Amos. Then I know I'll have pleasant dreams every night. Daddy will be home the day after tomorrow, and I'll be home the day after that. Meanwhile, you and A'isha will do something that will be fun every day." She gave the boy one last hug and handed him to Noah.

"I'll be home in two days, Amos," Noah said, hugging the child.

Just as Amos Ben-Chaiyim stepped from the car, Alexandra waved from the front door. He smiled and waved back.

"I'll be right there," she called out to him. A moment later she and Noah came out of the house and greeted Amos on the sidewalk.

"You take good care of her," Noah said as the two men embraced.

"Between the United States Air Force, the Israeli Defense Forces, the United Nations peace keepers, and even the Egyptian Army, you can rest assured that nothing is going to endanger Alexandra," Amos answered with a laugh. "I think she may be the most secure person on the planet for the next few days."

"You just keep your eye on her, Amos. I'd never let her do this if you weren't going to be there."

***

There was mostly inconsequential small talk on the half-hour ride to Camp Springs, Maryland, where Andrews Air Force Base blanketed most of the landscape.

"I never thought I would take an assignment that required me to travel back to the Middle East," she mused as they crossed over the Woodrow Wilson Bridge just south of Alexandria and on into Maryland.

"Well, I wouldn't say you *took* the assignment. It was more like you grabbed it as soon as the opportunity presented itself. Frankly, I'm surprised Noah would hear of it."

"Noah trusts my judgment, Amos. He knows these Kilometer 101 talks will be historic, and that I'll be the only journalist there."

"What about Markazie? Your boss had no qualms about your running off to Egypt?"

"Amos, it was like he was expecting me to figure out how to get there. He just laughed when I told him I could get credentials to be there through your embassy."

"I don't think my boss back in Israel would laugh, but Simcha Dinitz outranks him," Amos replied. "When I told him of your role in the Shoukri affair, he knew who you were immediately. I also think he liked the idea of being helpful to a journalist for a major Washington newspaper. It didn't take any convincing. Dinitz said to just make sure you understood that you were not to enter the tent when any of the negotiators or members of their respective teams are present."

***

The guard at the main gate at Andrews studied the travel documents the Ambassador had secured from the State Department. He peered for several moments into the car, looking from Amos to Alexandra, comparing them to the photographs on the papers he held in his hand.

"Welcome to Andrews Air Force Base," he said. "Proceed along the main road to the first group of hangars. Your transport is waiting at the first hangar you'll come to, about a half mile straight ahead." He then stepped back and waved them onto the base.

A Bell Iroquois Huey was awaiting their arrival. Its twin rotor blades and tail blades began rotating as soon as the sedan turned onto the tarmac. An airman hurried from the hangar and opened the rear door of the car.

"Mr. Ben-Chaiyim, Mrs. Greenspan, welcome to Andrews Air Force Base," he said as he helped Alexandra from the car. He escorted them to the helicopter and offered his hand to assist Alexandra. A few minutes later they were over the Chesapeake Bay, flying just to the north of the immense bay bridge. Alexandra smiled as she looked down at the magnificent five-mile-long span and remembered driving over the bridge with Noah shortly after her rescue from Khartoum. Her boss, Frank Markazie, had insisted that she and Noah get away for a few days and handed her the keys to his ocean-front townhouse in Ocean City.

It took only a few minutes for the Huey to reach the opposite shore on the Delmarva Peninsula and then fly on to Dover Air Force Base, home of the USAF 9th Military Airlift Squadron and its fleet of Lockheed C-5 Galaxies.

"My God, they're the largest planes I've ever seen," Alexandra said as the Huey flew along a row of ten C-5s and slowly descended between two of the huge aircraft. Alexandra noticed that nearly all of the gray cargo planes were in the process of being loaded with an enormous array of equipment. Some had dozens of pallets lined up waiting to be moved into the cavernous planes. Some had combat vehicles, even helicopters, waiting to be uploaded.

"I'm amazed they can even lift off with all that equipment," she said. "It looks as though you could fight an entire war with just one planeload of supplies."

"You probably could fight some wars with a C-5 load of arms," Amos replied. "I would imagine most of those pallets are loaded with munitions—you know, bullets, mortar rounds, small arms, anti-tank missiles, and the like. Those are consumables that will probably be shipped to the front as soon as they arrive. War has a monstrous appetite for that stuff."

"Amos, look, there are two tanks lined up ready to be loaded onto that plane," she said, pointing to a C-5 just to the right of where they were setting down.

"Yes, I see," he replied. "I'm surprised. My understanding was that heavy armored equipment was being shipped from America's bases in Germany. I didn't expect to see any direct shipments of tanks from the United States. They may be replacements being shipped to Germany or some other US base in Europe."

"Do you think most of these planes are being loaded for transport to Israel?"

"Yes, that's my understanding. They're flying pretty much around the clock from several air force bases here in the United States."

"Can Russia match what the United States is sending?" she asked as the Huey eased down onto the tarmac.

"I doubt it, Alexandra. And these cargo planes are just the tip of the iceberg. The US will be shipping far more into Israel by sea than by air."

A young airman was waiting to assist them off of the Huey and offered his hand to Alexandra as she stepped from the helicopter. "Welcome to Dover Air Force Base," he yelled above the din.

"Thank you," she shouted, taking the airman's hand and steadying herself on the portable stairs that had been placed below the door.

"This is the C-5 you'll be boarding," the young airman yelled, pointing to the cargo plane to their left. You've got about an hour before she's fully loaded, so you're welcome to wait in the hangar. You'll go deaf waiting out here. There's coffee and snack machines inside. There's also a lady's rest room in the hangar where you can change clothes. I was asked to give you these fatigues to wear while you're in our care," the airman said. "You'll be a lot more comfortable, and a lot less conspicuous. I'll come and escort you to the plane when she's ready."

"Oh, yes, of course," Alexandra replied, taking the package from the airman. "Thank you."

"How long is the flight?" Amos asked as he stepped from the Huey.

"Depends, sir. It's about five hours to Lajes in the Azores, depending on winds, and another six hours from there to Tel Aviv. Figure refueling and chow time in Lajes, and I'd estimate twelve to fourteen hours."

"Do you know what she's carrying in those pallets?" Amos asked, glancing over to the C-5 they would soon be boarding.

"Let's see, tail number 00461 … Yes, sir, you'll be sitting on top of thirty-six pallets loaded with ninety-seven tons of 105-millimeter Howitzer shells," the airman answered after skimming a manifest clamped to the clipboard he held.

"Sorry I asked," Amos answered, with a laugh. "Come on, Alexandra, let's get out of the way here and find some coffee in the hangar."

"Did he say we're flying with ninety-seven tons of Howitzer shells?"

"He did."

"Live Howitzer shells?"

"They wouldn't be of much use if they weren't."

"All these planes lined up here are sending munitions to Israel?"

"Looks that way to me."

"My God, these planes are the length of a football field."

"Almost," Amos answered.

"I'm surprised they can get off the ground with ninety-seven tons of cargo on board."

"Actually, they can load a lot more on the C-5 and it would still get off the ground."

"Unbelievable."

"Alexandra, the wheels alone on these planes weigh nearly sixty tons in total. Look at those wheel carriages. She has twenty-eight wheels, and each one weighs over two tons. What a sight. Can you imagine, these planes are flying from bases all over America?"

"And all headed to Israel?"

"Who would have believed it?"

"Six years ago, America didn't intervene like this?"

"You mean during the sixty-seven war?"

"Yes, Israel fought that war with mostly French equipment. After the *Liberty* incident, I'm surprised America has become such a staunch supporter of Israel."

"This is more about Russia than about Israel, Alexandra. You know that."

"Of course I do. I've written about that extensively, but this is the biggest airlift since Berlin."

"Well, that was also a contest between America and Russia. Russia will never be able to match America's production capability or its maneuverability. Think about it, Alexandra. Russia is a little over a thousand miles away from the fighting. America is over six thousand miles away, and if this becomes a contest about who can best support their ally, America will still run circles around Russia."

"Nice ally to have, huh, Amos?"

***

Daoud picked up Noah about fifteen minutes after Alexandra and Amos departed for Andrews Air Force Base. They arrived at the Eastern Shuttle terminal at National Airport about twenty minutes later. Daoud waited for an opening at the curb and quickly pulled in as soon as a taxi drove away. He jumped out of the car and rushed to retrieve Noah's overnight bag from the trunk. He handed it to Noah, along with an envelope from Marshall Flynn, Potomac Center's chief financial officer.

"Mr. Flynn said this is for you to read on the way to New York."

"Thank you, Daoud. I should be returning by Wednesday afternoon. I'll call and let you know what time I'm due in."

"Yes, sir, you just let me know and I'll be waiting right here."

The Eastern Airlines shuttle terminal was a no-frills, efficient people-moving operation. Departing passengers queued up all morning to board outgoing flights to New York and Boston, as incoming travelers rushed through the terminal, having just arrived from those same cities. The hall was especially chaotic during the morning and afternoon peak hours.

Noah made his way through the crowd, stopping briefly at a newsstand in the terminal to pick up the morning editions of the *Washington Post* and the *Daily News*. The war and speculation about whether the ceasefire would take hold dominated the front page of both papers. A map of the battlefield, with stark black arrows indicating where the Israeli Army had trapped the Egyptian Third Army, was displayed above the fold on the front page of the *Daily News*. The city of Suez was shown in bold letters, and Kilometer 101 was circled on the road leading from Cairo to Suez. A queasiness radiated through Noah as he contemplated Alexandra traveling to that very spot. A few minutes later, the Eastern Shuttle boarded and Noah slowly made his way to a window seat at mid-plane. As usual, the morning flight to New York was packed with commuters. Noah was unnerved, edgy. He glanced once more at the menacing map on the front page of the *Daily News* as the plane taxied away from the terminal. Then, as the plane turned onto the active runway, he laid his head back against the headrest, closed his eyes, and slowly sucked in a deep breath. He was off to Wall Street to talk to the suits about the outlook for retail sales in America during the balance of the fourth quarter. Alexandra was off to Kilometer 101, a sandy speck on the road to Cairo, just west of Suez City and the Suez Canal.

The plane, engines roaring, sat for an extra moment and then lurched forward and raced, full throttle, down the runway and, seconds later, lifted off over the Potomac. It headed west, with the Pentagon just below on the left side of the plane and the obelisk commemorating George Washington pointing skyward to the right. By the time Noah opened his eyes the Boeing 727 was over the David Taylor Model Basin at Carderock, where the river separates Maryland from Virginia. The plane arced slowly to the northeast, its flightpath set for New York's LaGuardia airport.

***

Both the nose and tail sections of the Lockheed C-5 Galaxy yawned wide open, pointing almost perfectly skyward, when Amos and Alexandra were escorted into the tunnel-like cargo bay. An airman directed them to the long, narrow iron staircase attached to the interior sidewall of the plane. It climbed diagonally to the seventy-three-seat passenger cabin, several stories above where they stood. Alexandra paused a moment to gaze through the plane. All thirty-six pallets loaded with Howitzer shells had been rolled into place and secured. She could see past the long row of pallets right through the plane, and out to the tarmac in front of the aircraft.

"I've never seen anything like it," she murmured to Amos as they made their way to the stairs.

"Neither have I, Alexandra. You really understand the might of this nation when you see something like this."

"I never imagined that such aircraft existed," she replied. "Do the Russians have anything like this?"

"They're using their Antonov 22s to supply the Egyptians and Syrians. They carry about ninety tons of cargo and they're turbo props, so they're not as fast. These C-5s will run circles around them."

***

Noah carefully opened the envelope Daoud had handed him and removed the memorandum Marshall Flynn had written.

Noah, I've been trying to determine whether the increased revenue our tenants are reporting in our malls is being driven by increased sales or merely increases in price. We automatically collect sales data directly from retailers' cash registers. But we don't track unit sales, only daily gross revenue. The good news is that revenue through the third quarter was up nicely, about six percent over last year. What is curious, however, is that traffic and, apparently, volume coming into the loading docks at each of our malls seem to be down a bit. I've also checked automobile counts at our lots and garages. Definitely down. I've asked our mall managers about foot traffic in the malls. Definitely not up. This is very preliminary, but if loading dock traffic is down, and parking and foot traffic are down or, at best, unchanged, while revenues are up, that could suggest our tenants may be getting more growth from price increases than from increases in unit sales. I hate to suggest this, as you're about to meet with analysts, but I think that prick Markanos might be onto something.

Regards,
Marsh

Noah folded Marshall Flynn's memorandum and slipped it into the inside pocket of his jacket. He glanced out the window as the Maryland countryside slipped by below. His mood, already discomforted by Alexandra's travel to the Middle East, now plunged deeper after reading Marshall Flynn's memo. It only reinforced his own sense of foreboding about the economy. He was now certain the meetings he was about to have in New York were a bad idea. Analysts always wanted to hear good news about the companies they recommended, or they wanted to be the first to sound an alarm if there were any hints of trouble on the horizon. Noah knew he couldn't tout steady sales growth without expressing caution that the increases in revenue could be coming from price hikes rather than increased sales. But that was

far from certain, and he wasn't about to go off and predict an impending recession when no economist or analyst in the country had expressed such a concern. Noah considered calling off the meetings. He
would call Karen as soon as he landed and discuss his concerns with
her. She would know what to do. Maybe Mid America Ventures could
notify the institutions that had been invited to the meetings that Noah
had a bad cold, nothing serious, and was advised not to travel for a
few days and that the meetings would be rescheduled. Noah rushed
to a pay phone and called Karen as soon as he deplaned at LaGuardia.
Karen listened patiently as Noah read Marshall Flynn's memorandum.

"I don't think we should be having these meetings until I have a
better understanding of what the hell is going on," he explained.

"You can't call off the meetings, Noah. That would raise immediate
suspicion that something was up."

"You could say I have a bad cold."

"Someone's antennae would go up immediately, Noah. And then,
should there be negative news, they would know you knew, and your
credibility would be zilch after that."

"What am I supposed to say, Karen, that business is strong?"

"Isn't it?"

"Yes, at the present time it is, but I think we have some indication
that things might not be as rosy as today's sales data suggest."

"You mean it's too early to project what your year end is going to
look like?"

"Yes, I think it is too early to have too much to say. Frankly, I'm a
little worried."

"Then say that."

"What, that I'm worried?"

"No, not that you're worried. Just tell them that you're having your
best year ever, that revenue remains strong, and, when they ask you to
forecast the year end, that you don't make projections and that it would
be too early to project year-end results anyway."

"You make it sound so simple."

"It is simple, if you don't get all caught up trying to cross *every t* and dot *every i*. Noah, you're not obligated to share every concern you have, nor are you obligated to share every scrap of information you have. The fact is, you don't know how the economy is trending at the moment. You have fragments of information that bear watching, that's all."

"So, you think I should just go on with the meetings and not give any indication that I've got some concerns?"

"Noah, you really don't know enough about what is going on with the economy at the moment. You've had some interesting, but very preliminary, indications that sales might not be as strong as they appear. Maybe it's the weather. Maybe it's the damn war over in the Middle East. You don't know precisely what's going on. There is nothing wrong with saying it's too early to tell how the year is going to wind up. Meanwhile, you have a healthy business that has made a lot of investors a lot of money. The year-end will be what it will be, and you'll report the results accurately and with far more information than you have right now."

"Speaking of the war in the Middle East, have you heard from Amos today?"

"Hah! Only that he's flying off with your wife to these talks that are about to take place."

"How about that?" Noah replied lightheartedly.

"I guess they're in the air by now. It's kind of exciting to think of them being there while history is being made."

"I'll be glad when Alexandra's home. I'm somewhat unnerved by the whole thing."

"Me too, but I'll have to get used to it. Amos is always going to be where the action is."

"Well, I would never let her do this if Amos wasn't going to be with her every step of the way."

"They'll be fine, Noah. Amos isn't going to let anything happen to Alexandra. Besides, they'll be with Israeli troops the whole time she's there."

"She'll have some great stuff to write when she gets back."

"Which will be before you know it. She might beat you back to Washington."

"I hope so. Anyway, I've got to run. Thanks, Karen, this has been very helpful."

"Just deal with the facts as you know them today, Noah. The meetings should go fine."

CHAPTER TWENTY-SIX

It was noon when Yusuf arrived at his sister's home, and Amos, who had been eagerly awaiting his uncle's arrival, ran to the door calling his name. Yusuf swept his nephew into the air and spun around as he hugged the child. Then he saw her. A'isha was at the end of the hall, arms crossed, and smiling broadly as she watched them. He paused for a moment to absorb the sight of her. She was not wearing her hijab, and her face was beautifully framed by her shoulder-length, radiant black hair. Her crisp white blouse smoothly draped the swell of her breasts and was tucked smartly into black stretch stirrup slacks, and the fashionable block-heel ankle boots she wore elevated her almost to his height.

"Hi," he said, momentarily at a loss for more of a greeting.

"Hi yourself," she replied.

"You …"

A'isha raised her eyebrows in anticipation.

"You look … lovely," he managed to say.

"We're going to the movies," Amos interrupted.

"We are?" Yusuf replied, his eyes still on A'isha as he lowered the boy to the floor.

"Yes, we thought that would be a good way to spend the afternoon," A'isha answered. "There's a film your sister found called *The Biscuit*

Eater, about young boys and a dog, that we thought Amos would enjoy. It's playing on Connecticut Avenue near Dupont Circle. We can have lunch here and, maybe, have dinner after the movie at the Hot Shoppe."

"Sounds great," Yusuf replied.

"I'm having Pappy Parker's Fried Chicken," Amos yelled.

***

"Oh my God," Alexandra murmured as they entered the passenger cabin. "The seats are all facing backwards and there are no windows."

"It looks like we're going to be the only passengers on this flight. There'll be plenty of room to stretch out."

"Do you know why the seats all face backwards?" she asked.

"It's safer. In an accident, your back can take more impact than your chest."

"That's really reassuring," she answered sarcastically.

"It's true, though. Passengers in rear-facing seats have come through accidents better than passengers in forward-facing seats."

"Why no windows?"

Amos shrugged. "I don't know. I assume it's cheaper to build this way. By the way, you look glamorously militaristic in those fatigues, Alexandra."

"Did you notice, they have my name stamped on the shirt?"

"I noticed."

At the sound of the engines revving up, Alexandra fastened her seatbelt and leaned back into her seat. "It's a bit disorienting moving backwards," she said.

"Actually, we're not moving yet. You'll know we're moving when they start to push us back onto the tarmac."

A few minutes later the plane lurched with a slight jolt as a pushback tractor begin pushing the nearly one million pounds of fully loaded C-5 Galaxy until it was in position to make its way forward under its own power. A moment or two passed before the unmistakable piercing whine of the C-5 engines signaled that the plane was moving on its own. It took about ten minutes for the C-5 to make its way to the active runway, where it sat for several moments while the pilot brought the engines up to full throttle. Then Alexandra felt her body push forward against the seatbelt as the pilot released the brakes and the largest plane in the US Air Force began hurtling down the runway, its powerful engines screaming at high pitch. It was like no sound she had ever heard before. The pilot set a great-circle route, flying northeast over the Jersey shore and then out over the Atlantic toward Newfoundland for about two hours, before gracefully arcing south and down to the Azores. It was a sight unseen in the windowless passenger compartment of the giant cargo plane. Alexandra found the flight in the C-5 surprisingly disorienting.

The plane, buffeted by wind, with the sound of heavy rain beating hard on the fuselage as they approached the airfield at Lajes, finally touched down as the unseen sun descended over the western horizon. Her head ached as she stepped from the cargo bay of the C-5 and peered out into darkness barely five hours after their morning departure from Dover.

"You don't look so well, Alexandra. Are you okay?"

"Just a headache, Amos. I'll feel better."

"You know, it's probably going to be around five or six a.m. by the time we make it to Tel Aviv, after we refuel here and fly over to the Mediterranean and on to Israel. You'll have to sleep on this leg of the flight or during the day once we get to Eilat, or you'll be in no shape to travel to Suez for the talks at Kilometer 101 tomorrow night."

"I'll have no trouble sleeping, Amos. I'm already exhausted even though it's only early afternoon on our body clock."

"Well, Ambassador Dinitz arranged for us to have dinner at the Officers' Club here at Lajes. Some food will do you good. You should be able to sleep for a while once we're out over the Mediterranean."

"Do you know how long we'll be here?"

"It depends on how long it takes to refuel the plane. We were flying pretty heavy. I don't know how much fuel we burned, but the C-5 holds over fifty thousand gallons. I would guess at least a half hour to refuel."

It was eight o'clock, and still raining, when the C-5 finally lifted off from Lajes and headed east toward the Straits of Gibraltar. There the pilot would begin threading a needle down the middle of the Mediterranean, between Europe, where they were unwelcome, and the coastline of Arab North Africa, where nation after nation was hostile to their mission. It was around ten thirty that evening when Lieutenant Rod Burke, co-pilot of the C-5, joined them in the passenger cabin.

"Not too crowded for you folks, I hope," he joked as he entered the narrow, dimly lighted cabin.

"I'm glad we didn't have to bump anyone to get a seat," Amos replied.

"You know, we've flown these birds to Nam with every seat filled. Trust me, this is a better way to fly on a C-5."

"No complaints," Alexandra answered. "Everything has gone very smoothly, and everyone has been very accommodating."

"So, I wanted to give you both a heads up on where we are in our flight and what precautions we've taken."

"Is there a problem?" Amos asked.

"No, and we don't expect one, but we don't assume anything and we prepare for everything," the young lieutenant replied. "We'll be passing through the Straits of Gibraltar in about fifteen minutes. As we head east across the Mediterranean, we'll be flying just beyond the flight control zone of a succession of Arab nations to the south, and we're obliged not to penetrate the air space of any of the European nations along the opposite coastline to the north. So, we're flying a very narrow corridor to keep away from both coasts. We're temporarily *persona non grata* with our European friends, and we have to assume some potential for mischief from the opposite coast."

Amos glanced over to Alexandra and could tell she was unnerved. Lieutenant Burke saw him reach over and squeeze her had reassuringly.

"It suddenly feels very lonely up here above the Mediterranean," she said, managing a weak smile.

"Well, I can assure you there's no reason to feel alone. We'll have a lot of company up here."

"Is that good?" she replied.

"Very good," he answered. "We have three aircraft carrier groups sailing at six-hundred-mile intervals on the line we're flying. From this point on, we'll have navy fighter jets escorting us every mile until we're only two hundred miles from Tel Aviv. At that point, the Israeli Air Force will accompany us right to Lod Airport. Like I said, no reason to feel lonely."

"Quite an operation," Amos said.

"You have no idea," Lieutenant Burke replied. "This airlift and all the logistics that go with it is absolutely extraordinary, especially when you consider how quickly it was all organized."

"Thanks for the heads-up, Lieutenant," Amos answered. "Much appreciated."

"You're Israeli, is that right?"

"Yes, I am," Amos answered.

"What you people have done on the battlefield in the past two weeks is extraordinary. It's rare that wars turn around so quickly and so decisively."

"Well, maybe that's because we're the only nation that can never afford to lose a war."

"Are you Israeli too, ma'am?"

"I was born in Jaffa," Alexandra replied.

"That's in Israel, right?"

Alexandra smiled. "It is now," she said.

Lieutenant Burke returned the smile, gave a quick, casual salute, and shook hands with both of them.

"Well, make yourselves comfortable. We have about four hours to go. It's really a privilege to have you both on board," he said, as he turned and left the cabin.

***

Yusuf gently held his nephew in his arms as A'isha unlocked the front door of the Greenspan house. Amos had fallen asleep almost immediately during the drive back to Georgetown, following dinner at the Hot Shoppe a few miles to the north on Wisconsin Avenue.

"He's out like a light," Yusuf whispered.

"Lay him down on his bed and I'll get him undressed and into his pajamas," she replied as they headed for the stairs.

Yusuf watched as A'isha carefully, but quickly, undressed Amos and slipped him into his pajamas. "Why don't you go downstairs and turn on the TV while I finish getting him ready for bed? I'll only be a few minutes."

"I'm enjoying watching you. You got him out of his clothes and into his pajamas like you've been doing it for years."

"It's not exactly rocket science," she answered. "Now, go before you wake him up."

"Don't be long," he replied, as he moved behind her, encircling A'isha in his arms.

She leaned back against him and looked up over her shoulder, smiling wistfully. Yusuf tightened his embrace and, after a moment's hesitation, brought his lips down to the side of her neck. "Hurry," he whispered.

A'isha carried Amos into the bathroom and softly ran a warm wash cloth across his face. He hardly stirred. She smiled down at him. *He's half Jewish and half Arab and beautiful and lovely in every way*, she thought. She lifted the sleeping child just high enough to softly kiss his forehead. She lingered with her lips pressed against his warm skin for an extra moment. *How could anyone hate this child simply because he's Jewish?* she thought.

A few minutes later, after she had lowered Amos onto his bed and pulled the covers up around his shoulders, she made her way down to the living room and sat down on the couch next to Yusuf.

"Well, there have been no shots fired for twenty-four hours," he said. "I guess the war is really over."

"For now," she replied in a whisper.

"Were you conflicted about the fighting?" he asked.

"Not about who would win or who would lose," she answered.

"About what then?"

"About whether or not it will ever end. I have family in the Middle East, not far from Hebron—grandparents, aunts, uncles, and first cousins. This constant fighting is going to define their time on this earth. Look, the Egyptians were not benign occupiers of Gaza. They were simply occupiers. It will mean nothing to me or my family whether or not they push the Israelis off of the Sinai, and who cares whether Syria or Israel sits on the Golan Heights? I think with Israel a separate Palestinian state might be possible, even necessary, someday, but with Egypt or Syria—never."

"Not likely with Israel either, I'm afraid."

"Let's not spend the evening talking about the fighting over there."

"Let's not spend the evening talking at all," Yusuf replied, as he leaned down to kiss her. A'isha looked up at him, a slight smile playing at her lips. As their lips met, she reached up and pulled him into a tight embrace. They held onto one another as he turned and effortlessly pulled her onto his lap, her legs straddling his thighs, her lips pressing against his. He lowered his hands to the small of her back and pulled her even closer. Feeling that he was aroused, she pressed hard against him. Her eyes were closed as she threw her head back and stifled the urge to cry out. It was then, at that moment, that the telephone began to ring from across the room.

"Let it ring," he moaned.

A'isha sat there for a moment, bringing her hands to her face as she tried to catch her breath and collect her thoughts.

"No, I can't just let it ring," she said, reaching back and removing his hands.

She stood and steadied herself and then hurried to phone, lifting it from the cradle on the fourth ring.

"Hello," she said, trying to steady her voice.

"A'isha, it's Mr. Greenspan."

"Yes, how are you?" she asked.

"Is everything all right? I was ready to hang up the phone and try again later."

"Yes, everything is fine," she answered. "I was watching television and must have dozed off."

"I was just calling to check in and make sure everything was going well."

"Yes, yes, everything is fine. Amos is sound asleep. We went to a movie and had dinner at the Hot Shoppe."

"Was Yusuf with you? He was going to drive over from Baltimore."

"Yes, he and Amos had a wonderful time together."

"Well, I'm just sitting here in my room at the Waldorf in New York and thought I would give a call and check to make sure everything was okay."

"Everything is fine, Mr. Greenspan."

"Yusuf must have headed back to Baltimore right after dinner."

"No, he stopped by the house and carried Amos up to his room for me. Amos fell sound asleep on the drive home after dinner."

"Is Yusuf still there? I'll say hello to him."

"No, he left a few minutes ago," she replied, cringing at the lie.

"Well, okay, you know where to reach me if you need me."

"Yes, at the Waldorf. I have the number on the fridge."

"Okay then, A'isha. Have a good evening."

"Thank you, Mr. Greenspan. Good luck with your meetings in New York."

She hung up the phone and turned to Yusuf.

"Saved by the bell, huh?" he said, as he stood to leave.

A'isha nodded. "I don't know why I told Mr. Greenspan you had already left."

"Well, once you said you had dozed off on the couch, it was the logical thing to say. I'd better head back to Baltimore, A'isha. Noah may call me there."

"When will I see you, Yusuf?"

"When would you like to see me?'

"On my day off. I'd like to fix you dinner at my place."

He smiled knowingly. If there was going to be romance, she wanted it in the privacy of her own apartment.

"Or I could fix you dinner at my place," he replied.

"I would like that, Yusuf," she said as she reached out and embraced him. "I would like that very much."

CHAPTER
TWENTY-SEVEN

It was a little after five o'clock, and the sun was beginning to rise over the eastern Mediterranean when the Lockheed C-5 Galaxy glided down toward the Israeli coastline, making landfall at Herzliyya, and banked south to the main runway at Lod, just east of Tel Aviv. Alexandra had slept fitfully for an hour or two during the flight over the Mediterranean from Lajes. She and Amos made their way down the long staircase into the cargo hold of the plane and were ushered by one of the crewmen to the rear of the C-5, where they waited for the giant cargo door to be raised. It slowly yawned open to reveal an Israeli ground crew eager to begin unloading the pallets of Howitzer shells stacked behind them. The morning air rushing through the open cargo door was warmer than Alexandra expected, and she found the fresh air invigorating. The tarmac was surprisingly busy, with the sounds of trams racing about with the war munitions from America. They were greeted warmly by the Israelis, some of whom welcomed them with applause.

"Welcome to Israel," someone shouted.

Amos waved as he and Alexandra walked from the plane onto the tarmac.

"Amos Ben-Chaiyim?" a voice called to him from behind the ground crew gathered in front of them.

"Yes!" he yelled back.

"I'm Lieutenant Gad," a young officer said, as he pushed his way through the assembled ground crew and greeted Amos and Alexandra. "We have a helicopter standing by to fly you down to Eilat. I understand there are rooms for both of you at Hotel Eilat where you can rest. We'll be flying you over to the Canal later this afternoon."

"How are things over there?" Amos asked.

"Quiet for the time being," Lieutenant Gad replied. "Hopefully it will stay that way."

"This is Alexandra Salaman Greenspan," Amos said, turning to Alexandra. "She'll be accompanying me to the talks."

"Yes, I know," the young lieutenant answered. "She is listed on the manifest. Welcome to Israel, Mrs. Greenspan."

Alexandra smiled and nodded. "Thank you, Lieutenant. I'm pleased to be back," she said.

"Ah, you've been to Israel before?"

"Oh yes," she answered. "I was born a few miles from here."

"Oh, I see," he said, as he glanced at the spelling of the name, SALAMAN, over the fatigue shirt pocket.

"Israeli?"

"Palestinian," she replied, matter-of-factly.

Lieutenant Gad looked from Alexandra to Amos.

"Mrs. Greenspan is a leading American journalist," Amos said. "Her columns are published under her maiden name. She was single when she began writing for the *Evening Star* in Washington. She's here to assist me with my assignment from Ambassador Dinitz."

"Well, you are here to observe history in the making. Hopefully it will be good history," Lieutenant Gad replied. "Come, my job is to escort you by jeep to the helicopter."

As they walked toward the waiting jeep Alexandra turned and saw that several of the pallets of Howitzer shells had already been unloaded. She knew they would probably be on the way to the Golan Heights before she and Amos reached Eilat.

***

Noah nursed an Amaretto on the rocks following dinner at the Waldorf's Bull and Bear. He casually thumbed through a copy of *Business Week*, and after he had read everything of interest, he ordered another Amaretto and reached into his jacket pocket for the memo Marshall Flynn had written. He carefully reread it. Flynn's observations troubled him. What if the country was about to go into a recession, as the memo suggested, and he didn't mention his concern to the analysts he would be meeting with in the morning? He had become one of the country's most respected retail developers. What would his credibility be if the bottom suddenly fell out of retail and he had appeared clueless at his meetings with analysts that growth looked shaky? That was the problem, he thought. He wasn't clueless—he did have a clue.

Noah signaled for the waiter and asked him for a pen and paper.

"Another Amaretto?" The waiter asked, as he returned with a pen and a small pad of paper.

"Sure," Noah replied, as he began writing a list of questions he knew he could expect from the analysts. He jotted down under each question bullet points to highlight possible answers.

How's business?
- *It will be a record year for Potomac Center Properties of America.*

How is occupancy running at your malls?
- *We are running at pretty near full capacity at all of our properties. Lowest vacancy rate ever.*

What new properties are on the drawing board?
- *We're looking at property in Prince George's County, Maryland and in Delaware between Wilmington and Philadelphia.*

Do you anticipate increasing your lines of credit?
- *No, we have all the borrowing capacity we need at the present time.*

Do you anticipate any new stock offerings?
- *No, we have no plans to issue additional stock and we are not planning any secondary offerings.*

What is your best estimate of year-end results?
- *We don't project earnings going forward, but we are comfortable with the estimates analysts are making regarding year-end results. We're one third of the way through the fourth quarter and we see no surprises in the final two months.*

What's the outlook for your tenants' same-store sales growth?

Noah paused, holding his pen in midair. This was the big question. This was the question that was sure to come and the one in which the analysts would be most interested. It differentiated between growth in revenue that came from price increases and growth in revenue that came from increased unit sales and customer traffic. Noah sat there for a moment and then laid his pen down. He took another sip of his Amaretto and sat back in his chair to consider how best to answer what he knew would be the most important question he would be asked. He hesitantly picked up his pen.

- *That's a question better directed to retailers you follow.*
- *Or, we have no better insight into that than you analysts do who follow the retail industry.*
- *Or, that's a question I should be asking you.*
- *Or, your guess is as good as mine.*

Noah laid down his pen again. He sat back and reached for the Amaretto. He knew these were all weak answers. They were all reasonable answers, but weak nonetheless. He could predict the immediate follow-up questions that would come. *How is customer traffic at your malls? How is volume at your receiving dock holding up? How full are your parking facilities compared with the last two quarters?*

Noah sat up straight and arched his back to relieve the strain he felt between his shoulders. He quickly drank the last of his Amaretto, folded the notepaper with the questions and answers he had jotted down, and placed them it in his jacket pocket. He was tired and a little woozy. *I probably could have done without that last Amaretto*, he thought as he signed the check. He pushed back his chair and stood up, steadied himself, and headed back to his room. He left the copy of *Business Week* he was reading on the table. Under it lay Marshall Flynn's memorandum.

The busboy handed the maître d' the magazine and memorandum Noah had left behind and pointed out the room number on the check he had signed.

"Mr. Greenspan left this behind. He's staying in room 2525 in case you want to call him," the busboy said.

"Yes, I'll do that," the maître d' replied as he held up the memorandum and skimmed its message. He reached for the phone to call room 2525 and, then, abruptly paused. The words jumped out at him.

> *I hate to suggest this as you're about to meet with analysts, but I think that prick Markanos might be onto something.*

The bespectacled maître d' ran his hand through his silver hair as he stared at the name—"Markanos." *It has to be the same Markanos that comes to the Bull and Bear so frequently*, he thought. *The same Markanos who tips so handsomely and even more generously when I tell him of interesting conversations I've overheard from the Park Avenue corporate regulars who come to the restaurant.*

He reread the memorandum, noting the bold letterhead, **Potomac Center Properties of America**, and there in the upper left-hand corner the name of the person who had penned the document, *Marshall Flynn, Chief Financial Officer.*

***

It was nearly midnight when Noah finished watching the local news. The coverage was the same on all the channels. The fact that Nixon was going to name a new Watergate prosecutor to replace Archibald Cox and the meeting Alexandra was traveling halfway around the world to witness were all any of the news anchors were talking about. Noah got up from the couch and lifted his jacket from the back of the desk chair, where he had hung it upon returning to his room from dinner. As he was about to hang his jacket in the closet, he reached into the inside pocket to reread the Flynn memorandum. That was when realized he must have left the memorandum on the table at the Bull and Bear. He lifted the phone and asked the operator to connect him to the restaurant. The maître d' answered immediately.

"This is Mr. Greenspan in room 2525," Noah began. "I think I may have left some reading material at my table following dinner this evening."

"Ah, yes, Mr. Greenspan, I'm glad you called. We're about to close and I didn't want to call your room this late, but you did leave a *Business Week* magazine at your table. Would you like us to send it up?"

"No, no, I've read the magazine. I'm calling about a memorandum I also left on the table. Was that turned in with the magazine?"

"No, I'm afraid not," the maître d' lied. "Just the *Business Week* magazine. The busboy gave it directly to me."

"I'm certain I left it on the table," Noah replied. "Are you sure you don't have it there?"

"Oh, quite certain, Mr. Greenspan. I even skimmed the magazine myself. Do you recall, was it a single sheet of paper?"

"Yes, it was a one-page memorandum."

"Ah, then it was no doubt simply thrown out as trash. I'm so sorry."

"Can it be retrieved? Can someone check the trash? It's rather important."

"That would be quite a task, Mr. Greenspan. By now the trash from the restaurant has been bundled and stored with scores of other trash bags from the hotel for pickup Monday morning."

"God damn it," Noah whispered to no one in particular. "Okay, I guess it's not really that big of a deal. Thank you."

"I'm so sorry, Mr. Greenspan."

"Yeah. Sorry to have bothered you. Like I said, it's not a big deal."

Oh, I think it must be a very big deal, the maître d' thought as he placed the phone back on the receiver.

Noah set the alarm on the clock radio for seven a.m. It was close to one o'clock before he turned out the light and fell into a restless night's sleep. He was unnerved not knowing exactly where Alexandra was, only that she was thousands of miles away, and he was angry with himself for leaving the Flynn memorandum on the table at the Bull and Bear. *Damn Amarettos,* he thought to himself.

The phone rang a few seconds after the buzzer on the clock radio sounded. He reached over and turned off the alarm and picked up the phone in one motion.

"Noah Greenspan," he answered.

"Noah, it's Karen."

"You're a pleasant wake-up call," he answered.

"Noah, what the hell happened? Did you have any meetings last night?"

"What are you talking about?" he answered, as he sat up in bed.

"You don't know?"

"Know what, Karen? I have no idea what you are talking about."

"Noah, Markanos put out a short on your stock"

"What? When? It's seven damn o'clock in the morning."

"It was on the business wire first thing. It must have been posted around midnight. My boss called me from his home to ask me if I knew anything about it. He saw it in the middle of the night."

Noah pulled back the blanket and got to his feet. "Why in the hell would Deutschland Trust issue a short-sell recommendation in the middle of the night?" he asked.

"I don't know. I can only assume they believe people will be selling after your meetings today and they wanted to get in the race before anyone else. Did you meet with anyone I don't know about last night?"

"No, Karen. I didn't leave the hotel. I had dinner alone here at the Bull and Bear."

"What a bomb he's thrown before your meetings in New York even get started. Investors are jumpy as hell anyway because of the damn Arab oil embargo. I think we're in for rough sledding."

"What does his sell recommendation say?"

"It says he thinks the country is going into a recession and that retail stocks are going to get murdered, and therefore PCPA is lousy stock to be holding right now. Given your high multiple, he thinks you're a great stock to short."

"In other words, he's predicting we're going to get clobbered."

"That's the only time short sellers make any money, Noah."

"Isn't that pretty unusual, putting out a sell recommendation in the middle of the night?"

"I can't remember anything like it, Noah."

"How did he justify his recession prediction?"

"He said he's been talking to retailers and they tell him sales have been softening since last March. Of course, he also referenced the likelihood of inflation, given the oil situation."

"I think that's bullshit," Noah said.

"What's bullshit, that sales have been softening?"

"No, that he's been talking to retailers. I don't think you send out a sell recommendation in the middle of the night because some retailers say their sales have been soft."

"Well, you can tell the institutions you'll be meeting with in a couple of hours that revenue at your malls is up nicely. If they start buying PCPA stock, Markanos and Deutschland Trust will take a bath. Look, pardon my language, but that would serve that prick right."

"What?"

"I said, if your meetings go well and the stock runs up it will serve that prick right."

Noah's mind abruptly focused on the Flynn memo. Karen's comment reminded Noah that his chief financial officer had referred to Markanos as a prick. *Oh shit*, Noah thought. *Someone picked up Flynn's memo after I left the restaurant last night and must have called Markanos.*

"I can't make that kind of a positive statement, Karen."

"Why not? It's true."

"Yes, but we don't know whether the increased revenue is from price increases or unit sales increases."

"Right, you don't know, and you don't have to speculate."

"It's not that simple, Karen. Marshall Flynn sent a memo to me in which he expressed concern that our revenue increases could very well be because our tenants have been raising prices, and not necessarily enjoying increased sales. In fact, from what we can see, traffic is down at our malls."

"He put that in a memo?"

"Yes, he did. He gave it to Daoud to deliver to me when he drove me to the airport yesterday morning."

"You know, you should tell your people to speculate *verbally* about something as sensitive as this. You don't need that kind of speculation floating around on paper in the office, Noah."

"Karen, it might be floating around Markanos's office."

"What are you talking about?"

"Karen, I was reading Flynn's memo at dinner last night."

"So?"

"I left it on the table in the restaurant when I went back up to my room. I called the maître d' around midnight when I discovered that I had left it on the table, and he said it had already been disposed of."

"Disposed of?"

"Thrown out."

"Noah, do you know what the odds are that the memo would have miraculously found its way to Markanos between last night when it was thrown out and when his sell recommendation hit the wire early this morning?"

"Stranger things have happened."

"Highly doubtful."

"Yeah, I know, but, Karen, I have to be careful. My chief financial officer is on record speculating to me that Markanos may have been right about the economy softening. Markanos might be a prick, but he's smart as hell."

"Well, if the memo or its message did find its way to Markanos, he's skating on very thin ice."

"Thin ice? Are you kidding? He couldn't have stronger evidence that we're concerned about a recession."

"Because?"

"Because if he has the memo or someone told him about it, he knows we share his concern."

"Noah, were that true and he ran and shorted the stock, he would have been trading on insider information. The SEC would absolutely nail him if they thought he shorted the stock based on a company memo that had not been otherwise made public."

"Well, we'll never know, will we?"

"Noah, here's what I think you should do. Just say the company is always sensitive to how the economy is doing. Say that you take many things into consideration, such as tenants' revenues and traffic at your malls. Traffic can be very variable and hard to interpret on a spot basis. A mom can come into a mall with four kids and not buy anything, or she can come in alone and spend like a sailor. Revenue, on the other hand, is totally objective. You can measure it day by day, and, as of now, it has been growing steadily. I don't think you have to say more than that."

"But what if he really has the memo?"

"The memo doesn't contradict what I've just suggested you say, and besides, it would be suicide for him to ever admit seeing or even knowing about an internal company memo—especially after shorting the stock."

"Interesting. I would have never thought of that."

"You don't have to argue with Markanos's opinion. You can even say you worry about the sustainability of growth every day, but as of now, revenue is continuing to grow nicely."

"Somehow, I just know that memo found its way to Markanos. I know the odds must be a million to one, but the timing of his sell recommendation and me losing Flynn's memo just can't be a coincidence."

"Noah, it doesn't matter. Look, your tenants are mostly very substantial retailers. They've weathered many recessions. They're not going to close up and flee your malls every time there's a business downturn. In fact, you, as the landlord, might be in the best position of all. You're pretty well protected by the leases you have. They're your dike"

"Maybe, maybe not. We haven't been through a recession yet. Analysts will be watching our vacancy rates, looking for cracks in the dike."

"Look, I don't know what the effect of Markanos's short will be. He's stuck his neck out and will do everything he can to drive down the price of your stock. Just go to your meetings and demonstrate that you're well positioned to weather whatever the economy throws your way. Your investors will want to see a cool steady hand at the helm. They might not buy more PCPA, but I don't think they'll bail on you either, not if you win their confidence."

"Have you heard from Amos?" Noah asked, changing the subject.

"No. He and Alexandra must be in Eilat by now. It's afternoon there. Maybe we'll hear from them before they head out to the talks tonight."

"Well, I won't, because I won't be reachable, but you might. Leave a message for me at the hotel if you do hear from them."

"Sure. It's pretty exciting, don't you think? The entire world will be waiting for word from this Kilometer 101, and they'll be right there."

"Frankly, I'd rather she was right here. She's wound up in danger every time she's been in that part of the world."

"She'll be fine, Noah. She'll be with the IDF nearly the entire time she's there, and Amos certainly isn't going to let her out of his sight."

"Yeah, I'm sure she'll be fine. I'll just rest easier when I know she's on her way back to Georgetown."

* * *

The mournful, long-abandoned dwelling halfway between Khirbet Zanuta and ad-Dhahiriya was perfect, just twelve miles south of

Hebron and only two-and-a-half hours by car from Eilat. It was hidden in the hills overlooking the desert, just over the Green Line on the West Bank, about thirty miles from the Dead Sea on an unused and unmarked dirt road that led nowhere. The building had the added advantage of being well off of Highway 40, the main artery running north through the Negev, and it was a safe distance from the neighboring towns. The uneven rugged stone walls, identical to the walls of the ancient dwellings of ad-Dhahiriya, had stood the test of time. The roughly hewn limestone and mud mortar had kept the elements out and would keep any sound in. Everything about the place served his purpose well. Omar Samir was pleased.

**

Alexandra and Amos were transported by IDF helicopter from Lod to Eilat Naval Base and then driven to their hotel overlooking the Red Sea. They checked in and agreed to meet in the lobby at five o'clock. Too tired to even undress when she got to her room, Alexandra just kicked off her shoes and fell across the bed. She didn't awaken until shortly before they were to leave for the two-hour flight to Kilometer 101, fifteen miles west of the Suez Canal.

Their helicopter was idling when they arrived, ready to depart from the same pad on which they had landed earlier in the day. Alexandra noticed the Star of David had been covered with the blue insignia of the United Nations. The pilot, seeing that Alexandra was puzzled, was quick to assuage whatever concern she had.

"While we have safe passage across the Sinai and will be traversing the peninsula through the Mitla Pass and flying almost entirely over Israeli-held land, we don't want to take any chances. That's why we've borrowed the symbol of the UN," the pilot said. "Just a little extra precaution."

"Does the UN know you've *borrowed* their logo?" she asked.

"Believe me, they would not want any Egyptians firing at an Israeli helicopter after three weeks of fighting."

She ignored his evasive answer and simply nodded. "No, of course not."

They flew on a slight northwestward course into the sun, heading in an almost straight line toward Suez City from Eilat. The landscape changed dramatically as they passed through the Mitla Pass and on toward the East Bank of the Canal. On the east side of the pass swells of desert sand simply blanketed everything. On the west side the hulks of burned-out Egyptian tanks were everywhere.

"All Egyptian," the pilot yelled to them, pointing down to the desert floor in a stabbing motion. "The biggest tank battle since Kursk in World War Two took place just below where we're flying. The Egyptians lost nearly five hundred tanks down there."

"And the Israelis?" she asked.

"A couple dozen for a few hours. We actually got most of them up and running again pretty fast."

Alexandra looked to Amos. "It's true. It was what you Americans call a turkey shoot. No one can figure out why Sadat ordered an open-field attack so far beyond his Russian missile protection."

As they approached the Canal, Amos pointed north between the Great Bitter Lake and Lake Timsah. "That's about where Sharon broke through the Egyptian lines," Amos said, jabbing his finger toward the misnamed Chinese Farms on the east side of the Canal. "The Egyptian Second Army is to the north, and the Third Army is to the south and completely cut off. Once we succeeded in crossing the Canal, our forces wanted to cut off the Second Army too, but the US supported an UN-sponsored ceasefire before we could do that. The Americans came to our rescue with the airlift, but they're determined not to let us finish the job."

"Another catastrophe for the Arabs," Alexandra said to no one in particular.

"It was a bigger catastrophe for us, Alexandra. Our losses have been horrible."

The helicopter crossed the Canal just south of Suez and flew for several minutes over a highway leading west from Suez toward Cairo.

"And there's Kilometer 101," the pilot said, pointing down toward a tent and clusters of men, some of whom were pointing up at the descending helicopter.

Amos looked over to Alexandra. "Excited?"

"More than I should admit," she answered.

Amos jumped down as soon as the Bell Huey landed and then turned and clasped Alexandra by the waist to ease her out of the helicopter.

"Have the two sides met yet?" Amos asked one of the young Israeli officers who walked over to greet them.

"No, there's been a hang-up on the road a few miles from here," the lieutenant replied. "I'm Lieutenant Asher Goren," he said, extending his hand.

"I'm Amos Ben-Chaiyim, on assignment here from the embassy in Washington. What kind of hang-up?" Amos asked as he shook the officer's hand.

"Well, it seems the Egyptians aren't going to come to talk until a truck caravan carrying medical supplies and food and water reaches the Third Army. That was a condition of the talks."

"So, what's the hang-up?" Amos asked.

"I'm not sure. But it seems our people are waiting for definite instructions to let them through. For some reason our troops on the road were not informed about the convoy and won't let them through until they get direct orders from headquarters."

"Why wouldn't they have received instructions to let the Egyptians through?"

The Israeli soldier just shrugged. "I think someone screwed up."

"You're telling me the non-military supplies for Egypt's Third Army are just sitting out there on the road while our people await orders?"

"Seems that way. They're trying to work it out with headquarters. We've insisted that our people, in addition to the UN inspectors, be allowed to check out what the lorries are carrying."

"I thought all of that had been worked out."

"It had, but somebody forgot to tell the Egyptians driving the lorries."

"Who are all these people?" Amos asked, gesturing to the men who were there apparently waiting for the talks to begin.

"UN personnel and quite a few of our people, mostly security and staff. We have communications set up so that General Yariv can step out and consult with Dayan if he needs to. The Egyptians have a similar capability."

"Good afternoon. I'm Alexandra Salaman. I'm here to assist Mr. Ben-Chaiyim," Alexandra interrupted, extending her hand to the Israeli lieutenant.

"You're an American?"

"Yes. I am now," she replied.

"How long ago did you leave Israel?" the Lieutenant asked.

"What makes you so sure I left Israel," she replied, smiling.

"I can spot Israeli women wherever they are."

"We all sound alike, do we?"

"No, but you're all beautiful," he replied, with a broad, friendly grin. "You have to be a Sabra. You have exotic Middle Eastern features."

"Maybe I'm just prickly like the sabra," she answered, referring to the cactus found throughout Israel.

"Ah, but the fruit of the sabra is sweet on the inside," he answered.

"Nice meeting you, Lieutenant," Alexandra replied, extending her hand.

"If all the women at the Israeli embassy in America are as charming as you, I may transfer from the army to the diplomatic corps."

"A real charmer," Amos said, as the young lieutenant turned and walked away.

It was close to midnight before General Yariv arrived with his entourage at Kilometer 101. He stopped to shake hands with a number of the Israeli officers. Amos noticed Lieutenant Goren gesturing toward him and Alexandra after exchanging a few words with General Yariv.

The general looked over to them, shook a few other hands, and made his way over to Amos and Alexandra.

"Mr. Ben-Chaiyim?" General Yariv said, more a greeting than a question.

"Yes, and this is Alexandra Salaman Greenspan," Amos replied.

The general glanced at the name on her fatigue shirt and smiled. "I presume you're not from the embassy," he said.

"No, I'm not," she replied.

"She's here with Ambassador Dinitz's permission. She's here to observe."

"Observe for whom, Miss Salaman?"

"I'm a journalist with the *Washington Evening Star*, but I'm not here to report directly from the talks—only to observe."

General Yariv looked into her eyes and then slowly nodded as though remembering something from the past. "What did you say your name is?"

"Alexandra Salaman Greenspan," she answered nervously.

"You were the young women, a student in Beirut, who warned us of a terrorist plot back in the early sixties."

"It was nineteen fifty-nine," she replied.

"I don't think I ever had the opportunity to say 'thank you,'" he said, extending his hand and clasping hers. "We owe you a great debt of gratitude." He paused a moment, continuing to hold her hand for an extra second or two. "Didn't you get yourself into a barrel of trouble in Khartoum following the sixty-seven war?"

"That would be me," she answered with a faint smile.

"You know we can't have press reporting on these talks just yet."

"I do, and I promise I'm only here to be at Kilometer 101 so that I can write that I was here when I am free to report."

"So, you came all this way to stand at a mile post and look at a tent?"

Alexandra nodded. "History is about to be made here, General. That mile post, Kilometer 101, will probably always be synonymous with these first face-to-face meetings between the Egyptian high command and the Israeli high command. Yes, I'm happy to travel halfway around the world to be able to say I was here."

"Nonsense. If I have your word that you're only here to observe and that you won't report directly on the proceedings of these talks, or quote anything anyone says, you're welcome to sit in the tent and observe. All ears, Miss Salaman, but no note taking. Like I said, we owe you a huge debt of gratitude." With that, he shook her hand once more and turned and walked toward a nearby group of Israeli officers.

Alexandra was speechless. She looked at Amos. "I did hear him say what I think he said, didn't I?"

"You just got an invitation to a ringside seat from the only person who could have made that invitation."

"Wait until Noah and Markazie hear about this," she whispered.

"Wait until Benjamin Bar-Levy hears about it," Amos replied. "He'll have my scalp."

CHAPTER
TWENTY-EIGHT

So, this is how it begins, Alexandra thought as the Israeli and Egyptian delegations filed into the makeshift tent around one thirty in the morning. Alexandra, seated next to Amos along with other Israeli and Egyptian staff, could almost reach out and touch the men who would soon be engaged in one of the most momentous negotiations of the twentieth century. It was a crude setting, given its historical significance—a large camouflage canopy stretched over the uneven floor of desert sand, and stark glaring lightbulbs hanging from hastily installed overhead electrical wiring. The warriors, deadly adversaries only days before, were seated opposite one another at two blanket-covered wooden tables no more than a few feet apart. Alexandra looked from General Yariv to General el-Gamasy. The negotiators, who had never met face to face, and who had little trust in one another, each sat for a moment taking measure of their adversary. The tension was palpable. The chill of the night desert air hinted more of hopelessness than of hope. The two nations facing one another at that table had, during the prior three weeks, been locked in mortal combat. Their armies had been responsible for the deaths of thousands of young men under the command of men sitting an arm's length away, across the table. General el-Gamasy, expressionless and seemingly aloof, evidenced no concern regarding the desperate situation that had befallen Egypt's trapped Third Army.

General Yariv sat for a moment taking measure of his Egyptian counterpart. He studied General el-Gamasy through his tinted horn-rim glasses. As a legendary former chief of military intelligence, General Yariv thought he knew all there was to know of Mohamed Abel Ghani el-Gamasy. El-Gamasy, who had been staring down at his hands, lifted his gaze to General Yariv. The two men peered briefly into each other's eyes. Then, after a moment's hesitation, Israeli Major General Aharon Yariv stood to face Egyptian General el-Gamasy, who quickly got to his feet. The two men faced one another and nodded, almost imperceptibly. Then Major General Yariv slowly and resolutely extended his hand. General el-Gamasy nodded slightly and clasped the Israeli's hand. It was a breathtaking moment, after which nothing was ever to be quite the same between the countries they each represented.

Such opposites, Alexandra thought. The Egyptians at the table were in either proper military uniform or civilian suits with dress shirts and coat and tie. The Israelis, all military, were dressed in more casual military uniforms and combat boots.

Amos leaned into Alexandra to whisper in her ear. He pointed out General David Elazar, the Chief of Staff of the IDF, who was seated at the opposite end of the table from General Yariv. Then he identified General Shmuel Eyal, who was seated next to General Yariv. "Our major issue tonight will be getting our prisoners of war back. That's why General Eyal is here and so prominently positioned at the table. That's his issue. It's his only issue." Alexandra nodded her understanding.

"Do you know the Egyptians who are at the table with General el-Gamasy?" she whispered.

"The only one I recognize is sitting next to him. That's Omar Sirry from the Egyptian Foreign Ministry. I assume he's here representing Egypt's Foreign Minister, Ismail Fahmy."

"What does that tell you?" she asked.

"I don't know, other than that Sadat is taking these talks very seriously. This isn't a one-off event, Alexandra. Sadat apparently wants this to be the beginning of something that is going to lead somewhere, somewhere that's going to change the status quo."

"I'll believe it when I see it," she whispered.

"I think you may be seeing it right now, at least the *start* of it," he whispered back.

"So, shall we begin?" General Yariv asked as the two men took their seats.

"We believe there are two pressing issues that must be resolved before any progress can be made at these talks," General el-Gamasy began.

Alexandra glanced to Amos. "This is history, Amos," she whispered. "My heart is absolutely pounding in my chest."

"I'm sure we both have issues that must be resolved at the outset of these talks, General," Aharon Yariv replied. "We have our own pressing issues, as well."

"The supply of non-military items such as food and water and medical supplies to our Third Army must be allowed transit without further delay. That was always a condition of these talks."

"We have agreed to an immediate convoy of such items, General. We have no objection to that."

"The convoy should have reached the Third Army by the time we began talking. That was the agreement."

"We agree the two events were to be simultaneous, but there were unexpected, very minor issues that had to be resolved, and that I believe have been resolved," General Yariv replied.

"We expect that such non-military supply convoys will now proceed without further interruption as needed. We cannot go through this with every convoy."

"There has been no discussion that I know of regarding an uninterrupted flow of supplies to the Third Army. We have no objection to non-military supply of the Egyptian Army, but there will have to be a procedure established to accomplish this. These talks cannot be held hostage to a protocol for the daily shipment of supplies."

"Exactly. So, let's agree that supplying our Third Army with non-military items will not require a separate daily negotiation. Let's just agree that that's acceptable."

"I'm sure that will be no problem, but there will be many details to work out and I have no authority to negotiate those details. This first convoy of non-military supplies was the only supply issue with which we were confronted, and we have agreed to that."

"But it has not gone smoothly. There have been endless and unnecessary delays."

"My understanding is that the convoy is proceeding as we speak."

"I would like your assurance that we will not have to go through this with every supply convoy."

"Yes, we would want to avoid wasting time discussing every convoy, but I must confer with our people. I have no authority to approve endless supply convoys at this first meeting."

"You will secure an understanding from Tel Aviv?"

"Yes, I will begin that process at our first break tonight. There is, however, an issue that is just as important to us as your Third Army problem is to you. We must facilitate an immediate return of prisoners of war."

"I have no authority to deal with prisoner of war issues at this time," General el-Gamasy replied.

"There is *no* issue of greater importance to us," General Yariv answered.

"I don't think we can address prisoners of war until your forces have returned to the October twenty-second lines. That was where both armies were when the UN resolution passed calling for a ceasefire. Those were the lines when you and we agreed to a ceasefire."

"Which your forces repeatedly violated, General el-Gamasy."

"You have used every skirmish to justify advancing beyond the October twenty-second lines," General el-Gamasy replied.

"We must deal with the current reality, General. The lines are where they are. There is no magical way to define precisely where we were on October twenty-second when your troops fired on our troops in violation of the ceasefire. It would be impossible."

"I believe there are satellite images available of the battlefield every day since the war began," General el-Gamasy replied. "It should be no problem at all to move your army back to the October twenty-second lines."

"A final disengagement agreement will establish your lines and our lines, General. Until then, we will waste time if we argue over hypothetical lines that were rendered meaningless a week ago when your forces fired on our forces during the ceasefire."

"These are very important issues for us, General Yariv. Your forces are holding our forces hostage, and you have now advanced onto the African side of the Suez Canal. This is entirely unacceptable."

"Let us not lose sight of who began this war, General el-Gamasy."

"We have not moved one inch into Israel, General Yariv. You forget, you have been occupying Egyptian territory for five years. All of our soldiers are on Egyptian territory. The Sinai Peninsula, all of it, *is* Egypt. The October twenty-second lines, and many miles to the east beyond, are all Egypt."

"From which your President Nasser amassed over one hundred thousand troops to attack my country in nineteen sixty-seven."

And so it went. Seemingly endless banter, but little progress toward any meaningful decisions.

Alexandra leaned into Amos again. "This isn't going well, is it? They've been bickering for over an hour," she whispered.

"It's going very well, Alexandra. It's dialogue between Egypt and Israel."

"General el-Gamasy, why don't we take a break and we can each confer with our leadership. We'll want to see what we can do to facilitate the non-military supply of your Third Army, and we would like a resolution of the prisoner of war issue. We'll be happy to exchange the Egyptians prisoners we hold for our men who you are holding." General el-Gamasy nodded his agreement.

The tent quickly emptied as the Israelis and Egyptians headed to separate areas to confer. Alexandra welcomed the break and the opportunity to stretch her legs after sitting on the hard wooden chairs that had been provided for the meeting. It was nearly three o'clock in the morning and there was a biting edge to the cold desert air. Alexandra shivered as they walked from the tent onto the uneven sand terrain that surrounded them and took hold of Amos's arm for support. He took off his jacket, draped it over her shoulders, and put his arm around her. She slid hers around his waist. "We've been through a lot together, you and me," she said.

"It seems like several lifetimes have come and gone since we first met when you were a student in Beirut."

"What an unlikely situation that was. It's still hard for me to believe. I and my stories for *The Star* were being used in such a horrible scheme to create mayhem. You figured out how the timing of my stories was being used by terrorists even though I didn't have a clue."

"Well, my colleagues at Mossad did. I was just dispatched to Beirut to determine who the plotters were."

"You came to either kill me or save me."

"Well, I obviously made the right decision."

"You saved my life in Beirut."

"All in a day's work," he quipped.

"Twice."

"Twice what?"

"You've saved my life twice."

"Ah, Khartoum. That was a bit more challenging," he answered. "I rescued you and—who was it?—ah, yes, Sabirah Najat."

"Don't remind me. That pseudonym almost cost me my life. That mad man, my jailer at Omdurman Prison in Khartoum, Mohammed Faisel, was determined to force me, or Sabirah Najat, to become his slave-wife. He believed he could do whatever he wanted to do to Sabirah Najat because he insisted she was an apostate. It took a long time for the bad dreams to stop after Khartoum," she said.

"But life is good now, Alexandra," he said, momentarily tightening his embrace, "for you, for Noah, for your child, my godson, Amos, and for Karen and me."

"Yes, life is good for us, but the world seems no better off. Think of the blood that has been spilled only a few miles from here."

"I don't want to think about it. It was absolute carnage for us."

"It seems a lot harder to end a war than to start one," she said as they slowly strolled under the light of a half-moon through the sand outside the tent at Kilometer 101.

"It always is, Alexandra."

"Do you think anything will really get accomplished here, Amos?"

"If it is up to General Yariv and Golda, absolutely. Neither side will want to lose whatever momentum has begun here. Yariv and el-Gamasy have broken the ice, Alexandra. They won't want to go back to business as usual. We've taken huge losses, and the Egyptians never expected to be bargaining with Israel for the survival of their trapped Third Army. A door has been opened. We would be crazy to close it."

"It's hard to be here witnessing all of this and not be able to report about it as it's happening."

"You'll have plenty to write about when you get home, Alexandra."

"I know. This has been the opportunity of a lifetime for me."

"Let's hope many positive stories begin with these meetings."

"It will be interesting to see if the tenor of the meeting changes after this break."

"Well, I can assure you both sides have been consulting with their leaders back in Cairo and Tel Aviv," Amos answered.

***

In Cairo, Anwar Sadat was brooding.

"The Israelis must go back to the October twenty-second lines. That's where both sides were when we accepted the UN ceasefire," he railed.

"But that isn't where we are now," General el-Gamasy replied into the phone. "And we are as much to blame for that as are the Israelis," he continued. "The Israelis can destroy the entire Third Army overnight, and they can probably decimate the Second Army as well. Frankly, I don't know why they are holding back. I wouldn't if I were leading their army."

"They're holding back because Kissinger is holding them back. The Israeli generals have no interest in compromise given their current advantage on the battlefield, but the old lady won't risk alienating the Americans. She's wiser than all of the generals put together."

"Mr. President, what do you want me to do? All the Israelis want to talk about are their men we are holding as prisoners."

"Continue to insist on the reestablishment of the October twenty-second lines. Do not back away from that. Demand free access to the trapped Third Army, and use the prisoner issue as your bargaining chip, but do not concede anything regarding the reestablishment of the October twenty-second lines. I want the Israelis off of the west side of the Canal."

Less than fifty yards away, Major General Aharon Yariv was conferring on a secure line with Defense Minister Moshe Dayan at the Southern Command Headquarters in the Negev and with Prime Minister Golda Meir in Tel Aviv. The old lady, as President Sadat referred to the Israeli Prime Minister, was resolute. "Maintain the status quo until we meet with the Americans in Washington next week. We'll have Major Generals Israel Tal and Shmuel Eyal sit in for you while you accompany me to Washington. Eyal's focus will be on the prisoners and nothing else until you return to the talks. We don't budge from the west side of the Canal unless the Egyptians abandon the east side of the Canal. Don't even entertain a discussion of our moving back to the so-called October twenty-second lines. They don't exist."

Defense Minister Dayan had little interest in the talks at Kilometer 101 and resented his Prime Minister's trust in Major General Yariv. Dayan saw the talks as an impediment and not a solution to the war. The Israeli Defense Forces had fought back from the abyss and were now prepared to kill off the invaders once and for all. The Egyptian

Third Army, which had inflicted so much misery on the Israelis only two weeks earlier, were now out-flanked, out-gunned, and totally at the mercy of the very army they had come so close to annihilating. And now they were being coddled in that damned tent at Kilometer 101 as though they were victims rather than the aggressors they were. It was, he thought, disgusting. Virtually all of his fellow generals agreed. Chief of Staff Dado Elazar quietly instructed his commanders to be prepared to resume the war. General Sharon—Arik the Lion, as his men referred to him—opined that the talks should be deliberately steered to a dead end so that the fighting could resume.

But the old lady was in charge, and no one, not Dayan or Elazar or Sharon, would challenge that; not in the ramshackle, boisterous democracy they themselves had fought so hard to establish a quarter century earlier.

When all was said and done, Golda Meir knew with every fiber of her being that all of these men had failed her. None, she thought—not one—had warned her of the impending calamity that Yom Kippur would usher in. She hung up the phone certain that had Major General Aharon Yariv still been chief of military intelligence instead of that incompetent General Zeira with his absurd Kontzeptziya, none of this would have happened. Only she understood that Israel at this moment of euphoric battlefield accomplishment was on life support.

***

Alexandra thought the atmosphere in the tent had, indeed, improved as General Yariv and General el-Gamasy took their seats opposite one another. Both negotiators seemed more relaxed; they seemed more like men who knew one another. General el-Gamasy pulled his chair closer to the table and absently rubbed his hands together to warm them. General Yariv quickly signaled one of the young Israeli officers who was standing nearby to come over to him and whispered something in his ear. A moment later the officer reappeared with an IDF field jacket and approached General el-Gamasy to offer the garment to help shield the Egyptian from the cold. General el-Gamasy looked up at the young Israeli and to the jacket he was offering him. For a moment it seemed everyone held their breath to await the general's reaction. He looked over to General Yariv, smiled ever so slightly, stood, accepted the jacket, and quickly put it on.

"*Shukran jazilan,*" he said softly to the young officer. He then, almost imperceptibly, nodded his appreciation to General Yariv.

"Wow," Amos whispered.

"What did el-Gamasy just say?" Alexandra whispered back.

"He said, *Thank you so much.*"

"So, I think we have a suggestion for supplying the Third Army," General Yariv began. "We will agree to having UN personnel along with unarmed men of the IDF inspect the lorries, which will then proceed to the Canal at Kilometer 138.5, near Shallufa. There, unarmed IDF troops and UN personnel will be allowed to inspect the cargo once again before it is loaded onto Egyptian amphibious vehicles that are already at the Canal, to be transported to the East Bank and on to the Third Army." General Yariv sat back in his chair to await General el-Gamasy's reply.

El-Gamasy tapped his fingers on the table top for a moment as he collected his thoughts.

"We believe what you propose seems workable, General Yariv, but it does not represent very much progress. The non-military supply of our Third Army resolves little more than a humanitarian issue that really doesn't require you and I to be here at Kilometer 101 at three o'clock in the morning. I cannot emphasize enough the importance to us of both sides moving back to where they were on October twenty-second, when the UN ceasefire was to go into effect."

"Well, we are pleased we seem to have agreement on the resupply of the Egyptian Third Army, and we too would like to now proceed to issues of disengagement. Our most important issue is that of the prisoners of war. We are disappointed that your side does not seem to see this issue with the urgency that our side sees the issue. You are holding many of our men, and we are holding many of your men. Their well-being should be of equal interest to both of us. To us, that is our number-one priority. We don't see how these talks can proceed until we at least have a list of all of our men held by your side, in return for which we will provide a list of your men who we hold. We especially want to know their condition, and we would like to arrange for immediate inspections of the prisoners by a neutral party, such as the International Red Cross. This, to us, is far more important than this preoccupation with establishing phantom lines that never existed at all in reality."

"It is difficult to discuss disengagement if we do not agree on the point on the map from which we are to disengage. Every ceasefire, every truce, every disengagement begins with a map. We believe the map must reflect the October twenty-second lines."

"And we believe the map should reflect the lines as they exist right now, because we both know where *we* are and we both know where *you* are. We cannot create a map of where we think both sides were when the fighting was supposed to stop on October twenty-second, but when the fighting, in fact, didn't stop. And I must say, General, exchanging prisoner lists is far more important than exchanging our respective views of where these fictitious lines were a week ago."

"I believe I can obtain a list of the captives we hold by tomorrow's meeting, General Yariv. I will do everything I can to have that list with me tomorrow, and I presume you will do the same."

"Of course," General Yariv replied.

"But we both know exchanging lists of prisoners cannot be our only accomplishment here."

"That is correct, General el-Gamasy. So, I believe we have a very constructive proposal for further progress."

"We are eager to hear it."

"We propose a real disengagement plan. Something far more meaningful than pretending we know where the lines really were on October twenty-second. We propose withdrawing all of our troops to a line ten kilometers beyond the east side of the Canal. We would totally abandon our positions on the west side of the Canal. Simultaneously, your side will withdraw from the east side of the Canal to a line ten kilometers from the water's edge on the west side. Once these new lines are confirmed ten kilometers on either side of the Suez Canal, with twenty kilometers separating our forces, a UN or some other separation force we each would agree to would be installed to oversee or maintain this new buffer zone. Normalcy would return to the Canal, quiet would return to the prior battlefield, and the prisoners would be reunited with their units or with their families at home. That would conclude the first phase of the disengagement. Then, at a time to which we both agree, and when the success of this first disengagement phase has been established, we could move to a second disengagement phase during which we would move our forces further east, and Egyptian forces could reoccupy a predetermined zone on the east side of the Canal. And so, in a few increments over a reasonable period of time, when good faith has been demonstrated by both sides, we would move still further east, relinquishing more of the Sinai to Egyptian control."

"This is a constructive suggestion you have made, General. I see some real problems with it from our point of view that I would like to reflect upon, but these are the issues we should be discussing. Let me suggest that we reconvene tomorrow and discuss this issue of disengagement after further reflection."

***

"So, what do you think?" Alexandra asked as they walked to the helicopter waiting to take them back to Eilat.

"Yariv has put the right question on the table, but I'll be surprised if he gets an answer tomorrow that he can live with."

"It seems like a very rational proposal to me," Alexandra replied.

"Rationally reasonable, but politically very difficult for the Egyptians," Amos answered. "First, the Sinai *is* theirs, so having us propose that they abandon the Sinai to this line ten kilometers on the west side of the Canal is a bitter pill for them. Second, what we've proposed would require their abandonment of every vestige of what they achieved on the battlefield. No, I don't think Sadat can buy that."

"Tomorrow's session should be very interesting when the Egyptians respond to Yariv's proposal."

"Yes, it will be. Yariv knows they are going to say no, but it's a start. They'll find common ground, eventually."

"Well, it will be dawn before we turn in. I'll try reaching Noah if the operator at the hotel can get a call through. It will be close to midnight back in the States. I'm not sure whether he'll be in New York or back in Washington. I'm eager to hear how his meetings have gone."

"Are there problems?"

Alexandra shrugged. "I'm not sure. He thought an analyst was about to urge investors to sell their shares of Potomac Center Properties of America. Everything Noah has is tied up in that company, so, yes, he's been very concerned."

The helicopter's rotors began to slowly turn as soon as Alexandra and Amos approached the awaiting aircraft.

"I can't wait to crawl into bed," she said. "I'm exhausted."

CHAPTER
TWENTY-NINE

"So, Noah, you think the retail business is as strong as ever, is that right?" George Markanos asked as soon as Noah began taking questions, following breakfast. The other analysts focused like lasers on Noah, all of them acutely aware that the Street's most aggressive short-sell analyst had just trashed Potomac Center Properties of America.

"I didn't say that," Noah replied.

"You said sales were up around six percent."

"I said our tenants' revenue was up six percent."

"Isn't that the same thing?"

"No, of course not. We only collect revenue data from our tenants' cash registers. We can't differentiate between revenue from unit sales increases or revenue from price increases."

"I think your revenue increases are from tenant price increases."

"I know you do. I read your short-sell recommendation."

"Do you quibble with it?"

"Nope, although I was surprised you would short the stock based on your conversations with a few retailers."

"If I'm right, retail is in for a drubbing."

"We're not retailers. We're developers and landlords, and we're here for the long haul. If the economy goes into recession, as you suggest it will, we'll come through it just fine. We have the strongest retailers in the nation in our malls, and they've all weathered recessions in the past, and if we're headed for a recession as you suggest, they'll weather this one too. Our malls are all at capacity, and I think they'll continue to enjoy very low vacancy rates."

"But if you're wrong, as I think you are, and your vacancy rates shoot up, I think your stock could take a beating."

"Of course, you do. You've placed a colossal bet on that opinion with your short-sell report last night. What time did you issue that report? It was two o'clock in the morning, right?"

"That's right. I just couldn't sleep, I was so worried about the economy. So, I just got dressed and took a taxi to the office and wrote that report. No hard feelings, right, Noah?"

"Absolutely right, George."

"So, none of your folks are worried about a recession, Noah?"

That son of a bitch wants to catch me in a lie, Noah thought. *That bastard has seen the Flynn memorandum.* "We have a variety of opinions floating around our office at any point in time, George."

"And your opinion is the only one that really counts, right, Noah?"

"We have a superb senior management team, George, and I value all of their opinions very highly. But yes, you could say the buck stops with me."

"Mr. Greenspan, I'm Andrew Teal with Boylston Equities in Boston."

"Of course. We're pleased you're here, Mr. Teal. Boylston has been a loyal shareholder from the very beginning. I certainly appreciate you coming down from Boston for our meeting this morning."

"Actually, I'm not from the buy side of the shop. I'm General Counsel at Boylston."

"Oh," Noah replied, somewhat taken aback. "Well, welcome. How can I help you?"

"Actually, you probably can't *help me*, as you say. I guess I'm just doing some due diligence. That short-sell report on PCPA must have a lot of investors rattled. We've never seen anything like it. I mean, an analyst rushing out a sell report in the middle of the night like Deutschland Trust did last night. Frankly, I'm just curious as hell. Is some shoe about to drop at Potomac Center?"

"I personally know of no material negative development of any kind at our company, Mr. Teal … but that's a question you have every right to ask the author of the report urging investors to sell our stock. After all, he's sitting just two tables away from you," Noah said, glancing to the table where George Markanos was sitting just in time to see the analyst shift a bit uncomfortably in his chair.

"Well, all right then," the man from Boylston Equities continued. "Mr. Markanos, you just issued a pretty draconian *sell* recommendation on Potomac Center Properties. I don't ever remember a report that was so urgent that it was released at two o'clock in the morning. You've got millions of shares represented here this morning, so is there something specific about Potomac Center you want to share with us?"

"You read my report. It's all there."

"No, sir. I wouldn't say it's all there at all," the attorney replied. "You suggest that the country may be heading into a recession and that Potomac Center Properties of America would be a good stock to sell if the country is headed that way, but there are hundreds of stocks that will be adjusted downward if a recession is coming, and yet you specifically targeted PCPA without identifying anything at all about PCPA's operations. That just seems strange to me."

George Markanos shrugged. "Sure, I could have recommended dozens of stocks to sell, and I probably will as time passes, because I do think a recession is coming, but, for starters, PCPA, which has thousands of leases with vulnerable retailers, seems like a pretty good short-sell situation to me."

"But do I understand that you're saying you have nothing specific, nothing negative, to report on Potomac Center Properties of America? You simply believe that they'll take a pounding if a recession is coming, and based on that, Deutschland Trust is shorting the stock?"

Noah watched Markanos scratch, in frustration, at the stubble on his chin before answering. He knew the short-sell analyst desperately wanted to tell the group that he knew foot traffic and parking traffic were down at the malls, but that he couldn't reveal that without also revealing that he was in possession of an internal memorandum and that his sell recommendation was based on undisclosed insider information.

"Yes," he finally answered. "I consider Potomac Center Properties of America a damn good proxy for retailing, and if retailing is going to take a hit, then PCPA is a good stock to unload."

"On the other hand," an analyst interrupted from across the room, "PCPA is really positioned to weather a storm well, given that its malls are leased to the strongest retailers in the country—those that will come through a business downturn in the future just as they have in the past. I'm not suggesting that recessions are of no concern, only that there are far more vulnerable companies than a company like Potomac Center Properties of America."

"Maybe so, but I wouldn't be out buying PCPA if I thought we were on the brink of a recession," Markanos answered.

"I might," came a voice from across the room. Noah recognized the analyst from Dearborn Securities from Chicago. They were a medium-sized money management group with a solid record for serving their clients well in good times and bad times. "Michael Kerlow here from Dearborn Securities. We like regional and national retail companies, and we might very well look at PCPA as a hedge if we thought a recession was coming. I read your report this morning. I think you might be right about a recession in the near future, but I'm inclined to urge our clients to consider Potomac Center Properties of America as sort of a safe harbor if headwinds are coming."

Noah glanced over to George Markanos. He was trying to remain nonchalant, but the stress was beginning to show. The short seller had been confident that his middle-of-the-night sell recommendation would produce a strong down day in the market for Noah's company.

If, however, the opposite turned out to be true—if the stock went up instead of down—short sellers would get caught holding the bag as their losses mounted in tandem with Potomac Center's rising stock price.

It's going to backfire on Markanos, Noah thought gleefully, as he tried to maintain an almost indifferent expression. He knew, of course, that getting into a pissing contest with the short seller would be a losing proposition, especially with the Flynn memorandum floating around.

***

Noah hurried back to his room at the Waldorf and placed a call to Karen in Chicago.

"Hi, Noah. So, how did it go?" she asked as soon as she heard his voice on the phone.

"Unpleasantly," he replied. "I just know Markanos has seen the Flynn memo, or knows what it says."

"It's a moot point, Noah. The market is down, your stock is down, and all indications are that Markanos is going to look like a genius."

"Why, because he predicted a recession?"

"More or less. The government just released consumer prices for the third quarter. Prices have skyrocketed to an annualized rate of nearly twenty-three percent. That makes Markanos look pretty smart."

"You mean, because he wrote that he thinks our revenue is up because prices are up?"

"Exactly. It stinks that he may have gotten his hands on the Flynn memo, but he was sniffing around the price issue before Flynn wrote his memo. Flynn just confirmed what he suspected was happening."

"Are we getting hit hard?"

"Pretty bad, Noah. All the so-called nifty-fifty stocks are getting pounded."

"What do you think I should do? What's the sense of holding analyst meetings while the sky is falling?"

"Well, you can't cancel your scheduled meetings, Noah. That would be a disaster. There's no time when your presence will be more appreciated than when you're facing the analysts during a bad time. Everybody comes when times are good. They'll appreciate you addressing their concerns when the market is jittery like this."

"I can't give them much comfort."

"Actually, you can. They all know you can't influence the economy, but they'll take comfort in the fact that your leases are the underpinning of your balance sheet. Talk to them about the solid companies that populate your malls. Give them comfort that even if the economy is headed south, your malls are populated by companies with solid balance sheets that are going to be here for the long haul. They're not going to vacate your malls, and they're not going to stop paying rent."

"Well, it's not quite that simple, Karen. Some of our tenants will want to renegotiate those leases. They'll sure as hell resist the automatic rent escalators in their leases. If we're in for a long slog, they'll insist on some rent abatement or accommodation. And when they know there isn't a line of retailers ready to take their space, they'll drive a pretty hard bargain."

"Yeah, you're right, but you're still better off than most."

"Maybe, maybe not, Karen. You know our loan agreements all have material adverse change clauses."

"I don't think a recession would qualify as a material adverse change, Noah."

"Who knows. There isn't a specific definition of a material adverse change. It's whatever a lender says it is. You just referred to our leases as the underpinning of our balance sheet. If our leases come under pressure because of a recession, I could see our bankers calling that a material adverse change."

"What could they do about it?"

"Well, in the worst case, I suppose they could call our loans. That's not very likely, but who knows what they might try to do. For sure, they could try to squeeze a few more basis points out of us."

"And higher interest cost would, of course, affect your earnings."

"And that would affect the price of our stock."

"Which, in turn, would increase the adverse effect on the company."

"Pretty vicious cycle, huh, Karen?"

"Well, it's all speculation, Noah."

"There's one other thing. I personally have a pretty large loan outstanding with Bank Parthenon in Athens."

"They're the banking house that facilitated Alexandra's ransom in Khartoum, aren't they?"

"Yes. We developed a pretty good relationship back then. Anyway, I borrowed twelve million dollars from Parthenon to finance some property I bought over on the Eastern Shore. They might call the loan or ask for better terms if this market sell-off turns serious."

"Can you pay down the loan?"

"Yes, if I sell some stock."

"Potomac Center Properties of America stock?"

"That's the only stock I own."

"Noah, under no circumstances do you want to be selling PCPA stock in a market like this. That would send a terrible signal."

"Yeah, Markanos would love to jump on that, wouldn't he?"

"You know, he has to be very familiar with your loan covenants, Noah. I suspect you'll hear from him inquiring whether or not your bankers are happy."

"Do I have to tell him anything?"

"Not that you haven't told the rest of the Street. Although he'll pick up on anything you say that's evasive. My advice would be to issue a statement if you wind up changing any of your loan terms."

"What's our stock doing now?"

"You sure you want to know?"

"Come on. What's happening?"

"You've lost a little over twenty percent of your market value. You're trading at forty-eight dollars and change. You opened at sixty."

"Funny, I don't feel any poorer."

"It's all paper, Noah. This will be the first recession you've been through as a public company. Don't obsess over each day's stock movement."

"No, of course not. I didn't obsess during the ride up, and I won't obsess during the ride down, if that's what we're in for."

"We're all in uncharted territory, Noah. The greenback is no longer tied to anything. Nixon is still playing with wage-price controls, it looks like we're in for some serious inflation, and who knows where, or at what cost, we're going to get the oil we need to fuel our economy."

"The government predicted three percent inflation at the beginning of the year. That should be manageable."

"Yeah, except our analysts say we're going to be closer to ten percent inflation by the end of the fourth quarter. Government estimates of inflation for the year back in January are going to be way off by the end of the year."

"You sure know how to cheer a guy up, Karen."

"Noah, we should probably arrange for you to meet with one of our high-net-worth financial planners. Your net worth is going to go for a roller-coaster ride. You have all of your wealth and income tied up in PCPA. It has served you well, but we might be in for some real market turbulence for the next several months, and given the personal debt you're carrying, this economy might prove pretty stressful to you personally."

"Karen, I know I should diversify my personal investments, but I can't very well do that with the Street looking over my shoulder and Markanos ready to pounce at the first sign I'm lightening up on my stock in the company."

"Well, hold onto your hat, Noah. PCPA has dropped another seven dollars a share while we've been talking."

"Huh," he murmured, absently, "I've lost fifty million dollars today."

"Well, you made one hundred and fifty million dollars the day you went public. Did you feel that much richer?"

"Not particularly."

"Then don't worry about being fifty million dollars poorer today. It's all noise, Noah."

"God, I wish Alexandra were home. I hate not being able to discuss what's happening with her."

"She'll be home soon enough."

"Yeah, she should be heading back the day after tomorrow."

CHAPTER THIRTY

Noah's net worth, by the end of the day, had been slashed by nearly fifty million dollars. He was losing two-and-a-half million dollars with every one dollar decline in the share price of Potomac Center Properties of America. Noah wasn't particularly worried about the ups and downs of the market and the corresponding fluctuation of his net worth, but his bankers were. By the time he got back to his room at the Waldorf there were urgent messages from his secretary to call.

"Hi, Barb, what's so urgent?"

"Are you kidding? The phone has been ringing off the hook here. Everyone wants to know what's happening with the stock."

"What are you telling them?"

"I'm not telling them anything. I'm transferring them to Marshall Flynn. A few of them insist on talking to you, though."

"Like who?"

"Myron Abrams at Capital City National Bank. He says he's calling as the representative of the banks that are on our line of credit."

"Who else is insisting on talking to me?"

"Some Greek guy from the New York office of Bank Parthenon. He says it's urgent."

"Well, it's too late to call them now. I'll call them in the morning."

"What the hell is happening, Noah?"

"Recession jitters. The market got pounded today and we took a huge hit. We're down thirty bucks a share."

"Thirty dollars a share! That's half of where we closed Friday."

"Yeah, I noticed."

"Are we in trouble?"

"Of course not. But we're a public company, and if the public is bailing on the market we'll take a hit like everyone else."

"But half the value of the stock?"

"Markanos shorted us last night. The market expects retail to go south in any recession, and Markanos said PCPA is a perfect proxy for retail and everyone holding the stock should sell."

"That's terrible."

"Look, we may be in for a bear market, but the market will recover and so will we."

"Is there anything you want me to do?"

"Yes. Stop worrying about the stock. It will be fine."

"Okay. By the way, that reporter from the *New York Times*, Mark Caztaneo, also called. I told him you were at the Waldorf, so he might call you there."

"Oh shit," Noah whispered. "That's trouble."

"I hope it's okay that I told him where you were staying, Noah. He knew you were in New York."

"It's fine, Barb. Like you said, he knows I'm here meeting with analysts. He would have just thought you were being evasive if you hadn't told him where he could reach me."

"That's what I figured."

"Is Marsh still in? If he is, I'd like to talk to him."

"Yes, I think he is. Hold on."

"Flynn," the familiar voice answered.

"Marsh, it's Noah."

"Boy, am I glad you called. That prick Markanos shorted us."

"Stop calling him a prick."

"He is a prick."

"Well, you don't have to put it in writing."

"Oh yeah, my memo to you yesterday. My use of the work *prick* offends you?" he replied, laughing.

"No, but it might have offended George Markanos."

"Well, I promise I didn't copy him on the memo."

"I think he has the memo."

"What? That's impossible."

"Remote, but not impossible. I left the memo on the table at dinner last night at the Waldorf. I think someone on the hotel staff picked it up and somehow got it to Markanos."

"That's ridiculous."

"Yeah, I know, but Markanos grilled me at the meeting this morning, and it sure sounded like he was trying to get me to contradict what was in the memo."

"Nah. Noah, that's really far-fetched."

"It was around eleven o'clock when I left the restaurant, and he rushed out a short recommend on the stock within three hours."

"Noah, if the memo made its way to Markanos, I'm really sorry. I feel terrible."

"He was preparing to short the stock anyway. It's no big deal, but we should assume anything we put in writing might wind up in the *Wall Street Journal* someday, so let's not write anything we wouldn't want to see in the papers."

"Yeah, I should have known better. Did Barb tell you the banks have been calling?"

"Yes, she did. I'll call them first thing in the morning."

"Myron just needs some handholding, but Bank Parthenon might be a problem for you, Noah. They want to call your personal loan."

"All twelve million?"

"Yeah, I think so. Their head of North American Operations, some guy named Papagoulos, said they're liquidating their outstanding personal loans in North America or demanding two dollars of collateral for every dollar outstanding. You haven't paid any principal, so they want to be paid in full or have you put up twenty-four million dollars' worth of PCPA stock."

"We don't know where the stock is going to settle in. The number of shares it will take to collateralize the loan could change day by day."

"Yeah, that's what Papagoulos said too. That's why they thought it might be best just to pay off the loan and be done with it."

"Well, I can't sell that kind of stock in a market like this, and where in the hell am I supposed to find twelve million dollars without selling some stock?"

"I'm sorry, Noah. I don't know what to tell you."

"I'll think of something. Maybe the stock will turn around tomorrow."

"Markanos is making a fortune with his short sale," Flynn said.

"If he based the short on your memo, it's probably illegal as hell."

"Well, with the entire market going south, that would be pretty hard to prove. The prick is a hero."

"Stop calling him a prick."

"Right, sorry. But the shmuck does look pretty smart to the Street right now."

"Goodnight, Marsh."

"Yeah, talk to you tomorrow."

"Marsh, transfer me back to Barb."

"Sure, here goes."

"Mr. Greenspan's office."

"Barb, can you patch me into a call with my father and Alexandra's dad?"

"Sure, Noah, give me a minute."

Noah sat there for a moment thinking about what he had to do next. It took only a couple of minutes before his secretary was back on the line. "Okay, Noah, here you go," she said.

"Hi, Noah, is everything all right? Are you okay?"

"Yes, Dad, I'm fine."

"Hello, Noah. I'm on," Sharif Salaman's voice interrupted.

"Dad, Sharif, I'm sure you've been following the stock today."

"Yes, of course," Sharif answered.

"Sharif and I have been talking about it all day," Hy Greenspan replied. "We saw the short-sell report from that analyst from Deutschland Trust."

"Yes, that's why I'm calling. As you know our stock has been getting pounded all day."

"We're not concerned, Noah," Sharif Salaman replied. "It's probably a good time to buy more PCPA stock."

"Well, here's the thing. I have a twelve-million-dollar loan with Bank Parthenon, and they want me to close it out because of the steep decline in the value of the stock I used as collateral. Obviously, this would be a very bad time for me to sell any of my stock to raise the money. I don't want to borrow the money from any of the banks on our credit line because that would raise questions too."

"You need twelve million dollars then, right?" Sharif asked.

"I do."

"Noah, is it okay for me to sell some of my PCPA stock," his father asked.

"I'd rather you didn't, Dad. That would be sure to get picked up by the business news wires. It wouldn't look good."

"I can advance you the money, Noah. I have about fifteen million in CDs. I'll cash in twelve million of my CDs and transfer the money to your account," Sharif interrupted.

"I've got a couple million in CDs too," Hy Greenspan said. "The rest of my money is in PCPA stock."

"Okay, Hy, if you can transfer two million to Noah, I'll transfer the remaining ten million," Sharif said.

"Thanks, Sharif, Dad. I don't know what to say, but I'll get the money back to you as soon as I can. Once the market settles down I'll arrange a secondary offering to raise some capital. That could take a year or two, depending on market conditions. Meanwhile, I'll have our attorney draw up loan documents for both of you."

"Don't worry about it, Noah. Pay it back whenever you can," Sharif said.

And with that, Noah's immediate problem was resolved by his father and his Palestinian father-in-law.

He sat at the desk in his room and began making a list, prioritizing what he needed to do during the next twenty-four hours. First on the list was to liquidate his loan with Bank Parthenon as soon as his father's and father-in-law's funds transferred to his account. Then he would call Myron Abrams at Capital City and try to calm his nerves. Noah was starting to list the points to make with the analysts at his meetings the following day when the phone rang.

"Noah Greenspan," he answered.

"Hi, Mr. Greenspan. It's Mark Caztaneo over at the *New York Times*."

"Ah, the angel of death."

"Ah, come on, Mr. Greenspan, you're my favorite CEO."

"Yeah, and you're my favorite *New York Times* reporter, but every time you call it's to tell me I'm being sued."

"Well, no one has filed a suit against you that I know of ... yet."

"That's very reassuring, Mark. How can I be of help?"

"I would just like a quote from you for the story I'm writing for tomorrow's paper."

"What story are you writing that involves me or Potomac Center Properties of America?"

"I'm writing the story that is going to say that shares of Potomac Center Properties of America suffered the biggest drop of any public company traded on any stock exchange today."

"You're kidding?"

"No, I'm not. I'm really sorry, Mr. Greenspan. But it seems you won the prize for dropping the farthest into the crapper today."

"Quite an honor," Noah replied.

"Markanos over at Deutschland Trust says you're still way overpriced if we're headed into a recession."

"Prick."

"Can I quote you on that, Mr. Greenspan?"

"No, you can't, Mark. That's off the record."

"You're supposed to tell me something is off the record *before* you say it, Mr. Greenspan."

"Come on Mark, you know …"

"I'm just kidding, Mr. Greenspan, you know, just pulling your chain. I wouldn't quote you calling Markanos a prick."

"I appreciate that, Mark."

"He is a prick though. He's always dumping on stocks he wants to short. He's always snooping around looking for dirt that he can use to recommend shorting a stock. What a way to make a living."

"Well, he makes a lot of money for Deutschland Trust's clients."

"He's a grease ball, if you ask me. You know that creep actually pays bellmen and waiters and maître d's for any negative information they overhear from corporate executives."

Noah froze. "You're kidding?"

"I can't prove it, but that's the scuttlebutt."

"What if you could prove it?"

"That would be one hell of a story. That's the kind of reporting Pulitzers are made of."

"Interesting," Noah thought aloud.

"Anyway, do you have a quote for me?"

"About the decline in the PCPA share price today?"

"Yeah, you should have something to say, don't you think?"

"Sure. You can quote me saying, 'Potomac Center Properties of America expects little if any change in its occupancy rates. We believe our tenants have strong balance sheets and that they, with few if any exceptions, will come through any economic slowdown the country might face.'"

"Got it. What do you have to say about Markanos calling your stock way overpriced?"

"He's entitled to his opinion, but we think he's wrong."

"That's it?"

Noah hesitated as he considered the quote he had just given the reporter. "No. Make that 'we think he's wrong *yet again* about Potomac Center Properties of America.'"

"Ah, that's a good needle you're jabbing him with. He lost big the last time he shorted your stock."

"How bad is the story going to be, Mark?"

"What can I say, Mr. Greenspan? Your stock got murdered today, worse than any other company. There's no way to put a smiley face on that."

"No, of course not."

"Sorry, Mr. Greenspan. I always enjoy talking to you. You're a class act, always have been."

"It's okay, Mark. You do your job. Maybe someday I can help you get that Pulitzer you referred to."

"Good luck tomorrow, Mr. Greenspan. Maybe your stock will bounce back higher than ever."

"You think so?"

"Nah, I think you're probably in for more pounding. Bad news feeds on bad news, and if the papers are full of recession talk, you'll get hit some more I'd guess."

"Have a nice evening, Mark."

"Yeah, you too, Mr. Greenspan."

***

Noah lay down on the bed, eyes focused on the ceiling as he contemplated what he had learned from the newspaper reporter. *Markanos pays waiters, maître d's, bellmen, and who knows who else for snooping and eavesdropping on the conversations of corporate customers. The waiter or maître d' gives him a tip about something they've overheard and he gives them twenty, maybe fifty bucks. Every once in while he gets a tidbit sufficient to short a stock, and he and his clients make a small fortune off of a tidbit of information. That son of a bitch got hold of the Flynn memo. I just know it.*

He was about to drift off when the telephone rang.

"Yeah," he answered, his voice sounding groggy.

"Noah, it's me. Did I wake you?"

"Alexandra!" he answered excitedly. "Alexandra, I'm so happy to hear your voice. What time is it there?" he asked as he sat up on the edge of the bed.

"It's dawn here. I just got back to the hotel in Eilat."

"You just got back?"

"Yes, Noah. The meetings at Kilometer 101 didn't begin until one thirty in the morning. Noah, General Yariv is letting me actually sit in on the meetings. I can't report directly or even take notes, but I'm right there in the tent while the talks are going on. I could almost reach out and touch the negotiators. It's the most exciting assignment I've ever had."

"I'm very excited for you, Alexandra, and I miss you terribly. I can't wait until you're home."

"How are things going in New York?"

Noah started laughing.

"Why are you laughing?"

"You have no idea what's happening here, do you?"

"No, of course not. What *is* happening?"

"Let's just say it's been an eventful day in the market."

"Good eventful or bad eventful?"

He started to laugh again. "God, I love you," he said.

"Were your meetings good?"

"Good as could be expected."

"But?"

"But our stock didn't do so well today. There's a lot of talk of recession, and George Markanos from Deutschland Trust shorted our stock."

"So, we were down today and will probably be up tomorrow. We've been through those kinds of days before."

"Well, not quite like this one," he said.

"How bad?" she asked.

"The stock lost half its value today."

"What do you mean it lost half its value?"

"We opened at sixty and closed at thirty. We own two-and-a-half million shares, so on paper we lost seventy-five million dollars today."

"Oh my God," she answered. "Noah, I'm so sorry. Was the entire market down?"

"Yes, but Potomac Center Properties of America got the raspberry for its shares losing more value than any other public stock in the United States. I'm afraid it's going to be a major story in the *New York Times* business section tomorrow."

"Oh, honey, I'm so sorry. I'm so sorry I'm not there with you."

"There's nothing you could do, Alexandra. We just have to hunker down until the economy settles down."

"Does this impact us in any way, or is it just a matter of waiting out the storm?"

"Well, I just borrowed ten million dollars from your dad and two million from my father."

"Why did you have to do that, Noah?"

"Do you remember the property I bought over on the Eastern Shore? It's a huge parcel that I paid twelve million dollars for."

"Of course I do. It was near Rehoboth, Delaware."

"Well, I borrowed the money from Bank Parthenon in Greece."

"Oh, right. They were the bank that you used to get me out of Khartoum."

"Well, they called the loan because it was collateralized with PCPA stock. I couldn't very well sell any of our stock in this market to raise the money, so I called your dad and my dad."

"And they advanced you the money to pay off the loan."

"Without batting an eye."

"That doesn't surprise me one bit."

"Your folks had fifteen million in CDs and they transferred ten to my account. My dad pretty much emptied his CD account and transferred two million to me. Everything else he has that's liquid is in PCPA stock."

"You've made both families very wealthy, Noah."

"Well, they're a lot less wealthy today. So are we."

"But it will pass, won't it?"

"Absolutely, but it might take quite a while, maybe a year or two if the market dives."

"Are you worried?"

"Nope. But it will probably be nerve wracking for a while if the recession everyone is worried about is severe enough."

"Well, I'm coming back on one of the air force cargo planes following the talks tomorrow night. I'll be home Wednesday."

"How was the trip over?"

"Tiring, but exciting too. Noah, you can't imagine how much the United States is shipping to Israel. These planes are beyond enormous."

"Well, look, you must be exhausted. Try to get as much sleep as you can, Alexandra."

"I will. I love you, Noah. I'm glad I came here, but I can't wait to get home. I sleep a lot better when you're next to me."

"Yeah, me too. I hate being separated. It's unbelievable how much my sense of well-being depends on having you nearby."

"I love you."

"And I you. Get some sleep."

"Goodnight, Noah."

"Goodnight, Alexandra."

***

Room service came with Noah's breakfast promptly at seven the next morning. He snatched the *New York Times* from the serving cart as the waiter rolled it into the room. He turned to the business section and immediately saw the bold headline on the first page and above the fold.

Potomac Center Properties of America Clobbered by Market
By Mark Caztaneo, staff writer

October 30, New York – Noah Greenspan, CEO of Potomac Center Properties of America, picked what turned out to be an unfortunate day to come to New York to meet with analysts. Yesterday, his company's stock scored the greatest decline in share price of any public company traded on any exchange in the United States. Based on the most recent SEC filings, Mr. Greenspan's own holdings in PCPA shares lost $75 million in value yesterday. Mr. Greenspan seemed unrattled by the beating his company's shares took. "Potomac Center Properties of America expects little if any change in its occupancy rates. We believe our tenants have strong balance sheets and that they, with few if any exceptions, will come through any economic slowdown the country might face," he said.

His company's shares are under pressure because of growing concern that the country is sinking into a recession that, according to a number of analysts, might be quite severe. To add insult to injury, Potomac Center Properties of America was also hit with a strong and widely quoted short-sell recommendation by George Markanos of Deutschland Trust. Mr. Markanos is a well-known and widely followed short-sell specialist. He referred to Potomac Center Properties of America as "way overpriced even at thirty dollars a share."

Mr. Greenspan seemed unconcerned by the short seller's strong sell recommendation. "We think he's wrong yet again," the beleaguered CEO said. Mr. Greenspan was referring to the last time Mr. Markanos shorted PCPA and the stock wound up for the day trading at its all-time high.

The consensus among economists seems to be that the economy is in for a long slog. The projections of three percent inflation the Nixon Administration made back in January have turned out to be woefully inadequate, with the current consensus among economists estimating inflation of close to ten percent by year end. "When things cost more, people buy less and that doesn't augur well for retail shopping malls," said Sheldon Skimore of Union Square Financial Management. Boris Gittelsohn of Westlake Securities opined that the prospect of long lines at gas stations if the Arabs really go through with their threatened oil embargo will play havoc with retail in general and shopping malls in particular. "Nobody is going to want to drive anywhere they don't have to drive," he said.

Shares of Potomac Center Properties of America closed at $30.00, down $30.00 from the opening.

CHAPTER

THIRTY-ONE

The doorbell rang as A'isha handed Amos the last piece of the puzzle they had been working on together on the living room floor. It was a cutout of the Statue of Freedom, the female character that sits atop the US Capitol building. Amos smiled as he inserted the piece in place.

"Do you want to pick out another puzzle?" A'isha asked as she got to her feet to see who was at the door. Amos went to his toy chest to pick out another puzzle as A'isha walked from the living room to the front door and pulled it open.

"Hi, I'm Sarah Jean Bogart," the young woman said, putting down her valise and extending her hand to A'isha.

"Oh, we weren't expecting you until this afternoon," A'isha answered, clasping Sarah Jean's hand warmly. "Please come in. You must be exhausted."

"Oh, I'm too excited to be exhausted," she answered, as she entered the foyer. Sarah Jean's Mississippi Delta accent sounded foreign and comical to A'isha, but she was immediately impressed by the young woman's firm handshake and confident manner. She was dressed in jeans, a white blouse under a plain brown button-down cardigan sweater, and scuffed, somewhat worn penny loafers. She also was, A'isha thought, quite pretty. About two inches shorter than A'isha, Sarah Jean had deep blue eyes, a pale, clear, almost luminescent complexion, and light brown hair that she had pulled back in a ponytail. She wore no makeup other than a light pink tint of lipstick.

"Are you Miss Salaman?" Sarah Jean asked, her eyes fixed on A'isha's hijab.

"No, no. I'm A'isha Abadi. I'm the nanny for Amos, the Greenspans' son."

"Is that all one name? That's a mouthful," Sarah Jean answered with a laugh.

"No, no. A'isha is my given name. Abadi is my family name."

"Are you Indian?" Sarah asked, glancing at A'isha's hijab again.

"No," A'isha answered with a broad smile. "Actually, I'm from Michigan, but I was originally from a small town near Hebron … in Palestine. Most of my family is still there. I came here to Washington to accept a job at the Qatari embassy, but it turned out to be a really boring job, so when I saw that the Greenspans were advertising for a nanny I jumped at the chance."

Sara Jean nodded. "So, you're A-rab."

"I am, yes."

"And so is Miss Salaman?"

"Yes. In fact, we were both born in Palestine. She is from Jaffa, near Tel Aviv."

"And Mr. Greenspan is …"

"Jewish," A'isha answered.

"I thought Jews and A-rabs didn't get along. I mean, isn't that what all the fighting is about?"

"Some Jews and some Arabs get along just fine, Sarah Jean."

At that point in the conversation, Amos came through the hall and into the foyer. He moved to A'isha's side and smiled at Sarah Jean.

"My goodness, aren't you the most handsome boy I've ever seen," Sarah Jean said, stooping down and extending her hand to Amos.

"I'm Amos," the boy answered, extending his hand to Sarah Jean.

"Have you ever seen such gorgeous eyes?" she asked to no one in particular.

"Come, let's go into the kitchen," A'isha said. "You must be starved."

"I could use a little something. I don't want you to go to any trouble or anything, but I am a little hungry—maybe a peanut-butter-and-jelly sandwich or somethin'. I made good time. I drove my old Dodge Polara all night to get here early. I have an appointment with Mr. Markazie at the *Star* this afternoon."

"You drove all night?"

"Yes. It was easy until I got to Washington. This city must have been designed by a crazy man or somebody with a strange sense of humor."

"It was designed by someone who thought cities should be easy to evacuate in time of war."

"It looked to me like it was designed by someone who wanted to sit back and watch people go around in circles."

"Come on, I'll show you your room and you can shower and freshen up. You might want to take a nap before you rush off to the *Star*. There's plenty of food in the fridge. You can have peanut butter and jelly if you want, but there's also fresh deli in the fridge too."

***

The telephone in Noah's room rang just as he was about to leave for his first meeting of the day.

"Noah, it's Karen."

"Hi, Karen, what's up?"

"Noah, it's going to be another bad day for PCPA."

"How do you know that? Trading on the exchange doesn't begin for another hour-and-a-half."

"Yeah, well, I just spoke with your floor specialist at the exchange. He has a ton of sell orders queued up for the opening bell and no buy orders. None, Noah."

"So, we're going to get clobbered again?"

"It looks that way."

"Any suggestions, or are you just calling to make me feel bad?"

"Actually, I do have a suggestion you should think about."

"I'm listening."

"What would you think about the company jumping in and buying back its own stock."

"What about our budgeted expansion plans? You think we should be buying our stock rather than real estate? Wouldn't a major stock buy-back signal that we're curtailing our growth plans?"

"Maybe. It could be viewed as a negative, or it could be viewed as seizing the opportunity to own more of your company at bargain basement prices. That could be seen as a very positive sign by the Street."

"I don't know. I have to think about it. I don't like curtailing our growth plans. We have capital budgeted to acquire land for new malls, and this market could also provide an opportunity to buy land for a lot less than we thought it would cost when we budgeted for the year. Let's keep a close eye on the trading today. Maybe we'll step in if the price continues to drop."

"How about giving me buy authorization for the company if the price drops to a predetermined level, say, twenty dollars a share?"

"Let me discuss it with Marshall Flynn and see what he thinks. I'll keep in touch with you or have Marsh call you."

"Okay. Good luck with your meetings today."

"Thanks, Karen."

***

Potomac Center Properties of America opened at twenty-six dollars a share, off thirty-four dollars from the prior day's opening. On paper, Noah had lost eighty-five million dollars in twenty-four hours.

His first meeting of the day was dreadful. Hudson Bay Financial had owned the stock from its first day as a public company. But now they were going to dump the stock. Nothing personal, they told Noah. They just were liquidating what they called their cyclicals, and the past twenty-four hours had convinced them that Potomac Center Properties of America was a very cyclical stock.

Noah asked to use the phone in an empty office and called Myron Abrams at Capital City National Bank as soon as his meeting ended.

Abrams had been Noah's banker from the very beginning. He was always a nervous Nellie, but very loyal to Noah. He was also the lead banker on Potomac Center's loans.

"Myron, it's Noah. I'm sorry it has taken a while to get back to you. As you can imagine it's been a hectic couple of days."

"My phone has been ringing off the hook, Noah. Every bank on your credit line wants to know what's going on."

"Tell them we're setting new records every day," Noah responded.

"Noah, this isn't funny. These aren't the kinds of records bankers want to hear about."

"Myron, we can't do anything about recession jitters. Our operations are humming, but we can't stop investors from running for the hills."

"Isn't there anything you can do to calm the Street?"

"Well, let me run an idea by you. Suppose we jump in today and start buying back our stock? That would show the Street that our confidence in our company is sky high."

"But you would be buying stock at the expense of buying property for expansion."

"It would be a damn good investment. PCPA is worth a hell of a lot more than twenty-six dollars a share."

"Twenty-four dollars a share."

"What?"

"Twenty-four dollars a share. That's what you're selling at right now."

"What do you think?"

"About what?"

"About the company buying back its shares."

"The banks loaned Potomac Center Properties of America money to expand, to buy great real estate, not to buy stock."

"But it would be a great investment. The stock is way underpriced."

"George Markanos thinks it's way overpriced."

"Fuck George Markanos."

"Noah, right now he's the brightest light on the Street. Do you realize how much money he has made for Deutschland Trust and their clients with his short-sell recommendation?"

"So, what do you think our banks will say if we start buying back our shares at these prices?"

"I think they'll probably declare a material adverse change in condition."

"You actually think they would invoke the MAC clause in our loan agreements?"

"You're damn right I do. They would want a hell of a lot more interest on your loans, maybe another point or two."

"That's ridiculous."

"That's reality. Why the hell do you think those MAC clauses are in those loan agreements?"

"Myron, I have to call Marshall Flynn. I'll keep you posted on what we decide to do."

"What should I tell the banks, Noah? They're calling every five minutes."

"Tell them we've seen no adverse effect on our business. Tell them Potomac Center Properties of America has never been in better shape. And tell them we're very appreciative of their support."

"Can I tell them you'll keep them informed if and when you do see any adverse effect on the business?"

"Absolutely."

"Okay. You know I'm in your corner, right, Noah?"

"Right, Myron. You've been there from the very beginning."

Noah hung up and immediately placed a call to his chief financial officer.

"Marshall, what would you think of our starting to buy back our stock?" he asked as soon as Marshall Flynn picked up the phone.

"I'd rather buy real estate."

"I'd like to stop the hemorrhaging."

"You can't be sure it would stop."

"I feel like we have to do something."

"I don't."

"We're getting the shit kicked out of us on the Street."

"It will turn around when the market turns around, Noah."

"What are we trading at now?"

"Twenty-two dollars a share."

"Jesus Christ."

"We have bigger problems than what the stock is selling for today, Noah."

"Like what?"

"Like Brightstar Fine Clothing has notified us that they are not renewing when their lease runs out next February in D.C., and that they are no longer negotiating to be the anchor for our Prince George's County Mall."

"Shit!"

"Forsman Theaters has also dropped out. They said they're not opening any new theaters until they have a better handle on what the economy is going to do in the next couple of years. We were talking to them about space in three of our malls."

"We can't have an empty anchor box."

"Well, I think we're going to have an anchor box without an anchor, Noah."

"This is a catastrophe."

"It's a temporary blip. It will even out as the economy evens out."

"Yeah, but I just told the lead bank on our loans that I would let him know if we saw any adverse effect on our business from all this recession talk."

"Oh boy. What did you tell him that for?"

"What's the difference? I have to tell him what you've just told me."

"We're going to have a MAC invoked, Noah."

"Won't that make a great story on the business pages."

"How many more meetings do you have in New York?"

"Just one. These meetings are torture, Marshall."

"Yeah, I'm sorry, Noah. But really, this is a bad day and it might be a bad year, but we're solid. Any space that winds up being empty will get leased. We've got plenty of staying power. This is our first economic downturn and it won't be our last, but we're strong. This will be a bad memory, but that's all it will be. Don't become obsessed with this awful market we're heading into."

"Yeah, thanks Marshall. I'll be fine. Like you said, we've never been through anything like this before. What is so frustrating is that we couldn't be running a smoother operation, and we're being hammered by events over which we have no control."

"Noah, you know you are the inspiration for our whole management team. You can't let them see you walking around like the world is ending. They're going to take their lead from you. If you're glum, they're going to be glum. When you're confident, they're confident."

"Yeah, I understand. Thanks, Marsh."

Noah hung up the phone and sat there for a moment with his head in his hands. *God, I wish Alexandra were here,* he thought. *I would give anything to just be able to hold her in my arms tonight.*

Noah breathed a long sigh and reached for the phone to call Myron Abrams back.

"Myron, it's Noah. Do you have a minute?"

"Twenty dollars a share, Noah. That's where you're trading now. Just in case you didn't know."

"Look, I said I would keep you informed of any adverse effect the bad economic news is having on our business. Well, Brightstar isn't going to renew their lease, and Forsman Theaters is going to wait out the storm before committing to any new leases."

"I'm sorry, Noah. I really am, but you know I'll have to inform the banks. Capitol City National is the lead bank, and I'm the banker who is responsible for keeping all the banks on the credit line informed."

"Yeah, I know, Myron. We've always been straight with one another and I certainly wanted to be straight with you now. We're in for some rough sledding, but the company is in solid shape, Myron. We may not grow like we thought we were going to grow nine months ago, but we're solid."

"I know that, Noah. Thanks for the heads-up."

***

It took only two hours before the story ran across the business news wire.

Banks Invoke MAC Clause on PCPA

A consortium of six banks led by Capital City National Bank have invoked the material adverse change clause in their loan agreements with Potomac Center Properties of America. This action followed a precipitous drop in the price of the company's shares, which closed at twenty dollars a share today, down forty dollars from the opening yesterday. Invoking the so-called MAC clause is certain to require renegotiation of the banks' loan agreements with the mall developer. The drastic drop in the price of the company's stock followed a short-sell report by George Markanos, the noted short-sell analyst at Deutschland Trust. Markanos, commenting on the banks' decision to invoke the MAC clause, said "the banks exercised the right judgment because Potomac Center Properties of America is a much more cyclical company than they realized, and the mall developer never deserved the high nifty-fifty multiple the Street was according it." Markanos went on to say he believed the company's management was worried about how the company would fare in a recession, but they never disclosed that concern to analysts. He said he thought the company was still overpriced at twenty dollars a share. "The banks are certain to demand a higher rate of interest from Potomac Center Properties of America, and that will adversely affect the company's bottom line," he said. "The banks might also demand some accelerated pay-down of their loans with Potomac Center, which would adversely affect the firm's development plans." Markanos predicted that the share price of PCPA could settle in at about ten to twelve dollars a share, which he thought would be about where it belonged. "The market ultimately reveals what a company is worth, and we'll soon see what the market thinks Potomac Center Properties of America is worth," he said.

Noah sat in the back of the taxi taking him to the Eastern Shuttle terminal at LaGuardia rereading the business wire story. Markanos was pounding away at him and the company and there wasn't a thing he could do about it. His net worth had declined by one hundred million dollars in less than two days, and if Markanos had his way Noah would be down one hundred and twenty-five million by noon the next day. He couldn't wait to get home, to be with his son and to await Alexandra's return from the Middle East. When he was with her, he felt he had everything that mattered. Without her, it sometimes seemed there was nothing much that did matter.

CHAPTER
THIRTY-TWO

Alexandra studied the terrain below as the helicopter crossed into Sinai air space from Eilat to take them to the second day of negotiations at Kilometer 101. The landscape was one of desolation. Nothing but sand and occasional rock outcroppings as far as the eye could see. Swirls of small sand spouts danced below them here and there as desert wind currents whipped through the area. Their flight path took them over the same road they had traversed the day before, across the Sinai from Eilat and through the Mitla Pass and on to Suez City. The hulks of Egyptian trucks and tanks, undisturbed from the prior day's flyover, were testament to the fighting that had taken place below them only days earlier. She had been told that the greatest tank battle since World War Two had taken place directly below them. But the scene was deathly quiet now. *How many dead are lying in the sand below us?* she wondered. It had to be thousands.

Alexandra and Amos walked directly to the tent at Kilometer 101 as soon as they landed, took their seats, and awaited the arrival of the two generals. General Yariv and his team arrived first, followed moments later by General el-Gamasy and the Egyptians. General Yariv stood and he and General el-Gamasy shook hands, a bit stiffly, Alexandra thought.

As the two men took their seats General Yariv gestured with a friendly sweep of an arm to General el-Gamasy that the Egyptian should begin.

"We have considered your proposal, and as I said yesterday, it was a constructive one. However, you will recall that I also mentioned that I saw some problems with it from our point of view. I'm afraid, upon thorough consideration, that we cannot accept your proposal. We have fought a war, General Yariv, and our forces, at great cost and considerable loss of life, liberated much of our land that your forces had illegally occupied since nineteen sixty-seven. Your proposal would require that we relinquish all that we achieved in the liberation of our own land. We cannot do that. I, as the commanding officer of all Egyptian ground forces, cannot recommend that and, politically, the people of Egypt would never stand for it."

"What we proposed, General el-Gamasy, was a mutual withdrawal. We would abandon our positions west of the Canal simultaneously with Egypt abandoning its position east of the Canal. My proposal was entirely reciprocal."

"But General, you yourself proposed that in a subsequent disengagement our forces would reoccupy the East Bank of the Canal as your forces withdrew further east. Inasmuch as you propose that we eventually reoccupy an area to the east of the Canal, what sense does it make for you to insist that we move our forces to the west side of the Canal only to have them return to the east side a bit later? Instead, I would propose that Israel, at this time, agree to a symbolic withdrawal of its forces from the west side of the Canal to the east side of the Canal. You have thousands of men on the west side of the Canal. Withdraw a few thousand meters to the East side of the Canal. That would establish intent and show good faith."

"In return for which Egypt would withdraw an equal number of its forces from the east side of the Canal?"

"General Yariv, we have no intention of withdrawing any of our forces from Egyptian land. The Sinai, all of it, is Egypt. Your forces do not belong in the Sinai, and we are not going to abandon any of the land we have liberated. That is not a reasonable thing for you to ask us to do and we cannot do it."

"Well, I think we are at a deadlock, General el-Gamasy. We can be very patient, but we cannot ignore the facts on the ground. We are taking great care not to take advantage of our position on the battlefield in the interest of reaching an understanding with your country."

"General Yariv, both sides have agreed to a ceasefire and you have agreed to allow non-military supplies to our Third Army, but your forces have made resupply unreasonably slow, and that is unreasonably endangering the men of our Third Army."

"We are anxious to make any reasonable modifications to procedure to expedite delivery of food, water, and medical supplies to your Third Army. We are, however, very disappointed that you have been unable to supply us with any information about Israeli troops who you are holding as prisoners of war. We see no reason why we should not be exchanging prisoners of war. As I said yesterday, that is our most important issue."

"I do have a list of forty-five wounded Israeli prisoners. We will agree to an immediate exchange of wounded prisoners of war."

"Well, that is something on which we can agree. I understand we are holding around seventy-five seriously wounded Egyptian troops."

Alexandra leaned toward Amos. "It sounds like Yariv's plan for a mutual withdrawal of Egyptian and Israeli forces from the East and West Banks of the Canal is dead in the water," she whispered.

"It seems that way. They're shifting to other issues."

"General Yariv, it appears we can make progress on the prisoner of war issue, which, as you say, is your most important issue. The welfare of our prisoners is, of course, of great concern to us as well, but our most pressing immediate issue is that of our Third Army. We are concerned that there are those on the Israeli side who do not consider the welfare of our Third Army to be of great concern. We have information that there are those on your side who would welcome a return to hostilities and who would be eager to attack the weakened forces of our Third Army."

"General el-Gamasy, there is probably no other army in the world other than the Israeli Army that would even be discussing the supply of aid to an enemy army that it had trapped after that army had attacked and inflicted such heavy losses."

"So, you are telling me that your fellow generals are all in agreement that our Third Army should be resupplied?"

"No, I am telling you that *I* am in agreement, and that *I* am the only general who is speaking for the Israeli government."

"And your government is in agreement that our Third Army should be resupplied?"

"That is correct. As long as the ceasefire is respected and maintained, no harm will come to your Third Army."

"And you will move your forces back to the October twenty-second lines?"

"There are no such lines, General el-Gamasy. The lines are where the lines are."

"No. The lines must be where they were when the UN called for the ceasefire that both sides agreed to."

"Please, General el-Gamasy. Your forces did not comply with the UN ceasefire."

"Nor did your forces, General Yariv."

"Our forces fought back valiantly and aggressively, and now the fronts are quiet and the lines are where they are."

"General Yariv, why don't we cut to the chase, as they say. We both know sooner or later my country and your country will find some modus vivendi. We can start that process now. Why don't you move your forces to a line, say, thirty-five miles east of the Canal, and we'll keep our forces close to the East Bank of the Canal. Once we have demonstrated that neither side plans aggression against the other, Israel can abandon the rest of the Sinai. We can agree to a generally demilitarized Sinai, other than whatever forces we might need for general security purposes."

"That is certainly a meaningful and interesting proposal, General el-Gamasy, but you know perfectly well that neither of us has the authority, sitting here in this tent at Kilometer 101, to undertake such an initiative. That is something that can only be decided upon by our governments in Cairo and in Jerusalem."

"Or, perhaps, in Washington," General el-Gamasy replied. "Our Foreign Minister Fahmy is on his way to Washington now, and I understand that your Prime Minister Meir will follow shortly thereafter."

"Yes, I will be leaving for Washington with her," General Yariv answered. "General Eyal and General Tal will sit in for me here for a couple of days. I will return to these talks around the fourth or fifth of November, and I promise I will have discussed what you have said directly with Prime Minister Meir. Meanwhile, we would like assurance from you that you will lift the blockade at Bab-el-Mandeb."

"First things first, General. When we know our Third Army is no longer in peril we'll deal with Bab-el-Mandeb. Our men are in need of food, water, and medical supplies, which, to us, is more important than your need for Iranian oil."

"We have committed to allowing non-military supplies through to the Third Army and we are doing everything we can to expedite the process."

"Then I can assure you the shipping lanes will be opened accordingly."

***

"So, what do you think?" Alexandra asked as she and Amos made their way to the helicopter for the flight back to Eilat.

"Nothing much is going to happen until Yariv has been with Golda in the United States and we know exactly what the Americans want us to do. When all is said and done, Kissinger will determine how this all ends."

"Well, that should be good for Israel. The United States now has a huge investment in Israel's survival."

"The United States stopped Russia from determining the outcome of this war. The Americans have been adamant, however, that Israel is not going to dictate the peace. Israel is focused on the short game. Utterly defeating the Egyptians. Kissinger is focused on the long game."

"What is the long game, Amos?"

"A process to end the cycle of fighting between Egypt and Israel. We have fought four wars in twenty-five years. If Kissinger thinks Sadat wants to end the perpetual state of belligerency, then that will be his focus."

"That would be good, wouldn't it?"

"Yes, of course, but it's going to be hard to convince Israel to look beyond the moment. Our people have fought back from near defeat and now have the enemy in a choke hold. The Americans will tell us this is the time to play nice. Golda has to contend with Dayan and Elazar and Sharon, and believe me, none of them will want to play nice, nor will our people who lost loved ones in this war, which is nearly everyone."

"What do you think is going to happen?"

"Whatever Nixon and Kissinger want to happen."

"What about Sadat?"

"Sadat will be easier to convince than Golda."

CHAPTER
THIRTY-THREE

The telephone rang at the Greenspan home in Georgetown just about the time the helicopter lifted off at Kilometer 101 to take Alexandra and Amos back to Eilat.

"Greenspan residence," A'isha answered.

"A'isha, praise be to Allah that you answered. You must come right away."

A'isha recognized Ahmed Sayed Kahn's voice. "Ahmed, is that you?"

"Yes, yes, it is me. You must come. It's your family in Hebron. There is trouble and they are going to call me shortly. You should be here."

"Trouble? What kind of trouble? I don't understand."

"I can't talk about it on the phone. You must come."

"I can't come now. I'm alone with the child. There is no one else here."

"Bring the child with you. It shouldn't take that long."

"But he'll need to have dinner soon. We have a guest staying here at the house. She works at the paper. Can't this wait until she returns from work and I can ask her to stay with Amos?"

"No, no, A'isha. You must come now and be here for the call from Hebron. Bring a snack or something for the child. You'll probably have him home by dinnertime. I don't think the call will take much time."

"Who is going to call? What has happened? What kind of trouble are you talking about?"

"We're wasting time, and you should be here when the call comes from Hebron. Your family may be in big trouble. I can't talk about it on the phone."

"You're at the embassy?"

"No, no, you must come to my apartment. I'm calling from home."

"Where is your apartment?"

A'isha reached for a pad on the counter and grabbed a pen to write down Ahmed Sayed Kahn's address.

"Amos!" she called into the living room. "Come, we have a little errand to run." A'isha grabbed a box of Klondike Pete's Crunchy Nuggets as a snack in case Amos got hungry before they returned for dinner. She helped Amos into a jacket and threw on her Burberry trench coat, and she and the boy hurried down to Wisconsin Avenue, where A'isha hailed one of the taxis heading north.

Ahmed Sayed Kahn opened the door as soon as she arrived at his apartment and urged her and Amos in.

"Come quick, the call should come any minute."

"Ahmed, what is this all about? What kind of trouble is my family in?"

"Big trouble. Come with me to my office and we'll wait for the call."

A'isha held Amos's hand and followed Ahmed Sayed Kahn to a room at the end of a long hall. The door to the room was open and he stood aside so that she and the boy could enter. A'isha moved quickly into the room and gasped at the sight. The room was bare except for two cots and two folding chairs. There were no windows, and the walls and ceiling were covered with acoustic tiles. She spun around to confront Ahmed Sayed Kahn in time to see the door slam shut and hear the click of the dead bolt.

"Ahmed, are you crazy?" she shouted. Amos, wide-eyed with fear, began to cry.

"You needn't shout, A'isha. No one can hear you," his voice said through an intercom. "No harm is going to come to you or the boy. You will both have to be my guests for a short time. That is all. I have provisions for food. There are blankets, and there is a toilet through the other door in the room. It is very small, but sufficient. I suggest that you keep the boy calm. Your stay here should be very brief."

"Why are you doing this, Ahmed?" she shouted. "Do you realize what could happen to you?"

"A'isha, why are you asking such silly questions? Do you realize what could happen to you and the boy if you do not do as I say? Now, be quiet and keep the boy quiet. I have no intention of harming you. As I said, you and the boy will have to be my guests for a short time. I intend no harm to you."

"Is the Qatari embassy having you do this, Ahmed. Why? Why are they doing this?"

"The embassy has nothing to do with this, A'isha. Nothing!"

"Then why are you doing this?" she shouted. There was no answer. She simply heard the intercom click off. A'isha held Amos tightly and tried to console him. "It's only a game, Amos. Don't be frightened. I'm with you. It's only a silly game."

"I ... I ... don't like this game," he managed to say between sobs. "I want to go home."

"So, do I, Amos. So do I."

"I don't want to sleep here," he cried.

She hugged him tightly. "Neither do I," she whispered. "We'll be home soon." A'isha wanted to scream for help, but she was afraid it would terrify Amos, and she saw that the room had been constructed with soundproofing material. She had no idea why Ahmed Sayed Kahn was doing this, but she knew it couldn't continue very long. The thought crossed her mind that Ahmed was involved in a kidnapping scheme. Perhaps someone wanted to demand a ransom for Amos.

***

"Yoo-hoo," Sarah Jean shouted as she let herself into the Greenspan house. "Anybody home?" *Huh?* she thought. *That's strange. A'isha said she would be fixing dinner for Amos about now.*

Sarah Jean removed her windbreaker and hung it in the foyer closet. She walked into the kitchen and noticed the door to the cabinet where cereals were stored was wide open. Sarah Jean looked into the living room and saw an unfinished puzzle spread out on the floor. An *Evening Star* note pad that had been stacked with a few other similar pads at the corner of the kitchen counter was instead next to the phone. A ballpoint pen that had been snatched from an *Evening Star* mug that held several other pens and pencils was lying next to the pad. She could make out an impression on the pad from a scribble that she assumed A'isha had made before tearing off the top page. Just to make sure she pulled a pencil from the mug and ran it lightly over the top page of the pad. *1973 AM* was all that had been written on the prior page.

Hmmm, she thought. *1973 probably was the year. AM could stand for morning. Or maybe 1973AM was a radio station.* Sarah Jean walked over to the radio sitting on the corner of the counter. The AM dial stopped at 1700. Just then the telephone rang.

"Greenspan residence," she answered. "This is Sarah Jean Bogart."

"Hello, Sarah Jean. I've heard very nice things about you. This is Yusuf Salaman. I'm Alexandra's brother. May I please speak to A'isha?"

"She's not here, Mr. Salaman. She and Amos must have gone out."

"Huh, that's strange," he answered. "She and Amos are always there at this hour."

"Yeah, but they're not here now. Do you want me to give A'isha a message when she and Amos return?"

"No, I'll try a little later. They didn't leave a note or anything?"

"No, but it looks like they left in a hurry. One of the kitchen cabinets was wide open, and there's a half-done puzzle on the living room floor. I haven't been here that long, but everything always seems neat as a pin."

"You're right. Their house always is neat as a pin. It sounds like she must have run out to buy something. Maybe she was out of something she was going to make for dinner."

"Yeah, that's what I was thinking too. Do you want me to have her call you when she and Amos get back?"

"Yes, would you? I'd appreciate that."

"Sure, Mr. Salaman."

Sarah Jean hung up the phone and walked through the entire house. Everything seemed in order, neat as a pin—except for the unfinished puzzle on the living room floor and the door of the kitchen cabinet that had been left wide open.

**

Alexandra and Amos arrived back at their hotel in Eilat and went directly to the dining room to order dinner before the restaurant closed for the evening.

Too tired to order a full dinner, Alexandra settled for a plate of hummus and pita with an assortment of cold vegetables on the side. Amos ordered shawarma, a Middle Eastern version of gyros, marinated lamb slowly roasted for hours on a spit.

"Well, I'm glad I came," she said as soon as they ordered. "I'm ready to go home in the morning, but I wouldn't have missed this for anything."

"You're one lucky journalist, Alexandra. These are historic talks. Maybe the most important in the history of the region."

"Having actually met General Yariv and having watched him and General el-Gamasy negotiate with one another gives me a perspective no other journalist will ever have about this slice of history."

"True. Most of the journalists and historians who write about these talks in the future will have never laid eyes on men like General Yariv and General el-Gamasy, let alone sat and observed them for hours as you have."

"I think Israel is at a defining moment."

"How so?"

"It's unimaginable to me that the Israeli generals who fought in this war, which doesn't include General Yariv because he was already retired, can stand by and let an invading army that they have trapped just go free with all its men, equipment, and weapons. When has that ever happened in warfare?"

"I have confidence in our democracy, Alexandra. We have civilian control of our country, just as you have in the United States. These generals you speak of aren't going to Washington to meet with Kissinger and Nixon. Golda Meir is. She can come out of those meetings with the United States as a strong ally. She may have to swallow hard and let the Egyptian Third Army go, but that will be her call, and I don't think any of our generals, not Dayan, not Elazar, and not even Sharon, will interfere. None of them were asked to accompany the Prime Minister, only General Yariv was. That's what I call *a tell,* Alexandra. Meir is determined to build on Israel's relationship with America. She's not going to let her generals' desire to annihilate the Egyptian Third Army ruin this new American-Israeli relationship. If the Americans say the Third Army is not to be molested or humiliated, that will be the end of it."

"What will Sadat have accomplished with all this bloodshed?"

"I think he'll eventually get his Sinai back, and I think he'll reestablish a relationship with the United States. Sadat can't stand the Russians, and he certainly doesn't want them back. Meanwhile, Kissinger has emerged as the savior of the Israelis and of the Egyptian Third Army. He's put the United States in the best position it has ever been in with regard to both Egypt and us. Quite a feat."

"Do you know if you'll be flying back with me tomorrow?"

"Yes, Ambassador Dinitz wants me in Washington while Prime Minister Meir and General Yariv are there."

"Do you think you'll come back here when the Prime Minister and General Yariv return?"

"I don't know. It will be up to Ambassador Dinitz. He'll probably decide where he wants me based on how the talks with Meir and Yariv go."

Alexandra and Amos finished dinner and chatted over coffee for a few extra minutes before leaving the restaurant. "I'll sleep well tonight," she said. "It's late and I'm absolutely exhausted."

"I'm going to run down to the docks. I understand that the blockade at Bab-el-Mandeb has ships backed up all over the harbor. I heard that ZIM Shipping has a dozen ships stranded there. I'll want to report, first hand, to Ambassador Dinitz just how bad the situation is at the port."

"We'll meet for breakfast in the morning?"

"Yes, the C-5 we're on is scheduled to depart Lod at nine. We should probably plan to leave here at seven."

"I'll be ready," she said and quickly embraced him. "I can never thank you enough for making this trip possible for me."

"We have done some interesting things together, haven't we?"

"You are a master of understatement, Amos Ben-Chaiyim."

"Goodnight, Alexandra. Sleep well, and I'll see you here in the lobby at seven."

Alexandra went up to her room and thought of calling home, but she realized that it would probably be at least an hour or so before Noah arrived back from New York. She knew he was planning to catch a late afternoon shuttle back to Washington following his meetings with analysts.

I hope today was a better day for him and Potomac Center, she thought. Alexandra sat down at the small desk in her room and pulled her wallet from the pocket of the fatigues she wore. She opened it and slowly flipped through the few photographs it held. She lingered for a moment on a color picture of her and Noah and their son, Amos. Their son was so beautiful, she thought, smiling at the photograph. The child seemed, to her, to be a picture of innocence. His smile was so joyous, and it accentuated the dimples he'd inherited from Noah. But his big dark eyes and his wavy black hair—there was no mistaking the Salaman in him. She brought the photograph up to her lips and gently kissed it. *See you tomorrow my darlings,* she whispered.

The telephone rang a moment later.

"Hello," she answered. "Noah, is it you?"

"Hello, Alexandra," the voice on the other end responded.

She froze. She knew the voice, and it terrified her.

"You must listen to me very carefully, Alexandra. Do you know who this is?"

She couldn't speak. She fought to catch her breath as a wave of nausea swept through her.

"Alexandra, you must listen to me. You must listen to me, Alexandra, or very bad things will happen very quickly."

Alexandra couldn't respond, nor could she think straight. She sat there, phone to her ear, as she tried to control her breathing, which had become rapid and labored.

"Do you know who this is, Alexandra?"

"Yes," she answered, feebly.

"Who are you talking to, Alexandra?"

"Omar. Omar Samir," she barely managed to say.

"Now, you must do exactly as I say, Alexandra. There is a black car across the street from the hotel. You must go to the car and get in the front seat next to the driver and do exactly what the driver tells you to do."

"You're insane," she managed to answer into the phone. "I'm calling for help."

"No, of course you won't, Alexandra. Why would you do such a terrible thing to your son?"

"My son? Are you crazy?"

"Oh no, Alexandra. I'm not crazy at all. I want to protect your son."

"You are crazy."

"Am I? You've known me for a long time, Alexandra. Do you think I'm crazy?"

"I'm not leaving this hotel. I'm going to hang up and call hotel security."

"Of course you're not going to do that. That would kill your son. Why would you do such a terrible thing to such a young child? I thought you loved him?"

"You're insane. My son is safe in our home in Washington."

"Is he?"

Alexandra's breathing became even more labored, more rapid.

"Yes, he is at home and safe."

"You mean with A'isha?"

Alexandra gasped. She couldn't speak.

"You think he is safe with his nanny A'isha, A'isha Abadi? She is one of us, you fool."

Alexandra was too shocked to speak, too short of breath to scream. She could hear the sound of her own panting against the mouthpiece of the phone.

"You have exactly seven minutes to be in the black car waiting across the street from the hotel. If you are not there in seven minutes you will never see your son again. Indeed, no one will ever see him again. He will cease to exist in eight minutes. I know you will try calling home. In fact, I encourage you to do that. That should take only about two minutes. That will leave five minutes for you to get to the car." Then there was a click and the phone went silent.

Alexandra brought her hands to her face and began to sob. Then she saw her wallet lying on the desk in front of her. There she saw the picture of her and Noah and Amos. Amos, so full of life, such joy on his face.

Alexandra reached for the phone and dialed the operator.

"Can I help you?" the voice said.

"Yes, this is an emergency," she cried. "You must place an immediate call to my home in America … in Washington D.C. You must do it right away. I'll talk to anyone who answers."

"Hang up. I have the number. I'll call you as soon as I have placed the call. It might take a few minutes."

"This is an emergency, a matter of life and death," Alexandra screamed into the phone.

"Hang up. I'll call you as soon as I have your party on the line," the operator answered.

Alexandra sat there motionless, unable to comprehend what was happening. She looked at her watch. She had no idea how much time had elapsed. She just watched the second hand sweeping around the dial. She stared at the phone, which sat there silent and ominous. Her eyes darted to her watch. The second hand continued to sweep relentlessly around the dial.

"Oh God, please don't let them hurt my baby," she murmured.

The phone began to ring and she snatched the handpiece from the cradle. "Yes," she screamed.

"Alexandra, is that you? This is Sarah Jean."

"Oh, thank God. Sarah Jean, let me speak to A'isha right away."

"She's not here, Alexandra."

"She not there? Is Amos there?"

"No, Alexandra, neither one of them is here."

Alexandra could hear the pounding of her heart reverberating in her ears. "Do you know where they are, Sarah Jean?"

"No, they were not here when I returned from the *Star*."

"Did A'isha leave a note saying where they were? They're always home at this hour."

"I thought it was strange that no one was here so close to dinnertime."

"Is there anything unusual that you can see?"

"Well, there is something a little unusual, I guess. There was an unfinished puzzle on the living room floor, and I know this isn't anything to make a big deal over, but one of the kitchen cabinets was hanging wide open. I noticed it right away, because I can see that you keep your house neat as a pin, like everything seems in place in your home. It sort of looked to me like A'isha and Amos left in a hurry."

"Oh my God," Alexandra cried aloud. "Oh my God."

"What is it, Alexandra? What's happened?"

"Has Mr. Greenspan called?"

"No, he said he might be home late for dinner, depending on what shuttle he was able to catch from New York."

"Sarah Jean, call the police and call the FBI. Find Agent Larry Hogan. Tell them our son has been kidnapped and that A'isha Abadi took him from our home."

"What? What are you saying, Alexandra? Are you sure you want me to do that?"

Alexandra looked at her watch again. She saw only that several minutes had gone by.

"Alexandra?"

"Do it!" she screamed. Alexandra slammed down the phone and raced from the room. She knew at least five minutes had elapsed, maybe more. She ran through the lobby and out the front entrance. She spotted the black car parked across the street from the hotel and dashed across the street. The driver of the car stared at her as she ran toward him.

"Get in!" he shouted as she approached the car.

"Get in!" he shouted again as she hesitated.

"Where are you taking me?" she cried out as he sped away. He did not answer. He just looked straight ahead as he drove.

"Have they hurt my baby?" she begged the driver.

"Sit quietly," he snapped. "No one wants to hurt your baby. Just do as you are told."

"Where are you taking me? Are they going to kill me?"

"No one wants to kill anyone. They just want to talk. Don't ask me any more questions. Just sit quietly."

They drove, in silence, for several minutes north toward the Negev.

"What is happening?" Alexandra finally screamed. "Why are you doing this?"

The driver, without warning, turned and slapped Alexandra hard across the face with the back of his hand. "Do not say another word!" he shouted. "Don't you realize what they are capable of if you anger them?"

Alexandra was too shocked to cry out. She sat there, stunned, holding the side of her face, trying to comprehend what was happening. Then, shortly after they left the city limits, the driver pulled over onto the dirt shoulder of the road. There was no traffic coming toward Eilat or leaving the city. It was after midnight and the road was deserted.

The driver reached across Alexandra and opened the glove compartment of the car. He withdrew a black cloth hood.

"Put this over your head," he commanded.

"No, I won't. Please don't make me do that."

"You will pull this over your head. Everything depends on you doing exactly what we tell you to do."

"I can't. I won't. Look, I've come as you've demanded. I'm not going to run away."

"Miss Salaman, you will do exactly as I ask. We are in control. It is not anyone's intention to harm you or the boy, but you know we will, like that," he said, snapping his fingers. "Why would you endanger your son because of something as simple as pulling that hood over your head?"

Alexandra nodded. "Please don't hurt my son," she cried softly, as she pulled the hood over her head. "Please don't hurt him."

Alexandra sat there in the car trying to control her breathing, which had become more labored with the hood covering her head. Then suddenly the driver grabbed her left hand, and holding her hand tightly in his grip, he snapped a handcuff over her wrist.

"No," she screamed, as he grabbed her right hand and she felt the metal dig into her flesh as the other handcuff snapped into place.

"Shut up," the driver commanded. "Be quiet. We have a two-hour drive and I don't want to hear another word from you."

Alexandra sat there, head bowed, crying softly as the car continued driving into the Negev desert. Her world had turned upside down in a matter of minutes. Somehow, incomprehensibly, she was a prisoner—as was, it appeared, her child. She knew Omar Samir, or any of his colleagues, would kill her son, Amos, without batting an eye. He was the child of a Jewish man and a woman they considered to be a traitor. She assumed they also knew the child's name and that he was named after the Mossad agent they detested, the man who had foiled a plot they had meticulously planned for months and the man they held responsible for the death of their sheik, Ali Abdul Shoukri.

CHAPTER THIRTY-FOUR

Noah, anxious to get home in time to see Amos before A'isha put him to bed, hurried from the shuttle into the terminal. He spotted Daoud as soon as he exited the jetway and immediately saw the two men standing with him.

"Is there a problem?" he asked as he approached Daoud and the two men.

"Mr. Greenspan, I'm Detective Bollinger of the Metropolitan Police Department. This is Detective Greely," the man said.

"What's the problem?" Noah asked.

"Let's move over to the side of the terminal, where we can speak privately," Detective Bollinger answered.

"What is it?" Noah asked as they moved out of the flow of passengers rushing in and out of the terminal.

"We think your son may have been kidnapped and your wife may be in some trouble in Israel. We're assuming you might be in danger as well, and that's why we're here."

"The police had me paged here in the terminal, Mr. Noah. That's why they were waiting with me at the gate when you got off the plane," Daoud said.

"You think my son has been kidnapped? Is that what you are telling me?" Noah asked, panic in his voice.

"Yes, that seems to be what has happened, Mr. Greenspan. We're here to escort you home. There are other officers at your home, as well as some FBI agents. We're taking this very seriously. We think it would be best if you drove with us."

"Do you know … do you know if he was hurt?" Noah asked, trying to maintain his composure.

"We have no indication that anyone was hurt, but we really don't know."

"We think we should get you home, Mr. Greenspan."

"Yes, I'll come with you."

"I come too, Mr. Greenspan. I follow you home. Anything you need me to do, I'll be right there to do it," Daoud said.

Noah nodded. "Yes, thank you, Daoud."

"How did anyone get to my son?" Noah finally asked. "He's never alone."

"I think the officers and agents who are at your home will have more information," the detective answered.

"Was A'isha hurt?"

"That's your son's nanny?" Detective Bollinger asked.

"Yes. She would never leave him alone."

"She's missing too," Mr. Greenspan.

"They were both kidnapped?"

"Really, the officers and agents at your home will know more than we do."

Noah nodded.

∗∗∗

Noah recognized FBI Special Agent Hogan as soon as he walked into the kitchen, where everyone was gathered.

"Hello, Mr. Greenspan. It's been a long time. I'm sorry we're meeting again under such terrible circumstances," Agent Hogan said as he approached Noah to shake his hand. "The Bureau assigned this case to Agent Atkins and me because of the work we did involving your company back in nineteen sixty-eight."

"Mr. Greenspan, I'm Sarah Jean Bogart. I'm Miss Salaman's new assistant at the *Star*."

"Of course, of course. My wife told me all about you. Can someone tell me what we know?" Noah asked as he shook Agent Hogan's hand.

"Miss Bogart here called us. Why don't you go over what you've told us?" Agent Hogan said, looking to Sarah Jean.

"I came home from the *Star* and the house was empty. It looked like Noah and his nanny left in a hurry. There was an unfinished puzzle on the living room floor and that cabinet where the cereals are kept was wide open," she said, pointing to the still open cabinet door.

"And that's why everyone thinks they've been kidnapped?" Noah asked.

"No, there's more, Mr. Greenspan," Sarah Jean, continued. "Your wife called from Israel about an hour after I got home and found the house empty. She asked for A'isha, and when I told her she and Amos were gone, she sort of broke down. She said to call the police and to call Special Agent Hogan at the FBI. Then she just hung up like she was in a big panic. I mean, really in a hurry."

"And that's all we know?" he asked, his voice strained and pleading.

"There was a strange note by the phone. Actually, it was an impression from a note that had been ripped off the pad," Sarah Jean replied.

"We don't think it means anything. At least, anything we can make sense of," Agent Hogan interrupted.

"No disrespect, sir," Sarah Jean answered, "but I sure as hell think it means something. The pad was sitting by the telephone and the ballpoint pen was lying next to it. I think she wrote on that pad, dropped the pen, and ran with Amos from the house."

"We can't make anything of the note. It doesn't seem to tell us anything."

"What did it say?" Noah asked.

"It just had the year, nineteen seventy-three, and the letters AM next to the year. That's all. The telephone company is trying to trace where the call originated. That might tell us something," Agent Hogan answered.

"My God, I can't believe this is happening," Noah said, his voice shaken.

"Mr. Greenspan, how did you find the woman you hired as your boy's nanny?" Agent Hogan asked.

"She answered an ad in the help wanted section of the *Evening Star*," Noah replied.

"Did you check her references?"

"She worked at the Qatari embassy. She said she was very bored with her job and she was familiar with my wife's writing at the *Star* and wanted to apply for the job."

"Did you and your wife interview her?"

"Actually, I interviewed her before my wife did. She's a very impressive young woman."

"Her name is A'isha Abadi?"

Noah nodded. "Yes, that's her name."

"She's an Arab woman?"

Noah nodded. "Yes, she's from Palestine."

"Given the circumstances of our last time together, I'm a bit surprised you would hire an Arab woman to look after your child," Agent Hogan said.

"I'm married to an Arab woman, for God's sake, Agent Hogan," Noah answered impatiently. "I can't believe A'isha would be a part of anything that could harm Amos," he continued.

"I agree with Mr. Greenspan. A'isha seemed to really love Amos, and he was certainly comfortable with her," Sarah Jean said.

"I understand what you are saying," Agent Hogan replied. "However, we can't dismiss the fact that your son's Arab nanny apparently received a telephone call and rushed from the house with your son in a big hurry, and no one has heard from either of them since. Doesn't it seem odd to you that she hasn't called? Surely she knew you would be worried sick."

"Maybe she was kidnapped too," Sarah Jean interrupted.

"No one gets kidnapped by a telephone call, Miss Bogart."

"That note means something," Sarah Jean said.

"Nothing that's going to help us very much though," Agent Hogan replied. "*Nineteen seventy-three AM* isn't much of a clue to anything. We don't know that it means anything at all, nor do we know when the note was written. Mr. Greenspan, I think you're probably going to get a demand for a ransom. That's the most likely scenario we can expect."

"And you think A'isha, our nanny, is in on it?"

"We can't rule that out. We'd like to set up a team here to monitor all calls that come in and try to trace them. That's pretty standard procedure in cases like this. If someone calls and demands a ransom we'll coach you on how to respond."

"If this was just about a ransom why would my wife have called from Israel in such a panic?"

"I don't know."

"Have you tried to reach her?"

"No, we wanted to wait until you were here."

"You're not going to be able to reach her," Sarah Jean interrupted. "I'm telling you, she was rushing when she called here earlier. There was panic in her voice, and when I said A'isha and Amos weren't here, she said to call the police and the FBI. She knew something was terribly wrong. I could hear the dread in her voice, and I'm telling you, she was rushing and she was panicked. She knew something bad was going on."

The conversation was suddenly interrupted by the ring of the telephone. Agent Hogan asked if there was an extension nearby. Noah pointed to the living room as he went to answer the call.

"Noah Greenspan," he said, picking up the phone.

"Noah, it's Amos in Eilat. Have you heard from Alexandra?"

"She called a couple of hours ago in a panic. I wasn't here. She asked for A'isha, and when she was told A'isha and Amos were not here she told our house guest, Sarah Jean Bogart, to call the police and the FBI. Then she apparently hung up, and no one has heard from her since."

"Oh shit," Amos said. "I wasn't in the hotel when she called home, but the desk clerk told me when I returned that she ran through the lobby and out the front door of the hotel around midnight. She never returned."

"Did the desk clerk see where she went?"

"He said she ran across the street and got into a car. He said no one seemed to force her or anything."

"Where could she have gone ... and with whom?"

"There's more. The hotel operator said Alexandra placed a call to your home just before she ran from the hotel, and that she pleaded with the operator to hurry ... she said it was a matter of life or death. We checked her room. She obviously left in a hurry. All of her stuff is in the room. Even her wallet was lying on the desk. Noah, have the police checked A'isha's apartment?"

"Mr. Ben-Chaiyim," Agent Hogan interrupted, "this is FBI Special Agent Hogan. We met five years ago when Potomac Center was opening and there was a bomb threat."

"Yes, I remember."

"We have agents going to the nanny's apartment now. We've called there but there's been no answer. We don't think that's where they went."

"Noah, you know I've had an uneasy feeling about A'isha Abadi from the time you hired her," Amos said.

"I can't believe she's involved in this," Noah replied. "She wouldn't let anyone harm Amos. I'm telling you, she loves that boy."

"But she *did* take him from your home at an unusual hour of the day, and Alexandra did call in a panic looking for her after she left with Amos. It seems as though Alexandra knew something was wrong when she called."

Noah didn't respond.

"Look, I was supposed to return to Washington with Alexandra, but I'm going to see if I can hang on here for a few days. I want to do all that I can to find her."

"Do you have any thoughts?" Noah asked.

"I'm guessing they would have headed north through the Negev to the Palestinian territories. They're probably there by now. Then there's no telling where they've taken her. But we have good intelligence sources there. We'll find her, Noah."

"Please … please … find her," Noah pleaded. "Find her, Amos."

"Amos, it's Agent Hogan. I don't think we can accomplish anything more on this call. Please call me if you learn anything. I presume that, for the time being, we can reach you at the hotel in Eilat. We have that number. You can reach me at area code 202-555-2000. Just ask for me."

"Yes, okay. Please keep me informed."

"Yes, we will be sure to do that."

Sarah Jean wiped away her tears as she watched Noah cry into his hands. "They have my son and my wife," he cried in agony. "They never gave up and now they have them."

Sarah Jean walked over to the kitchen counter, took one of the pens from the mug, and copied the note A'isha had written, *1973 AM.*

"I assume you'll want the actual pen and the sheet of paper with the impression of the note," she said to Agent Hogan.

"Yes, please don't handle either one. We'll check them for prints, but I'm sure we'll find it was written by the nanny. It doesn't really tell us much … not anything, really."

"Oh, I think it tells us somethin'. I don't know what, but it means somethin'," Sarah Jean said.

"It no doubt means something, Miss Bogart, but we'll never guess what the nanny's abbreviation refers to."

"It could refer to a place."

"Like what?" Agent Hogan asked.

"I don't know. Maybe Armenia. AM is the abbreviation for Armenia."

"Do you or your wife have any connections in Armenia, Mr. Greenspan?" Agent Hogan asked.

"Armenia? No, of course not."

"Well, I just meant it as an example," Sarah Jean replied.

"Miss Bogart, maybe it would be best if you left the investigating to us," Agent Hogan said.

"Oh, don't worry. I never interfere with police work, but I'm investigating things all the time. That's what I do for a living too. It's as natural for me as breathing."

"Well, I suggest you concentrate on breathing," Agent Hogan answered impatiently. "And please, we do not want anything about what's happened in the newspapers. Not yet anyway."

"Of course not. The *Star* will wait until there's some kind of an announcement from you people before we write anything. Frank Markazie won't do anything that could place Alexandra in any kind of jeopardy," she said.

"Who is Frank Markazie?" Agent Hogan asked.

"He's our boss at the *Star*. He thinks the world of Alexandra. He hired her when she was still in high school."

"Mr. Greenspan, we'd like to have someone here all night just in case there's a call from the perpetrators."

"Yes, of course," Noah replied. "Anything you need to do is fine with me."

"I suggest you get as much sleep as you can, Mr. Greenspan. The next few days are going to be very stressful," Agent Hogan said.

"I have to call the Salamans. They have no idea what's happened," Noah replied. Noah reached for the phone and dialed Yusuf in Baltimore. He explained that Alexandra and Amos were both missing and that terrorists are suspected.

"Is Alexandra missing in the Middle East?"

"Yes, it looks that way," Noah answered.

"And someone got to Amos too?"

"Yes."

"In Washington? How could that be? Who took him?"

"Right now, it seems A'isha did."

"What?"

"It looks like she received a phone call and hurried from the house with Amos. That's all we know."

"But …"

"Yusuf, we have to keep the line open. The FBI is here, and we're expecting whoever is responsible to call. You'll have to tell Samira and Sharif, and, of course, you're welcome to come over in the morning. I'll call my folks and break this horrible news to them."

It was a miserable night. Noah was too distressed to even contemplate showering and changing for bed. Instead, he just sat in a club chair, fully clothed, staring into the darkness of the sitting room adjacent to their bedroom. Images of Alexandra and Amos kept passing through his mind. The thought that they were prisoners in hostile hands, captives of people who he feared would kill them without an ounce of remorse, was overwhelming. That night, he was certain he would never see them again. "Oh please, God, don't let anyone hurt them," he said, sometimes to himself, sometimes out loud, over and over again. "Don't let anyone hurt them," he cried.

A few steps down the hall, in the Greenspans' guest room, Sarah Jean Bogart lay in her bed staring at the ceiling. She, too, was wide awake. Sleep was the furthest thing from her mind.

God damn it, she thought to herself. *I know that message A'isha left means something important. But what? I think the phone rang. Amos was doing a puzzle on the living room floor. She ran to the phone. Someone told her somethin'. She pulled the sheet of paper from the pad and wrote a note. She threw the pen down on the kitchen counter, grabbed Amos, and ran from the house. Why did she write the year nineteen seventy-three and the initials AM? Or was it the year? Maybe it was a place, an address in AM. What the fuck does AM mean? And why was the cabinet door left open? There's nothin' in that cabinet but cereals. Who the hell runs from a house with a child and a box of cereal? God damn it, that note means somethin'. I know it does.*

It was almost eight o'clock in the morning before Noah finally dozed off. His brief slumber was interrupted, however, by the ring of the telephone.

"Greenspan," he answered.

"Noah, it's Marshall. We've got to discuss what kind of statement to make to the press."

"You decide and just make it. I'm in no shape to make any business decisions."

"What are you talking about?"

"Not a word to anyone, Marsh, okay?"

"Yeah, yeah, okay. What's wrong?"

"Alexandra and our son, Amos, have been kidnapped."

"What?"

"They're gone, Marsh. I've got the FBI here and the police, and I don't know what the hell is going to happen. We're all just waiting. You can't breathe a word of this, Marsh. But I can't be bothered with work. I've been up all night and I can't see or think straight."

"Jesus Christ, Noah. Are you sure?"

"That's the way it looks. I don't know what to do. Nobody does."

"I don't know what to say, Noah. I've never heard anything so awful. Are they asking for money?"

"They haven't asked for anything yet. We haven't heard a word from anyone. I don't think it has anything to do with money."

"Why would anyone kidnap your wife and child if it wasn't for ransom?"

"We think terrorists have them."

"Is Alexandra still over in the Middle East?"

"Yeah, we think they grabbed her in Eilat and drove her into the Palestinian territories."

"Holy shit."

"It looks like Amos's nanny ran off with him at about the same time."

"Here in Washington?"

"It looks that way."

"Oh hell, I don't want to bother you with all this Wall Street shit."

"What's happening?"

"Our specialist called this morning. He says to expect our stock to be in free fall again today."

"You deal with it, Marsh. I can't even think about that shit."

"Yeah, yeah, sure. I'll take the calls. What should I say about you? Everyone is going to want to know where you are while everything is going to shit."

"Tell them I have a cold or pneumonia or something."

"No one is going to believe that, Noah. They're all going to want to hear from you, and they'll think you're ducking their calls."

"I am."

"Jesus Christ, Noah."

"You handle it, Marsh. I'm in no shape to deal with the Street. We pay you big bucks. Go earn them. You'll handle it fine. Tell them the truth: we're in a fucking recession and we'll have to see what happens like everyone else."

"Mr. Greenspan, this is Agent Mike Atkins. I hate to interrupt your conversation, but we should keep this line open as much as we can."

"Who in the hell was that on the line?" Marshall Flynn asked.

"We have the FBI here monitoring all our calls. They've been here all night."

"Jesus. I'll come by and talk to you in person if there's anything I have to talk to you about."

"Good idea, Marsh. Goodbye."

"Yeah. Talk to you later, Noah. I'm praying for you."

Moments later, the telephone rang again.

"Greenspan."

"Noah, it's Karen. I just spoke to Amos from Eilat. He's filled me in on everything. I'm coming to Washington."

"What are you going to do here, Karen?"

"I just want to be there to give you any support I can."

"You can give me support best by staying at Mid America Ventures in Chicago and helping Marshall Flynn deal with the vultures on the Street."

"Noah, it's like a tsunami has hit your stock. There's nothing anyone can do in the short run. Right now, everyone is listening to Markanos. He says the stock should be between ten and twelve dollars a share, and that's probably where it will be before the day is out."

"I can't be bothered."

"I understand. You shouldn't be. Do I understand that Alexandra and Amos are *both* missing?"

"Yes, they're both missing. We think terrorists have them both."

"Mr. Greenspan, I'm sorry to interrupt, but ..."

"It's all right, Agent Atkins. Karen, we have to keep this line clear."

"Who was that on the line?"

"The FBI."

"Jesus Christ."

"Goodbye, Karen. I'll call you later if we have any news."

"Noah, I'm so sorry. I'll talk to you later."

Noah made his way down to the kitchen to make himself a cup of coffee. He was dressed in the same clothes from the day before, minus his suit jacket and wingtip shoes. He was wearing slippers.

Sarah Jean was sitting at the kitchen table opposite Agent Atkins.

"You sit right down, Mr. Greenspan. I'll pour you some coffee," she said, jumping to her feet. "How do you take it?" she asked.

"Black. Thank you, Sarah Jean."

"Anything new?" he asked Agent Atkins.

Agent Atkins shook his head. "Nothing yet," he answered.

"Here you go," Sarah Jean said as she placed a mug of coffee down in front of Noah.

"Thanks, Sarah Jean. Say, I've heard wonderful things about you from Alexandra. She says you're one of the most natural investigative reporters she's ever seen."

"Well, thank you. Alexandra is a wonderful role model."

Noah nodded. "Yeah," he replied, "she is that."

They sat there for several minutes without speaking. The ticking of the clock on the kitchen counter was the only sound in the room.

Noah lowered his head into his hand. "I'm exhausted," he finally said. "I didn't sleep at all last night."

"You're going to need to rest, Mr. Greenspan. Like we said last night, things are going to be very stressful for a while."

"I don't know if I'll ever see them again," he whispered. No one spoke. No one knew if he ever would see his wife and son again. After several minutes, the silence was jolted by the ringing of the phone.

"I'll get it," Agent Atkins said.

Noah and Sarah Jean both watched Agent Atkins as he listened to the caller.

"Okay, Larry. I'll let them know," he said.

Agent Atkins hung up the phone and walked over to the kitchen table and pulled up a chair.

"The person who called the nanny yesterday called from a public phone booth on the street."

"On what street? Where did he call from?" Noah asked.

"He called from one of the phone booths on the street at Eighteenth and Columbia Road. It doesn't tell us much. He could be anywhere in the city, but that's where he called from."

"Where is that?" Sarah Jean asked.

"It's not that far. It's a couple of miles from here, but they could be anywhere in the city now. In fact, we can't be sure they're even still in the city."

"Great," Noah whispered sarcastically. "That's just great."

"You know, I think I'll drive over there. I'd just like to look at those telephone booths," said Sarah Jean.

"There are telephone booths a lot closer you can look at, Miss Bogart. There are some on the corner of Wisconsin and M Street, right around the corner. They're all identical."

"Nah, I want to look at the phone booths at the intersection where the caller called from."

"Okay," Agent Atkins answered with a shrug of his shoulders. "It's an easy drive from here. Take M Street here in Georgetown over to

Eighteenth and take a left on Eighteenth and go straight north until you reach Columbia Road. It's only a couple of miles."

Sarah Jean got up from the table and threw on her jacket, which she had hung over the back of one of the kitchen chairs the night before. Hy and Esther Greenspan and Sharif and Samira Salaman were about to ring the doorbell when Sarah Jean opened the door to leave. She shook hands with them after introducing herself as Alexandra's new assistant at the *Star*. They smiled and shook her hand but didn't speak.

Sarah Jean followed Agent Atkins's directions and arrived at Eighteenth Street and Columbia Road in about twenty minutes. She found a parking spot not far from the intersection. She strolled to the intersection and quickly spotted the telephone booths right on the corner, just where Agent Atkins said they were. She studied the multitude of stickers that had been plastered on the sides of the phone booths. Most were political. "Impeach Nixon!" one read. "Out of Vietnam!" another screamed. Several advertised massage parlors and escort services. *Lordy, I didn't expect to see that in our nation's capital,* she mused.

Sarah Jean stepped back and slowly looked over the intersection. Just across Columbia Road, to the north, she saw a huge apartment complex. *Must be thousands of apartments in those buildings,* she thought. *They could be anywhere.* Then she looked up at the street sign and squinted to make out the small lettering under the large print that identified Columbia Road. "Holy Shit," she said aloud. "Holy Shit, this neighborhood is called Adams Morgan. That's what the AM stood for, Adams Morgan! Nineteen seventy-three isn't the year. It's an address in Adams Morgan."

CHAPTER
THIRTY-FIVE

Alexandra felt the car slow down and pull off to the side of the road. She heard the driver open the car door and get out of the car. A moment later her door was pulled open and she was yanked from the car. She was positive that this was the spot where her life was going to end. Suddenly the hood was pulled from her face, but before she could cry out or say anything, the driver grabbed her under her chin and squeezed hard, forcing her mouth open. She didn't know what was happening or why. She was terrified and shaking with fear. Suddenly, and without warning, he forced a small rubber ball into her mouth and quickly slapped a piece of duct tape across her mouth. It all happened so quickly she didn't have time to think. She was certain this was the end. The driver pulled the hood back over her head and pulled her to the rear of the car. She heard the trunk open and, a second later, he pushed her back against the bumper, causing her to trip backwards into the trunk. She was too panicked to fight or struggle. It was all happening so fast. She felt him tug at her legs and could hear the tearing sound of the duct tape as he began wrapping it around her ankles. She felt him lift her legs and suspend them in midair to a hook hanging from the top of the trunk. She could neither cry nor kick at the inside of the trunk. She concentrated on breathing through her nose as her mouth was so tightly sealed shut. And then the trunk slammed shut. The car began moving once again. She heard nothing but the hum of the tires on the highway and the low roar of the engine as it raced through the desert. Then the car slowly began to decelerate, slowed down, and then rolled to a stop. There were voices. It was Hebrew. She was positive she was hearing men talking in Hebrew. She realized they had come to the so-called Green Line separating Israel from the Palestinian territories, probably near Arad. She tried to kick at the trunk, but her legs, bound and hanging from the hook in the trunk, just jerked aimlessly. She tried to scream, but no sound came. Alexandra listened to the border guards talking to the driver. She couldn't make out what they were saying but could tell the guards and the driver seemed to know one another, as though the driver was a frequent traveler through this particular crossing. She even heard them laughing.

"*As-salamu alaykum*," she heard the driver say.

"*Shalom*," the border guards answered,

And then the car began to drive on, picking up speed as it drove from the checkpoint. No more than about a half hour later, she felt the car turn off the main highway, as it slowed to maneuver over ruts in the sand. For several minutes she was tossed about in the trunk as the car drove through what seemed more like a sandy field than a roadway. Then, the moment she dreaded. The car came to a stop and she heard the driver open his door. Her chest heaved as she tried to control her breathing. She had never known such fear, not even in Khartoum. The driver pulled open the trunk lid and yanked her from the car. He pushed her back and hoisted her up onto the top of the trunk, and as she lay there trying to catch her breath, she felt him cut the duct tape from her ankles. He yanked her to her feet and, holding tightly to her arm, led her forward for several feet. She heard a door open as someone pulled her inside. The driver grabbed her wrist and unlocked the handcuffs. Then he abruptly pulled her right arm behind her back and snapped the handcuff back on her wrist. A moment later he did the same with her left arm and snapped the handcuff onto her left wrist. She stood there hooded and gagged, with both arms bound behind her back. Alexandra knew that someone, maybe several people, was standing inches away watching her as she tried to catch her breath, watching her shake with fear.

Someone, she assumed the driver, yanked the duct tape from her mouth. She felt him force his fingers into her mouth and extract the rubber ball. She staggered slightly and fought to steady herself. A hand gripped her forearm and pulled her upright. Then, suddenly, the hood was pulled from her head. Her eyes closed tightly, rebelling against the light in the room. Slowly she struggled to open her eyes.

Then she saw him standing only a couple of feet in front of her. She nodded her recognition.

"Good evening, Alexandra."

"Omar, do what you will with me, but leave my son alone," she managed to say.

"We don't plan any harm to your son, Alexandra. In fact, our preference is not to harm you either."

"I know you didn't do this to me just to talk. What is it you want of me?"

"We have plenty of time to talk, Alexandra. Let me look at you. It has been so long."

He stood for a moment and took his time looking at her. She watched his eyes roam over her from head to foot. "You are as beautiful as ever, Alexandra." Her heart pounded in her chest.

"You hardly look any older then when we were students in Beirut, Alexandra," he said as he reached out and placed his hands on her shoulders. "Yes, you look just the same," he said, moving his hands from her shoulders to each side of her.

"Do you remember how much we trusted you?" he said as he moved his hands down the sides of her body. "Alexandra, you're shaking. Why are you shaking? I said we aren't planning to hurt you."

"Please, don't hurt my son," she managed to say. "I know you are going to kill me, but please don't harm him."

"Why do you think we are going to kill you?"

She didn't answer.

"I asked you, why do you think we are going to kill you?"

"I have no idea what you want me to do, only that I probably won't do it."

"And then you think we would kill you?"

She didn't answer.

"We won't kill you for disobeying. One way or another you will do what we say. But if you are not cooperative, if you make this difficult, you will be responsible for what happens to your son. So, you see, everything is up to you."

"Please, Omar, tell me what you want of me."

"We are going to pick up where we left off in Khartoum."

"I don't know what you are talking about."

"You remember Khartoum?"

"Of course I remember Khartoum."

"Then what we expect you to do should be very clear to you."

"Nothing is clear to me."

"You remember Muhammed Faisel?"

"Of course I remember that mad man."

"He divorced his wife because of you."

"He was crazy. He wanted me to become his slave."

"He wanted you to become his wife."

"That would have been the same thing."

"You would have been safe. No harm would have come to you. All you had to do was be a good wife, an obedient wife."

"He was an awful man. I would have rather died."

"And your son. You would rather he had died too?"

"I had no son then, Omar."

"But you do now."

"What are you saying?"

"You are a very lucky woman, Alexandra. Muhammed Faisel is a free man now and he has forgiven you."

"What? What are you saying?"

"Hello, Sabirah," came the voice from behind her, the voice that had taken so long to fade from her consciousness, the voice of Muhammed Faisel, her tormentor in Khartoum who had insisted that she was Sabirah Najat. It was the pseudonym she had used five years earlier when she traveled to Khartoum to cover the Arab League Conference with fellow journalist Dany Haddad after the six-day war. Muhammed Faisel had her thrown in a cell at that horrible prison in the Omdurman section of Khartoum. Her subservience to him was to be the price of her freedom. Only her rescue by Amos and Mossad with the help of a Greek shipping magnate saved her.

"As I told you, Alexandra, we intend to pick up where we left off five years ago in Khartoum," Omar Samir said. "It's that simple. That way, everyone will be safe—you, your son, everyone."

With that, the driver who had brought her there grabbed her arm and spun her around. Muhammed Faisel stood facing her, only a foot or two away.

"It will be good, Sabirah. I forgive you, and now you will show me your appreciation."

Only the firm grip of the driver held her up as she began to shake uncontrollably.

"I have brought you a proper abaya and niqab to wear. These American army clothes you wear are offensive. They disgust me. We will give you a day or two to come to your senses. Then you will return to Sudan with me, where you will become my wife. You will be a good, obedient wife, Sabirah. And then no harm will come to you or to your boy. We will arrange to get the boy to you someday, and then we can make sure he has a proper education in a proper madrasah."

"I will never accompany you to Sudan, and I will never be your wife," she answered.

With that, Muhammed Faisel suddenly grabbed Alexandra's jaw behind her chin, squeezing her tightly in his hand. He tilted her head and pulled her in an upward motion, causing her to stand on her toes to keep her balance.

"Who do you think you are talking to, Sabirah? Do you think I'm asking you? Do you think I'm proposing? I am telling you what you will do to save your son. Do you want to save your son?" he shouted, squeezing her jaw tighter. "Do you?" he screamed.

Alexandra jerked her head in a nodding motion. She couldn't open her mouth to speak, so tight was the vice-like grip in which he held her.

"Do you think I have forgotten the grief you caused me in Khartoum five years ago? Do you?" he shouted, squeezing her jaw even tighter. He could feel her jaw quivering in his grip.

"You will do everything as I command, Sabirah. That is how you will protect your son. Do you understand?" he shouted again. "Do you?"

Again, she jerked her head to signal that she understood.

"Now, there's a hose against the wall connected to the cistern on the roof. We will remove the handcuffs so that you can clean yourself. Take off the disgusting American army clothes you are wearing, clean yourself, and then put on the abaya I brought for you to wear. You will need to get used to covering your face with the niqab when you are in Sudan, so you will wear it here at all times unless I tell you to take it off. Get used to the abaya and niqab, Alexandra. From this day on the abaya is all you will ever wear except when you are doing your duty as my wife, and then you will be wearing nothing."

***

Sarah Jean took her time walking through the Adams Morgan neighborhood to familiarize herself with the area. She walked along Columbia Road and turned onto Nineteenth Street. There were so many streets that intersected Nineteenth Street where the addresses ran between 1900 and 2000, and so many buildings with 1973 addresses were large apartment complexes.

I know they're in one of these buildings, she thought, *but which one?* Sarah Jean quickly determined that Columbia Road was the main thoroughfare through Adams Morgan and decided to see if there was a 1973 address on Columbia Road.

Oh Lordy, she thought when she finally reached 1973 Columbia Road. *It's one of the largest apartment buildings I've seen in Adams Morgan.* It was a ten-story building that seemed to be as high as any of the buildings in the area, and she guessed there were twelve, maybe fifteen, apartments on each floor. *There could be a hundred and twenty, maybe a hundred and fifty, apartments in this one building*, she thought. *And this Adams Morgan neighborhood is crawling with apartment buildings. Well, I've got to start somewhere*, she thought.

Sarah Jean walked the entire length of the building. It seemed pretty up-scale to her, maybe the nicest building she had seen so far in Adams Morgan. She came to an alley at the end of the building and decided to walk through it to see the backside of the building. Dozens of garbage bags lined the rear of the building. A rat scurried away as she approached. The side of one of the bags had been ripped open and some of the refuse had spilled out into the alley. *Probably the rat*, she thought. She hurried by the spilled garbage, anxious to get through the alley. But then Sarah Jean stopped dead in her tracks. Something had caught her eye. She slowly walked backwards and peered down into the spilled garbage. She stooped down and looked closely. Beneath a couple of empty beer bottles, she saw something that looked familiar—colorful print on carboard that was partially obscured by the bottles. She swept away the bottles with her hand.

"Sweet Jesus," she whispered aloud. It was an empty, miniature box of Klondike Pete's Crunchy Nuggets, the same cereal Amos liked. Sarah Jean squatted over the spilled garbage, picturing the open cabinet in the Greenspan kitchen, the one in which they kept cereals, the one in which she had seen a stack of those same miniature Klondike Pete's Crunchy Nuggets boxes. She hesitated for a moment and then pulled the cereal box from the refuse. That's when she saw the crumpled piece of paper that had been torn from a familiar notepad. Her hands trembled as she read the hastily written note just below the Evening Star logo, *1973 AM.*

Think, girl, think. What are you going to do now? she asked herself. Sarah Jean stood and walked from the alley out onto the front sidewalk and to the main entrance of the building. The glass door swung open as the building's doorman greeted her.

"How can I help you, young lady," the uniformed black man asked.

"Hi," she answered, glancing at his name badge. "Mr. Carter, I'm Sarah Jean Bogart of the *Evening Star*," she said, fishing though her shoulder bag to find her identification badge from the paper.

"We're doin' a feature story about the doormen in the nation's capital. You know, sort of a human-interest story."

"Well, I'll be," he answered. "I've been working this job for twenty years and you're the first person that ever showed a speck of interest in what I do."

"Well, you doormen are what helps make this city so special," she replied. "We don't think people appreciate the role you play in this great city."

"Now, that's the truth," he answered.

"So, how would you describe the tenants in your building?"

"They all fine people."

"Mostly young people, older people, married people, single people?"

"Mostly married couples. Not all of them married, but most are."

"Uh huh," she said, scribbling notes on the notepad she always carried with her.

"Many kids in the building?"

"No, not many kids here. Mostly retired people, and a few embassy folks live here too."

"Uh huh," she continued. "You got any ambassadors living here?"

"No, no. They all live over on Massachusetts Avenue. We have a lot of nice embassy employees though."

"From major countries like France or England or Germany?"

"Nah, a few from Africa and one or two from the Middle East. We got a nice man from Algeria living here and one from Qatar. Mr. Kahn from Qatar has relatives staying with him now. I think it might be his sister and his nephew. She wore one of those scarves Arab woman wear—cute little boy too."

Oh my God, Sarah Jean thought. "Oh, maybe I can arrange to interview them while they're here. That could be a nice touch in our story. You know, relatives coming to Washington to see what their family members who work in embassies do. And we could have a picture with you and the visitors, maybe looking over a map of the city or somethin' to show how the city's doormen act as ambassadors."

"Well, wouldn't that be something," the doorman replied. "He'd be a good person to put in your story. He's a very interesting man. He's very quiet, but he loves music, and just last week he built a little music studio in his apartment."

"A music studio? That really is interesting," she said.

"Oh, it's nothin' fancy, just soundproofed a small bedroom and turned it into a studio by putting those special tiles on the walls and ceiling and even the floor so that he wouldn't bother the neighbors."

"So, does this tenant from Qatar spell his name C-O-N-N?"

"No, I think he spells it with a *K,* but you can come in and copy his name off the mailbox. Them Arab names are a mouthful to remember. I'll show you where the mailroom is."

Sarah Jean followed the doorman into an alcove off the lobby and into the mailroom. *There must be at least one hundred and fifty mailboxes,* she thought.

"This here is Mr. Kahn's mailbox. See, he spells it with a K."

"Uh huh," she answered, as she copied Ahmed Sayed Kahn's name from the mailbox. She noted the apartment number. It was 807.

"You want me to call up to his apartment and see if he's in?"

"No, not now. Let me see when I can schedule a photographer to come back with me, and then we'll call to schedule a photograph with Mr. Kahn and his relatives and you."

"Now, won't that be somethin'," the doorman replied.

"Please don't say anything to anyone about the story we're planning to do, not even to Mr. Kahn, before I call him to make an appointment to come back with the photographer. We don't want the *Washington Post* to learn about the story and scoop us."

***

Noah was sitting at the kitchen table with Agents Atkins and Hogan and Yusuf when Sarah Jean burst through the front door.

"I know where Amos and A'isha are," she called out excitedly as she hurried into the kitchen.

"What are you talking about?" Agent Atkins asked, making little effort to hide his irritation. "What do you mean, you know where they are?"

"They're in apartment 807 at 1973 Columbia Road."

"Sarah Jean, how do you know that? What makes you think they're in an apartment on Columbia Road?" Agent Hogan asked.

Sarah Jean didn't say anything. She just reached into her jacket pocket, pulled out the empty miniature box of Klondike Pete's Crunchy Nuggets and the notepaper with *1973 AM* hastily scribbled across the sheet, and handed them to Agent Hogan.

"Where ... how did you get this, Sarah Jean," Agent Hogan asked as he laid the cereal box and note on the kitchen table for everyone to see.

"Oh my God," Noah said, his voice shaken. "Oh my God."

"I was at the apartment building where they are," she answered.

Noah looked over to Yusuf, and then to Agent Atkins. They were both, momentarily, speechless.

"Sarah Jean, tell us exactly why you went to the address on Columbia Road where you found these items and what you did when you got there," Agent Hogan asked, leaning forward, his gaze fixed on Sarah Jean's eyes. Where, and how, did you find the cereal box and note."

"First thing I learned is that Columbia Road runs through a neighborhood called Adams Morgan. *That's* what the AM meant in A'isha's note. Nineteen seventy-three is an address in Adams Morgan."

Agent Hogan nodded. "Go on, Sarah Jean," he said, taking the young reporter very seriously.

I figured Columbia Road was probably the one street that A'isha didn't think she had to write down, because, being such a major street, she wasn't going to forget it. I think A'isha knew the street really well and didn't see a need to write the name down, but she did write down the neighborhood where that address was on that street, because Columbia Road probably runs through more than one neighborhood. So, you see, she just wrote down the initials of the neighborhood, AM for Adams Morgan."

"What's at 1973 Columbia Road, Sarah Jean? You've obviously already been there," Agent Atkins interrupted.

"A big apartment building."

"Sarah Jean, why do you think Amos and A'isha are in apartment 807 at 1973 Columbia Road, over in Adams Morgan?" Agent Hogan asked.

"I walked around the building from the front on Columbia Road through the alley behind the building."

"And you found the cereal box and note? Sarah Jean?" he asked.

"I sure did, in the alley."

"In the alley?" Agent Atkins asked.

"Yes, in the garbage."

"You looked in the garbage? Why in the world did you do that, and what did you see in the garbage that told you the nanny and the boy are in that building?" Agent Hogan probed.

One of the garbage bags was ripped open. I think rats got to the bag. Anyway, I recognized the cereal box just lying there in the garbage, and when I picked it up I saw the notepaper with the message A'isha had written on the Evening Star notepad—the one just like the one's on the kitchen counter over there," she said pointing to the notepads on the counter.

"Oh my God," Noah whispered.

"What did you do then, Sarah Jean," Agent Hogan asked.

"Well, I knew I couldn't just walk away, having seen that cereal box and A'isha's note. The only other time I ever saw that kind of cereal box was right there in that cabinet," she said, pointing to the kitchen cabinet that had been left open when A'isha had rushed from the house with Amos.

"Alexandra told me you were amazing," Noah said.

"I'm not amazing, Mr. Greenspan, just curious."

"But why do you think the nanny and the boy are in apartment 807, Sarah Jean?" Agent Hogan asked.

"I went to the Columbia Road entrance to the building and met the doorman. I told him I worked for the *Evening Star* and that I was doing a story about the city's doormen. You know, what an important part they play in making the city so special."

"Incredible," Agent Hogan murmured admiringly.

"Anyway, Mr. Carter, that's the doorman, he starts telling me about the different kinds of tenants who live in the building and mentions that some work for various embassies in the city. So, I asked him about the embassies that have employees who rent in the building. And so Mr. Carter tells me about a tenant from the Qatari embassy, Mr. Ahmed Sayed Kahn, who has two relatives visiting. He thought they might be Mr. Kahn's sister and nephew."

"The Qatari embassy! That's where A'isha worked before she came to work for us," Noah said.

"So, I'm sure you asked about these relatives who are visiting." Agent Hogan interrupted.

"Of course I did, I knew they had to be A'isha and Amos. Mr. Carter said the woman was wearing one of those thingamajigs on her head. He also said the man they were visiting had just built a sound-proof room in the apartment. He told the doorman he was building a sound studio because he loves music and he doesn't want to disturb the neighbors."

"And what did you say the man's name was?" Agent Hogan said.

"Ahmed Sayed Kahn. His name is Ahmed Sayed Kahn," she answered.

"Let's get over there," Noah said, getting to his feet.

"Hold on, Mr. Greenspan. We're going to have to get a search warrant. We can't just bust in."

"Are you kidding me?"

"This Ahmed Sayed Kahn works in the Qatari embassy, so he must have a diplomatic passport, which means we have a file on him. I'm going to make a quick phone call and see what we can learn.

It took only a few minutes before the FBI called back with information about Ahmed Sayed Kahn.

"So," Agent Hogan began as soon as he finished talking to the Bureau, "here's what we know about Ahmed Sayed Kahn. He's a Qatari citizen, age thirty-five, and is a fairly low-level employee at the Qatari embassy. He's primarily a gofer. He also drives for the embassy. He's well educated and has a degree in political science from Phoenicia University at Beirut."

"Phoenicia University! Alexandra went to Phoenicia University, and so did Omar Samir and Ali Abdul Shoukri," Noah cried. "They were terrorists. Samir still is. This guy Kahn must still be connected to terrorists."

"I'll rush through a search warrant request, Agent Hogan said. We'll get immediate access to that apartment."

***

Elias Carter, the doorman Sarah Jean had spoken with only hours earlier, opened the door to apartment 807 for the team of FBI agents and Metropolitan Police officers. They quickly located the locked, soundproofed room and used the intercom to tell A'isha they were from the FBI and that she and the boy were safe. Using a Halligan bar, they easily knocked the door from its hinges and found A'isha with Amos in her arms huddled against the opposite wall.

Agents Hogan and Atkins accompanied A'isha and Amos back to the Greenspan house to interview them there rather than at FBI headquarters. The FBI agents and Noah were quickly satisfied that A'isha had been as much of a victim as Amos. Agent Hogan told Noah he had seen few agents with better investigative instincts than the spunky young woman from Blytheville, Arkansas. He admitted that he and his fellow agents may have never discovered where A'isha and Amos were being held. "Sarah Jean Bogart is one brainy, tenacious young woman," he told Noah. "However, we have a much more difficult problem finding Alexandra," he said. "We have to assume from what we learned from your friend Amos Ben-Chaiyim that the only reason these people wanted A'isha and your child, Amos, out of the house was to convince your wife that the boy was in their hands. They convinced her that his life depended on her doing what they demanded, which was that she go with the driver they had waiting at the hotel in Eilat. So, when your wife called here and learned that A'isha and your son were gone, and that they apparently had left in a hurry, she believed she had no choice but to obey the terrorists or they would kill your son. Once they had Alexandra she would have no way of knowing whether A'isha and your son were safe. For all she knows, they are still holding your son. It makes no difference to them now that he is safe and with you. As long as Alexandra believes her son's life is still in their hands, she'll do what they demand, or they'll threaten to kill the boy."

"She'll endure anything if she believes it will keep them from hurting Amos," Noah replied.

"So, the reality is that your wife has no way of knowing that her son is safe. As long as they have her thinking they have the boy, she is pretty much under their control," Agent Hogan said.

"We have to reach Amos in Israel. It seems as though the outcome of this horror is going to be determined there and not here," Noah said.

"I'm afraid that's probably true," Agent Hogan agreed. "We'll try to question this Kahn fellow, but I doubt that he'll know very much, or that the Qataris will allow him to be questioned. He seems to be a flunky who was apparently trying to please Omar Samir. The Qataris will probably get him out of the country anyway. They may hang him, but they'll do it in their country, and they'll do it their way."

Later that evening they finally got through to Amos in Eilat and filled him in on what had taken place since they had last spoken.

"Amos, it seems they wanted A'isha Abadi and Amos out of the house when this character Omar Samir called Alexandra in her hotel room," Agent Hogan explained. "He used his knowledge of their absence to induce Alexandra to follow his instructions. Miss Abadi and the boy are both safe now, and the fellow who held them for nearly two days will be prosecuted either here by us or by the Qatari government. He was just a pawn. I doubt that he knew he was participating in a plot to kidnap Alexandra, but we can't be sure. Our immediate need is to try to find a way to let Alexandra know that Amos is safe. And, of course, we have to figure out where she is and get her the hell out of there before something really bad happens."

"Yes, I understand," Amos replied. "We're assuming they're holding her somewhere between Hebron and the so-called Green Line that separates Israel from the Palestinian territories. You are right, though. We have to figure out how to get word to Alexandra that Amos is safe. She'll do whatever they command her to do if she thinks they have their hands on her son. If she knows he's safe, she'll use her ingenuity—and she has plenty of that—to resist until we can get to her."

CHAPTER THIRTY-SIX

Benjamin Bar-Levy was furious. Once again, Alexandra Salaman, the Palestinian woman married to the Jew in America, was in Israel, or, more accurately, in the Palestinian territories, and she was in serious trouble. Amos Ben-Chaiyim, his most trusted agent, who was supposed to be in Washington assisting Ambassador Dinitz, was, instead, still in Israel preoccupied with extracting the Salaman woman from the hands of terrorists. This was the last straw. Amos Ben-Chaiyim had finally broken the camel's back with his preoccupation with the Salaman woman.

Amos knew his career with Mossad was in jeopardy, but there was no way he was going to leave Alexandra in Omar Samir's hands.

"You are needed in Washington helping Ambassador Dinitz, Amos. We are at the most crucial point in this God-damned standoff with the Egyptians, and you want to focus your attention on the plight of the Salaman woman."

"Our debt to her is eternal, Benjamin. She stopped a massacre of our people fifteen years ago, and the perpetrators have been after her ever since. They have her now, and we have to do everything possible to rescue her."

"You had your own dalliance with her, Amos. It still clouds your judgment."

"You mean because I once fell in love with her? That has nothing to do with what we owe her. We should leave no stone unturned to help her. Her enemies are our enemies, Benjamin."

"Amos, you have to prioritize. You can't be serving Ambassador Dinitz in his most important assignment ever and also be distracted trying to save this one woman, who shouldn't have been anywhere near here anyway."

"She was at the talks with Ambassador Dinitz's permission, and she was an observer in the tent at Kilometer 101 at General Yariv's invitation. The terrorist, Samir, came after her and succeeded in grabbing her right under our nose, and I'm going to find her."

"You know she's probably dead by now."

"I don't think so. They could have killed her in Eilat, Benjamin. They have planned something far worse than death for her, and we have to stop them."

"We don't even know where they're holding her, or what they're planning."

"No, we don't."

"What do you propose doing?"

"The first thing we have to do is get word to her that her son is safe."

"That's the child who is named after you?"

"Yes, I am his godfather."

Benjamin Bar-Levy nodded. "So, there really was an Amos Project?"

"It looks that way."

"Those scribblings I told you about were what we suspected."

"Yes, but the boy is safe. They used him as a decoy to trap his mother. She doesn't know he's safe. He's at home with his father, Noah."

"So, she will do what they say as long as she believes they have him and will kill her son if she doesn't do what they tell her to do?"

"That is correct."

"Well, if we don't know where she is, I don't know how we can get word to her that her son is safe, let alone attempt to rescue her."

"I think our first task has to be to let her know her son is safe. There may be a way to do that."

"Your schemes always fascinate me."

"Sometimes they work."

"Actually, they work almost all the time. Look how you plucked her out of Khartoum in sixty-seven."

"Benjamin, I think they have to be holding her somewhere near Hebron, probably between Hebron and the Green Line just twenty or so miles south of Hebron."

"There are thousands of houses and other buildings in that area from Hebron to the Green Line. You know they won't let her read a newspaper or listen to the radio or watch television. What do you want to do, deliver circulars to every building?"

"Actually, that's close to what I have in mind."

"What do you have in mind?"

***

Omar Samir and Muhammed Faisel were certain they had Alexandra exactly where they wanted her. She would do nothing to anger them or defy them, so certain was she that they would kill her son at the slightest provocation and then kill her. She had little concern for her own life anymore, but she could keep Amos alive by not angering her captors. And so she did what she was told. She stood naked in front of them and bathed with the cold water from the hose, and she didn't object when they took her shoes, clothing, and undergarments away as she bathed. Muhammed Faisel handed her a coarse cloth with which to dry herself, and then handed her the black abaya. She donned the abaya and niqab as he commanded and stared into the room through the narrow slit that partially obscured her vision. She knew escape was futile because her son's life was too high a price to pay for her freedom. She was told to sit quietly on the floor against the wall while the men talked. When they grew tired they stood and walked over to Alexandra. She sat motionlessly and didn't speak.

"It is time for sleep, Sabirah. You will sleep on your own mattress between our mattresses."

They laid three thin, old, and used mattresses down in the center of the room and Alexandra was told to undress and lie on her back on the middle mattress. They threw a rough blanket over her, and Omar Samir and Muhammed Faisel moved to the mattresses on either side of her. They handcuffed each of Alexandra's ankles, one to Omar Samir's left ankle and the other to Muhammed Faisel's right ankle. "You will lie still and lie quietly and not disturb us while we sleep."

Alexandra nodded, but said nothing. The two men drifted off quickly, pulling her legs uncomfortably as they moved restlessly in their sleep. Sleep was a luxury she would not know that night.

The next morning, Omar Samir and Muhammed Faisel uncuffed her and left her lying on the mattress. Later, the two men sat at a wooden table against the wall eating their breakfast of pita, labneh, and boiled eggs, and called to Alexandra, who was sitting on the floor in the corner of the room eating what they shared with her.

"So, Sabirah," Muhammed called over to her, "in a few days it will be safe to leave for Sudan. We will drive to Amman and fly to Khartoum from there. I even renewed the travel documents I took from you in Khartoum. The travel document issued by the Arab League to Sabirah Najat. We have a ticket for you in that name, Sabirah. When you are with me you will always answer to the name Sabirah Najat. Do you understand? You are never to use the name Alexandra around me. Not ever. You will be Sabirah Najat from the time we land in Sudan. Now tell me, who will you be in Sudan?"

"I will be Sabirah Najat," she answered.

"You will not cause trouble on the road or in the airport if we are questioned by the Jordanians."

"No, I will cause no trouble," she replied.

"You will learn to like my house near El-Obeid. It's not too far south of Khartoum."

Alexandra nodded

"Are you comfortable in your abaya and niqab?"

"I will get used to them."

"Yes, Sabirah, you will have much to get used to."

She nodded.

"The shit in the bucket needs to be thrown out," Omar said. "Empty the bucket in the ditch in back of the house and use the shovel that's there to cover the shit with sand."

She nodded and got to her feet and walked, barefoot, across to the corner of the room and picked up the bucket.

"Hurry, I don't want you outside more than a minute."

Alexandra opened the rear door and walked out into the morning air. She poured the contents of the bucket into a shallow trench that ran along the back of the house and shoveled sand into the trench as she had been instructed to do. The area was desolate. She could scream and no one would hear her. It was deathly quiet except for the distant drone of a small airplane overhead. Alexandra looked up into the sky and squinted through the slit in her niqab. Her heart raced at what she saw. There against the blue sky a small single-engine plane finished skywriting its message: "Amos - Safe." Alexandra gasped as tears ran from her eyes. In the distance, to the north, she saw another plane skywriting against the sky. While she couldn't make out what the other plane was writing, she knew Amos had found a way to let her know her son was safe, and that Omar Samir could no longer threaten him.

"Sabirah, come back to the house," Muhammed Faisel called angrily from the open doorway. "Come back inside, now!" She hurried back to the house, before Muhammed Faisel could step out and see the plane and the message it was delivering. Every hour or so, she could hear the faint sound of the single-engine plane as it returned throughout the day to deliver its message. Alexandra knew she was in no less danger, and that her captors would probably see or learn of the message that was now observable all over the West Bank. She understood that her life depended on behaving as though she was unaware of the message the skywriters were sending and still feared for her son's life.

CHAPTER
THIRTY-SEVEN

At Agent Hogan's suggestion, they agreed that Amos and the FBI agents would talk each night at six o'clock in the evening, Washington time. They would attempt to develop a plan to locate and rescue Alexandra, assuming she was still alive. The call would be made to the Greenspans' Georgetown home so that Noah could be apprised about what they were learning and what rescue plans might be feasible. Noah also wanted A'isha and Sarah Jean to be on the call. He had a telephone speaker from his office installed so that everyone participating would hear the same thing.

"Well, I think it's a safe bet that everyone on the West Bank knows your son is safe," Amos said as soon as he got on the line.

"We have to assume that includes Omar Samir," Agent Hogan answered.

"Yes, but that's a chance we had to take. Hopefully, Alexandra knows her son is safe."

"Anything else we should know?" Agent Hogan asked.

"Yes, we have some intelligence that I think tells us a great deal about what Omar Samir plans to do with Alexandra."

"Go on."

"We've been routinely getting our hands on the passenger lists for flights to and from Amman. We assume there's a chance Samir will try to get Alexandra as far from Israel and Mossad as he can. Well, we've come across something really fascinating. There is a Muhammed Faisel and a Miss Sabirah Najat booked on Royal Jordanian Airlines from Amman to Khartoum in three days."

"Muhammed Faisel!" Noah interrupted. "Muhammed Faisel is the mad man who terrorized Alexandra five years ago in that awful prison in Khartoum, when Alexandra was travelling under the name Sabirah Najat."

"I know, it has to be the same man. We think he's teamed up with Omar Samir and they've kidnapped Alexandra and are planning to have her return to Sudan with Muhammed Faisel. That would be their ultimate retribution." Amos replied.

"She would die before she would return to Sudan with that sadist. How do they think they could get her through a crowded airport? She would scream for help," Noah answered.

"I'm not so sure she would scream if she thought it would cost Amos's life."

"Where did he fly in from?" Agent Hogan asked.

"Good question," Amos answered. "He flew in from Khartoum."

"So, it has to be the same Muhammed Faisel," Noah replied.

"Yes, we certainly have to assume it's the same man."

"What do you make of this, Amos?" Noah asked.

"Omar Samir hates Alexandra. We know he was responsible for Alexandra's arrest in Khartoum five years ago. And his accomplice, who also turned out to be Alexandra's tormentor, was a prison official named Muhammed Faisel. If Omar Samir wanted to plan a fate worse than death for Alexandra, he might try to force her into Muhammed's hands again. We know the Muhammed Faisel at Omdurman Prison wanted Alexandra to be his personal house slave. He was going to force her to become his wife."

"And you think Omar Samir's plan might be to deliver Alexandra to Muhammed Faisel?" Noah asked.

"It would be the ultimate horror for Alexandra," Amos answered.

"Would the Jordanians cooperate with us and intercept them at the airport in Amman?" Agent Hogan asked.

"It's hard to say. The King tried to warn us about the war, and we ignored his warning. Also, there is no love lost between the Jordanians and the Israelis. I don't know if we could count on Jordan to help us, given the war and the anti-Israel sentiment in the Kingdom. The risk is that if an intercept at the airport in Amman fails, and Muhammed Faisel and Alexandra leave on a flight to Khartoum, it would be next to impossible to ever extract her from Sudan. I just don't think we can count on an intercept at the airport, and if that failed and they flew to Khartoum we'd never see Alexandra alive again," Amos answered.

"So, we have three days to find Alexandra," Agent Hogan said.

"Or hope that she escapes and finds her way to friendly people somewhere near Hebron," Noah interrupted.

"Noah, if she's being held by Omar Samir and Muhammed Faisel, I don't think escape is likely. They're not going to be careless enough to give her that opportunity. They let her slip through their fingers once. They're not likely to make that mistake again. If we're going to save Alexandra, we, or someone cooperating with us, are going to have to find her and take her from them."

"How are we supposed to do that?" Noah asked. "It sounds like a pipe dream to me."

"Maybe not," A'isha interrupted. Everyone suddenly grew silent.

"What do you mean, A'isha?" Noah asked.

"I think we have to leave this to professionals, Miss Abadi," Agent Hogan said.

"I agree," Amos said.

"You professionals didn't find my son and A'isha when they were locked up in that apartment in Adams Morgan," Noah interrupted. "Sarah Jean found them. A'isha, please go on. What were you going to say?"

"Mr. Greenspan, I have a large family in the Hebron area. They are well established and well respected and there isn't much they don't know or can't determine about what is going on anywhere on the West Bank. I have young cousins there around my age. They're smart and they can be pretty tough when they have to be. I think the Abadis can do more than the Jordanians and certainly more than the Israelis to help Alexandra. If she is anywhere near Hebron they can find her."

"Noah, I have real reservations about relying on private parties we don't even know, especially people we can't direct and who answer to no one," Amos interjected before anyone could respond.

"I don't like it either, Noah," Agent Hogan replied. "This would be a very unorthodox way to proceed. No one we know or have reason to trust would be calling the shots."

"A'isha, how would we even arrange to brief your family? This is going to be very complicated … lots of details and huge risk. Who would be in charge and run this effort?" Noah asked. "How would your family coordinate with the FBI or, for that matter, with Mossad?"

"I would fly to Jordan and meet with my family and brief everyone who would be involved. Mr. Greenspan, I believe with the Abadis we would have a chance. Relying on Israeli military or Mossad or, certainly, the FBI around Hebron would be fraught with danger. You might kill Omar Samir or this Faisel monster, but the chances of Alexandra surviving would not be good."

"You know," Sarah Jean interrupted, "if this were happening in Chickasawba, Arkansas, I'd rely on the local good old boys before I'd rely on the FBI coming in from Washington."

"Mr. Ben-Chaiyim, how effective do you think Mossad or Shin Bet would be around Hebron, especially while Israel and Egypt are in a standoff in Sinai?" A'isha asked.

Amos was momentarily silent.

"And Agent Hogan, what, realistically, can the FBI do in Hebron, or anywhere else on the West Bank?"

The silence on the phone spoke volumes to everyone on the call.

"I am telling you, my family can do more on the West Bank to, God willing, help Miss Salaman at this particular time than anybody from Israel or the FBI."

Sarah Jean looked to Noah and then Agent Hogan. Agent Hogan sat thinking, tapping his fingers against the table top. Noah leaned back against his chair, hands clasped behind his head, his eyes fixed on the ceiling as he contemplated the case A'isha had just made.

"Shoot! What is there to think about?" Sarah Jean finally interjected impatiently. "It seems to me we're lucky as can be that we have a resource like A'isha's family to help us."

"Amos?" Noah prodded.

"A'isha makes a good point," Amos answered. "I think our people stirring things up around Hebron right now could do more harm than good."

"Agent Hogan?"

"Truthfully, we have no real capability to do much anywhere on the West Bank, especially in an area as tense as Hebron. It's not like we have a field office there."

"A'isha, this could be very dangerous for your family," Amos said. "I don't just mean the operation itself, but their safety after word gets out that they helped us or that they helped the FBI."

"My family can take care of itself, Mr. Ben-Chaiyim, and besides, they wouldn't be doing it to help you or the FBI. They would be doing it to help Alexandra, a fellow Palestinian, and because I asked them to."

"When could you leave, assuming we agreed to what you propose?" Noah asked.

"I've already checked. There's a noon flight from BWI in Baltimore to JFK in New York that connects with a Royal Jordanian Airlines flight directly to Amman. I could leave tomorrow. There are flights originating at Dulles here in Washington, but they leave later in the day. I could save six hours by leaving from Baltimore. I could be meeting with my family in Hebron within twenty-four hours."

There were several moments of silence as they contemplated A'isha's response.

"Excuse me … Mr. Greenspan?" Sarah Jean interrupted.

Noah nodded to her.

"What are you gentlemen waiting for? I don't mean to put in my two cents or nothin', but I think I just heard a plan."

"Amos … Agent Hogan?" Noah asked.

"A'isha, I have to ask you this," Amos replied. "What led you to apply for the nanny job with the Greenspans? I've asked you that question before, but I thought your answer was always a bit evasive. I don't mean to put you on the spot, but I have to ask, given the proposal you just made."

"Ahmed Sayed Kahn brought me the nanny ad and asked me to apply for the job," A'isha answered without hesitating. "In fact, he insisted that I apply for the job."

"What?" Noah interrupted.

"Dear Mary, mother of Jesus," Sarah Jean whispered.

Agent Hogan didn't say anything. He just stared at A'isha, his mouth slightly agape as he contemplated her response.

"It's true," she continued, as tears welled up in her eyes. "Ahmed brought me the ad and insisted I should apply for the position. He said it would be good to have someone working with a prominent Palestinian journalist like Alexandra Salaman who would know what stories she would be writing. The job seemed perfect for me. I didn't think much about his comment about being interested in whatever I heard concerning what Alexandra was planning to write. It never came up again, and I never reported anything to him. We spoke from time to time, and I probably told him more about my work than I should have, but I never reported anything to him. I thought he was just curious. I would never have said or done anything to jeopardize the responsibility with which you and Alexandra entrusted me, Mr. Greenspan. You are like my own family now, and I truly love your son, Amos. I love him very much. I would protect him with my life."

"I believe you," Noah whispered.

"I am sickened every time I think of how he tricked me into leaving the house with Amos just before Alexandra would be calling to make sure Amos was home and safe."

"Noah, I think we can dismiss Miss Abadi's proposal to help. In fact, if I were you, I would dismiss Miss Abadi as well," Amos said.

Sarah Jean and Agent Hogan turned to Noah.

"No, I'm not dismissing A'isha, nor, I am certain, would Alexandra. A'isha was duped. She wasn't knowingly a part of the plot against us. If you have a better plan for trying to free Alexandra, I'll listen, but right now A'isha's plan is all we have."

"If this was the Bureau's decision, A'isha would be dismissed. We just don't tolerate anything in a job application or interview that isn't one hundred percent truthful. However, A'isha isn't applying for a job at the FBI; she's trying to help free Mrs. Greenspan, and I haven't heard a more promising proposal then the one she's made."

"Amos, do you or Mossad have a better plan than having A'isha and her family in Hebron trying to help us?"

"No, I guess we don't," he answered.

"Agent Hogan?"

"I don't think there is very much the Bureau can do in this situation. We might cause more harm than good."

"A'isha, find out what the trip will cost. I'll write you a check," Noah said.

"I've saved some money. I'll pay for my ticket. It's the least I can do."

Noah reached over and placed his hand on her arm. "No one is blaming you for what happened, A'isha. I think we're fortunate to have you, and I hope you'll be with this family for a long time. Of course I'll pay the cost of your travel."

***

By noon both Omar Samir and Muhammed Faisel had seen the writing in the sky. They had stepped outside to discuss their plans for traveling with Alexandra to Amman and from there on to Khartoum.

That's when they saw the plane skywriting. They knew the Americans and the Israelis were trying to get word to Alexandra that her son was safe.

"They know we have her here on the West Bank," Muhammed said.

"No, they don't know, they're guessing. If they knew where we were they would be all over the area."

"Do you think she has seen the skywriting?"

"She's never outdoors."

"She was this morning. Remember, we had her empty the shit."

"She was only outdoors for a minute. I don't think the plane was overhead that early."

"We have to find out if she knows her son is safe. If she does, she'll have nothing to do with you and we'll have to kill her and throw her body in the ditch with the shit, and then get away from here," Omar said. "That would be too easy a fate for her, but she'll only obey us and travel with you to Sudan if she thinks her son's life depends on it."

"I've dreamed of having her, of controlling her, for five years."

"Yes, and that would be the perfect fate for her. She detests you, Muhammed. It would be a fate worse than death for her. It would be the perfect retribution for the grief she has caused us. It would be a life of hell for her and a fitting punishment for the death of Ali Abdul Shoukri. She would dread every day of her life, having to obey you, having to clean your house and sleep in your bed."

"Yes, her dread would make it all the better."

"We must determine if she knows about the damn planes overhead and the message they are leaving up there for all of the West Bank to see."

Alexandra, of course, knew that by now Omar Samir and Muhammed Faisel were aware of the skywriting. What they had no way of knowing was whether she knew. If they thought she was aware of the message, Alexandra was certain they would kill her on the spot. They knew she would die before letting them force her to Sudan with Muhammed Faisel. She knew she would be tested and that her life would depend on whether they believed she was unaware of the sky-writers telling all the world that her son was safe.

Omar went into Hebron in the afternoon to buy food for dinner and left Muhammed Faisel alone with Alexandra. She sat on the floor, leaning against the wall, and contemplated what she should do. She knew they would kill her the moment they suspected she knew her son was safe and that her obedience was no longer assured.

"Sabirah, we will be having our dinner meal soon. You should clean yourself before the evening meal. Come, take off your abaya and niqab and cleanse yourself with the water from the hose."

Alexandra stood and walked to Muhammed.

"Take off your abaya and niqab," he said, staring into her eyes, searching for any sign of defiance. She disrobed and handed him the abaya and niqab.

"Stand over the drain," he said, "and I'll hold the hose." Alexandra did as she was told and stood there as Muhammed Faisel trained the hose and the stream of cold water on her.

There was little conversation as the two men ate their dinner of taboon bread and rice with small chunks of meat mixed in. "Alexandra, you must eat. Come here and have some food. You must be strong for our journey to Sudan."

She stood and walked to the table.

"Hold out your hand," Omar Samir commanded.

Alexandra held out her hand and Omar scooped some rice from the bowl and dropped it into her bare hand.

"Now go back to where you were sitting and eat," he said.

Alexandra seemed as compliant as she had been the day before, giving no hint that she had seen the message that Amos was safe.

She sat on the floor with her back against the wall for hours as the two men talked. Alexandra tried to determine whatever she could from their conversation, but they often spoke in hushed tones and it was impossible to understand what they were saying. Then she heard her name mentioned and that of Phoenicia University in Beirut. She watched as both men shifted in their chairs and turned to look at her. Her heart raced as they got up from the table and dragged their chairs over to her. They sat down a foot or so in front of her and peered down at her.

"Alexandra, I was just telling Muhammed about your treachery in Beirut. I told him how you ran to Israel with the Jew after divulging what you had learned about our planned operation in Ma'alot-Tarshiha. I told Muhammed about how you led on our sheik, Ali Abdul Shoukri, and how he trusted you, and then how you betrayed him and how you were responsible for his death. Muhammed knows about the Jew you married in America and the boy you had with him, whose life is now in our hands." Omar Samir glared down at her. "But Muhammed knows you were but a foolish young girl then, and he is willing to forgive you. He is willing to spare your son. All he expects of you is obedience. You are grateful for that, yes?"

She nodded. "Yes," she whispered.

"I didn't hear her. Did you hear her, Muhammed?"

"No, I heard nothing but a mumble. I didn't hear anything that sounded contrite or sincere."

"I am very grateful, Muhammed … Omar. I am very grateful," she answered.

Omar bent down close to her and looked into her eyes through the slit in the niqab she wore.

"I'm not ready to forgive you, Alexandra. Not yet. Maybe by tomorrow, eh?" he said menacingly. "Come, let's finish our meal, Muhammed." They turned and dragged their chairs across the floor and back to the table.

Alexandra sat there on the floor, her back against the wall, her breathing labored, her arms wrapped around her knees. She knew they would return soon to test her, to determine if she still feared for her son's life. She had little doubt what they would do to test her. Alexandra reached under the abaya and dug her finger nails into the perineal flesh between her legs and stifled a groan as the skin tore.

Soon the two men rose from the table and walked over to her. Her heart was pounding, but she sat impassively.

"Alexandra, it is time for sleeping. Are you ready to sleep?" Omar Samir asked.

"Yes, I am ready," she answered, jerking her head affirmatively.

"Good. We have decided that tonight we will only sleep on two mattresses. You will lie with Muhammed and then you will lie with me. Is that understood?"

She jerked her head, signaling that she would comply. Her heart pounded as she choked back her tears.

"You will behave? You will do as you are told?"

Again, she nodded. "Yes, I will do whatever you ask. But promise me you haven't harmed my son. Promise me you won't hurt him," she begged.

"We have no desire to harm the boy. Someday, when it is safe, we will arrange to get him to Sudan. We will enroll him in a madrasah as I told you," Muhammed replied.

Alexandra nodded convincingly. "He mustn't be harmed," she said.

"No, no. Of course not. I promised you we won't harm the boy ... not as long as you do what you are told."

"I will do as you say," she replied.

"Good, take off your abaya and niqab. It is time to show your appreciation for your son's safety."

Alexandra removed the niqab and pulled the abaya over her head. She rose, naked, in front of them.

"What is this?" Muhammed yelled as he looked at the rivulet of blood running down her leg.

"It is my time of month, Muhammed. I can do whatever you ask of me, but I can't stop my monthly flow," she answered.

"It is forbidden!" he yelled.

"Only intercourse is strictly forbidden," Omar said. "She can still lie with us. She can still show us her appreciation for how we are taking care that no harm comes to the boy."

Muhammed glared at Alexandra. "Why didn't you say anything?"

"What could I say? What could I do? It's a light, intermittent flow. I'm sure it will be over in two or three days?"

"Clean yourself. You can lie with Omar tonight. I don't want you on my mattress in this condition. It is forbidden. Go clean yourself. The sight is disgusting."

Alexandra walked to the hose and washed the blood from her thigh. "See, it is barely a trickle now," she said.

"I'm not so strict, Alexandra. You'll lie with me tonight," Omar said. "You will keep me warm."

Alexandra dried herself with the cloth they had given her earlier and walked back to the mattress where Omar stood waiting for her.

His hands were outstretched, holding the handcuffs with which they had bound her when they brought her from Eilat.

"No, no," she cried. "Please."

"Turn around and put your hands behind your back," he commanded.

"Please, I beg you, don't make me do that. You don't need to use the handcuffs. I'm not going anywhere."

Omar Samir, without warning, slapped her hard across her face.

"When will you learn to do as you are told, Alexandra?"

She nodded, obediently. "I'm sorry, Omar," she said, sobbing as she turned her back to him and placed her wrists together behind her back.

"Now get on the mattress and wait for me," he said in a steady, menacing voice.

He held onto her arm as she lowered herself onto the mattress.

"I won't be able to sleep with my arms cuffed behind my back," she said.

"We'll see, Alexandra. We'll see how you behave."

"Omar, it is forbidden," Muhammed Faisel said.

"I will not do anything that is forbidden," Omar Samir replied. "It is not forbidden to look or to touch or to be kept warm. You will want to help me keep warm, won't you, Alexandra?"

"Yes. Yes, of course," she nodded. She would do what she had to do to survive until they were in a more public place such as the airport in Amman. Then she would flee from them at the first opportunity. She would scream for help as soon as they entered the terminal at the airport. That was her plan.

CHAPTER
THIRTY-EIGHT

There was little conversation as Noah drove A'isha to Baltimore–Washington International Airport the following day. He gave her ninety-five hundred dollars, enough, they thought, for expenses she might incur, but less than the amount she would have to declare at the airport. He also purchased first-class tickets for her all the way through to Amman.

"We'll follow in two days and, God willing, meet you and Alexandra in Jerusalem."

"If she is alive, we will find her, Mr. Greenspan."

"Good luck, A'isha," he said, as he pulled up to the curb at the airport. "Stay safe."

"God willing, Mrs. Greenspan is unharmed and we will all meet this weekend in Jerusalem," she said. "If she is anywhere near Hebron, my family will find her and we will bring her back to you."

Noah nodded. "God willing."

***

Noah sped along the Baltimore–Washington parkway contemplating the torment Alexandra must have experienced since being taken by Omar Samir. He wondered if she was even alive. What might be happening to her at that very moment, he wondered. It was all but unbearable. His world had become so dark, he thought, as he drove through a bucolic countryside forested with trees aflame with autumn colors. He had never been so miserable.

"Hello, Barb," he said as he entered his office suite. "I thought I would get away from the house for a while."

"Any news, Noah?" she asked.

"Nothing good, Barb," he answered. "I don't know what to expect. It's all so awful."

"Noah, Marsh needs to talk to you. He said to have you buzz him if you came in. He's tried calling you at home several times this morning."

"Yeah, I should have called him earlier. I drove A'isha to BWI this morning. I'll call him now."

Noah walked into his office and stood for a moment surveying the room. So much of what he had accomplished was on display, the photographs, the framed covers of *Time Magazine* and the *Washingtonian*, the various plaques that adorned the walls and stood on the shelves, and on his desk and the credenza behind his desk. *None of it matters*, he thought.

He walked over to his desk and picked up the framed photograph that Alexandra had given him on his last birthday. He looked at the color image of Alexandra and their son, Amos. She looked radiant, so alive, so loving, so beautiful.

"Oh God, what have they done to you?" he cried, clutching the frame to his chest. "What have they done to you?"

Noah placed the photograph back on the credenza and sat down at his desk. He took a minute to regain his composure, and then reached for the phone and dialed Marshall Flynn's extension.

"Flynn."

"Marsh, it's Noah. Sorry it has taken me so long to get back to you."

"I'll come right down to your office. We need to talk."

"Come on over. I'll have Barb hold my calls."

A few moments later Marshall Flynn entered Noah's office and took a seat opposite him at his desk.

"Any news?"

Noah shrugged. "Not really. We have an effort underway to locate her, but I have no idea how realistic it is. We know jack shit about what's happening over there. We've concentrated on getting the message out that Amos is safe at home, but we have no idea if the message has reached her. We're actually skywriting above the entire West Bank, *Amos - Safe*."

"I don't know how you're holding up."

"Not very well, Marsh. I've never been so miserable in my life. If anything bad happens to Alexandra, I don't know how I'll survive."

"You'll survive, Noah. She would expect no less of you."

"So, what's up, Marsh?" Noah finally asked.

"I received a call from Markanos. He tried calling you several times and when he couldn't reach you he called me."

"What did the prick want?"

"I thought we weren't supposed to call him a prick," Marshall quipped.

"I said *you* shouldn't call him a prick. I'll call him anything I want."

"Well, I think you'll have to come up with something worse than prick."

"Why, what's he done now? He's already cost me over one hundred and twenty-five million dollars of net worth in the past week."

"He called and told me that a client of Deutschland Trust wants to buy a controlling interest in Potomac Center Properties of America."

"He *is* a prick."

"He said Deutschland's client is willing to pay two-and-a-half times PCPA's current share price."

"So, his so-called client is offering to pay twenty-five million for stock that was worth three hundred million a week ago?"

"That's what he said."

"Tell him to go fuck himself. I own fifty-one percent of the company."

"Noah, he threatened, or he said his client sort of threatened, to tender a public offer to our shareholders of twenty-five dollars a share, contingent upon you selling ten percent of your shares in their offering. They're also demanding the election of a new Board of Directors, on which they would nominate five of our seven directors."

"Why does he think we would even entertain such a ridiculous proposition?"

"Noah, he has a ton of leverage."

"I don't think he has jack shit."

"He can offer twenty-five dollars a share tomorrow, and thirty dollars a share next Monday, and thirty-five dollars a share a week later and still have a lot of room to raise his offer and still steal the company. Do you know what the stock is selling for right now?"

"No, I've been distracted," Noah answered sarcastically.

"It's at nine and a quarter," Noah.

"What does Karen say we should do?"

"Karen says we should reject the offer and call it insulting."

"Then we'll listen to Karen."

"Karen also says that we could damn well lose control of the situation if Deutschland's client keeps upping the offer."

"Not if I don't sell."

"Deutschland could try to force the election of new outside directors."

"We'll cross that bridge when we get to it, Marsh. For now, if Deutschland's client actually makes the offer, we'll respond as Karen suggested."

"Okay. You're the boss."

"Marsh, tell me exactly how your conversation with Markanos went."

"Well, I pretty much did. He did say he's going to keep on hammering Potomac Center shares."

"So, he's hammering our stock with his short-sale recommendation, and representing a group that wants to buy our shares at the same time?"

"Yeah, I guess that's right."

"What else did he say?"

"He said he believed that if we checked with our parking management company, he'd bet traffic was down, and that deliveries to our loading docks were probably down, and that foot traffic in our malls would be down. He said he believed all of our increases in tenant revenue were coming from retail price increases and not increases in unit sales."

"In other words, he got ahold of your memo."

There was an awkward moment of silence.

"Marsh?"

"Yeah, I think he got ahold of my memo to you that, essentially, said all of those things."

"If we could prove that, especially with his proffering an offer for the company, we could nail him at the SEC. He's trading on non-public information based on an internal company memorandum."

"Well, there's no way in the world we could prove that, Noah."

"Maybe. Maybe not."

"What are you thinking?"

"I'll let you know when I decide what I'm going to do. At the moment, I have far more pressing matters to deal with."

"Of course. I understand, Noah ... but you've lost a fortune, over one hundred and twenty-five million dollars of net worth this week ... and, Noah, your entire management team has taken a beating too."

Noah nodded and sighed. "I know, Marsh. I know."

"Not to mention your parents and the entire Salaman family."

"My wife is being held by terrorists, Marsh. I haven't the slightest idea whether she's even alive."

"I understand, Noah. I really do. We all feel for you, and God knows everyone is worried sick about Alexandra. But you can't just ignore the havoc that prick Markanos is causing all of us. On paper, at least, we've all been ruined."

"Nobody has been ruined, Marsh. We'll get through this."

"You seemed to have an idea about how to deal with Markanos a few minutes ago."

"So?"

"So, it's time to deal with him, Noah."

Noah nodded that he understood.

"I'll stay in touch, Marsh."

"I'm really sorry you have to deal with this shit at a time like this, Noah."

"No, you did the right thing by having this conversation with me, Marsh. Really, thanks."

Noah sat there for a moment after his chief financial officer left his office, contemplating what to do next. He reached for the phone on his desk and buzzed his secretary.

"Yes, Noah?" she answered.

"Barb, see if you can reach Special Agent Hogan for me at FBI headquarters."

***

Alexandra experienced the worst night of her life.

Omar Samir did not rape her that night. Even he wouldn't violate Islam's strict prohibition against sexual intercourse during menstruation. But that didn't stop him from holding her, naked, against his body during the night, or kissing her passionately, or letting his hands roam over her. Sleep was not something she would experience that night—not for a moment. Her arms, bound behind her back, ached unbearably, and the searing pain in her shoulders burned like fire. She pleaded with Omar Samir to release her from the handcuffs.

"Where am I going to go, Omar? What can I do? What is the point of constraining me this way?" she cried. "What's the point?

"The point is, I enjoy having you constrained, as you say. Relax, Alexandra, your arms will only get in the way," he said, as his hands roamed her body. "You know, I envy Muhammed Faisel," he whispered into her ear as he gripped her arms. "You are a beauty," he said pulling her tightly against his body. "By the time your bleeding stops he'll have you to himself in El-Obeid. Once you are in Sudan, no one will be able to help you. He can enjoy you, or he can have you hanged. It is that simple, and it is what you deserve for what you did to Ali Abdul Shoukri," he whispered.

"I didn't betray Ali, Omar," she answered softly to avoid waking Muhammed Faisel. "He and you betrayed me. I was just a girl, a young student. You used me. I wrote articles about your student movement that all of you said you liked. But you used the timing of the articles to notify your friends of arms shipments. How did I betray you or Ali Abdul Shoukri?"

"You ran off with the Jew from Israel."

"What was I to do? Ali was going to kill me."

"Because you betrayed us."

"I tried to stop a massacre, but I demanded that the Israelis not kill anyone. I protected your accomplices in Ma'alot-Tarshiha. None of them were killed."

"No, they are rotting in Israeli prisons. They would have rather died."

CHAPTER THIRTY-NINE

Heinz Stutenhof, maître d' of the Bull and Bear at the Waldorf Astoria, was busy looking through the evening's reservations. It was three o'clock in the afternoon and, but for a few lunch stragglers still chatting at their tables in the far corner of the room, the restaurant was empty. The white-haired maître d' looked over the rim of his bifocals as the two men entered the restaurant.

"I'm sorry, gentlemen, we won't be open for dinner for another two hours," he said.

"Heinz Stutenhof?"

"Yes, I'm Heinz Stutenhof," he answered.

"Good afternoon, I'm Special Agent Laurence Hogan from the FBI, and this is my colleague, Special Agent Mike Atkins," Agent Hogan said, flashing his FBI credentials for the maître d' to see. "We've come up from headquarters in Washington and we were wondering if we could have a moment of your time."

"But of course. Please, let's sit at a table," he said with a sweep of his arm, gesturing to a nearby booth. Heinz Stutenhof loved being in the know and was immediately intrigued about whatever the two FBI agents wanted to discuss. Information could be like currency in New York, and whatever the two FBI agents had come to New York to discuss would almost certainly provide grist for the mill.

"Can I offer you gentlemen something to drink?"

"That's very kind of you, but no thanks," Agent Hogan replied.

"Actually, I'd have some coffee if that's convenient," Agent Atkins said.

"Of course, no trouble at all," the maître d' answered. He snapped his finger at a nearby busboy who was setting out drinking glasses on the tables. "Andre, some coffee for the gentleman," he said. "Agent Hogan, are you sure we can't get you anything"

"Well, maybe a glass of cold club soda," Agent Hogan replied.

As soon as the coffee and club soda were served, Heinz Stutenhof sat back, anticipating whatever information he was about to learn from the two agents.

"This is, of course, an entirely voluntarily interview," Agent Hogan began.

"Of course, of course. But you can always feel free to come and chat with me. I am always glad to be helpful. You see and hear a lot in this job."

"Thank you very much, sir," Agent Atkins said as he placed a small tape recorder on the table and pressed the "on" button.

"Interview between Heinz Stutenhof and Agents Laurence Hogan and Michael Atkins, November second, nineteen seventy-three," Agent Atkins said into a small microphone attached to the recorder.

"We appreciate that very much, Mr. Stutenhof. You would be surprised how many people clam up when we come to chat."

"It is an honor to assist the FBI," the maître d' replied, with a smile.

"It really is, and we appreciate your spirit of cooperation, Mr. Stutenhof," Agent Hogan said.

"Certainly, certainly," Heinz Stutenhof answered.

"We really appreciate upstanding citizens like you, Mr. Stutenhof," Agent Atkins interrupted. "It makes our work so much easier. You should see how some people react when we remind them that even though these discussions are voluntary, it's still a felony for anyone to lie to us. You'd be amazed how skittish people get when we tell them that."

"Yes, yes, I'm sure," the maître d' replied. Agents Hogan and Atkins both noticed Heinz Stutenhof was no longer smiling.

"So, last week a Mr. Noah Greenspan was a guest at the hotel and dined here and left a memorandum on the table that one of his employees had sent to him."

The maître d' shrugged nervously. "I wouldn't know …"

"It was the memorandum that you passed on to George Markanos over at Deutschland Trust after Mr. Greenspan left the restaurant," Agent Atkins said, interrupting the maître d'.

Agent Hogan leaned forward, his blue eyes peering into the maître d's bifocals.

"I … I don't know what you're …"

"Don't finish that statement, Mr. Stutenhof. You don't want to say anything to us that isn't true," Agent Hogan interrupted.

"Maybe I should have a lawyer here," the maître d' answered, his voice shaking, his fingers quivering ever so slightly.

"Sure, sure," you can do that, Mr. Stutenhof. Everyone is entitled to have a lawyer present when they talk to us if they choose. Of course, then we'll have to arrange to have this discussion downtown at the criminal investigation section in our New York City field office," Agent Hogan said.

Heinz Stutenhof reached in his pocket for a handkerchief and patted away the beads of sweat that had suddenly appeared on his forehead.

"Criminal investigation section?" he stammered.

"Yeah, that's where we usually talk to targets of our investigations. But you're not a target, Mr. Stutenhof. Right now, you're a cooperating citizen. We don't have any interest in seeing you get into any trouble. That's why I stopped you from lying to us a moment ago," Agent Hogan answered.

"You see, *you* didn't break any law when you passed that information on to Mr. Markanos. Well, you probably did if he compensated you for the information, but believe me, we have no interest at all in catching you on a technicality. By the way, how much did he pay you for the information in that memorandum?" Agent Atkins said.

"One hundred dollars," the maître d' replied, his voice barely above a whisper.

"Yeah, you see, you were suckered into something much bigger than you realized at the time. Mr. Markanos, on the other hand, has probably made several million dollars on the information he paid you a hundred bucks for," Agent Atkins explained.

"Did you short any shares of Potomac Center Properties of America, Mr. Stutenhof?"

"No, none. None at all," he answered.

"That's good, because that would have been a very serious felony," Agent Atkins said.

The maître d' lowered his head into his hand. "Am I in trouble?" he asked.

"Nah, I don't think so," Agent Atkins answered. "You're helping the FBI. You didn't know you were doing anything illegal. That's the way we see it right now, isn't that right, Agent Hogan?"

Agent Hogan nodded. "That's exactly the way we see it … right now."

"Mr. Stutenhof, you still got that memorandum Mr. Greenspan left here on his table last week?"

The maître d' nodded. "Yes, I still have it. I used the hotel's Dacom 412 to send a copy to George Markanos and I kept the original," he replied.

"You sent it to him here in New York?"

"No, he was at his home in New Jersey. I sent it to him there. He has a Dacom 412 too." Agent Hogan looked up at Agent Atkins. "Wire fraud," he said. Agent Atkins nodded. "Sure as hell is."

"I committed wire fraud?" the maître d' asked, panic now evident in his voice.

"You as the sender and Mr. Markanos as the receiver both did, but the Bureau isn't interested in charging you with anything, Mr.

Stutenhof. You're not the criminal here," Agent Hogan replied. "I believe the Dacom 412 records the time, date, and destination of all transmissions. Can you retrieve that information for the transmission you made to Mr. Markanos for us?"

"Yes, I can do that. Just give me a few minutes," he answered.

"Also, we'll need the original memorandum as well. We'll have to take possession of it," Agent Atkins said.

"Yes, yes, of course," the maître d' answered. "I'll get it for you right away."

***

"So, what do you think Director Clarence Kelley would say about what we just did?" Agent Atkins asked as he and Agent Hogan drove over the George Washington Bridge on the way back to Washington.

"I think if we had come up empty handed, he'd really be pissed, but we just nailed one hell of a big white-collar crime case to refer to the SEC and the Justice Department for prosecution."

"Yeah, I feel pretty good about it, even if we were acting like a couple of private eyes. That's the part the new director of the FBI wouldn't like. You know, us going off on our own without authorization, without a case file having ever been opened," Agent Atkins replied.

"We did the right thing. Noah Greenspan is going through so much right now, we couldn't just sit by and watch him being ruined by a vulture like Markanos. Markanos committed a major crime here and I think we've nailed him. I can't wait to see Noah Greenspan's face when we hand him the missing memorandum his chief financial officer wrote to him last week. That damn memorandum in Markanos's hands has cost Greenspan well over one hundred and twenty-five million dollars of net worth."

"And the poor bastard doesn't know whether his wife is dead or alive," Agent Atkins said.

***

Noah's call to FBI Agent Larry Hogan had paid off. Agents Hogan and Atkins went out on a limb launching their own one-day, unauthorized investigation of George Markanos and Deutschland Trust. Noah's hunch that Markanos had gotten hold of the memorandum he had left on the table at the Bull and Bear proved to be correct, and the two FBI agents nailed the case at the cost of gasoline for a drive up to New York and back. Their case against Markanos was so solid that the Justice Department was able to rapidly bring charges based on an *Information*, an alternate procedure to a grand jury indictment.

Deutschland Trust and George Markanos Charged by Feds

New York, New York - The US Department of Justice has charged Deutschland Trust and the bank's controversial short-sell analyst George Markanos with one count of wire fraud and one count of stock fraud and one count of stock manipulation pertaining to Mr. Markanos's recommended short sale of Potomac Center Properties of America last week. The bank and its analyst were charged with an Information, which is an expedited procedure used when the evidence is so great that the presentation of testimony and other evidence to a grand jury is considered superfluous by the prosecutor and the defendant.

According to the Information, an internal memorandum written last week by Marshall Flynn, chief financial officer at Potomac Center Properties of America, to Noah Greenspan, CEO of the shopping mall development company, was given to Mr. Markanos by the maître d' of the Bull and Bear restaurant at the Waldorf Astoria in New York City after it was inadvertently left on a table in the dining room by Mr. Greenspan.

The Information states that the memorandum expressed concern that the United States was headed toward a recession and cited reduced automobile traffic into the malls' garages, reduced incoming deliveries to the malls' receiving docks, and reduced foot traffic in the malls.

The Information further alleges that the memorandum was sent over interstate wires to Mr. Markanos, who was at his home in New Jersey at the time. Mr. Markanos, according to the Information, then returned to New York and issued a short-sell recommendation sometime after midnight on October 30.

Mr. Markanos was also charged with stock manipulation, because he allegedly contacted the chief financial officer of Potomac Center Properties of America, Marshall Flynn, on behalf of an unnamed client of Deutschland Trust to make an offer to purchase in excess of fifty percent of the outstanding shares of the company for twenty-five dollars a share.

Maximum sentence for all three charges, were Mr. Markanos found guilty, could be as high as fifty-five years in federal prison as well as millions of dollars in fines. Mr. Markanos has plead not guilty and says he plans to vigorously defend himself.

Shares of Potomac Center Properties of America plummeted from sixty dollars a share to ten dollars a share over the last three trading days.

Mr. Greenspan said he was shocked by the charges against Deutschland Trust and Mr. Markanos but had no further comment at this time.

CHAPTER FORTY

Noah, FBI Agents Hogan and Atkins, and Sarah Jean Bogart were gathered around the Greenspan kitchen table when Amos's call came through from Eilat, as scheduled, promptly at six o'clock.

"Hello, Amos," Noah answered as soon as the phone rang.

"Hello, Noah. Who do we have on the call?"

"Same cast of characters. Agents Hogan and Atkins are here, along with Sarah Jean Bogart."

"Good. Good evening, everyone. Sarah Jean, we haven't met, but I understand you're quite the investigator."

Agent Atkins rolled his eyes impatiently.

"Yes, she's been very helpful, Amos," Noah answered. "Is there anything new to report?"

"Well, we have nothing new, but here's what we know at this time. We know A'isha arrived in Amman on schedule and should be with her family in Hebron. We assume she has briefed them by now. They are really good, respected people in the area, well connected. They may be of real help."

"Let's hope so, Amos. I'm worried sick."

"I know, Noah. We all are."

"Are we still skywriting?"

"We are, but we assume if she hasn't seen it by now her captors have and they'll make sure she doesn't see it."

"I hope she knows Amos is safe. That would relieve a lot of stress for her."

"There is something we should discuss, and, Sarah Jean, this will probably involve you."

"Yes, sir. I'll do whatever you tell me to do."

"We've maintained a tight news blackout regarding Alexandra being kidnapped by terrorists."

"Yes, sir," Sarah Jean replied. "The *Star* hasn't printed a word, and as far as we know, no other paper even knows she's over there."

"Well, our people over here aren't sure the news blackout regarding Alexandra is a good idea. They think it might be a mistake at this point."

"Why?" Noah asked. "What's the point of giving what Samir has pulled off any publicity?"

"We know these people follow any news of their operations very closely. So, here we have a major terrorist act: the kidnapping, and for all we know the murder ... I'm sorry, Noah, but I'm just giving you the thinking here ..."

"It's okay, Amos, go on."

"So, we have the kidnapping and maybe the murder by terrorists of a prominent American journalist and not a word is being printed in any American newspapers. Our people are concerned that might suggest there's a news blackout because we are planning some operation of our own to try to find and rescue her. Our people believe that might cause Samir to get very nervous and do something drastic with Alexandra."

"You mean kill her?"

"We can't rule that out, Noah."

"Let me interrupt for a moment," Agent Hogan said. "I think the Bureau would prefer the blackout. We'd rather keep the kidnappers guessing."

"Ordinarily, we would agree," Amos replied. "But this blackout has gone on for days now, and we're concerned that that is going to make Omar Samir very jittery. That worries us."

"So, your people think the total news blackout might make Samir and Muhammed Faisel nervous and that they might kill Alexandra and be done with it?"

"Samir must have expected major headlines in the American press by now, and the total lack of coverage would probably seem very suspicious to him. So, yes, he might get concerned that we're about to mount an operation of our own, and we're concerned he might do something drastic."

"So, you're suggesting that we publish a story that Alexandra has been kidnapped?" Sarah Jean asked.

"Yes, our people think that would be better than continuing the news blackout. They're concerned that the absence of news coverage is just too unusual in a case like this, and that it might cause the terrorists to do something precipitous."

"Precipitous? Is that your way of saying murder?" Sarah Jean asked impatiently.

"Yes, Sarah Jean. I guess that's what I'm saying," Amos answered.

"I'll talk to our editor, Mr. Markazie," Sarah Jean answered. "He will absolutely hate to see this in our paper. I'm told he's been Alexandra's mentor since she was sixteen years old. The people I work with at the paper say he loves her like a daughter."

"He's a consummate professional, Sarah Jean. He'll understand the logic of what Amos is suggesting," Noah said.

"How do you feel about this, Noah?" Amos asked.

"I can't stand the thought of something like this being in the paper. It will just kill the Salamans. Every paper in the country will pick it up within twenty-four hours."

"That's the point, Noah. It will send a signal that we're in the dark, and that's a better signal than that we're planning an operation that necessitates a news blackout."

"I think we have to go with your judgment," Noah replied.

"I'll go over all of this with Mr. Markazie. It's going to be his decision," Sarah Jean replied.

"Amos, is there anything we can do to help?" Agent Hogan asked.

"I'm afraid not, Larry. There's not even anything *we* can do to help. I think it's all boiling down to A'isha and her family. We know that

Muhammed Faisel and Sabirah Najat, and we assume Omar Samir, are booked on a flight to Khartoum out of Amman the day after tomorrow. There is really only one highway into Amman from the West Bank, so, hopefully, the Abadi's will be able to intercept them. We're assuming, of course, that they are on the West Bank and probably near Hebron. The Abadi's are our best hope. Frankly, they're our only hope."

"How will they know who to intercept?"

"They'll be looking for two men and a woman traveling by car from Hebron to Amman."

"Won't they need a picture of Alexandra?"

"Well, A'isha can identify Alexandra once they've stopped them."

"But they'll need some way of identifying Alexandra as a passenger in a car, won't they?"

"Noah, you can be sure they'll have Alexandra in an abaya and a niqab. She won't be recognizable from the window of a car."

"This rescue sounds like a very, very long shot to me, Amos."

"It is, Noah, but it's all we've got." My guess is that the Abadis will try to narrow the field by spreading out and checking the few hotels in the area, or any activity in houses that are supposed to be vacant. There are a number of pretty isolated old stone structures that have been empty for years in the surrounding desert. The Abadis are well connected in the Hebron area. They won't be completely in the dark. Word will get to them if there is anything unusual or out of the ordinary."

There was silence for several moments. "I guess we're all hoping for a miracle," Noah finally said.

"Yeah, a miracle wearing a red hijab," Sarah Jean replied.

***

Sarah Jean was already in the kitchen waiting for Noah to come down for breakfast the following morning. She had brought Amos down with her and poured some Klondike Pete's Crunchy Nuggets into a cereal bowl for him.

"Hello, Mr. Greenspan," she greeted him when he walked into the Kitchen.

"Good morning, Sarah Jean. Have you seen the morning paper?"

"I have it, Mr. Greenspan," she answered, holding one arm behind her back. "It's upsetting. It's a bad way to start the day."

"I may as well have a look, Sarah Jean. It's going to be in every paper in the world by tonight."

"I'm so sorry, sir," she said, handing him the morning edition of the *Star*. "I'm so sorry."

"Let's stop with the *sir* and the *Mr. Greenspan*, Sarah Jean. I'm Noah. Just call me Noah."

"Yes, sir … I mean, okay, Noah … sir."

Noah held out his hand for the paper, and Sarah Jean, haltingly, handed it to him.

"Oh my God," he whispered as soon as he looked at the front page. A large photograph of Alexandra, two columns wide and three column inches deep, appeared under the headline.

Evening Star Reporter Kidnapped in Israel Feared Dead

Washington D.C. – Alexandra Salaman, 34, columnist for the Evening Star went missing in Eilat, Israel, last Tuesday and authorities fear for her life. Ms. Salaman traveled to Egypt last Saturday to cover the Egyptian-Israeli disengagement negotiations near Suez City at Kilometer 101 on the road to Cairo.

Miss Salaman was last seen getting into an automobile around midnight in front of Hotel Eilat, where she was staying. Hotel personnel said Miss Salaman rushed from the building seemingly distressed, and it appears that she was somehow coerced into the automobile.

US and Israeli authorities appear to be in the dark regarding her whereabouts, and there is fear that she may have been killed and buried somewhere in the desert.

"No one has heard a word about her whereabouts since she went missing, and that is a very bad sign," said one State Department official, whose name cannot be divulged because he is not authorized to speak on the matter. Another knowledgeable official at the Defense Department said she could be anywhere in the Middle East by now. "If her abductors succeeded in getting Miss Salaman across the so-called Green Line separating the Palestinian territories from Israel she could be captive on the West Bank, or she could have easily been moved into Jordan, Iraq, Syria, or Lebanon. There is no telling where she is or what has happened to her, or if she is even alive," he said.

FBI agent Laurence Hogan acknowledged that the Bureau was involved in the case and said, "We're working with the Israelis and with Interpol," but declined to comment further.

Miss Salaman has had other brushes with danger in the past. When she was a student at Phoenicia University in Beirut, Lebanon in 1957, she was employed as a student correspondent by the Evening Star. A group of Palestinian students at the university were involved in terrorist activities and, unbeknownst to Miss Salaman, used the timing of her stories to tip off fellow conspirators in Israel about arms shipments to be used in a terrorist attack on the Arab-Israeli town of Ma'alot-Tarshiha. Miss Salaman was warned by Israeli operatives that she was being used by terrorists, and she was subsequently able to determine where the attack was to take place and notify the Israelis. She had to flee Beirut with the clothes on her back.

Ms. Salaman spent several years in Israel before returning to the United States in 1964. Three years later, she returned to Israel in June 1967 to cover the six-day war. In August 1967, she travelled, under the pseudonym Sabirah Najat, to Khartoum, Sudan to cover the Arab League summit that produced the so-called Three No's Declaration by the Arab states—no peace, no negotiation, and no recognition. As she was preparing to leave with another correspondent at the conclusion of the summit, she was arrested and held captive in a notorious prison in the Omdurman section of Khartoum. She was rescued in a daring operation by Israel's Mossad, and the details of the rescue operation are still not fully known.

Miss Salaman is married to Noah Greenspan, 35, who is the chief executive officer and founder of Potomac Center Properties of America, which has developed and operates several regional shopping malls, including one on the banks of the Anacostia River here in Washington. Mr. Greenspan declined to be interviewed for this story.

Sarah Jean watched Noah carefully as he stood there reading the Star's coverage of Alexandra's kidnapping. He finished the story, tears in his eyes, and lowered his head into his hand.

"This is such a nightmare," he finally said, looking up to Sarah Jean. "The thought of her being in the hands of these terrorists and at their mercy is just unbearable."

"I am so sorry, Mr. Greenspan, I mean, Noah. I feel so helpless … useless as a wooden frying-pan."

"So far, Sarah Jean, you're the only person who has accomplished anything since this awful business began. You were responsible for finding and rescuing Amos and A'isha, and right now A'isha and her family are the only hope we've got."

CHAPTER
FORTY-ONE

Omar Samir had been gone since early morning and Muhammed Faisel was largely avoiding Alexandra. There was, to him, nothing enticing about a menstruating woman. It was, he thought, a disgusting time of the month, a time when women should keep to themselves. Men should have no more contact with a menstruating woman than necessary. She was sitting on the floor, half asleep, resting against the wall, exhausted from the sleepless night she had spent on Omar Samir's mattress. She was too tired to eat and longed to sleep, even if only for a few minutes. She dreaded the passage of time when the afternoon sun would set, and evening would emerge, and Omar Samir would lead her to his mattress, and her body would again become his plaything. She knew that she would soon have to slowly rip the scab from her perineum so that she would bleed and thereby limit the liberty he would take with her. Her head nodded as exhaustion slowly began to descend into sleep. Her head fell forward, pushing her chin down until it almost rested against her chest. Then, for a few moments, sleep came, freeing her from the agony that occupied her every waking moment. But it was not to last. Omar Samir came through the door waving a copy of *Al ra'i*, the daily newspaper published in Amman.

"Muhammed, Muhammed," he yelled, waking Alexandra from her brief respite. "Look, on the front page of *Al ra'i*, a big story about what we've done, what we've accomplished. Look, it even has her picture."

"Let me see," Muhammed Faisel said, grabbing the paper. "Praise be to Allah, what we have done is news all over the world."

"Sabirah, Sabirah, look. Look at what we've done. They think you are dead. They won't even try to find you. We will be left alone in El-Obeid."

"What?" she said. "What are you talking about?"

"It's all here, reprinted, it says, from the *Washington Evening Star*. They think you are probably dead, buried somewhere in the desert. You really will belong to me."

"Let me see."

"See, here is your picture," he said, holding the paper up to her face. "It is written in Arabic, of course. Shall I read it to you?"

"No, I can read Arabic, but just tell me what it says."

"It says they think you are dead and buried in the desert, or possibly held as far away as Iraq or Syria or maybe Lebanon or Jordan. They have no idea where you are or whether you are even alive," he said joyously. "You really will be mine," he said, taking her by the chin and pulling her head up so that she was staring into his eyes. "All mine."

"Come, Omar, let's go to the table and read the entire news story," he said, abruptly releasing Alexandra's chin from his grip.

She sat there against the wall, her chest heaving as she tried to catch her breath. She looked at them sitting at the table with the paper spread out in front of them.

Alexandra's head sagged toward her chest as she wept. Then she looked up at Omar Samir and Muhammed Faisel gloating over their accomplishment, and for the first time since her abduction, she felt only anger. She reached under the abaya, took a deep breath, and pulled the scab from her flesh. She felt the warm blood on her fingers and knew she could still resist. She moved her fingers, wet with blood, forward from the wound. Alexandra leaned back against the wall and let the bleeding trickle down onto her thigh. A few drops of blood fell to the floor where she was sitting.

She knew her son was safe and that neither Omar Samir nor Muhammed Faisel knew that she knew. They would assume she would be compliant all the way to Sudan if that's what it took to protect her son, but she would shock them once they were in the terminal at the airport in Amman. She would scream for help. She would kick at them and claw at them if they tried to silence her there. The Jordanians were wary of the Palestinians anyway, and were reluctant allies of the Egyptians and the Syrians in the recent fighting. They would free her, arrest her captors, and return her to America. Time, she was certain, was on her side.

Omar Samir and Muhammed Faisel finally got up from the table and walked over to her. Omar Samir reached down and yanked the niqab from her head.

"How are you feeling, Alexandra?"

"Exhausted," she answered. "I didn't sleep last night. You know that."

"Well, you've done nothing all day. You should be rested."

"What do you want of me?" she asked.

"How do you feel? Are you still sick?"

"I'm not sick, Omar. A woman isn't sick because she menstruates."

"Are you … bleeding now?"

She nodded.

"Let me see."

She pulled the abaya up enough for him to see the rivulet of blood on her thigh and the droplets on the floor.

"Disgusting," he snapped.

"How long will you be like this?" Muhammed Faisel demanded to know.

"Probably only another day or two" she answered.

"Go clean yourself and then scrub the floor where you've been sitting. It's disgusting."

Alexandra got to her feet and pulled the abaya over her head and handed it to Muhammed Faisel. She stood before the two men naked and defiant.

"Do you really think I'm disgusting, Muhammed?"

"I envy you, Muhammed. Look at what you will have in El-Obeid," Omar said, taking Alexandra by the shoulders and turning her slightly so that she was standing directly in front of Muhammed Faisel. He nudged her forward, closer to him. She could feel Muhammed Faisel's breath on her face.

"It will be all the retribution I could have ever imagined," he said as he moved behind Alexandra. He placed his hands on her shoulders and tightened his grip on her. "Feel how warm she is, Muhammed. Feel her arms."

"Not while she is like this," Muhammed answered. "It is forbidden."

"I am not so strict as Muhammed," Omar said. "You will keep me warm again tonight won't you Alexandra?" She didn't answer.

"Won't you?" he repeated, moving his hands to her breasts.

She began to breathe heavily and she could feel her heart pounding in her chest. "Yes, Omar. I will keep you warm tonight," she answered.

"Good. Now, go clean yourself for bed. We have a long day tomorrow. We need to rest."

***

Noah and Agents Hogan and Atkins were sitting around the kitchen table waiting for the nightly six o'clock call from Israel. Sarah Jean let herself into the house and called out to them from the foyer.

"I hope everybody is hungry," she yelled. "We've got hot Mighty Mo's, fries, and shakes from the Hot Shoppe." Amos came running into the kitchen and climbed up on his father's lap.

"Hi, everybody," Sarah Jean said as she followed Amos into the room. She handed out the cheeseburgers and shakes to everyone and placed the fries in the middle of the table.

"Any news?"

"No," Agent Hogan replied, reaching for a french fry. "We're waiting for Amos's call now. We do know the *Star*'s article has circulated throughout the Middle East. It's big news there."

The sudden ringing of the telephone interrupted the conversation.

"Amos, it's Noah. We're all here. Is there anything to report?"

"Good evening, everyone. Here's our thinking. With that flight from Amman to Khartoum tomorrow, the Abadis will try to screen traffic and intercept them before they get to the airport," Amos said. "We've made contact with the family and I think they're very sharp. A'isha did an excellent job of briefing them on the situation."

"How is an intercept on the way to the airport even possible?" Noah asked. "The traffic going into the airport must be very heavy."

"That's true, but the traffic from the West Bank into Amman may not be so heavy, and there's only one road from the West Bank. The Abadis know the flight time, so all of their effort can be focused on the few hours before the flight is scheduled to depart."

"It sounds like a very long shot to me," Noah said.

"But it's the only shot we have," Agent Hogan replied, "and it may not be such a long shot after all. The Abadis will have to make some basic decisions. Cars with no women will get a pass. I would guess cars with children will get a pass. A car with a man and a woman or two men and a woman will be what they will focus on."

"They could have her in the trunk or on the floor," Noah replied.

"They could, but that's awkward for them," Amos said. "They would not want to do anything that aroused suspicion at the airport, like opening the trunk or getting someone off the floor of the car. Ever since the open warfare between the PLO and Jordan three years ago, the Jordanians are very vigilant, especially at the airport. No, I think they'll drive up to the curb at the airport like any other travelers. And that's our ace in the hole. Even if the Abadis don't intercept them before they get to the airport, I think Alexandra will scream her head off once she's in the airport."

"Which could be a pretty dangerous thing to do," Noah replied.

"Not as dangerous as getting on that plane to Khartoum," Agent Hogan said. "If they succeed in getting Alexandra to Sudan, it could take years to get her out, and that's assuming we could even prove she was there."

"So, they're just going to stare at passengers in cars and decide whether they think Alexandra is in one of the cars?" Noah asked.

"Well, they do have other plans as well," Amos said.

"Such as?"

"As I understand it, there are clusters of old abandoned stone houses south of Hebron, not far from a town called ad-Dhahiriya. From time to time vagrants have occupied these structures for brief periods. Anyway, there are too many to inspect, but the Abadis do think one of these abandoned structures would be a likely place for them to have taken Alexandra. They feel the hotels in the area would be too dangerous to take an unwilling female. The hotel management would call the police immediately if they suspected anything immoral. They could be holed up with a family friendly to their cause, but the Abadis pretty much rule that out too, because they feel word would get back to them quickly. They are very well connected in the community. No one would want to have a problem with the Abadis."

"So, how will they check out all of these abandoned structures?" Noah asked.

"That wouldn't be possible. But these clusters of old one-room stone structures are all off the main highway south of Hebron. You have to drive along a rough sand path for a few miles to get to them. There are only a handful of paths leading from the highway to these abandoned structures. The Abadis will have someone parked, beginning midnight tonight, at each junction where these paths intersect with the main highway. They'll keep a watch there until an hour before flight time tomorrow. If a car that looks suspicious exits from one of these paths onto the main highway, the sentry will radio ahead using a walkie-talkie. Keep in mind, all of these old structures are supposed to be abandoned, so a car exiting one of these sand paths will automatically be viewed as suspicious. Should that happen, I can assure you that car will be stopped before it gets out of Hebron, and if Alexandra is in the vehicle, it will never reach the airport."

"We have something interesting," Agent Hogan said. "The Bureau received word from Interpol that an O. Samir traveled by air from Aswan to Amman a week ago. We don't know where he went from Amman, but O. Samir must be Omar Samir, and it's only about fifty or sixty miles from Amman to Hebron."

"Interesting," Amos said. "If I had to guess, I'd say the traveler was Omar Samir. I don't think Muhammed Faisel could have devised this operation on his own. This has all the markings of something Omar Samir would do. I believe the only reason Muhammed Faisel is involved at all is because he represents the ultimate nightmare for Alexandra. He is Omar Samir's tool for creating misery for her."

"Anything else to discuss Amos?"

"No, I think that pretty much wraps it up from here."

"Okay, let's stay in touch, Amos," Noah said before ending the call.

"When is Mommy coming home?" Amos asked as soon as Noah put down the phone.

Agent Hogan looked at Agent Atkins and just shook his head. Noah started to respond, but words simply wouldn't come. He was too choked up to respond.

"Well, Amos, I bet your mommy is going to be home before you know it," Sarah Jean said, picking up the boy and hugging him tightly.

"But when?" he insisted.

"You know what I think we should do, Amos? Let's go and find some paper and crayons and make a great big Welcome Home sign for your mommy. How does that sound?"

The men at the kitchen table looked at Sarah Jean as she hugged Amos. They saw the tears streaming down her face as she tried to cheer up the child. "Your mommy is coming home soon," she said, her voice quivering with emotion as she forced a smile.

CHAPTER
FORTY-TWO

"It's time to lie down for the night, Alexandra," Omar said as he propped himself up on the mattress with an elbow. "Come here and lie next to me."

"Omar, you saw the bleeding. How can you lie with her?"

"I'm not going to do anything that is forbidden, Muhammed. She can lie with us."

"I won't have her on my mattress, Omar. Not when she's like this."

"Good, then I'll have her all to myself again tonight. Alexandra, come here and lie down next to me," he commanded, a sharp edge to his voice. "We have a busy day tomorrow and we must rest now."

She nodded and walked to the mattress.

"Take off your abaya." She complied as he watched.

Omar reached over to the side of the mattress and picked up the handcuffs that were lying there.

"No, Omar. Please, I can't spend another night like that. My shoulders burned all day. Please don't make me do that again."

"If the handcuffs hurt your arms we won't put them on your wrists behind your back. Come stand here next to me."

She moved closer to the mattress. Omar kneeled in front of her and picked up the handcuffs from the floor. He smiled up at her and snapped the cuffs onto her ankles.

"See, I don't want you to be uncomfortable," he said, suddenly pulling her off balance and down onto the mattress. "We don't want you to get hurt walking in your sleep, do we, Alexandra?"

Alexandra, actually thankful not to have her hands bound behind her back again, slowly shook her head. "No, Omar, we wouldn't want that to happen," she said.

"You see, I trust you. I'm not worried about what you might do with your hands when I am asleep."

"Yes, Omar. You can trust me," she answered.

"Listen, Alexandra, Muhammed is snoring already. We mustn't disturb him."

"No," she whispered.

"You know I could have killed you, don't you?" he asked in a low voice.

"Of course I do."

"But I have spared you, Alexandra," he whispered.

"Yes, I know."

"Do you know why I have spared you?"

"Of course I do."

"Tell me why, Alexandra," he asked in a hushed voice.

"You've found a punishment worse than death," she answered.

"Yes, yes," he answered. "It will be hell for you every day with that oaf."

"And that will make you happy, Omar? That you have devised a hell on earth for me?"

"Oh yes. Death isn't punishment. Not really. It is only a release. Why would I want to release you after what you did to us?"

"I did nothing to you. I tried to spare innocent men, women, and children of Ma'alot-Tarshiha."

"And all of our comrades are still in Israeli prisons, and sheik Ali Abdul Shoukri is dead. All because of you, Alexandra."

"We shouldn't be having this discussion, Omar. I'm not sorry I helped prevent a massacre of maybe scores, even hundreds, of people.

And you know perfectly well that I was not responsible for Ali's death. He kidnapped me, and the Israelis tracked us down and he was killed in a fire fight. How am I responsible for that?"

"You lived with that Israeli Jew, Alexandra, and now you're married to an American Jew"

"And is that worth all of this? Is that worth the trouble you have gone to just to make sure I am miserable for the rest of my life?"

"You are a Palestinian woman. The way you comport yourself is a disgrace."

"I have done nothing to disgrace the Palestinian people, Omar. Nor would I."

"You think we are so ignorant of your transgressions against our people, Alexandra? Nothing escapes us."

"I don't know what you're talking about."

"Don't you?"

"No, I don't."

"Even now you lie. You are totally under my control and still you lie. You realize that I control whether you live or die?"

"Yes. I know you could have killed me and I know you can still kill me."

"But still you lie."

"I'm not lying to you."

He turned on his side and reached over and pulled her onto her side so that she was facing him, their bodies only inches apart.

"You promote the Zionist cause. You think we don't know, Alexandra, but we know everything."

Alexandra hesitated.

"Oh, so now you are lost for words, eh, Alexandra?"

She didn't respond.

"Did you say something, Alexandra? I don't think I heard you. I was talking about how you promote the Zionist cause. You seem to have an answer for everything, but now you are silent."

"I don't promote the Zionist cause," she answered, her voice hesitant, her heart beat pounding in her ears.

"Stay where you are," he said menacingly. "Don't move."

Omar Samir got to his feet and walked across the room. She watched as he opened his satchel and pulled a paper from it. He turned and walked back to the mattress and tossed the paper down to her. "You think we are so stupid?"

"No, I don't," she answered as she picked up the clipping from the newspaper, the one with the full color picture of her sitting at the dais in the Grand Ballroom of the Mayflower Hotel under the Israeli flag.

"Oh my God," she whispered.

"You see, we know all about you and what you do among the Jews in Washington," he said, spitting out the words angrily.

"I was only accompanying my husband," she said, her voice unsteady and unconvincing.

"The Jewish businessman and his Arab Palestinian wife celebrating with the Zionists," he snapped.

Alexandra didn't respond. She knew it would be futile.

"Nothing to say, eh? Your silence is your confession. You see why we haven't killed you. Killing you would be too easy, Alexandra. You are married to a Jew Zionist and you happily consort with the Zionists. There is no punishment too severe for you. Sleeping in Muhammed Faisel's bed for the rest of your life will be hell on earth for you. That's why you are here, Alexandra. That's why tomorrow night you will be in Muhammed's bed in El-Obeid, Sudan. Then, all hope will be lost for you. Look at him sleeping there, Alexandra. Look at him. Get used to it. That will be what you see every night for the rest of your life. Do you have any idea what he will demand of you, Alexandra? How long do you think you will remain beautiful? Look at you," he said, pushing her onto her back. "You could have had any man in the Middle East, but instead you wound up with the Jew Greenspan, in America, and now you will wind up where you belong, with that cretin, Muhammed Faisel. You saw how he treated the women at Omdurman Prison. How do you think he will treat you in the privacy of his own home?"

She didn't respond to Omar Samir. Instead, she began to plan when she would yell for help at the airport. At the security checkpoint, she decided. *That would be the best place*, she thought. The Jordanians had welcomed thousands of Palestinian refugees, but they hated the terrorists. Ever since the Black September war three years ago they had hated the terrorists. Yes, that's when she would begin to scream and identify Omar Samir and Muhammed Faisel as terrorists—as soon as they reached the security checkpoint.

***

Noah was at his desk at Potomac Center making sure everything was in order. He had arranged a jet charter to fly him and Yusuf to Tel Aviv to await news of Alexandra and, hopefully, to bring her and A'isha back to America if she was still alive and able to travel. He tried not to think about what her condition might be, or of returning home without her. She had to be alive. The rescue effort had to succeed. He banished any thought of life without Alexandra. The very thought that she wasn't going to be at his side for the rest of his life was unthinkable, and the thought that their son, Amos, might have to grow up without Alexandra was unbearable. He called Sarah Jean, who had arranged to stay at home with Amos, to thank her once again for all she had done.

"Mr. Greenspan, please don't thank me for anything. Alexandra is the best thing that's ever happened to me. And you and this boy," she said, pulling Amos onto her lap, "well, you're all the family a girl could ever pray for."

"Well, while you're praying, pray for all of us, Sarah Jean, but mostly pray for Alexandra."

"I'm praying so hard to Jesus, Mr. Greenspan, I just know you'll be coming back with Alexandra. I just know you will."

Noah teared up but smiled for the first time in days. "Keep praying, Sarah Jean," he said. "Keep praying."

As soon as he hung up the phone, Barb buzzed him on the intercom. "Yes, Barb, what's up?"

"You're not going to believe who's on the phone asking for you."

"Don't keep me guessing. Who's on the phone?"

"That crazy class-action lawyer from Philadelphia, Saul Kronheim, who keeps suing you."

"I don't have time for him. If he wants to sue me tell him to call our lawyer, Stan Sherman, over at Higgins and Harper."

"He doesn't sound like he wants to sue you, Noah. He sounded very nice. He told me how dreadful he felt when he saw the story about Alexandra. I'm guessing he's just calling to wish you luck."

"I doubt it, but I'll take the call."

Noah paused a moment to decide whether he should call his law-yer before taking a call from Saul Kronheim. *What the hell*, he thought.

"Noah Greenspan," he answered as soon as Barb put the call through.

"Noah, it's Saul Kronheim in Philadelphia."

"Yes, I know. What can I do for you, Saul?"

"Well, I just wanted you to know how awful I felt when I read about your wife in the *Philadelphia Inquirer*. It's just dreadful."

"Thank you, Saul. We're hopeful she may still be alive. I'm getting ready to leave to fly over to Israel with my brother-in-law, Yusuf, in just a few minutes. God willing, we'll find her and return with Alexandra."

"I hope so, Noah."

"So, let's cut to the chase, Saul. Are you about to file another class-action suit against me?"

"Heavens no. Why would I do that?"

"Well, it's what you do."

"*Touché*, Noah. But no, that's not why I'm calling. But now that you've brought up the subject, it's an interesting thought you have."

"I don't know what you're talking about."

"Filing a class-action suit."

"Huh? You've lost me."

"Well, maybe I just misunderstood you. You see, it would be highly unethical for me to promote a class-action suit that I would then bring in court, but I thought I just heard you use those words to me."

"Saul, I was only …"

"Noah, stop!" the class-action lawyer interrupted. "It sounded to me like you were inquiring whether or not you had a case against Deutschland Trust because their analyst, what's his name, George Markanos, has cost you and the other shareholders of Potomac Center Properties of America about a quarter billion dollars of lost share value by shorting PCPA shares based on an internal company memorandum that somehow found its way to Deutschland Trust. I thought you were asking whether that constituted an illegal stock transaction because it was based on insider information that wasn't generally available to the investing public."

Noah paused before responding and smiled into the phone.

"Right, Saul. That's just what I was about to ask."

"Well, now that you mention it, I think you would have an open-and-shut case, Noah. You have shareholders in Pennsylvania, so I could bring a suit against Deutschland Trust, if that's what you were suggesting."

Noah smiled. "Yes, that's exactly what I was suggesting."

"Well, thanks for thinking of me, Noah. They'll settle and they'll settle fast. I usually get thirty-five percent of the settlement, but I don't think this case will cost hardly anything to bring. Twenty-five percent for me okay with you, Noah?"

"Sounds like a plan, Saul."

CHAPTER FORTY-THREE

Alexandra sat up and leaned forward to rub her ankles as Omar Samir removed the handcuffs. Muhammed stood at the foot of the mattress, watching.

"So, Alexandra, I don't see any fresh stains on the mattress. You're through bleeding?" he asked.

"Almost," she said. "I'm sure it will be over by the time we get to Sudan."

Muhammed Faisel nodded approvingly. "Good," he said. "That will be good."

"Get cleaned up and put on your abaya and niqab," Omar Samir said. "I don't want to have to look at you. I'll find something for us to eat before we leave for Amman."

Alexandra didn't respond. She just walked over to the hose and splashed cold water on her face and body, and then dried herself off and slipped on the abaya and niqab.

"Go sit against the wall, Sabirah," Muhammed commanded. "I'll prepare a bowl of rice for you to eat. It will be our last meal until we are on the plane to Khartoum this afternoon."

She did as she was told. She leaned back against the wall and tried to imagine the airport in Amman. She wondered whether the security area would be crowded when she began to scream for help. She knew most Jordanians spoke at least some English, and the security guards were sure to speak English. She began to rehearse in her mind what she would say and do. She would break away from them and scream, *These men are terrorists and they have kidnapped me. I am Alexandra Salaman, an American citizen.* That's all she would have to do. The guards would then separate her from them and she would be free. She tried to remember who the American Ambassador to Jordan was. She would demand to be in his protection. *Yes, that was it, Lewis Dean Brown.* She would demand that Ambassador Brown be notified immediately. Then, when she was safely in the American embassy, she would call Noah. She knew he had to have been worried sick. She would ask the Ambassador to arrange for her to call Noah. She couldn't wait to hear his voice and to hear her son's voice. She couldn't wait to get to the airport in Amman and then to the American embassy. *The Jordanians will know how to deal with Omar Samir and Muhammed Faisel,* she thought. *They will both be shocked when I finally cry out, when they learn that I've known all this time that Amos was safe.*

***

Noah met Yusuf at the private departure terminal at Dulles. They embraced and, moments later, they met the crew of the Grumman Gulfstream II that would take them to Tel Aviv, where they would wait to learn of Alexandra's fate. The captain, Sean Brially, introduced them to the co-pilot, Buzz Macintosh, and the flight attendant, Suzanne Worsley. He explained that Suzanne would serve dinner—an assortment of cold cuts, shrimp, and pastries—during the flight to Gander, Newfoundland, where they would refuel. From there they would fly to London Heathrow, refuel again, and then continue on for another thirty-two hundred miles to Tel Aviv. "Buzz and I will alternate flying the left seat so that we can both get some shuteye during the flight over to Tel Aviv," Captain Brially said.

"Gentlemen, with good tailwinds we'll be in the air about twenty hours. Add refuel time in Gander and Heathrow, and you can pretty much figure about a twenty-four-hour journey. We'll do everything we can to make your journey as pleasant as possible. We know a little bit about what this trip is for, and we hope we'll be bringing back a plane-load of very happy people."

"Thank you, Captain. We're counting on it," Noah answered.

They buckled up and the G-II lurched forward and screamed down the runway, lifting off around three o'clock.

"It's going to be a long twenty-four hours, Noah," Yusuf said as the plane leveled off and headed north along the East Coast.

"You know, I don't care how long the flight is as long as we come home with Alexandra," Noah replied.

"I know. They just *have* to find her."

"They have to find her *alive*," Noah added.

"Look, we know, or at least we think we know, that Samir and this Faisel character's plan is to get her to Sudan. That bastard Muhammed Faisel is booked to Sudan from Amman with another passenger, named Sabirah Najat. That has to be Alexandra."

"You would think so. After all, she used that pseudonym when she traveled to Khartoum in sixty-seven," Noah replied.

"Could there be another Sabirah Najat?" Yusuf asked.

"Traveling with Muhammed Faisel? I doubt it, but, you know, he kept Alexandra's travel documents that were in the name of Sabirah Najat when he was holding her in Omdurman Prison. He could be using the same travel documents to bring someone else, illegally, into Sudan."

"Why would he do that?"

"I don't know, Yusuf. Maybe because he's a creep."

"It's hard to believe we're going through this. We've been through so much together. Do you realize it's been a quarter century since we first met?"

"Yeah, we were eleven years old when your family immigrated to America and wound up in LeDroit Park, right down the street from my parents' grocery store."

"I remember when you asked my sister out that first time."

"Yeah, to go on a hayride with my Jewish friends from uptown."

"My father was apoplectic."

"Well, it all worked out pretty well."

"Yeah, you've been like a third child to my parents for years."

"And my folks got two new kids in the bargain too."

They sat there for a moment reflecting on the long history the two families shared.

"You were my best friend long before you were my brother-in-law," Noah said.

"Noah, do you think my sister ever saw the skywriting that would have told her Amos was safe?" Yusuf asked, redirecting the conversation back to Alexandra.

"Who knows? I hope so. No matter what has happened to her, I'd feel better if I thought she knew Amos was safe."

"I think she's alive, Noah. I really do."

"If she is, I think we'll find her."

"Have the Jordanian authorities been notified to try to intercept them at the airport?"

"Yes, the FBI notified the Jordanians, but we really don't know how much they'll try to help. They were nominal belligerents in the war and it's hard to assess the extent of the animosity there toward America, given the aid America is providing to Israel. They were not receptive to having the FBI send agents to Amman to help in apprehending Samir and Faisel. They said there was no extradition treaty between Jordan and the United States, so it would be inappropriate for anyone from the FBI to be on the scene at the airport. Besides, relying on interception at the airport is a last-ditch, all-or-nothing gamble. If it fails, Alexandra winds up in Sudan, where our options are non-existent."

"Do you think A'isha's family can really help? If the odds aren't great that Alexandra would be intercepted at the airport, what are the odds that the Abadis will intercept them at some unknown point somewhere between the West Bank and Amman?"

"Not great, I suppose, but at least we get two shots at intercepting them instead of just one."

"I can't imagine what she's been through," Yusuf said.

"I can. I know how long it took her to fully recover, emotionally, from her ordeal in that hellhole of a prison in Khartoum five years ago. This Muhammed Faisel character was obsessed with Alexandra, and he's a real psycho. Between him and Omar Samir, she's been through hell. She'll live with this for a long time, Yusuf. We all will. She'll need all the support we can give her."

"Well, she'll have that for sure."

"Maybe by the time we get there, she'll be in friendly hands and this ordeal will be over."

Yusuf nodded. "Let's hope," he replied.

"So, you've been seeing A'isha?" Noah asked, changing the subject.

"We've been on a couple dates. I like her a lot. She's very special, Noah."

"Yeah, we all think so."

"I never believed for a minute that she was involved with Amos's disappearance, other than as a victim herself."

"Agent Hogan said she was holding tight to Amos, protecting him, when they broke into the room they were locked in."

"She really loves Amos."

"It's reciprocal. He adores her too."

"Alexandra's new assistant is staying with him now?"

"Yeah, Sarah Jean Bogart from Blytheville, Arkansas. She is staying with us until she can find a place of her own. She's pretty amazing too. Damned if she didn't figure out where A'isha and Amos were being held. I mean, she figured it out down to the address of the building and the apartment number while the FBI was still sitting at my place waiting for a ransom call."

"Between Alexandra and A'isha and Sarah Jean, you and my nephew have three pretty amazing women in your lives."

There was a long pause. "Let's hope it stays that way," Noah answered.

CHAPTER
FORTY-FOUR

Muhammed Faisel pulled off her niqab and stooped down so that he was almost face to face with Alexandra. She squinted against the rush of light striking her eyes.

"Omar Samir has shown me this newspaper clipping. Sabirah, is this really you sitting with the Zionist under the Zionist flag?"

"It was a banquet that I attended with my husband. I had no choice about where they placed me to sit."

"But it is a Zionist gathering, is that right?"

"It was a Jewish gathering. My husband is a leader in the Jewish community. I attend these events with him. At the event pictured in the newspaper they were gathering to hear about the war."

"But they have the Zionist banner on the wall right over your head, Sabirah."

"It's the flag of Israel. The Jewish communities in America feel an attachment to Israel, just as the Sudanese people feel an attachment to the Arab side. There was also an American flag on the wall, but you just don't see it in this photograph."

"Were all the people in the room Jews, Sabirah?"

Alexandra looked down at her hands as she considered how best to answer Muhammed Faisel's question without angering him.

"Why are you not looking into my eyes, Sabirah?" he asked, taking her by the jaw and tilting her face up toward his.

"I was just trying to gather my thoughts … trying to find the right words to explain how the Jewish community had gathered to hear about the war."

He tightened his grip on her jaw as he spoke. "You are a disgrace, Sabirah, but that will soon change. What has happened to you since you left Islam?"

"I've never left Islam. I was never born into Islam. Please, I mean no disrespect, but I was born a Christian. My parents are Christians. My brother is a Christian."

"Yes, I remember how you tried to convince me of that at Omdurman Prison. But you forget I saw your travel documents and your credentials at the summit. Don't you know the punishment for leaving Islam?"

"I meant and mean no disrespect," she said.

"Do you know how embarrassing it would be to me if the people of El-Obeid knew I brought home someone who consorted with the Zionists in America?" he said, tightening his grip on her jaw.

"You're … hurting me," she managed to say.

"You think this hurts, Sabira? You would be publicly flogged in my country, if not stoned, for the way you behaved in America," he answered. "Do you understand?"

Alexandra nodded. "I understand."

"Do you understand that only I can protect you?"

"I understand," she said, nodding as she answered.

"Do you want me to protect you when we are home in El-Obeid?"

Again, she nodded.

"Say it!"

"I want you to protect me when we arrive in El-Obeid."

"So, you will be obedient?"

"I will be obedient," she answered.

"You will be a good wife?"

She looked into his eyes, his face blurred by her tears.

"Say it!"

"I will be a good wife," she sobbed.

"What are we going to do with you to make up for this?" he asked menacingly, holding the newspaper clipping up to her face.

"What do you want me to say? Whatever you want me to say, I'll say."

"It's not what I want you to say," he yelled. "It is what I want you to feel, Sabirah."

She nodded. "I'll feel as you want me to feel," she answered.

"You will feel gratitude!" he yelled.

"Yes, I will feel gratitude."

"You will show your gratitude by wanting to please me," he shouted.

Once again, she nodded, her jaw now numbed by his grip.

"Say it!" he bellowed.

"I will want to please you."

"Always!" he yelled. "Say it!"

"I will want to please you always," she answered.

"Do you know how humiliating it will be for me if this photograph of you with the Zionists shows up in El-Obeid?" he asked, holding up the newspaper clipping in front of her face.

"I'm sorry," she answered.

"What kind of Muslim are you, Sabirah?"

"I'm not a Muslim," she cried softly. "I'm not a Muslim."

"Enough, Muhammed," Omar Samir called from across the room. "The yelling is giving me a headache. We have a long journey ahead of us today. Once you have her at your home in Sudan you can do with her as you like, but we still have to travel from here to Amman, and then on to Khartoum."

"Yes, you are right, Omar. I don't want to be agitated with her while we're traveling."

"No, we want to appear like any other travelers. We want no yelling and no crying," Omar Samir said as he walked over to them.

"Alexandra, go and splash some water on your face. Your eyes are puffy from all the crying. I will give you my hairbrush. You will brush your hair. You look a mess."

She nodded. Omar Samir extended his hand to Alexandra and pulled her to her feet.

"Clean yourself up, Alexandra."

She walked to the wall where the hose was hanging and turned on the spigot. Cupping her hands, she caught enough water to splash on her face. Alexandra held her hands there for several moments, savoring the cool feel of her palms against her cheeks.

***

The Abadis knew they had a narrow sliver of time and a limited area of geography in which to identify Alexandra and rescue her from her tormentors. They also knew they would have to be very lucky. They assumed she was being held somewhere on the West Bank between the Green Line and Hebron. Areas just north of the Green Line but well south of Hebron around the towns of ad-Dhahiriya, El-Samu, Yattah and a few others could be monitored for cars leaving sparsely used side roads to enter Route Sixty, the main corridor running from south to north. The only thing the Abadis knew for sure was that Omar Samir and Muhammed Faisel would be travelling north on Route Sixty to get to the King Hussein Bridge over the Jordan River on their way to the airport in Amman. Monitoring the entire length of the highway through the West Bank would be impossible, so they bet everything that somewhere in the area between the Green Line and Hebron was where they were holding Alexandra. The Abadis assumed that Omar Samir and Muhammed Faisel had Alexandra in one of the clusters of old deserted stone dwellings off of the well-traveled thoroughfares leading north from the Green Line. They were certain they couldn't be staying in a home occupied by residents of the West Bank without word getting back to them. They reasoned that they had to be in a structure that was deserted and off the beaten path. The side roads that lacked recent tire marks were eliminated from their surveillance, as were the other back roads on which no abandoned structures were known to exist. They knew if their assumptions were correct there was a slim chance they might spot and intercept them. They also knew that if they failed no one would ever hear from Alexandra again.

And so, that morning the men of the Abadi family spread out over a stretch of forty miles along Route Sixty, positioning themselves at key points where backwater dirt roads intersected with the highway. There they would watch for cars turning onto Route Sixty from one of these dirt roads with one or two men and a woman. Some of the Abadi men were armed, but most were not. They all did carry, however, Motorola HT-200 walkie-talkies supplied to them by Mossad.

***

The time passed slowly as Omar Samir and Muhammed Faisel spoke to one another in hushed tones at the table. Alexandra was, as usual, sitting on the floor leaning back against the stone wall, trying to hear what they were discussing across the room. Every few minutes one or the other of them would glance over to her as they spoke. She could not make out what they were discussing, but she had little doubt that she was the topic of their conversation. They were not sure whether Alexandra knew her son was safe or whether she believed Amos's fate depended on her behavior.

Meanwhile, Alexandra continued to concentrate on what she would do when they reached the security checkpoint at the airport in Amman.

She knew her planned outburst had to take Omar Samir and Muhammed Faisel by surprise. They would have to be caught off guard and be slow to react, and the security detail had to immediately understand that she was a kidnap victim being trafficked through their airport. While she couldn't know how her captors would react, she was confident she could get the security guards at the airport to immediately intervene. Alexandra couldn't wait to be on her way to Amman. She looked around the stone-walled room, knowing she would never forget it, that it would haunt her for the rest of her life. The stone floor on which she was forced to sit every day. The mattresses on the floor on which she was ordered to lie, naked, next to them, the cold-water hose dangling from a rusty pipe on the wall, and the table at which she was never allowed to sit. She thought of Omar Samir and Muhammed Faisel ordering her to stand, naked, while they trained the hose on her. But in Amman the tables would be turned. She would become their antagonist. They would be publicly exposed as terrorists in a country that abhorred terrorism.

Alexandra watched Omar Samir and Muhammed Faisel as they whispered to one another while glancing at her. Then, the thought first occurred to her. What if they really were not going to take her to Amman? What if, instead, they planned to kill her in the deserted house and simply leave her body there? It could be months, even years, before anyone came to the house. They got up from the table and walked over to Alexandra and stared down at her.

"Are you ready to leave for Amman? We will be leaving shortly."

"I'm ready to go," she answered.

"Do you have to use the bucket before we go? It will take about two hours to get to Amman. Do you want to relieve yourself before we start out for the airport?"

"May I have some privacy?"

"Of course, Sabirah," Muhammed replied.

"Would you like to go outside with the bucket?"

Alexandra nodded.

"Get up and take the bucket outside and relieve yourself. I will have to put the handcuffs on your ankles."

"But you haven't had to do that before. I haven't run. Where am I going to run?"

"We think you might get some foolish idea before we fly off to Khartoum together. We couldn't have that, so you'll have to wear the cuffs if you are going to need privacy outside."

"Let me go to the ditch in the back to relieve myself. You can watch me from a distance."

Muhammed Faisel looked to Omar Samir, who nodded impatiently.

"All right, Sabirah, but hurry."

Alexandra took the bucket and walked to the ditch in the back of the house to relieve herself. They stood at the door and continued talking as they watched her.

As soon as she returned, Omar Samir ordered her to sit back down on the floor. She did as she was told and sat down with her back against the wall.

"Alexandra, we will be leaving for the airport very shortly," he said. "You will have to wear the handcuffs until we are past Hebron. It is a busy city with a lot of people. There will be heavy traffic, and we can't take any chance that you will try to do anything foolish."

"Please don't do that to me. I've obeyed everything you've asked me to do."

Omar Samir knelt down beside her, gripped her by the shoulders, and spun her away from the wall.

"Put your hands behind your back," he said as he grabbed her wrists.

"Oh God, don't do this, Omar," she cried.

Muhammed Faisel knelt down and snapped the handcuffs in place and pushed her back against the wall.

"That wasn't so terrible, was it Sabirah?" he said, tilting her head up playfully by her chin.

Alexandra didn't reply. She just looked away and closed her eyes against the tears.

"Alexandra, I promised you the handcuffs would only be needed for a brief time. You will see that I was being truthful. Now, try to relax. We will be leaving for Amman and the airport shortly."

Alexandra nodded. "The handcuffs aren't necessary, Omar. I haven't tried to run away from you."

"We can't be too careful, Alexandra. We've come this far, and soon we'll be on the final leg of our journey."

"Why are we waiting? Why aren't we in the car and driving to Amman?"

"We've planned our journey very carefully, Alexandra. Down to the minute, as they say. We'll be on our way soon enough—very shortly."

"Are you going to kill me before you leave for Amman? Is that why you've bound my hands behind my back like a prisoner about to be executed?"

"Is that what you think, Sabirah?" Muhammed Faisel answered. "You think we are going to kill you? You think I came all this way just to kill you? Why would I come to this godforsaken place if that was what we were going to do to you? Omar here could do that very efficiently without me, I assure you. No, Sabirah, you are coming to El-Obeid with me."

"He is telling you the truth, Alexandra. I could have certainly killed you, and I could still kill you if that was what I wanted to do. But that is not my wish. My wish is that you spend the rest of your life with Muhammed here. Whether that is a long life or a short life will be entirely up to you, but you are going to spend the rest of your life with Muhammed Faisel."

"And I can assure you, Sabirah, that I intend for you to live a long life. How long you live will be entirely up to you, but I am a very forgiving man. Already I have forgiven you for consorting with the Zionists in Washington. But I am going to keep the newspaper article with the picture of you sitting with the Zionists under the Zionist banner. And if you aren't appreciative every day of my forgiveness, I will give the newspaper article to the authorities in Sudan and let them deal with you. But I think you will learn to like living with me in El-Obeid."

Alexandra didn't reply. She just looked away and reminded herself that soon she would be the one who would be free, and that they would be in the hands of people who knew how to deal with terrorists. Then she heard the sound of a car coming to a stop in front of the house. Her heart quickened as the moment of their departure neared.

Alexandra was surprised when a woman walked through the door. She had assumed they would be using the same driver who brought her from Eilat.

Instead, the driver of the car was a woman, a tall woman, unsmiling, stern, and perfunctory in greeting Omar Samir and Muhammed Faisel. She was dressed in work clothes—what appeared to be a hospital worker's gray scrubs.

"This is our traveler?" she said, walking over to where Alexandra sat against the wall. That's when Alexandra first noticed the small satchel she was carrying, the kind doctors carry.

The woman knelt down in front of Alexandra and withdrew a penlight from the pocket of the smock she wore. She took Alexandra by the chin and shined a light into her eyes, first her right eye and then her left eye.

"What are you doing? Why are you doing this?" Alexandra cried out.

"This is Doctor Nazari, Alexandra. She has come to make sure you are well to travel."

"Of course I can travel. I don't need to be seen by a doctor."

"The motor and sensory functions of her eye are perfectly normal," the doctor said to the two men, ignoring Alexandra.

"I'll check her heart. That will be important," Doctor Nazari said, reaching into the satchel.

"Why are you doing this?" Alexandra asked anxiously, sensing that something was terribly wrong.

Again, the doctor ignored her as she withdrew a stethoscope from the satchel, placed the ear tips in her ears, and pressed the diaphragm against the abaya and over Alexandra's heart. Doctor Nazari moved the diaphragm to a few other positions over Alexandra's chest and then abruptly removed the stethoscope from her ears and dropped it back into her satchel.

"Good, strong heartbeat," she said to the men.

"What is going on?" Alexandra demanded. "Why are you doing this?"

Doctor Nazari, ignoring her, reached behind Alexandra's back and grabbed her lower arm, placing a finger on the underside of her wrist for several seconds as she looked at her watch.

"Her pulse is somewhat rapid, but that's not surprising given that she's very agitated," the doctor said to the men. "She'll tolerate the Ketamine quite well, I'm sure."

"What are you talking about?" Alexandra screamed.

"I'm going to give her a very strong dose," Doctor Nazari said to the men, as she continued to ignore Alexandra. "A typical dose for anesthesia usually puts an adult woman her size out for about ten to twenty minutes. It's generally used for brief medical procedures. The dose I'm going to give her will put her out for at least an hour, I'm sure."

"No! Don't do this to me," Alexandra screamed. "Why are you doing this? I haven't resisted anything you've asked of me. Please, Omar don't do this. Please, I beg of you, don't let her do this to me," Alexandra begged, her voice overcome with panic.

"Now, it will be important to re-administer the drug every hour, or whenever she shows signs of waking up," the doctor said, talking to the men as though Alexandra wasn't there. "The booster shots are of lower dosage, but given while she is still under the influence of the prior shot they should subdue her for another hour or so each time you administer them."

"Oh God, Omar, don't do this. Muhammed, don't let her do this. I beg of you, please, don't do this to me," Alexandra cried frantically.

"I've called ahead to Amman, Muhammed, and they've been told you are travelling with your wife, Sabirah Najat, who has suffered a severe stroke. Ask for Achmed Kazziam. He's a security supervisor and he will be expecting you. You have travel papers for her?"

"Yes, I have her travel documents from the Arab League. I've renewed them for her."

"Good. Security will pass you through as soon as you arrive. Your plane is already at the gate in Amman. It arrived last night. They will put you onboard as soon as you arrive. They're very sympathetic, and I was told you've been upgraded to first class, so you'll have a lot more privacy. I have a wheelchair in the trunk of my car for you to use to get her to the car and through the airport. You'll need it when you land in Khartoum as well."

"And she will stay subdued the entire way to El-Obeid?" Muhammed asked.

"As long as you inject her with the booster shots every hour she'll stay subdued. It won't matter too much, though, if she comes around before you get to give the booster. Her speech will be entirely slurred and very slow, and she certainly won't be able to walk. In fact, with the dosing we're giving her, she will look and act pretty much like a stroke victim for a few hours after she's awake."

"Oh my God, I beg you, don't do this to me," Alexandra cried out again.

Doctor Nazari pulled up the sleeve of the abaya and examined Alexandra's upper arm.

"She's pretty slender," she observed. "I think I'll give the first injection in her upper thigh, where there's more muscle. She's very agitated and her heart is going to be very rapid, so I'm going to inject this first dose very slowly. I don't want the Ketamine to overwhelm her ability to absorb it. It will take about a minute," Doctor Nazari said, and as she spoke she pulled the abaya above Alexandra's waist.

"No!" Alexandra screamed, kicking out at Doctor Nazari.

"What is this?" the doctor asked, pointing to traces of crusted blood that ran along the crease where the front of Alexandra's thigh curved into her inner thigh.

"She's had her menstrual flow while she's been here," Omar replied.

"Oh God, make them stop. Please, I beg you, don't do this. There is no need to do this. I'll do whatever you tell me. I won't run or scream at the airport."

Doctor Nazari looked up at them, her expression incredulous.

"No, I don't think so," she replied, and with that she grabbed Alexandra's ankles and yanked her away from the wall and pulled her legs up into the air.

Alexandra began to sob uncontrollably.

"You see that scab, gentlemen?" Doctor Nazari asked, holding Alexandra's legs apart. "She scratched at her perineum until it bled so that you would think she had her menstrual period. She's a smart one. I could almost admire her," she said, dropping Alexandra's legs to the floor.

"Oh, she will pay," Muhammed said angrily as Alexandra lay there crying and trying to catch her breath.

"I wouldn't be too hard on her. She's smart. Smarter than both of you, I suspect. Like I said, as a woman, I could almost admire her."

Alexandra, lying on the stone floor, now realized her plans to break free at the airport in Amman had just been shattered. She lay there utterly exhausted.

Omar bent over Alexandra and held her head still as he spoke. "You asked why we are doing this, Alexandra. I'll tell you why. Because you think we are stupid. Did you think, for a moment, I would have let you walk through an airport, free to scream and free to run? There is no escape, Alexandra. You will be wheeled through the airport as placid as a baby."

"Already she has deceived me," Muhammed said. "She knew I would never lie with her while she bled."

"You'll have plenty of time to lie with her, Muhammed. And if she resists, just give her a shot of Ketamine. I've brought two dozen vials and syringes. The vials I'm giving you have doses that will immobilize her for ten to twenty minutes. You will have plenty of opportunity to—how did you say it?—yes, lie with her. After the strong injection I am going to administer now in her thigh, you'll inject her every hour, *here*," she said, jabbing Alexandra's upper arm. "In fact, I'll draw a circle here on her arm so you'll know just where to inject," she said, pulling a pen from her pocket. She grabbed Alexandra by her upper arm with one hand and with the other drew a circle where Muhammed was to administer the booster shots.

"Now, Alexandra," Doctor Nazari began, "I'm going to administer a long injection into your thigh, here. It might burn a bit. You will go under in about ten seconds. Ketamine is what we call a dissociative drug. You will feel detached from your surroundings, almost like you are watching what is happening rather than experiencing it. You won't be able to talk, not so that anyone could understand you anyway. It's not a bad experience. Some people use it for fun, although in much smaller doses."

Alexandra's demeanor suddenly changed from momentary exhausted docility to fierce anger. She kicked at them, all of them, any of them she could try to reach.

"Hold her still," Doctor Nazari said as she reached into her satchel and withdrew a small packet of gauze and a bottle of antiseptic solution. Muhammed grabbed Alexandra's legs and Omar Samir grabbed her around the shoulders. She tried to struggle, but she was held still in their grip.

"Alexandra, when did you have your last menstrual period?" Doctor Nazari asked.

Alexandra didn't reply. "Don't do this," she pled, barely above a whisper. "Please don't do this."

"Shall I examine you right here on the floor and try to come up with a pretty good estimate, give or take a day or two, of how far along in your cycle you are? Do you want to tell me when you had your last period, or shall I do what I have to do to make a good guess?"

"Last week," she answered, her voice pathetic, defeated.

"Muhammed, I would say you will have about three weeks to enjoy your honeymoon in El-Obeid," Doctor Nazari said, looking up to Muhammed Faisel with a sympathetic smile.

She tore open the paper packet of gauze and poured a small amount of the antiseptic solution onto it and swabbed Alexandra's thigh. Then she reached into her satchel again and withdrew a syringe and a vial of Ketamine. Alexandra watched in horror as Doctor Nazari inserted the needle into the vial and withdrew a quantity of Ketamine sufficient to fill the syringe. Doctor Nazari then gripped Alexandra's upper thigh with one hand and carefully inserted the needle into her flesh with the other.

"Okay, here you go, Alexandra," she said.

"No, no, stop, please don't do this. Pleaaase dooonn't doooo thisss. Plea … plea … plea …"

Doctor Nazari slowly continued the injection, letting the Ketamine seep into Alexandra's thigh for a solid minute.

"Have a good journey, gentlemen," Doctor Nazari said as she withdrew the needle and handed Muhammed Faisel the satchel. "I'll keep the stethoscope," she said, taking it from the satchel and placing it around her shoulders. "The satchel contains about two dozen vials and syringes and some gauze and antiseptic solution. Use the antiseptic before each injection. Remember, inject every hour on the hour, or whenever she appears to be coming out of it, whichever occurs first. These are much lighter doses. She should tolerate them well. You should be able to keep her immobile until you can put her to bed in El-Obeid. I would keep her restrained while she is coming out from under the Ketamine in El-Obeid. She is going to be very confused for several hours afterwards."

"I'm a former jailer, Doctor Nazari. I have all that I need to keep her restrained."

She nodded. "Come, let's get the wheelchair from the trunk of my car. It will probably take the two of you and your driver to get her from the floor into the wheelchair."

The driver who brought Alexandra from Eilat pulled up just as Doctor Nazari was about to drive away. They acknowledged one another with a brief nod as his car drifted to a stop and she turned her car around to head back toward Hebron.

"You're just in time. We need you to help us get the woman in the house off of the floor and into this wheelchair," Omar Samir said. The three men went into the house and stood over her for a moment. Muhammed Faisel picked up the niqab from the floor and carefully pulled Alexandra into a sitting position with her back against the wall. He positioned the niqab over her head as best he could, and slowly moved the niqab until he saw that her eyes were behind the slits in the fabric. It took all three of them to lift Alexandra off of the floor and into the wheelchair. She was limp and motionless when they wheeled her to the car and lifted her onto the back seat.

Omar Samir sat in front next to the driver, and Muhammed Faisel got in the back and positioned himself as close to Alexandra as he could, until their bodies touched. After a moment's hesitation, he put his arm around her and very gently pulled her toward him until her head fell to his shoulder. He reached over and took her hand into his hand and held it firmly, almost affectionately, as the car pulled away from the old deserted stone house.

The driver steered around potholes as best he could and slowed down to a crawl to ride over ruts that spanned the entire width of the road. It took close to a half hour to reach the paved road that would take them to Route Sixty, which they would take north all the way to the King Hussein Bridge. As the driver brought the car to a stop to let traffic pass, Omar Samir noticed the pickup truck parked on the side of the road opposite where they were waiting to turn. The driver of the parked truck was kneeling beside the left front tire and had a jack set up next to the left fender. The pickup truck driver, who appeared to be no more than twenty years old, glanced across the roadway and waved to the driver of the car. Just as the driver began to make his turn onto the roadway, the pickup truck driver ran across the roadway waving his arms for help. He ran right toward them, blocking their turn.

"Can you give me a hand?" he shouted as he ran toward the car.

"Drive around him," Omar ordered the driver.

"I can't without running over him," the driver answered, honking the car's horn.

"Peace be with you," the pickup truck driver shouted as he stood in front of the car.

"We're in a hurry. We have a plane to catch," the driver of the car yelled.

"Can you lend me your jack for ten minutes?" the pickup truck driver shouted. "Mine is broken."

"Get out of the way!" the driver shouted.

The young man hurried to the driver's side of the car and asked again, as he peered inside. "Can't you help me? It will only take ten minutes, maybe only five."

"Get out of the way," the driver shouted again, as he pressed down on the accelerator and sped away. The driver of the pickup truck ran to his vehicle across the roadway and reached into the open window for the Motorola walkie-talkie.

"What was that all about?" Muhammed asked from the back seat.

"It was nothing. Just someone who needed help with a flat tire," Omar said.

They drove on for about a mile before coming to the rear of a line of ten or fifteen vehicles that had slowed to a stop on the roadway.

"What now?" Muhammed asked anxiously.

The driver leaned out of the window and stretched to see what was holding up traffic.

"It's a big herd of goats in the road," he answered.

"Can we go around?" Omar shouted.

"No, both sides of the road are blocked," the driver shouted back. "I'm sure they won't block the road for more than a minute or two."

"Can you see anything else?" Omar shouted. "Are they trying to get the goats off the road?"

"I can't tell. There's a group of about six men coming down the road. I'll ask them what is going on."

"Ask if there's any way around the backup," Omar replied.

"Hey, over here," the driver yelled, waving to the men.

Just as the men approached the car, the driver of the pickup truck with the flat tire drove up and swerved into the space in front of the car. The men in the road rushed the car, pulling the driver through the window and pulling the other doors open. They reached in and pulled Omar Samir and Muhammed Faisel from the car and threw them into the cargo bed of the pickup truck, climbing in after them and pinning them to the hard metal floor.

"What are you doing?" Omar Samir yelled angrily. "Are you crazy?"

"Who is the woman in the back of your car? Why is she unconscious?" one of the attackers, who seemed to be in charge, demanded to know. "She is a traitor to our cause. I am Omar Samir, a fighter for the Palestinian cause."

"You are Omar Samir, a disgrace to the Palestinian cause," the man shouted as the pickup truck sped away.

Alexandra slumped over in the back seat as one of the men got behind the wheel and did a U-turn, speeding off in the opposite direction toward ad-Dhahiriya.

CHAPTER FORTY-FIVE

Alexandra had trouble opening her eyes even though the lights were dimmed in the bedroom. She was lying on a bed, cradled in someone's arms. She tried to lift her head, but the weight seemed too great. She tried to focus.

"You're safe, Alexandra. It's all over. You're safe."

Alexandra tried to make out who was holding her. She couldn't open her eyes enough to see who it was. The voice was familiar. She turned her head to look up, but her eyes wouldn't focus. All she could make out was the hijab the woman was wearing, the familiar red hijab.

"A'isha?" she whispered.

The woman tightened her embrace, hugging Alexandra.

"Yes, Alexandra, it is me, A'isha. You are safe. No one can hurt you."

"Where am I?"

"You are safe in my uncle's home, not far from ad-Dhahiriya."

"What about …?"

"Muhammed Faisel and Omar Samir?"

Alexandra nodded.

"They will never threaten you again, Alexandra. They will never threaten anyone again."

"And my son?"

"Amos is safe at home in Georgetown."

"I'm so confused."

"You've been asleep for hours, Alexandra."

"I still don't know what happened. Omar Samir convinced me on the telephone that they were going to kill Amos if I didn't do exactly what I was told."

"It's a long story, Alexandra. I was tricked into hurrying from your house with Amos and rushing to the home of a former colleague of mine at the embassy. He said I had to be there to receive a call from my family here in Palestine. I was told there was terrible trouble and that I had to get there right away. I grabbed Amos and rushed to my former colleague's apartment. Amos and I were locked in a soundproof room. They just wanted me and Amos out of the house when you called from Eilat. It was all a carefully planned plot to make you think I kidnapped Amos and that he was in grave danger unless you did what Omar Samir instructed you to do."

Alexandra lowered her head into her hand and tried to concentrate.

"How did you and Amos get away?" she finally asked, as she became more alert.

"Your assistant at the paper, Sarah Jean Bogart, actually figured out where we were. It's an incredible story."

"Sarah Jean?" Alexandra replied, managing a weak smile. "I've never even met her. I've only spoken to her on the telephone."

"She's wonderful, Alexandra. She did her own investigation while the FBI was waiting for a ransom call. She's a guest at your house, you know."

Alexandra nodded. "Now I remember. I said she could stay with us until she found a place of her own."

"She's staying with Amos now. Noah and Yusuf are nearby in Jerusalem waiting for you."

"They are here, in the Middle East? They are in Jerusalem?" she asked excitedly.

"Yes. They are at the King David Hotel. My uncle will take us to them as soon as you are alert enough to travel. We're only about an hour away. I think your friend Amos Ben-Chaiyim is with them."

"Can we go now?"

"You should have something to eat first, and we should make sure you are steady on your feet. They must have given you some kind of drug to knock you out."

"They did. It was so awful. They brought in a doctor, a horrible woman named Doctor Nazari. She gave me the shot. I think she said it was a drug called Ketamine, or something that sounded like that."

"Do you feel as though you could sleep some more, Alexandra?"

"I think I'm okay. How long have I been asleep here?"

"You've been out, in this bed, for about four hours. My cousins brought you here when they took you from the car Omar Samir and Muhammed Faisel were traveling in with you. They were taking you to Amman."

"We were on the way to Sudan. I don't even want to think about it," Alexandra said, as her eyes drifted down to her clothes.

"Whose clothes am I wearing?"

"Mine. My slacks and blouse fit you perfectly. I thought you would prefer this outfit over the abaya and niqab you were wearing when we found you."

"Oh my God, don't remind me."

***

Noah, Yusuf, and Amos Ben-Chaiyim waited anxiously for Alexandra and A'isha at the entrance of the King David Hotel in Jerusalem. Arrangements had been made by Benjamin Bar-Levy to expedite travel for Ibrahim Abadi and his two passengers—his niece, A'isha Abadi, and Palestinian American Alexandra Salaman Greenspan. They drove from ad-Dhahiriya north through Hebron and on to Bethlehem, and from there into Jerusalem. IDF personnel at the checkpoint between Bethlehem and Jerusalem, having been alerted to their travel, waved them through after carefully examining Ibrahim Abadi's papers. A few minutes later, just beyond the old city, they turned into the driveway of the King David Hotel.

***

"Noah!" Alexandra shouted, tears streaming down her face as she saw him running down the driveway toward the car. He pulled the door open, and almost pulled her from the car, lifting her off the ground, as they both wept, too overcome with emotion to speak.

"Let me look at you," he finally managed to say.

"I was so afraid I was never going to see you or Amos again," she cried into his shoulder as he held her firmly in his arms. "Oh Noah, it was horrible … the way they tormented me, and what they had planned for me was even worse," she sobbed.

"They'll never threaten you again," Alexandra. "Not ever."

"They drugged me, Noah. They were going to take me to Sudan and make me Mohammed Faisel's slave," she cried.

"It's been a horrible nightmare," he said. "We were all worried sick, but you're safe now, Alexandra. It's over."

"A'isha … A'isha's family saved my life."

"We know," he answered. "A'isha was a Godsend, and her family was absolutely determined to find you. We don't think anyone else could have put a stop to what they were planning. But now you're safe, Alexandra. No one is going to hurt you," Noah said, holding her as close as he could.

Yusuf and Amos had followed Noah down the driveway but stood back, not wanting to interrupt Noah and Alexandra at that moment.

"What a scare you gave us," Amos finally said, hugging her.

"You have no idea how awful the past several days have been," she said, reaching out and pulling Yusuf into her embrace. "I didn't think I was ever going to see any of you again."

Amos turned to A'isha and Ibrahim Abadi and reached out to them.

"These are the people who made this possible. They are why we are together tonight," he said. "When we were stymied about what to do, A'isha convinced us that her family was our best hope. No one had a better option to offer. Not me, not Mossad, not the FBI. A'isha convinced us that our best hope was with her family, and we have you to thank, sir," he said, reaching out to clasp Ibrahim Abadi's hand. "You were a Godsend, a miracle."

"*Inshallah, inshallah,*" Ibrahim Abadi replied, shaking Amos's hand. "If God wills it."

Noah turned his attention to A'isha and her uncle. "I'm forever indebted to you both. I don't know what would have happened if it weren't for you."

"Actually, I think we do," Amos said. "I don't want to even think about it. You were our last, best hope of saving Alexandra. Thank God, everything worked."

"*Inshallah,*" Ibrahim Abadi said again.

"Can you stay for dinner here at the hotel, Mr. Abadi?"

"Thank you, but I must start back to ad-Dhahiriya before it gets any later," Ibrahim Abadi said. "Thanks be to God that it all worked out. But I must go. It was easy getting here through the checkpoint. It may not be so easy getting back this late."

"I can't begin to thank you for what you have done," Noah said, embracing A'isha's uncle.

"You must come when there is real peace," Ibrahim Abadi replied. He shook hands with the three men and embraced Alexandra and his niece. "God be with you both," he said, and with that, he turned and walked back to his car.

They stood there and watched in silence, and in awe, as Ibrahim Abadi got into his car and began his journey, alone, back to the West Bank and ad-Dhahiriya.

"I've arranged a table for dinner in the hotel dining room for the three of you," Noah said as they headed back to the hotel, "but I thought Alexandra and I would dine in our suite tonight, so that we have some time to talk alone." Alexandra leaned into him and laid her head on his shoulder as they walked through the lobby.

"How are we getting home tomorrow?" Alexandra asked.

"Ambassador Dinitz has arranged with Doctor Kissinger for us all to return on a C-5 tomorrow morning at eight o'clock," Amos replied.

"We'll save a lot of time because the C-5 will fly directly to Lajes to refuel and then directly on to Dover, Delaware. They'll have a helicopter fly us from Dover to National Airport."

"It seems like it was years ago when you and I came here from Dover, Amos."

"Barely a week," he replied. "By the way, did you ever see our skywriting?"

"I certainly did. I was emptying the shit bucket, excuse my language, A'isha, behind the house where I was being held and I saw the words *Amos - Safe* emblazoned across the sky. I knew from that moment on that he hadn't been harmed, but I couldn't let Omar Samir or Muhammed Faisel know that I knew he was safe. They would have killed me."

Noah reached down and squeezed Alexandra's hand.

"Say, I have some news to share with you," Amos announced to everyone as they all waited with Noah and Alexandra at the elevator.

"I've arranged to be transferred to the Israeli embassy in Washington, and Karen is moving to Washington to be with me."

"Amos, that's wonderful," Noah said, clasping Amos's shoulder.

"Long overdue," Alexandra agreed, as she leaned over and hugged him.

***

Noah and Alexandra dined alone, picking at a light meal in the suite Noah had reserved. They avoided any further talk of Alexandra's ordeal.

"Noah, what happened with all the trouble with the stock? Did that all get worked out?"

"I think so. It's a long story, Alexandra, but Markanos really hurt us … for about a week."

"Him again."

"Yes, him again, but this time he went too far, and I think he's going to pay a stiff price for his shenanigans."

"What happened?"

"It's a long story. He shorted us, and our stock absolutely tanked. But we were able to prove he used an internal Potomac Center memorandum that he got his hands on as the basis of his short sale. Then we found out that he was trying to engineer a takeover of the company based on the very low stock price. Anyway, the FBI was able to prove that he used an internal company document, and he was charged with fraud and stock manipulation by the government."

"Did that help us?"

"The stock has been recovering nicely, so, yes, it helped us a lot."

"And no shareholder suits this time?"

"Actually, I think there is one."

"Kronheim again?"

"Yep," Noah replied.

"That's awful," she said.

"Ordinarily, it would be, but this time he's representing us and our shareholders. We're suing Deutschland Trust."

"For how much?"

"I'm not sure, but I would guess somewhere between a half-billion and a billion dollars."

"And Saul Kronheim is our lawyer?"

"Looks that way."

"You called Saul Kronheim?"

"Not exactly. He called me."

"I guess I missed all the fun," she said.

***

Later that night, when Alexandra and Noah were alone and in bed, he reached out and ran his fingers gently across the side of her face. "I've never loved you as much as I do now," he said.

"I know, Noah. I feel the same way."

He started to pull her closer.

"Noah, we can't make love to one another for a little while," she said, tears in her eyes.

Noah propped himself up on an elbow.

"What did they do to you, Alexandra?"

"A lot of horrible things, but I stopped them from forcing me to have sex with them. Noah, I knew they intended to rape me, so I secretly dug my fingernails into myself down there and tore my flesh enough to bleed. When they saw the blood on my leg, I told them I had my period. I knew it was forbidden in Islam to have sex with a woman during her period. Anyway, it's pretty raw down there."

Noah pulled her into his arms and held her tightly in his embrace.

"Those bastards. I'm so sorry, Alexandra. I'm so sorry."

***

Amos was waiting at the table for Noah and Alexandra the next morning at breakfast.

"Good morning," he said. "I hope you both got a good night's sleep. We have a long day ahead of us."

"I think I slept off the last of the Ketamine," Alexandra answered. "I slept like a rock."

"Me too. How about you, Amos?"

"I never sleep very long, but, yes, I slept well."

Just then, Yusuf and A'isha entered the dining room holding hands. Noah looked at Alexandra, his expression bemused.

"Hmm, how about that?" he said.

"Pretty damn good-looking couple, I'd say," she replied, smiling at them as they approached the table.

The conversation soon turned to Sarah Jean Bogart and how instrumental she was in finding A'isha and young Amos in the Adams Morgan neighborhood of Washington. "She has an incredible head on her shoulders—incredible investigative instincts," Amos said. "She figured out that the United States had raised the nuclear threat condition while virtually everyone in the country was still in the dark."

"I know," Alexandra agreed. "That's why I hired her on the spot. I hadn't even cleared it with my boss."

"That might just be one of the most important decisions you ever made, Alexandra," Amos said.

"By the way," he continued. "I thought you would all be interested in an item that will be in tomorrow's *Jerusalem Post*. Benjamin Bar-Levy was sent an advance copy, and he had one of our people slip it under my door."

"What does it say?" Noah asked.

Amos took a sheet of paper from his shirt pocket and pushed it across the table for them to read.

Two Found Dead at Quarry Near Beit Fajjar

The Israeli Defense Forces reported the discovery of two male bodies on the floor of one of the quarries near Beit Fajjar. It appeared as though the men had been pushed or jumped off the ledge of the excavation and fell to their deaths about two hundred and fifty feet below. The deceased men were identified as Omar Samir and Muhammed Faisel. Omar Samir is a wanted terrorist with a long history of violence. Identification on Muhammed Faisel indicated that he was from El-Obeid, Sudan.

Alexandra finished reading the story and pushed it back across the table to Amos.

"Good riddance," she whispered under her breath.

***

CHAPTER

FORTY-SIX

Amos ran for the foyer from the kitchen as soon as he heard the key in the door.

"Momma!" he screamed as he leapt into her arms when she came through the front door.

Alexandra hugged and kissed Amos frantically, squeezing him to her body as hard as she dared.

"Oh, my baby, how I missed you," she cried.

"I missed you too, Momma," he answered.

Noah, A'isha, and Yusuf stood off to the side, not wanting to interfere with this moment between Alexandra and Amos.

As Alexandra lowered Amos to the floor she looked up and saw Sarah Jean Bogart standing there.

"Sarah Jean!" she said, as she walked over to her new assistant and hugged her.

"I understand I owe you a lot, Sarah Jean. Amos Ben-Chaiyim told me you figured out where to find A'isha and Amos long before anyone else even had a clue."

"Oh, they had a clue, all right, Alexandra. They just didn't know they had a clue."

"I understand you figured out where A'isha and Amos were by yourself without any help from anyone. Is that right?"

"Well, not really. I got a pretty good tip from someone."

"Really? Who gave you the tip?" Alexandra asked.

"A guy named Klondike Pete," Sarah Jean replied. "As soon as I saw Klondike Pete looking up at me from a pile of garbage, I knew Amos was somewhere in that building."

"Ah, from B-52s in Blytheville, Arkansas to Klondike Pete's Crunchy Nuggets in Adams Morgan. That's pretty impressive, Sarah Jean."

"Say, I saw you were suing somebody, Mr. Greenspan," Sarah Jean said.

"I am? I mean, where did you hear that?"

"I didn't hear it. There's a story about it in the business section of today's *Evening Star*. It's on the kitchen counter."

"Really? That was fast," Noah said.

Noah walked into the kitchen and picked up the *Star* from the countertop and quickly turned to the business section. *Kronheim doesn't waste time*, Noah thought.

PCPA CEO and Others File Suit Against Deutschland Trust

A civil class-action shareholder suit has been filed in the US District Court, Eastern Division of Pennsylvania, against Deutschland Trust and the bank's controversial short-sell analyst George Markanos, alleging that the bank committed fraud and engaged in stock manipulation of shares of Potomac Center Properties of America (PCPA) in an attempt to take over the company.

Earlier in the week, the Justice Department criminally charged Deutschland Trust and Mr. Markanos with essentially the same offenses. Plaintiffs' attorney, Saul Kronheim, filed the suit last night and released a statement saying what Deutschland Trust and Markanos did constituted "a monstrous crime" against the shareholders of Potomac Center Properties of America and that the plaintiffs were entitled to substantial damages. "A billion dollars wouldn't be out of the question," Kronheim said.

The bank issued a statement saying the suit was without merit and called the damages sought by the plaintiffs "ridiculous."

Noah Greenspan, CEO of Potomac Center Properties of America, who himself has in the past been a defendant in suits filed by Mr. Kronheim, was not available for comment.

"Hmmm, *a monstrous crime*. I like that," Noah said as he tossed the paper down onto the countertop.

The telephone rang just as Noah turned to pick up his son.

"Greenspan residence," he answered, as he lifted Amos into his arms.

"Noah, it's Frank Markazie. I'm just checking to see if everyone made it home all right."

"We're all here, safe and sound, Frank. Thanks for asking."

"Noah, is Alexandra up to talking on the phone?"

"She's standing right here, and she's fine, Frank. Hold on."

"Alexandra, it's for you. It's Frank Markazie."

"Hi, Frank," Alexandra said, taking the phone from Noah.

"Welcome home, kid," her boss said as soon as he heard her voice.

"Thanks, Frank. It's great to be home," she answered. "I have a lot to write about."

"You up to a little shop talk?"

"Sure, I'm fine."

"I wanted to talk to you about that assistant of yours, Sarah Jean Bogart."

"Shoot," she answered.

"I think you're going to have to get along without her."

Alexandra looked across the room to Sarah Jean. "Frank, maybe I should take this on another phone in the house."

"Why, is she around?"

"Yes, she's standing right here," Alexandra answered, looking to Sarah Jean curiously

"You don't have to move to another phone, I've already spoken to her."

"You spoke to her without talking to me first?"

"Yes, I did."

"Look, Frank, if it's about budget, I'll personally split the cost of her salary with the paper."

"I didn't say I was firing her, for fucksake. I said, you're going to have to get along without her. You can find another assistant any time you want, Alexandra. That kid is too good to be an assistant here at the *Star*. The *Post* has cleaned our clock with the Pentagon Papers story and now the Watergate story. I'm putting together an investigative reporting unit and I want Sarah Jean to be one of our key investigative reporters. She's amazing, Alexandra."

"Yes, she is, Frank. Let me talk to her. Can we talk in the morning?"

"Sure, kid. You going to have copy for me for Sunday's paper?"

"Jesus, Frank, I just got home."

"I'm just kidding. Why don't you and Noah head over to my place in Ocean City for a few days?"

"We might just take you up on that, Frank. I'll give you a call in the morning."

"Okay, kid. And welcome home."

Alexandra hung up the phone and looked over to Sarah Jean.

"I'll do whatever you want, Alexandra. I really mean that," Sarah Jean said before Alexandra could say anything.

"What do you want to do, Sarah Jean? Frank is right, you know, I can find an assistant any day of the week. A natural investigative reporter, that's not so easy to find."

"I wouldn't be up here in Washington if it wasn't for you, Alexandra."

"That doesn't make you an indentured servant, Sarah Jean. What would you really like to do?"

"I do love to snoop around and figure things out."

"Yes, you do, Sarah Jean. I don't think I would be here if you hadn't snooped around, as you say."

"But, it's an honor to work for you, Alexandra, and I wouldn't be disappointed if you asked me to turn down Mr. Markazie's offer."

"You would really like to be one of the *Evening Star*'s new investigative reporters, wouldn't you, Sarah Jean?"

Sarah Jean hesitated a moment and then nodded eagerly.

"Then you go for it, Sarah Jean."

Sarah Jean walked over to Alexandra and hugged her.

"You're the best thing that's ever happened to me, Alexandra. You got me out of the Chickasawba district of Mississippi County, Arkansas."

"And you helped get me out of a place I didn't want to be either, Sarah Jean. Let's call it even."

EPILOGUE

Egyptians and Israelis to this day debate which side really won the 1973 bloodbath that the Israelis call the Yom Kippur War and the Egyptians call the Ramadan War. Given that neither side was able to dictate to the other the final terms of a ceasefire, neither side can be said to have won the war. If any nation prevailed, it was the United States. If any nation utterly failed, it was the Soviet Union.

Egypt succeeded in crossing the Suez Canal with extraordinarily few casualties, a feat that Israeli intelligence said was impossible. Egypt also planned and prepared for the war brilliantly and, by and large, fought the war heroically.

Israel paid an enormous price for its complacency and its underestimation of the Egyptian and Syrian foot soldiers' ability to stand and fight. Conversely, once Israel regained its footing after initial devasting losses on the ground and in the air, its armed forces fought back brilliantly. In a matter of days Israel commanded both fronts—against Egypt on the Sinai and against Syria on the Golan Heights. The Israelis, in a couple of weeks, were within striking distance of both Cairo and Damascus. Israel's battlefield success during the war, especially in light of its initial devastating setbacks, is one of the greatest achievements in the annals of warfare.

Nonetheless, when the fighting was over, Israel no longer commanded the East Bank of the Suez Canal. It was in Egyptian hands and has remained in Egyptian hands ever since. While Egyptian forces never left the East Bank of the Suez Canal, all Israeli forces did abandon their positions on the West Bank of the Suez Canal.

The Kilometer 101 disengagement talks went on from October 28 until November 29, 1973. None of the major issues over which the war was fought were resolved during the Kilometer 101 talks, but the talks did constitute the first step toward a formal, lasting peace between Israel and Egypt. The talks also constituted the first face-to-face contact between Egypt and Israel since the founding of the Jewish state. The talks at Kilometer 101 also resulted in something no one foresaw—the two negotiators, Israeli General Aharon Yariv and Egyptian General Muhammad el-Gamasy, actually grew to respect and like one another.

If one wishes to determine who exerted the most influence on the outcome of the talks, the answer is simple—that would be US Secretary of State Henry Kissinger. The talks achieved what Secretary Kissinger wanted the talks to achieve, no more and no less. He saw the Kilometer 101 talks as a stepping stone to a Geneva conference and, ultimately, a formal peace between the two warring nations, which was finally achieved with the Camp David Accords facilitated by President Jimmy Carter five years later. Henry Kissinger, however, was the visionary and, in many respects, the architect of the peace between Egypt and Israel that no one believed could be achieved.

The Kilometer 101 talks, which almost cost our fictional character Alexandra Salaman Greenspan her life, did finally result in formal agreements on six points of contention:

1. Egypt and Israel agreed to observe scrupulously the ceasefire called for by the UN Security Council.
2. Both sides agreed that discussions between them would begin immediately to settle the question of the return to their positions on October 22 (the day the UN-brokered ceasefire was supposed to go into effect).

3. The town of Suez began receiving daily supplies of food, water, and medicines, and all wounded civilians in the town of Suez were allowed to be evacuated.

4. There was no further impediment to the movement of non-military supplies to the embattled Egyptian Third Army on the East Bank of the Suez Canal.

5. The Israeli checkpoints on the Cairo-Suez road were replaced by UN checkpoints, although at the Suez end of the road, non-uniformed and unarmed Israeli officers were allowed to participate with the UN in verifying the non-military nature of the cargo destined for Egypt's Third Army.

6. And finally, it was agreed that there would be an exchange of all prisoners of war as soon as the UN replaced all Israeli checkpoints on the road from Cairo to the surrounded Egyptian Third Army.

Today, Egypt and Israel are at peace, as they have been for over forty years.

Made in the USA
Columbia, SC
14 August 2018